Past Masters

Front cover images (left to right, top to bottom): Cyril M. Kornbluth, H. Beam Piper, William Tenn (Philip Klass), Eric Frank Russell, Edgar Pangborn, R.A. Lafferty, Leigh Brackett, Hal Clement (Harry Stubbs), Clifford D. Simak, Fredric Brown, Nelson Bond, Murray Leinster, Catherine L. Moore.

Past Masters,
& Other Bookish Natterings

by Bud Webster

The Merry Blacksmith Press
2013

Past Masters, and Other Bookish Natterings

For information, address:

The Merry Blacksmith Press
70 Lenox Ave.
West Warwick, RI 02893

merryblacksmith.com

Published in the USA by The Merry Blacksmith Press

ISBN—0-61584-282-8
978-0-61584-282-0

Table of Contents

This book is dedicated to:

William Sanders and Lawrence Watt-Evans, who gave "Past Masters" its first home; Gordon van Gelder, who encouraged me to write about all the weird books I've collected over the years; Dr. Jerry Pournelle, who can stand to write with me; Robert Silverberg and Barry Malzberg, who have answered every silly little question I've asked them over the years; John O'Neil, who gave me not only blog space but a place in his terrific magazine, *Black Gate.* To Bwana Mike Resnick for the terrific introduction. And, as always, to Mary, once my Significant Other and now my wife.

Finally, to Ariel and Gus, the two damn cats, and most of all, to my golden Baby Boy Puck, who will purr in my heart for all eternity.

Preface:
So, What the Hell Am I, Anyway?

> Mrs. [Rosel George] Brown is just about the only one of *F&SF*'s former gaggle of housewives who doesn't strike me as verging on the feebleminded; in fact, I think her work has attracted less attention than it deserves.

That's James Blish (writing as William Atheling, Jr.) being nice. He was talking about Brown's story in the August, 1962 issue of *F&SF* (then edited by Avram Davidson). He doesn't name the story—odd that a critic wouldn't, even in a review published at the time—but a little online research shows it to be her novelette "The Fruiting Body." It's a pretty good read, too, as most of Brown's work is.

For me, though, the salient point of the quote above is the off-hand contempt he throws on such fine *F&SF* contributors as Zenna Henderson, Katherine MacLean and Miriam Allen DeFord, a blatant disdain that is both unfortunate and unwarranted. Looking over the first Blish/Atheling volume, *The Issue at Hand* (Advent Publishers, 1964), in fact, the reader finds similar contempt for one writer or another on nearly every page.

It got worse. In the March, 1954 issue of Campbell's *Astounding*, a story by one Arthur Zirul titled "Final Exam" appeared. It was the author's very first story. Blish/Atheling, in the Spring 1954 issue of Redd Boggs' fanzine *Skyhook*, devoted almost his entire column (which translated to an incredible six pages in book form) to tearing this story to shreds; calling it "...one of the worst stinkers ever to have been printed...", and on and on *ad nauseum*.

Why? What was the point? Is there some reason why a writer, either self-defined as a critic or anointed as such by others, must heap that kind of scorn on something they don't care for? Spending approximately 2000 words to slam the first story by a presumably-young writer is worse than just needlessly cruel, it's deliberate sabotage.

(Sam Moskowitz had an explanation for this fervid attack on a writer Blish had never even heard of before. Writing in *Science Fiction Studies #70* in November of 1996, Moskowitz says, "It turned out that a Blish story was supposed to go into the issue [of *Astounding*], but at the last minute Campbell rejected it and substituted the Zirul story!" Was this, in fact, the case, or was SaM just being a mixer as was his wont?

Try as I might, I was unable to confirm the story's veracity, and frankly, considering both his avid willingness to feud with anyone and his personal dislike of Blish, my guess is that he made it up. After all, Blish had been dead for more than twenty years and couldn't argue. Barry Malzberg, himself a respected critic, states categorically that "Sam just hated Blish, had hated him for twenty years, old feuds, old loathing... Lying about the motive for the Zirul attack would be among the least vicious of his rodomontades.")

The perception of "Critic" as "Butcher" is omnipresent in our culture. Every cop, lawyer or detective show on television, every mystery novelist has offered at least one episode or book based around the plot that a local TV or newspaper critic has been shot, poisoned, strangled and/or defenestrated by someone he had gleefully eviscerated earlier and in each instance said Critic is portrayed as snide, embittered, egotistical and arrogant. Is it any wonder that so many who find themselves in a position to act as critic assume that unfortunate posture as a matter of course?

I wish I could say that this sort of venomous self-indulgence was unusual, but I can point to a number of examples by other critics just in our own field that are every bit as intentionally contemptuous and harsh, albeit not necessarily as omnipresent in those critics' *oeuvre* as in Blish/Atheling's.

The real purpose of a critic, it seems to me, is to evaluate the creative output of an artist (in whichever medium) in a way that establishes a historical and/or cultural context and makes that context comprehensible to the reader. In order to do that effectively, the critic may not have to know more about the subject than the audience he/she is writing for, but for damn sure he/she has to know enough about it to be able to both articulate his/her opinions *and* authoritatively substantiate them.

(This is to differentiate critics from reviewers, whose job is to give their readership a head's-up on individual, currently available works in order to help said readership make up their collective minds whether to buy that Blu-Ray set of the first—and only—season of *Firefly* or another six of Amstel Light, a more than worthy objective as far as I'm concerned.)

Where is it written, though, that the Critics' Chair should be a bully pulpit, with the accent on "bully?" Why are so many critics seemingly determined, even eager, to show so much unreserved disdain for their subjects, to cross the lines of civility to devastate the reputation (not to mention the feelings) of the artists they write about? Is the answer as simple as their wanting to portray themselves as clever, to prove that they're more so than the writers they slam?

I honestly think that's true in many cases, I really do. Do I think James Blish, author of the Cities in Flight stories, and the "After Such Knowledge" books had nothing more in mind than savaging his fellow scriveners and their work, though?

No. In all fairness, and as extreme (and objectionable) as I find much of his commentary, there's plenty of legitimate insight in his criticism. He knew what he was doing as an author, and although he may have been afflicted with the same institutional bitterness so many other writers suffer from—and allowed that acidity to color his critical writings—he was certainly able to shine his analytical light with accuracy and vigor. So, I can't be but just so, er, critical of him.

Nevertheless, "Critics" (as differentiated from "critics") have a reputation for cynicism and mockery that I find not only distasteful, but diametrically opposed to the very thing they're supposed to be doing; i.e., communicating a persuasive and reasonably accurate overview of the subject to their readers. I don't expect complete impartiality (and I ain't gonna get it anyway), but I would like at least a modicum of civility.

There's a reason, over and above the fact that my mother brought me up right. Critics, upper- or lower-case, have a twofold audience: first and foremost are the fans of whichever creative endeavor they take it upon themselves to evaluate - for our purposes, fantastic literature. Fans are far more likely to be interested in detail than more casual readers, and they tend to seek out information above and beyond that commonly given by reviews. They want to compare their opinions with those expressed by people they respect, if only to see if they agree with each other.[1]

The second part of that audience is the authors about whose work they write. Lemme tell you something about most creative types, if I may.

1. There is also that unfortunate faanish contingent which dearly loves to see one Name rip another Name apart, much like mundanes watching Keeping Up with the Real Housewives of the New Jersey Shore; as inevitable as that fact might be, however, I'd as soon not dwell on it.

We who write (or paint or quilt or play Theremins or whatever) tend to possess a less-than-half-full bottle of Self-Confidence Cola. There are notable exceptions, of course, but on the whole we're a neurotic and over-anxious lot, and *any* criticism is seen as a possible encounter with Jack the Ripper, no matter how gently worded. If our Critic is harsh and/or snarky, that means our Significant Others have to run around the house hiding all the sharp pointy things from us.

(Paradoxically, a lack of self-confidence doesn't preclude Ego; almost all creative types – barring those who secrete their work in closets, either actual or metaphorical – operate under the audacious notion that someone out there actually wants to read what we scribble in our lonely garrets, surrounded by hungry cats and tattered reference books. This ambiguity can cause much serious emotional heterodyning, like a psychosomatic ring modulator. What this means, in essence, is that all the various slings and arrows that plague us normally increase geometrically and start bouncing around in our heads like balls of psychic Flubber studded with nails. Ow.)

Here's another example, not quite as egregious. In Damon Knight's collection of critical writings (like the Blish/Atheling, originally published in fanzines and collected by Advent), Knight eviscerated A. E. van Vogt's *The World of Null-A*, titling the essay "Cosmic Jerrybuilder: A. E. van Vogt." The title alone gives the reader a clue as to Knight's opinion of the writer's work, and any doubts are dispelled quickly by phrases like "[van Vogt] is a pygmy who has learned to operate an overgrown typewriter."

The difference between Blish and Knight is subtle, but important: Knight wrote what he did not out of simple meanness or, if Moskowitz is to be believed, revenge, but because of a very genuine feeling of frustration at seeing a bright and extremely imaginative writer doing what he considered to be sloppy work. Did Knight enjoy the same degree of amusement that Blish did in flensing a work he didn't like? I honestly don't know, but I suspect not; I think he saw it as his duty, however unpleasant, to offer his considered opinion.

All that above is me trying hard to figure out just what the hell I am. When people mention one of my columns in their blog or on FaceSpace-Place, they frequently refer to me as a "critic." In reviews of *Anthopology 101: Reflections, Inspections and Dissections of SF Anthologies* (Merry Blacksmith, 2010), others have done the same.

I've always cringed away from the appellation, for several reasons, not the least of which is that I'm not willing to be as malicious as the stereotypical Critic is supposed to be. However…

However. The key reason is that I've just never felt qualified. Of course, I never thought I was qualified to write about old anthologies or unjustly forgotten authors, either, but I've been doing it for more than a decade now. Mary, who always knows better (don't tell her I said that, okay? If you do, I'll never hear the end of it) had been urging me all along to include more of my own opinions; little by little, I began to sneak some in and was surprised to find that my editors were pleased. This is a good thing, *n'est-ce pas*?

This shouldn't be taken as a claim that I have to force my opinions out. Anyone who's ever spent more than, say, five or ten minutes in a room with me knows better than that. There's something so terribly permanent, though, about committing those judgments to the cold light of print, isn't there? I mean, it's one thing to say "Cordwainer Halvah's last book really sucked!" in the con suite at 2:00am when everyone's bleary and barely conscious, but quite another to put it out there where your listeners/readers are clear-headed and ready for an argument, right?

So, it seems to me that you have an obligation to make sure that your statement that said novel "really sucked" can be supported by reason and analysis, and isn't just a poopy-headed expression of your dislike for the cover art, or because that cute girl in the chain-mail across the room won't smile back. That means you have to know something about whatever it is you're talking about. That means you have to have an *informed* opinion.

Do I got one o' those? Well, I'd like to think I do. I've certainly read widely in the field, both the fiction and the criticism. Not out of some directed intent to become what I was reading, mind you, but out of plain old curiosity. I did the same thing when I was collecting records and rocks.

So, what the hell am I, anyway? Some people have referred to me as a critic, as I said before, but then I've been called a Commie-Fag-Junky, too, and I'm not any of that. I can state categorically that I *am* a historian of the field of science-fiction and fantasy, that I'm a biographer of those who helped create it, and that I am (to a lesser extent, admittedly) a bibliographer (and please note that there are others out there more accomplished in these areas than I am). I will admit further that I have developed strong opinions about the subjects I have written about over the years, and that I'm more at ease expressing those opinions now than I was a decade ago. However…

However. I am not, and never will be, concerned solely with their literary work. As anyone who's read any of my columns (or even these blog entries) can tell, I'm a bull-goose process freak with an insatiable curiosity about the men and women who have created and shaped this wonderful literature, which means that as far as I'm concerned, it's all relevant and all grist for the journalistic mill.

If you will forgive me yet another "however," this doesn't mean that I have any interest whatsoever in making fun of, or being rude/cruel to/about, any of the authors or editors I write about. If I mention a flaw or foible, it's because I honestly believe that it affected the subject's work, not to "dis" from a distance in order to make myself look clever, or to elevate myself above the very people who have engaged my enthusiasm.

If I don't like a book or an author, I can find very little reason to write about it. Why bother? I'd rather spend the same time and energy covering someone with whose work I have connected in some way than go on and on about a book or writer who leaves me cold. Isn't it a better use of my efforts to advise readers about what they should actively seek out, not rail for page after page about stuff they should go out of their way to avoid?

Yeah, I have opinions, informed ones at that. Yeah, I have a lot of fun expressing them. But first and last, I am a *writer* and I'm only too conscious of what it must feel like for some uppity criticizer to go postal for six pages on a five-thousand word story just because they can get away with it. I've been harassed by bullies, and I try very hard not to be one. There's enough of that in the world as it is; I don't need to add to it. If that makes me *not* a critic, I'm content.

So, what the hell am I, anyway? Well, as long as you like what I write, it doesn't really matter, so call me whatever you like (as long as you don't call me late for dinner).

Although this volume is titled to reflect its primary content, *Past Masters* includes a number of other articles I've written over the years, all related to literature on one level or another. Most of them come from the column I've been doing for various online publications beginning with *Helix SF* and currently running (sporadically, due to the vicissitudes of Reality) in *The Grantville Gazette*. Aside from a one-off chapbook of the installment on Murray Leinster done in a very limited edition of fewer than a dozen copies by a friend, none of the "Past Masters" pieces have seen actual print. Of the others, the short-short bits on off-the-wall SF/fantasy books ran in *Fantasy and Science Fiction* as "Curiosities" pieces, the three "Alternate Dialogues" originally ran in the *SFWA Bulletin*, and I've included my history of the *SFWA Bulletin* itself, which was published in the 200th issue. The lone singleton, an examination of Tom Reamy done for the print edition of *Black Gate*, is the first of what I hope will be a new column series, "Who?!", devoted to promoting those fine authors even less well-known (now, anyway) than those I cover for "Past Masters."

"Past Masters" began in 2006 when a group of us (headed up by William Sanders and Lawrence Watt-Evans as editors) started *Helix SF*, an online semi-pro quarterly supported by donations from readers that lasted ten issues. The first installment originated as a speech I gave in 2005 at a Williamsburg, Virginia library as part of a conference on the planet Mars. I was asked to do a lecture on the literary explorations of our nearest planetary neighbor, and as the research was fairly simple I said "Oh, all right."

Helix's Editor-in-Chief Sanders had asked me to do a column for the magazine (as well as act as Poetry Editor), and I proposed several ideas for one; we decided on a series addressing classic-but-no-longer-famous authors, but for the first issue William allowed me to recycle that Martian lecture. I left the title of the column up to him and he chose "Past Masters," an appellation I considered perfectly apt.

There are nine of those columns collected herein, lacking only the tenth; that one was a farewell to the readers of *Helix* and none of us felt that it would add anything to the continuity if included.

After *Helix SF* folded, the column moved to Eric Flint's onliner *Baen's Universe* for a few issues until its demise, and thence to its current home, *The Grantville Gazette*, edited by Paula Goodlett.

A note about the columns: you can see the way they developed over the past few years, from general treatments of a theme (Mars, flying saucers) to examinations of specific authors. In each case I tried to include a bibliography, although those for the first two columns were more jokes than serious attempts to give the readers a direction in which to look.

The actual bibliographies are as complete as I can make them, and should not be considered whole or complete; nevertheless the more than casual reader will find them useful, I hope, in tracking down material they haven't yet encountered and of course that is my purpose in including them in the first place.

My thanks to William and Lawrence for giving "Past Masters" the opportunity to exist in the first place, and to Eric Flint and Paula Goodlett for giving it new lodgings. Also, my extreme gratitude goes to Phil Stephensen-Payne for his help more than once in assembling the bibliographies, and to the denizens of the FictionMags and PulpMags e-mail lists for their in-depth knowledge of the history of fantastic literature and its perpetrators. Thanks as well to Mary, who reads every line of what I write and tells me not only when it sucks but *why*, and to the trio of felinical beings who inhabit the parts of my heart not already claimed by Mary.

– Richmond, December 2012

❑

Introduction to Past Masters
by Mike Resnick

***PAST MASTERS* IS AN IMPORTANT BOOK.** Which figures. The columns from which it has been put together were (and are) important columns.

You see, Bud Webster knows not only the practitioners of the field, but also its history. And in this day and age, when the average SAT score is nose-diving toward two digits, it's a good thing to remind us of what came before.

Bud knows, for example, that H. G. Wells didn't simply write *The War of the Worlds* in 1898, wave a hand, and intone: "Let there be science fiction." He knows that Mary Shelley was writing it eighty years earlier with *Frankenstein*, and he knows that she came more than a century and a half after Cyrano de Bergerac, who may or may not have had a long nose and a romantic disposition, but had enough imagination to write about life on the Moon back in 1657 (and on the Sun, which seems a trifle hot, in 1662.)

And just as Wells didn't create the field, our most famous giants – Asimov, Heinlein, Clarke and Bradbury – didn't throw out what came before and shape it into what we know as modern science fiction. As you'll see when you read these remarkable biographies, they were predated by many fine and imaginative writers, many of who remain in print today.

His list includes one of my two or three all-time favorites, the brilliant C. L. Moore, who was married to a pretty major talent himself, Henry Kuttner. (In an introduction I just wrote for a Kuttner collection, I acknowledged his mastery of the form and finally forgave her for marrying him rather than waiting for me to be born and grow up.)

Another lady whose fan following hasn't diminished much is Zenna Henderson, who would be just as popular even if William Shatner hadn't starred in a painfully mediocre TV movie about her brainchild, "The People".

Another of my favorites you'll meet in the pages up ahead is the multi-talented Fredric Brown, who wrote fiction far better than he spelled "Frederick". He created the first true recursive science fiction (which is to say, science fiction *about* science fiction) with the classic *What Mad Universe?*, he was the absolute master of the short-short (today known as "flash fiction"), he could write serious extrapolative stories as well as funny and cynical ones—and while we claim him as our own, he actually produced about four times as many mystery stories, including one, the brilliant *Night of the Jabberwock*, that's *almost* science fiction (or fantasy, anyway).

There's Stanley G. Weinbaum, still being read, his "A Martian Odyssey" still considered perhaps the most influential short story in the field's history—and until you read Bud's piece on him, you won't know just how short his career actually was.

There are some friends I knew personally lurking in the pages up ahead.

There's Hal Clement (real name: Harry Stubbs), who was as thoughtful a man as you'd ever want to meet. When NASA announced that a high school teacher would be going along on one of the moon flights, the whole science fiction community began bombarding them with requests and demands that it be Hal, and we were even more heartbroken than he when he wasn't selected.

There's Phil Klass (pen name: William Tenn), second only to Robert Sheckley in pushing the boundaries of sophisticated humor back in the early 1950s, who just stopped writing one day, though he showed up at enough conventions to serve as the Worldcon Guest of Honor about eight years ago. He was a man who loved to talk, and it's just damned fortunate for the rest of us that he had so many witty things to say, as I suspect no one could shut him up.

You'll meet Will Jenkins (pen name: Murray Leinster), who'd been writing science fiction a decade before Hugo Gernsback coined the name for it, and was the Guest of Honor at the first Worldcon I attended back in 1963 at the ripe old age of 21. And there's Cliff Simak, the newspaper editor who wrote with remarkable sensitivity and created a pair of absolute classics in *City* and *Way Station*, and was probably the sweetest, gentlest man I ever met.

There will be those who are still popular, as least within the field, such as Cyril Kornbluth; those who are fondly remembered even as they fall out of print, such as Eric Frank Russell and Judi Merril; and those whose brilliance might well be forgotten but for people like Bud Webster who simply will not let you forget the likes of Edgar Pangborn or Cordwainer Smith.

And let me conclude this introduction by saying a few words about the most remarkable of all the people who appear in this volume, and that is Bud Webster himself.

Bud is in love with science fiction, and he puts his effort where his heart is. I guarantee you that whatever he's been paid for these articles and this book, it doesn't begin to pay for his time—his lifetime—of studying and assimilating all this information.

But he does more than write about it. He, more than any other living human being, keeps these writers in print. Not primarily as an editor, but in his work—*gratis*, of course—as the Estate Liaison for the Science Fiction and Fantasy Writers of America. Every anthologist, and almost every editor, in the field knows that if you need to find who controls a dead author's literary estate, there is only one person to go to, and that is Bud Webster. Without him, an awful lot of these names and their contemporaries would fall permanently out of print. I can't even begin to guess how often I've used his services, and I am far from the only one.

So if this book is a celebration of the writers who helped shape the field (and it is), it is no less a celebration of my friend Bud, who has made sure that their contributions have not only not been forgotten, but that they continue as shining examples to each new generation of writers and readers.

❑

Mars—
the Amply Read Planet

I will preface my remarks here by admitting freely that my primary expertise is in written SF and not other media. Were I to more than merely mention the titles of a representative number of the innumerable SF movies set on Mars, good and bad, this essay would go on forever—and you would all have logged out hours before. So take it for granted that there are plenty of them out there, perhaps fodder for another article at another time.

IN 1877, Giovanni Schiaparelli looked through his telescope at Mars and saw… STUFF. He didn't know what it was, although he sketched out what appeared to be (and which he described as) an elaborate system of "canali," or channels. What were they? Well, it would be wonderful to be able to confirm that they were, in fact, canals, or vegetation, or anything else that would put some kind of life above the level of the microbial on the fourth planet, but the fact is that he probably saw some craters, a few shadows, and the combination of excitement and not terribly good optics by our standards naturally turned them into a pattern his brain could accept.

And thus it began, really. 20 years later, Percival Lowell was pretty sure that Mars was hot and dry, but certainly able to sustain life. With that kind of build-up by astronomical heavy-hitters, was it any wonder why writers glommed onto the Red Planet as a stage on which to place their actors? Mars was romantic, it was mysterious, it was right up there in the sky where we could see it. I mean, who knew what was going on up there, right?

Of course, speculation about what was going on up there had happened before this: Athanasius Kircher, a German priest and scientist, speculated about Mars in his *Itinerarium Exstaticum* back in 1656; Emanuel Swedenborg went all mystic in 1744 or so and wrote about Mars in *The Earths In Our Solar System* in 1787; and Anglican clergyman Wladislaw Lach-Szyrma wrote about a winged Venusian named Aleriel who traveled to Mars (among other planets) in 1874 in *Aleriel, or A Voyage to Other Worlds.*

And it went on after Schiaparelli, if anything at an even more heightened pace. Percy Greg wrote one of the first interplanetary novels, *Across the Zodiac: The Story of a Wrecked Record*, in 1880, in which the hero uses antigravity to send his spaceship to Mars where he finds a scientifically advanced society that nevertheless has its dark side: "wrong thoughts" are against the law, and women are bought and sold. Sort of like Cleveland.

UK writer Hugh McColl wrote *Mr. Stranger's Sealed Packet* in 1889, which tells of two Martian races, both originating on Earth, and of the Utopia created by one of them. This book may very well have been a major influence on HG Wells.

Antigravity shows up again in Irish author Robert Cromie's *A Plunge Into Space* from 1890, where we find yet another Utopia and a fatal romance. The 1891 edition of this book, by the way, had a preface by Jules Verne.

1894 saw the publication of Gustavus W. Pope's *Romances of the Planets No. 1: Journey to Mars*, where his Army officer hero falls in love with the Princess of an advanced Martian race. This was almost 20 years before Burroughs's *A Princess of Mars,* by the way.

In 1897, Kurd Lasswitz, who is to the Germans what Verne was to the French and Wells was to the English, wrote his best and longest novel, *Auf zwei Planeten*, which starts with the discovery of a Martian outpost in the Arctic. Humanity is placed under the benign protection of the superior Martians and begins to improve while the Martians (at least the ones here on Earth) get more and more decadent. Finally we throw off the yoke, rebel against our repressors, and equality is established between the two planets. We're given the feeling that a Utopia will ensue. There were lots of Utopias in those days.

But of course, the Big Daddy of them all, the one we keep going back to (and back to and back to, it seems) is Wells's *The War of the Worlds*, which burst on the scene in 1889 and hasn't had more than a couple of weeks vacation since. Wells really managed to tear it up in this book, utterly destroying several English towns including Wimbledon (apparently, the Martians weren't tennis fans), thus bringing his Interplanetary War right smack dab into the laps of his British readers. As many of you may know from having read the book yourselves, we humans don't fare too well in the battle, at least until someone sneezes. At that point, it's just a matter of time.

It's impossible to overstate the importance of *The War of the Worlds* and the influence it's had over the years. Not only has it been filmed several times, and a TV series based on it, but it entered the non-reading public's psyche in 1938 when another guy named Welles did it as a radio play and scared a significant number of his listeners into near-hysteria. Along with Jules Verne's *20,000 Leagues Under the Sea* and Wells's own *The Invisible Man*, it's probably the single best-known science fiction novel ever published.

Hard on the heels of this one—almost literally, it was published six weeks later—was the supposed sequel to the Wells, Garrett P. Serviss's *Edison's Conquest of Mars*, the first non-juvenile edisonade[1]. Seemingly a precursor to the radio play (while predating it by almost half a century), it deals with the destruction the Tripods rained down on America, specifically New York and New Jersey, thus allowing Thomas Edison to get involved, along with Lord Kelvin and Herr Roentgen. Edison figures out how the heat-ray works, finds a way to counteract it, then develops a "Ship of Space," and a disintegrator, all through the clever application of electricity, which, if Serviss's fervor is taken at face value, was also invented by Edison.

I'll quote just a bit here to give you some idea about both Serviss's enthusiasm about the wizard of Menlo Park and his skills as a writer:

> "'Let the Martians come,' was the cry. 'If necessary, we can quit the earth as the Athenians fled from Athens before the advancing host of Xerxes, and like them, take refuge on our ships—these new ships of space, with which American inventiveness has furnished us.' [So much for Kepler and Roentgen.]
>
> And then, like a flash, some genius struck out an idea that fired the world.
>
> 'Why should we wait? Why should we run the risk of having our cities destroyed and our lands desolated a sec-

> ond time? Let us go to Mars. We have the means. Let us beard the lion in his den. Let us ourselves turn conquerors and take possession of that detestable planet, and if necessary, destroy it in order to relieve the earth of this perpetual threat which now hangs over us like the sword of Damocles.'"

Hugo Gernsback couldn't have said it better. Seriously.

Moving into the 20th Century, Louis Pope Gratacap published his best-known novel, *The Certainty of Future Life on Mars: Being the Posthumous Papers of Bradford Torrey Dodd* in 1903. The narrator theorizes that dying humans here on Earth are reincarnated on Mars as embodied spirits, and radio communication with his late father from the Fourth Planet proves it. And here we have another Utopia, in which the native Martians are servants to the reincarnated humans. Schiapiarelli himself wrote the afterword for this one.

1905 saw Edwin Lester Arnold's *Lieut. Gulliver Jones: His Vacation*, in which yet another military officer, this one a sailor, falls in love with yet another Martian princess, although he has a fiancée at home, so being an officer and a gentleman, he does the Right Thing. By the way, Jones's transportation, far from being a "ship of space," is a flying carpet. Well, I guess anti-gravity is anti-gravity.

Finally, we come to someone who could have made a career of writing just about an army guy having Martian adventures, had he not already been too busy writing about white ape-men, civilizations at the center of the Earth, and guys having Venusian adventures: Edgar Rice Burroughs. The first of the Barsoom stories, *A Princess of Mars*, was published in 1912 in *All-Story Magazine* with the title "Under the Moons of Mars" and under the pseudonym of "Norman Bean." In it we first meet the intrepid Capt. John Carter, the lovely (if red-skinned and egg-laying) Dejah Thoris, Princess of Helium, the brave, four-armed Tars Tarkas, and banths and thoats and zitidars and all the other utterly impossible things that Burroughs populated Barsoom with.

And you know? It doesn't matter that John Carter got to Mars magically, or that the Mars depicted by Burroughs didn't make any sense even by 1912 scientific standards, or that he could never quite keep all the details straight. It's *Barsoom*, the stories are terrific, and what else matters? There would be ten more Barsoom novels by Burroughs's hand, and all of them would be read avidly and passionately by his fans.

Over the next 20 years, Mars became something of a cliché in the pulps. Austin Hall's 1923 story, "The Man Who Saved the Earth," was reprinted in the first issue of *Amazing Stories* three years later; space operatic maestro Edmond Hamilton published "Monsters of Mars" in the April 1931 *Astounding*; there were many others. Mars is, after all, an obvious choice: it's next in line, it's more or less visible with the naked eye, and there were all those "canals;" it's no wonder it was at the top of the list for SF writers. It's the Alter-Earth, in many cases the Über-Earth, and at times when it's impossible to think of Earth as romantic, Mars still beckons.

But Stanley Weinbaum's magnificent and seminal "A Martian Odyssey" in the July 1934 *Wonder Stories* put paid to those clichés. Oh, there had been a few stories that challenged what had become just another formula: P. Schuyler Miller's "The Forgotten Man of Space" with its sad, put-upon Martians, and C. L. Moore's wonderful "Shambleau" just to mention two. But the Weinbaum stepped outside almost all bounds. Told in an airy, brash style quite different from the stiffness of lesser pulpsters, "A Martian Odyssey" features the first really *alien* aliens in SF. Up until then, Martians were monsters or thinly disguised human. Weinbaum gave us weird stuff that he made little or no attempt to explain or justify. Hey, this is an *alien planet*, right?

Tweel, the first alien our hero meets, is vaguely bird-like and travels by leaping 100 feet at a jump, then landing on his "beak" in the ground. There's a creature, thousands of years old, that builds a series of pyramids to house itself, each one slightly larger than the other. Why? Because it's a *Martian*, and apparently that's one of the things Martians do. Weinbaum died at an early age, but not before his easy-going story-telling style would influence a whole generation of SF writers.

Clive Staples Lewis created a decidedly spiritual mythology for Mars in the first book of his Space Trilogy, *Out of the Silent Planet*, in 1938, supplanting Darwinism with Christian ethics as the basis for his version of the inevitable Utopia. Scientifically it's not much more accurate than the Burroughs stories, but as an allegory it works just fine.

Eight years later, something important happened: Ray Bradbury, a writer of some reputation even then, published "The Million Year Picnic" in *Planet Stories*. It was the first of his Martian stories, and would lead to his career outside the pulps. His 1950 collection, *The Martian Chronicles*, may very well be the single most important single-author collection in the field. Hugely popular, it not only influenced the writers who came after, but generations of readers as well. If your school library only had a single SF book in it, it was almost certainly *The Martian Chronicles*.

No more accurate scientifically than any of the others I've mentioned, and quite likely much less so, it remains a true classic. It doesn't matter whether or not the events in "Mars is Heaven" or "Way Up In the Middle of the Air" *could* happen, they *did* happen each and every time we opened the book. Such is the power of genius.

In 1949, Robert Heinlein began making notes on a novel based on the idea of a human raised from infancy by aliens. Six years later, he set aside the 54,000 words of *A Martian Named Smith* as unsalvageable. Five years after that, in 1960, Heinlein's agent submitted the final draft—all 160,000 words!—of *The Man From Mars* to Putnam. It wouldn't be until 1961 that it would acquire the title *Stranger in a Strange Land*. The rest is history. Nobody, including its author, was prepared for the response the book garnered over the years. Chapters of the Church of All Worlds popped up everywhere, and the book was a campus favorite for decades. Had he written nothing else after that, Heinlein would have lived quite comfortably off the royalties for the rest of his life.

Of course, this wasn't the only book he wrote about Mars, not even the first. *The Red Planet*, a juvenile, was published in 1949. Mars and its political interests were central to 1956's *Double Star*, as was the case in 1951's *Between Planets* to a somewhat lesser extent, and would be central to the classic *Podkayne of Mars* from 1962. But like Burroughs, there's a definite lack of consistency in Heinlein's Martians—they keep changing shape, size, and spiritual make-up from book to book. This always confused me as a kid.

Moving ahead a couple of years, the then-little known Roger Zelazny, only a year after publishing his first SF story, made his mark indelibly with the exquisite "A Rose for Ecclesiastes." Seemingly reversing the idea of Heinlein's *Stranger*, a poet-turned-preacher leads a decadent Martian race to a cultural revival. It would not be the last time Zelazny would take on religious themes, but it was certainly one of his finest.

Philip K. Dick went to Mars twice in the same year: *Martian Time-Slip* and *The Three Stigmata of Palmer Eldritch*, both 1964, deal with human colonies in typical Dickian fashion, with reality shifts running more or less rampant. Much has been said by better than I about the seemingly perfect juxtaposition of the dry Martian desert environment and Dick's bleak psychological landscaping, so I'll merely mention it here and, for the sake of brevity, move on. He would, of course, return to Mars in "We Can Remember It For You Wholesale," which I understand was made into a movie starring some politician guy.

Fred Pohl's 1976 Nebula winner, *Man Plus*, concerns not Terra-forming but *terran*-forming. A human is cybernetically enhanced to survive in the Martian environment, but not for the reasons he thinks. It's a grim story, with little romance.

However, Terra-forming is exactly what Kim Stanley Robinson's Mars Trilogy is all about, or rather, to Terra-form or NOT to Terra-form. *Red Mars* (1992), *Green Mars* (1993) and *Blue Mars* (1996) are perhaps the most important books on the subject in a good thirty years, and certainly the most important work to date by the author. Described as "...the most detailed and impressive portrayal of the exploration and colonization of another planet ever published," this is Robinson's masterwork. His fellow writers agreed, as did his readers: the first of the trio won the Nebula for best novel and the other two won Hugos in the same category.

Its scope is impressive. The story begins 21 years from now, but by the end, some of the characters are two centuries old. In the beginning, a collection of 100 scientists (many of whom don't survive the story) are carefully chosen to be the first human colonists. After a "trial by ice"—a year spent together in Antarctica—they're sent on, Earth authorities having been convinced that they're compatible and stable as a group.

Except, of course, that they're *people*, and they form secret alliances, factions, schisms, and generally blow apart when they hit dirt. Divided into those who want to make Mars like Earth and those who just as passionately want it to remain as pristine as possible, and further into those who want to remain independent and those still loyal to Earth, feuds erupt into terrorism, and the Center can no longer hold. Things fall apart.

In the second book, the Original Hundred are hunted by Earth's corporate "metanations." They scatter, go underground, and otherwise rebel against what they see as Earth trying to turn the fourth planet into just another resource to exploit. Reluctantly re-joining, and teaming up with a corporate metanat who seems to be the least of many evils, they do what they can to influence the new colonists to view Mars as an independent planet, not just a corporate enclave. In the last book, Mars has oceans and—pace, Schiaparelli—canals. It also has an increasing dichotomy between the Reds, who want it to return to its original state (or as close as can still sustain life) and the Greens, who want it as Earth-like as possible. No Utopia here.

I will not go into further detail about this story. If you've read it, you already know; if you haven't, I wouldn't want to take the surprises away from you. But I will urge each and every one of you with any love for hard SF to find these books and read them. It's a high-water mark for the genre, one that isn't going to be equaled by anyone anytime soon. In a very real way, it restores much of the romanticism that our increasing knowledge of the realities of Mars takes away. If you like science fiction, you owe it to yourself to read the Mars Trilogy.

1999 saw the publication of a truly bizarre Mars tale: Larry Niven's *Rainbow Mars*. Originally planned as a collaboration between Niven and Terry Pratchett, it features Niven's hapless time-traveler, Hanville Svetz, and his journey to Mars to bring back the builder of the Martian canals. What he finds is, as usual, decidedly *not* what he was sent for. Instead, he finds elements from the Burroughsian, Wellsish, Bradbury-ite, and Heinleinian Marses, along with a Princess (who learns to surf!) and enough recursive science fictional in-jokes to float a largish thing that otherwise wouldn't float. It's his best in years, and even if you don't get all the jokes, it's fun to hunt for them.

So, how has science fiction treated Mars? Quite well, I'd say. Leaving aside importing Menlo Park inventors to wreak havoc, I think we've done pretty well by Ol' Red. And, of course, it's been very, very good to us. We've stayed pretty well up with the facts as they became known, and if we didn't, well, call it poetic license. Face it, facts should never be allowed to get in the way of a good yarn. It's still up there, of course, waiting for us to send something it can really use, and not just all these crawlers and probes and stuff. Mars wants us, just as much as we want it, and it's waited a long, long time for us to be ready.

Now, I realize I've left many, many books and stories out, and if I've missed your favorite, I apologize. Chalk it up to the limits of time, both in preparation and in presentation. Believe me, if I could have, I'd have mentioned every single one of them, and everybody but me would have been bored toothless. To help make up for that, and just for giggles, I've made a list of what I consider to be the 100 best story titles that mention Mars, and here they are:

"A Martian Sends a Postcard Home"
"All the Beer on Mars"
"An Occurrence on the Mars-to-Earth Run"
"Are There "Bears" on Mars?"
"Arthur Sternbach Brings the Curveball to Mars"
Atom War on Mars
"Atomic Airship of Mars"
Bad Dog and Those Crazee Martians!
"Bat-Men of Mars"
"Beast-Jewel of Mars"
"Because We Need No More Good Stories About Mars"
"Bingo Night at a Martian Sportsbar"
"Black Amazon of Mars"
Black-Wings of Mars
Blue Mars
"Brain Stealers of Mars"
"Can a Martian Help It If He's Colored Green?"
"Chameleons of Mars"
"Chicago Invaded - By the Men from Mars!"
"Coffins to Mars"
"Coyote on Mars"
"Death Walks on Mars"
"Don't Come to Mars!"
"Dope On Mars"
"Dream-Dust from Mars"
Egg Monsters from Mars
"First Graders From Mars"
"Foreign Legion of Mars"
"Foxholes of Mars"
"Frogs of Mars"
"From the Shores of California to the Sands of Mars"
"Grandma Goes to Mars"
"Great Wall of Mars"
Green Mars
"Holes Around Mars"
"How Green Was My Martian"
"Human Pets of Mars"
"I'm in Marsport Without Hilda"
"Innkeeper of Mars"

"Instant Maids of Mars"
"It Didn't Come From Mars"
"Janitor on Mars"
Jesus on Mars
Kent Montana and the Really Ugly Thing from Mars
"Let's Give Away Mars!"
"Lost City of Mars"
Lost Race of Mars
"Lost Treasure of Mars"
"Madmen of Mars"
Magic Ball From Mars
"Make Mine Mars"
"Man Who Bought Mars"
"Man Who Hated Mars"
Man Who Loved Mars
"Mars Confidential"
"Mars in the Parlor"
"Mars Invites You"
"Mars is a District of Sheffield"
"Mars Is Heaven!"
"Mars Is Home"
"Mars is No Place for Children"
"Mars Is Ours"
"Mars Is Waiting!"
"Mars Needs Beatniks"
"Mars Needs Women"
"Mars Will Have Blood"
"Martian Memorial to Elvis Sighted"
Martian Sexpot
"Martian Through Georgia"
"Martians, Go Home"
"Martians, Keep Out!"
"Me and Flapjack and the Martians"
"Mildews of Mars"
"Minnie of Mars"
Miss Pickeral Goes to Mars
Moving Mars
"Mr. Zytztz Goes to Mars"
"Mrs. Bagley Goes to Mars"

"Mushroom Men of Mars"
Mystery Men of Mars
"Mystery of the Blue Mist of Mars"
"Never Trust a Martian!"
"No Jokes on Mars"
"Of Course There Are Martians"
"Old Cosmonaut and the Construction Worker Dream of Mars"
"Once and Future Mars"
"Oscar, Detective of Mars"
"Pied Piper of Mars"
Rainbow Mars
"Red Death of Mars"
Red Genesis
Red Mars
Red Men of Mars
"Red Slag of Mars"
Return to Mars
"Rise and Fall of Paco Cohen and the Mariachis of Mars"
"Roughing It During the Martian Invasion"
"Sapphire as Big as the Marsport Hilton"
Sex Life on the Planet Mars
"Sherlock Holmes Versus Mars"
"Starving Children on Mars"
"Strictly from Mars"
"Summons from Mars"
"That's Just Like a Martian"
The Brave Little Toaster Goes to Mars
"The Day After the Day the Martians Came"
"The Day the Martians Came"
"The Martian and the Milkmaid"
"The Martian and the Moron"
"The Martian and the Vampire"
"The Martian in the Attic"
"The Martians and the Coys"
"The Martians and the Leadfoot"
"The Sacred Martian Pig"
"The Toad Prince or, Sex Queen of the Martian Pleasure-Domes"
"There Are No More Good Stories About Mars"
"They're Alive on Mars"

Tomatoes from Mars
Twisted Giant of Mars
"Uncle Clem and Them Martians"
"We Finally Go Back to Mars"
"We're Off to Mars!"
Welcome to Mars!
White Mars
"Windwagon Smith and the Martians"
"You Can't Escape from Mars!"
"You'll Like It on Mars!"
Zombie Surf Commandos from Mars

"There Are No More Good Stories About Mars Because We Need No More Good Stories About Mars"

Notes

1. Ah, the edisonade, that most basic and American sub-genre, in which a (usually) young, (always) American inventor uses his (never her) ingenuity to save his country, and the world if necessary, from alien invaders, evil super-scientists, Chinese dacoits, women of loose morals, and anything else the author can think of to throw at him. The Skylark books by Doc Smith are edisonades, as are, of course, the Tom Swift books.

❑

Way Up in the Middle of the Air

I WAS A KID ONCE, you know. A sweet, funny, innocent, credulous kid. I even had a friend: Billy McIlhaney, who lived down the block and was two years (and thus ages) older than I was. Billy was into things I'd never even heard of, like magic, pornography (or what passed for it in 1962—*Dude*, *Gent*, *Rogue*, *Swank*), and flying saucers. And the John Birch Society, but that was too weird even for me.

He was, as you might imagine, given that I was credulous and innocent, something of an influence. I took up magic, buying cheaply-made wooden boxes and tubes and silks and trick cards; I eschewed the skin-mags (hey, I was, like, ten years old and a Baptist), but I fell all over the flying saucers.

Billy had books, magazines, even some old newspaper clippings, and they formed a significant amount of my reading material for several years, supplementing the SF I was already reading voraciously.

I read Howard Menger's *From Outer Space to You*, Major Donald Keyhoe's books, and all the faux-Ripley collections of bizzarities assembled by Frank Edwards; I read about the Men in Black (who, although a lot of you damn kids don't know it, predate the movies and comics by decades), the Mothman of West Virginia, and about the very first modern sighting of a UFO by Kenneth Arnold back in 1947. I did not, interestingly enough, read much of anything about Roswell. Whatever happened at Roswell has become "important" only comparatively recently. Go figure.

And, of course, I read books by the Grand Old Man of Contactees, George Adamski.

Adamski was born in Poland in 1891 and moved to the US with his family two years later. When he was 22, he joined the US 13th Cavalry and served with them for six years. After settling in Laguna Beach, California, he set himself up as a philosopher and lecturer, as well as an ardent amateur astronomer and photographer. (These last two would become important later.)

Further biographical details may be found at Wikipedia, amongst other places; note carefully that said details will vary widely depending on the point of view of the biographer. Such is George Adamski, the legend and the myth. However, our subject here is Adamski the writer and the books he left behind, not Adamski the short-order cook.

His first foray into the world of publishing was a collaboration with British filmmaker Desmond Leslie titled *Flying Saucers Have Landed* (published simultaneously by Werner Laurie in the UK and the British Book Centre in the US, 1953). There's nothing terribly outstanding in most of the book, aside from the photographs (about which more later), until you get to the last two chapters; up until then, most of the information/speculation about UFOs is not much different from any of the other books on the subject at the time, but in those final two chapters Adamski managed to blow away the competition by claiming to have met and spoken to actual Venusians.

Uh-*huh*. Now, understand me, I believed every word of it. I make no apology; I offer no excuses, other than the fact that I was twelve and desperate to believe that there was life on other planets. Why? For the same reason that thousands of others at the time wanted to believe: if there was Someplace Else, it had to be better than Here.

Bear in mind what we grew up with in the late '50s and early '60s—the Cold War, race riots, a presidential assassination, another war in some Oriental place called Veetnam or something. The UFO subculture, at the time, was suffused not with the paranoia that would later turn the subject to darkness and malignance, but with hope and salvation. Oh, sure, there was some paranoia, but it was aimed at the government and military, not at our Space Brothers who, it was fondly believed, would step in just before we atomically annihilated ourselves and show us the way to Peace and/or Prosperity. One of my earliest clear memories is of playing in my yard and stopping from time to time to look out over the mountains, searching for the mushroom cloud I—we!—were convinced would eventually and inevitably come.

So Adamski's revelation that he'd been contacted was a thing devoutly to be wish'd, evidence that perhaps we wouldn't be allowed to blow ourselves up. Fair enough, I'm sure my grandparents thought the same thing about angels.

I recall holding Billy's copy of that first book reverently in my hands, turning the pages slowly in his room (he would never let me borrow his books—one of the few of his habits that survives in me today) and reading about magnetic propulsion systems, non-ballistic flight characteristics, and Madame Blavatsky. No shit.

The book itself was unassuming; a plain green binding with a jacket that featured a painting of one of Adamski's saucers in muted colors. Certainly nothing pulpish about it for all that, at the time it came out, there was still some crossover between the SF and UFO crowds. Adamski, far more interested in courting the mundane, non-SF-reading public than Ray Palmer ever was, had a carnival barker's feel for what the mainstream would find acceptable and what it wouldn't, and he knew (for all his self-assurance) that they might swallow the idea of flying saucers landing in his back yard, but *not* if he did the cover in primary colors.

Inside, though, there were photographs, actual *photographs* that Adamski took through his own telescopes. How cool is that? I didn't doubt them for a minute, of course. I mean, the book said they were real, and they couldn't print that if it wasn't true, right? Just like with the Internet?

So, okay, I had a lot to learn. I learned it, eventually, but in the meantime there were more books by Adamski to be astonished and excited by. Two years after his first came *Inside the Space Ships* (Abelard Schuman 1955), from a respected press that also published Shalom Aleichem and Isaac Asimov.

Inside was, if you'll forgive the expression, a solo flight, albeit one with a foreword by erstwhile collaborator Leslie. This time the cover was monochrome, showing a photo of the mothership surrounded by (presumably adoring) scout-ships, a photo which was printed in the first book (thus establishing that Adamski was an early recycler).

The basic contention was that not only were the denizens of the saucers still visiting Adamski at his remote home on Mt. Palomar, they were picking him up in the lobby of the hotel where he'd been drinking and "lecturing" and driving him in a sedan (black, of course) to see his old Venusian pal from the first book. The two gents giving him the ride were a Martian named Firkon and a Saturnian named Ramu. The Venusian was Orthon, but you knew that already, right? You have been following along in your own copy, haven't you?

The pictures weren't as cool as the ones in the first book, being mostly dark blobs behind light blobs, but what was cool was that these Space Brothers actually took him for a ride! Now, c'mon, who would lie about that? They only go 50,000 miles up, though, no trips to the moon or anywhere really interesting. However, they do get to talk to a couple of "Masters," who spell out their lugubrious warnings and philosophy:

> My son, our main purpose in coming to you at this time is to warn you of the grave danger which threatens men of Earth today... In your first meeting with our Brother here, he indicated to you that the exploding of bombs on Earth was of interest to us... It is possible that the body of your planet itself could be mutilated to an extent that would destroy her balance in our galaxy.

And so on and so on, ad aspera per nauseam. Nevertheless, this book caused as much furor in the saucer-nut culture as the first one did. It was a *Close Encounter of the Third Kind*, an adventure in space, a trip not quite to the moon on metaphorical gossamer wings. It was also either a heartfelt plea for some kind of peace in an increasingly unstable world (Hiroshima and Nagasaki were only a decade behind, the Cuban Missile Crisis less than a decade ahead), or one of the most cynical and opportunistic long-cons on record. Toss a coin.

We come to the third book in this little trilogy of Terra, the aptly-named *Flying Saucers Farewell* (Abelard Schuman 1961). Published four year before his death, this was Adamski's attempt to "sum up" what was known about UFOs, as well as to put forth his claim that aliens not only visited the Earth with some regularity, but were actually living among us in disguise. Once again, we're assured that (contrary to our own history) the Venusians/Martians/Saturnians/Whatevers only want the best for us and will guide us to greater health, wealth, prosperity, and, for all we know, red socks that won't run in the laundry and turn our underwear pink.

First, though, we have to get through the book's account of Adamski's world tour, which culminated not only in an audience with Queen Juliana of the Netherlands, but an encounter in Zurich with the Silence Group, his version of Albert Bender's Men in Black; they heckled his lectures, asked embarrassing questions, and somehow managed to make him look foolish without actually doing anything effective to stop him from talking—like cutting his tongue out and his fingers off, or simply shooting him in a dark alley.

I should point out that the Silence Group, or Silencers as they're known, were a matter of some discussion in the saucer sub-culture, both then and now. Much is blamed on them, as is true of all conspiracies, without any real investigation into their membership lists or e-mail addresses; apparently, the Silencers are anything the UFO enthusiasts really, really want them to be, as long as they're Evil and want True-Believers to shut up and just be laughed at by the rest of the world.

At which, I might add, one or the other of those two groups has been half-successful.

From the standpoint of those few of us who actively collect "sauceriana," the Adamski books are an absolute must-have, but they are by no means scarce: the first two went through multiple printings, and the third… well, it ain't got no pictures, so who cares? Pictures are everything in a UFO book. You could put together a set of all three, nice copies in jackets, for under $100. First editions might cost a little more, but if you're a total book-tweak and saucernut (like me), you'll have to have them. Add $25-30 to the total for firsts, and it still isn't very much to pay if you're a serious collector. There are far rarer and more valuable saucer-nut books out there, believe me.

Adamski died in 1965, one year before John G. Fuller's blockbuster *The Interrupted Journey* told us that UFO pilots were actually little gray men with big heads and eyes who experimented on us and then erased our memories of it; so much for the Space Brothers. Adamski was soon forgotten by the sub-culture he helped found, replaced by anal probes, abductions and government conspiracies that covered up what *really* happened at Roswell. He'd have hated it, I think; he had no capacity to sell fear and loathing, just peace and brotherhood. He died with little more money than he started out with, but the kid I once was still misses those Space Brothers, and I still get a thrill when I see a photo of those coool flying saucers.

Thanks for the memories, Prof. Adamski. I cherish them.

And now, lest any of you accuse me of being lugubrious in the extreme, here is a list of the 36 best flying saucer titles:

"A Flying Saucer with Minnesota Plates"
"A Saucer Has Landed… Probably"

"A Saucer of Loneliness"
"Captain Starlight and the Flying Saucer"
"Cassidy's Saucer"
"Dennis and the Flying Saucer"
"Eight Things Not to Do When the Alien Steps Out of Its Saucer"
Flying Cups and Saucers
"Flying Saucer Rock & Roll"
Flying Saucers and Common Sense
"Flying Saucers on the Attack"
Flying Saucers Uncensored
"Gravity Strings and Saucers"
"I Did Too See a Flying Saucer"
"In a Saucer Down for B-Day"
"Is the Government Hiding Saucer Facts?"
Menace of the Saucers
Night of the Saucers
"Operation Saucer"
"Our Saucer Vacation"
"Outer Space Saucers – A Myth!"
Rogue Saucer
"Santa Rides a Saucer"
Saucer Sluts
Space, Gravity and Flying Saucers
"Suppose You Met a Man in a Flying Saucer"
"The Last of the Saucers?"
"The Locked Saucer Mystery"
"The Man Who Rode the Saucer"
"The Mississippi Saucer"
The Saucers Speak!
"The Saucers Still Patrol Our Skies
"The Solipsist Lands in a Flying Saucer, With a Surprising Message for Himself and His Troops (Ready to Shoot)"
"When the Flying Saucers Land, Will You Be Ready?"
"When the Saucers Came"
"Why I Hunt Flying Saucers"

❑

Nelson Bond

"Past Masters." That's a pretty generic title for a column that features tiny slices of obscure science fiction history. Why that title? It's glib, it's inclusive without being specific, and it permits me to do pretty much what I want to do. As a rule, this is an advantage.

Sometimes, however, it's necessary to do that which I'd just as soon not have to do, as is the case with this installment. This time, I'm going to use the rubric of "Past Master" in a very real and particular sense: to venerate the recently deceased author, Nelson Slade Bond, who left us only four days ago as I write this.

I'll make no attempt at objectivity this time around, no effort to View Askance From Lofty Heights. Nelson was a friend, and he deserves better than that from me. His passing, although certainly not unexpected at the age of 98(!), came not even a week ago, and it still hurts. I'll run down the usual information, of course, but this isn't an examination of a writer I've heard of and/or studied, but a tribute to a man that I knew.

I grew up in Roanoke, Virginia, where Nelson and Betty Bond spent most of their married lives, raising two sons. One of them, Kitt, even dated the younger of my two sisters a few times. And as a reader from a very early age, I was at least peripherally aware that there was an AUTHOR in my home town, even though I'd never met him. I knew he was active in local dramatics, as was I while in high school, but our paths didn't cross.

Skip ahead a few years, several moves, and a couple of semesters of college in Richmond. I became active in fandom, attending conventions and cranking out my own fanzine, which I traded with whoever would trade back. At some point, this brought me to the attention of a nascent

fan organization which called itself the Nelson Bond Society, which published a clubzine called "The Jinnia Clan Journal" - a reference to Nelson's Meg and Dayv stories, which took place in a far-future America. They invited me to join, and I did, partly because when one first encounters fandom after a lifetime of segregation from the mainstream one tends to join everything, but mostly because I had become more familiar with Nelson's stories in the intervening years and looked forward to finally meeting him.

In 1974, the WorldCon was held in Washington, DC, and I was told that Nelson might attend. Now, bear in mind that I still had not actually met the man; all I had to go on were rather crude portraits the JCJ "staff artist" did of him, which showed an older man with a neat van Dyke. When I saw someone fitting this description at the "Meet the Pros" party at DisCon II, I approached him and asked if he was Nelson Bond. Nodding gravely, the gentleman in question replied, "Yes, as a matter of fact, I *am* L. Sprague de Camp."

For the next fifteen minutes or so, de Camp alternated between regaling me with stories of the old days when he'd known Nelson, and asking me questions about what Nelson was doing now. "Christ," I recall him saying when I hastily apologized for the mistaken identity and explained. "I didn't even know Nelson was still *alive*!"

This was to be a typical response by other SF writers when I mentioned Nelson to them: story after story about him, and surprise that he was still around.

Nelson's first SF story was "Down the Dimensions" in the April 1937 *Astrounding*, but this followed two years of humor, romance and sports stories. In fact, for the first four years of his writing career, the vast majority of his sales were to the sports pulps. His final story, "Proof of the Pudding," was published in the October/November, 1999 *Asimov's* by direct invitation of then-editor Gardner Dozois after Nelson's well-deserved (and superbly performed) stint as SFWA's Author Emeritus in 1998. Aside from one other story, "Pipeline to Paradise" in the Roger Zelazny-edited anthology *Wheel of Fortune* (AvoNova 1995), it was his first publication since 1958.

And that is all the faux-academic bibliographica I will impose on you this time.

I did, finally, meet Nelson in 1975, when he agreed to be interviewed for my fanzine and invited me to visit him and Betty. Betty brought sandwiches and beer (Canadian, of course), and I asked this fascinating man every question I could think of about his career in the pulps, his interaction with other writers, and his life-long love for antiquarian books while a cassette recorder whirred quietly in the middle of the table.

Among the bits and pieces of his writer's life that he passed along to me that afternoon was the advice he'd given a young Isaac Asimov when he'd boasted of selling his first story in 1939. Nelson, by then a seasoned vet of four years and more than four dozen stories, said, "Son, anybody can sell one story. It's the second one that proves you're a writer." He gave me the same bit of advice decades later after I sold my first yarn.

Harlan Ellison asked him to contribute a story to *The Last Dangerous Visions* after one of the younger Bond Society members wrote him saying that the book wouldn't be complete without one, and so Nelson wrote his first fiction in almost two decades: "Pipeline to Paradise." When the anthology still hadn't appeared after six years, Nelson withdrew the story with a sharp letter to Editor Ellison. This caused a breach between the two men, one that was healed in September of 2001 when a group of ex-Bond Society members and others paid tribute to Nelson and Betty. After a sumptuous lunch (with a special cake depicting the cover of Nelson's first book), letters from various writers, editors and publishers who had known and worked with Nelson were read by those present. In part, the letter from Ellison read:

> There have been few writers in my well-read life whose work I've been more in love with than yours. I came upon you when you were in fullest flower. I was in high school, 1950 I think, and I was a reader of Blue Book magazine. And it was there that I came across "And Lo! The Bird," which I suspect I've reread more than a hundred times; suspect I've read it aloud to high school and writing classes possibly half a hundred; and don't suspect, but *know*, I've recommended it to readers *more* than a hundred times.

Nelson positively beamed when this letter was read, and all differences between the two men were forgotten.

Nelson and I shared a love of books, not only as repositories of information, but as artifacts as well. He was an antiquarian, with a general knowledge of books and their history that I could never equal in a lifetime. My interests were more specialized, and I was thrilled on those occasions when he would call me or send e-mail asking about a specific SF or fantasy title with which he was unfamiliar.

His library was, if not all-encompassing, certainly extensive and eclectic. Among other things, he had a nearly complete collection of Cabell, and any number of signed first editions, which he would lovingly pull down and share with those he trusted to handle them. He had been close friends with Ray Bradbury, and among the treasures on that particular shelf was a copy of the asbestos-bound edition of *Fahrenheit 451*, one of only 200 copies, and the first edition of *The Illustrated Man* which Bradbury not only warmly inscribed, but in which he drew a sketch of the title character.

Nelson's catalogs were witty and frequently contained hoax titles, such as the autobiography of one Irene Wanda, who married first Howard Hughes and then Henry Kissinger, resulting in the title *I. Wanda Hughes Kissinger Now*. They were also sprinkled by bits of light, if perfectly scansioned, verse which were tied to specific books, such as this from one of his 1970s lists, referring to a H. P. Lovecraft book, and titled "Nyarlathotep is Petohtalrayn Spelled Backwards:"

> I never subscribed to the Cthulhu cult.
> I certainly don't denounce it,
> But the reason I never joined it is
> Because I cannot pronounce it.

Over the years, Nelson was warm, generous with his time and potables, incisive and insightful when reading one of my stories before I sent it out ("Remember," he told me more than once. "Great stories aren't written, they're re-written."). He was both funny and witty, and would laugh as hard at my jokes as I did at his.

He could also be acerbic and stern, as any number of people around him (including me) discovered when there were disagreements, but in every case, he was the epitome of an old-fashioned gentleman. I regret now that I didn't call him more often, but as has been pointed out to me, had I called him once a week I'd feel badly that I didn't call *twice* a week.

Over the years, a lot of Nelson's stories were rescued from potential obscurity by anthologists who knew good stuff when they saw it. "Conqueror's Isle," perhaps his most commonly-reprinted story, appeared in no fewer than eight anthologies, "And Lo! The Bird" in a half dozen, and the breathtaking "Magic City" stayed in print for decades though its publication in Anthony Boucher's massive *A Treasury of Great Science Fiction*, which was kept alive and very much kicking through the SF Book Club. This is, perhaps, the anthology in which many—if not most—young readers first encountered Nelson's playful, intricate prose.

Much of Nelson's work, however, remains unreprinted. In the case of the sports stories, this was fine with him; he recognized them for what they were, bread-and-butter yarns intended to keep a roof over his head. However, there have never been definitive collections of some of his most famous characters: Squaredeal Sam McGhee, Pat Pending, and Horse-Sense Hank remain out of print, barring a singleton reprint here and there. Perhaps this can be rectified in the future.

It's customary in these sorts of things to say something along the lines of "We'll not see his like again." Well, yes, but that's practically universal, and hardly does anyone justice, let alone someone who was the master craftsman that Nelson was. He was one of the very few remaining links with our shared history, one of the last of the Giants. In the words of Lord Buckley, he stomped upon the Terra, and left his mark not only on the readers he touched, but the other writers with whom he shared pages.

I'll miss your laugh, Nelson, and your grace and honesty. May the earth rest lightly on you.

A Brief Bond Bibliography (books only)

Mr. Merganthwirker's Lobblies – Coward-McCann 1946
Exiles of Time – Prime Press 1949, Paperback Library 1965
The Thirty-First of February – Gnome Press 1949
The Remarkable Exploits of Lancelot Biggs, Spaceman – Doubleday 1950, Wildside 2000
The Postal Stationary of Canada – Herman Herst 1953
No Time Like the Future – Avon 1954
Nightmares and Daydreams – Arkham House 1968
The Far Side of Nowhere – Arkham House 2002
That Worlds May Live – Wildside 2003
Other Worlds Than Ours – Arkham House 2005

❑

Zenna Henderson, People Person

There was a time, not so far back that it's slipped from living memory, when sentiment was accepted as a legitimate tone for a writer to use. To be sure, it was frequently abused, especially in the pulps, but in the hands of a skilled and sincere writer it could be—and often was—what elevated an otherwise common idea (robots and humans) to the level of near-genius ("Helen O'Loy," by Lester del Rey).

This is not, apparently, the case today. Instead of sentiment, all too often, we have irony. Instead of an examination of a character's emotions, we're given glib, therapy-inspired excuses for why they do what they do. Why should a writer work hard to create a memorable character when they can simply use a clip-artifact with a funny hat instead?

Of course, this is not the case across the board, or I would have given up reading for pleasure long ago, but it's true enough often enough to be dismaying. I can't help but feel that this trend towards thinly-veiled mocking of sincerity shows contempt for both the reader and the subject matter, and that is an offense no writer should be guilty of.

Yes, I realize that this makes me sound like a cranky old fart bitching about kids today, and the music they listen to being a bunch of noise, but deal with it. I have to. And I happen to *like* noisy music, myself, not like those old farts over *there.*

And I like sentimental fiction, unashamedly and unabashedly, as long as it doesn't descend into gratuitous and blatant button-pushing. Clifford Simak's *Way Station* and *Goblin Reservation* are just fine; PSAs by for-profit "charities" featuring dewy-eyed kids scrabbling in trash heaps ain't.

Zenna Chlarson Henderson (1917-1983) may have pushed the odd button or two, but she certainly didn't whang on them like a lab-rat jonesing for kibble. She tweaked them gently to remind us that they were there for a reason, then held those reasons up for us to marvel at.

Henderson was a school teacher all her life, but that wasn't her goal; it was just the only track she could get at her local college. Nevertheless, the daily experience of dealing with perhaps the strangest animals on the face of the Earth—children, in all their myriad and steadfast wonder—gave her an insight into humanity which was absolutely necessary for her avocation: writing with empathy and compassion about aliens among us.

During World War II, she taught children at the Japanese-American internment camp in Sacaton, Arizona for a year; it's not a stretch to consider that this, as much as almost anything else in her life, enabled her to address the role of the Stranger in a Strange Land.

But there's something else that might have had at least as much an impact: Henderson was born and raised in the Church of Jesus Christ of Latter Day Saints. Being a Mormon in Arizona wasn't easy; as recently as 1953, Arizona police arrested leaders of the Church. Currently, the LDS is listed by the Southern Poverty Law Center as a hate group because they consider some Church dogma to be racist and sexist.

Whatever the realities, Henderson almost certainly suffered prejudice at the hands of non-Mormons to one degree or another. Taken with her experiences at Sacaton, is there any wonder that this theme informs most, if not all, of her work?

That work began with the sale of her first story, "Come On, Wagon!" to *F&SF* in 1951. Not a story of "The People," it nevertheless tells of a child with odd mental powers who is forbidden to use them by his uncle, with tragic results.

Many of Henderson's stories involve tragedy of one sort or another. In fact, her People stories are founded on their calamitous shipwreck on Earth, with each story illuminating the aliens' emotional and physical responses to their disaster within the context of trying to hide amongst us.

But not false tragedy, or mere bathos—in that first story, little Thaddeus loses his psi ability as a result of his uncle's proscription, and someone dies as a result. If Henderson were a lesser writer, this story would resemble nothing more than a fantasy-oriented version of the death of Little Nell; that it doesn't can be explained by two facts: first, that Henderson began writing from an early age and worked a lot of the clichés out of her system. As she said in a self-penned author's bio in the August, 1953 issue of William Hamling's *Imagination*:

> I wrote poetry and 'plays' from the fourth grade on up, but it wasn't until about four years ago that I really started writing fiction in earnest.

The other fact is… well, not to put too fine an edge on it, the editors requested it. In a letter dated 3 December 1950, J. Francis McComas said, in part:

> …we don't think you have fully developed your situation. We'd like to offer the following suggestions for revision, with the hope you'll see fit to work on them and let us see what happens. If you can do a satisfactory rewrite, we'll want the story.

She could, and they did. Their suggestions, although perhaps implied in the original story, nevertheless turned it from a pretty good yarn into one of the most affecting first stories I've ever read.

Not far behind "Come On, Wagon!" was the first of the stories she would become best known for, her other life's work, if you will: "Ararat." Almost all of the People stories have biblical titles, very much in keeping with the spirituality that informs her entire body of work. And, indeed, the People were visited with cataclysms of biblical proportions: fleeing a doomed planet, human-like aliens with odd psi powers crash on Earth and are scattered. The stories in the series detail the difficulties the People have attempting to find each other while staying hidden from the rest of the world.

Like all of Henderson's work, the People stories are funny, moving, wistful, and in many places, bitter. There is no rest for the People, no safety except in isolation and secrecy. That the youngest of the People, those who don't remember their home, rebel against this isolation is inevitable; that this creates conflict and tension within their closed community makes for terrific story-telling.

But Zenna Henderson was about more than just this one series, however wonderful it might be (and it is, in every sense of the word). Her insights into the alien world of children are, on the surface, engaging. It's difficult not to like the likeable kids in her stories, and even the unlikable ones seem to have at least a few redeeming qualities.

It's down deep in the stories, though, that the real value is found. Her children may seem innocent and naïve, but some of them harbor dark secrets. In "The Anything Box," a young girl finds solace and relief from her

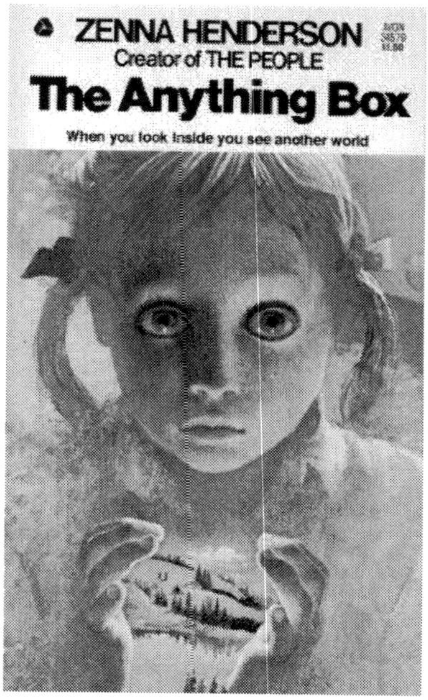

dreadful life (her father is a thief) in what her teacher at first believes to be vivid imagination. Cupping her hands around an invisible box, the girl can see whatever she wants most to see. Her real life becomes so unbearable, though, that she tries (unsuccessfully) to put herself into that imaginary world and is only saved when her teacher realizes what's going on and quite literally pulls her back.

In a very real way, "The Anything Box" can be seen as Henderson's attempt to portray autism. Any school teacher who puts in any time at all sees children who suffer from one degree of autism or another, and Henderson's experiences at the Japanese internment camp must have shown her children—and even adults—lost inside themselves trying to escape the harsh reality of their ruined lives.

There's more than a little bitterness, too, in the seldom-reprinted "The Grunder." Henderson wisely left children out of this story about a man's pathological—and unwarranted—jealousy over what he imagines are his wife's infidelities. On a camping trip intended to save their marriage, he is confronted with yet one more possibility that she's cheating, this time with two men who dropped by the campsite and, being the kind of fictional characters who do this sort of thing, tease him about being alone with his wife. He seems to deal with it well enough, encouraging his wife to relax, but then his compulsion gets the better of him. Before he can hurt her, he stumbles away into the rainy night and, sick of his own paranoia and willing to do anything to do away with it, seeks and finds the legendary grunder (a fish that swims in the earth). Using the formula given him earlier in the story by a grizzled local, he catches the earth-fish and uses it to literally rip the sickness out of himself.

There's both myth and madness in the resolution of this one, and if the characters here don't seem quite as clear-cut as their young counterparts in other stories, well, Henderson just knew kids better.

Myth and madness feature in "Walking Aunt Daid," one of the few truly creepy stories Henderson wrote. Even here, though, there's sweetness of a sort. The story involves a family curse/tradition, and the coming of age of the viewpoint character who must take his turn to walk Aunt Daid. What happens to them—what has happened many times, in fact—is both wonderful and terrible. The pair's moonlit journey changes them both, one of them forever, and the knowledge that it must happen again and again is another example of Henderson's surprising tinge of bitterness.

Zenna Henderson's output was small, comparatively speaking—three collections and a fix-up novel during her lifetime—but each story, each vignette, is a polished gem that outshines the work of lesser, more prolific writers. All four books were published in hardcover: three by Doubleday and one by the UK SF giant Gollancz. The press runs, however, were even more miniscule than was usually the case with Doubleday's SF line; I wouldn't be at all surprised to learn that there were only a few hundred of them ever bound, although the later Avon paperbacks were cranked out in huge numbers and, with the exception of *The Anything Box*, are quite common even today. For whatever reason, I see a dozen or more copies of the other Avon books for every single copy of *Box*, and I try and scarf them up whenever I can.

As should all of *you* out there reading this. Trust me; I wouldn't waste my time or yours with hacks or those numberless writers who've been forgotten for good reason. If I bring 'em up here, it's because I think they're in danger of fading from the SF Consciousness forever, and it's my job to do what I can to prevent that.

The NESFA collection mentioned below contains all the People stories, including one previously unpublished story, and belongs on the shelf of every serious SF reader. There's no space opera here, no battles, robots, blasters, or BEMs. It's not military in the least; there are no magic rings or dragons. But there is lyricism, and gentility, and emotion, and yes, not a little sentimentality. Zenna Henderson's kids may not wave wands and make potions, but they can grab a handful of sunlight and platt twishers with the best of them.

The People, and all the rest of her characters, children and adults alike, are worthy of your attention and affection. I sez, "Get into them."

Books

Pilgrimage: The Book of the People – Doubleday 1961, Avon 1964
The Anything Box – Doubleday 1965, Avon 1969
The People: No Different Flesh – Gollancz 1966, Avon 1968
Holding Wonder – Doubleday 1971 (contains 12 original stories), Avon 1972
Ingathering: The Complete People Stories – NESFA Press 1995 (contains one original story)

Stories

"Come On, Wagon!" (*F&SF*, December 1951)
"The Dark Came Out to Play..." (*Imagination*, May 1952)
"Ararat" (*F&SF*, October 1952)
"Loo Ree" (*F&SF*, February 1953)
"The Grunder" (*Imagination*, June 1953)
"The Substitute" (*Imagination*, August 1953)
"Hush!" (*Beyond*, November 1953)
"Food to All Flesh" (*F&SF*, December 1953)
"Gilead" (*F&SF*, August 1954)
"You Know What, Teacher?" (*Ellery Queen Mystery Magazine*, September 1954)
"Walking Aunt Daid" (*F&SF*, July 1955)
"Pottage" (*F&SF*, September 1955)
"The Anything Box" (*F&SF*, October 1956)
"Wilderness" (*F&SF*, January 1957)
"The Last Step" (*F&SF*, February 1957)
"Turn the Page" (*F&SF*, May 1957)
"Captivity" (*F&SF*, June 1958)
"Jordan" (*F&SF*, March 1959)
"And a Little Child..." (*F&SF*, October 1959)
"Something Bright" (*Galaxy*, February 1960)
"The Closest School" (*Fantastic*, April 1960)
"Things" (*F&SF*, July 1960)
"Return" (*F&SF*, March 1961)
"Shadow on the Moon" (*F&SF*, March 1962)
"Subcommittee" (*F&SF*, July 1962)
"Deluge" (*F&SF*, October 1963)
"No Different Flesh" (*F&SF*, May 1965)
"The Effectives" (*Worlds of Tomorrow*, May 1965)

"Angels Unawares" (*F&SF*, May 1966)
"Troubling of the Water" (*F&SF*, September 1966)
"The Indelible Kind" (*F&SF*, December 1968)
"J-Line to Nowhere" (*F&SF*, September 1969)
"The Believing Child" (*F&SF*, June 1970)
"Through a Glass" - Darkly (*F&SF*, October 1970)
"That Boy" (*F&SF*, November 1971)
"As Simple as That" (in Holding *Wonder*, Doubleday 1971)
"Three-Cornered and Secure" (in Holding *Wonder*, Doubleday 1971)
"The Taste of Aunt Sophronia" (in Holding *Wonder*, Doubleday 1971)
"Swept and Garnished" (in Holding *Wonder*, Doubleday 1971)
"One of Them" (in Holding *Wonder* Doubleday 1971)
"Sharing Time" (in Holding *Wonder*, Doubleday 1971)
"Ad Astra" (in Holding *Wonder*, Doubleday 1971)
"Incident After" (in Holding *Wonder*, Doubleday 1971)
"The Walls" (in Holding *Wonder*, Doubleday 1971)
"Crowning Glory" (in Holding *Wonder* Doubleday 1971)
"Boona on Scancia" (in Holding *Wonder*, Doubleday 1971)
"Love Every Third Stir" (in Holding *Wonder*, Doubleday 1971)
"Thrumthing and Out" (*F&SF*, October 1972)
"Katie-Mary's Trip" (*F&SF*, January 1975)
"The First Stroke" (*F&SF*, October 1977)
"There Was a Garden" (in *Cassandra Rising*, ed. Alice Laurence, Doubleday 1978)
"Tell Us a Story" (*F&SF*, October 1980)
"...Old...As a Garment" (in *Speculations*, ed. Isaac Asimov and Alice Laurence, Houghton Mifflin 1982)
"Michel Without" (*Ingathering: The Complete People Stories*, NESFA Press 1995)

❑

Gats, Six-Guns and Blasters

> "The company dicks were good. They were plenty good. Hugh Starke began to think maybe this time he wasn't going to get away with it."

NOW, THAT'S HARD-BOILED. Hell, that's a twenty-minute egg, pickled in brine. But it boils harder:

> His small stringy body hunched over the control bank, nursing the last ounce of power out of the Kallman. The hot night sky of Venus fled past the ports in tattered veils of indigo. Starke wasn't sure where he was anymore… Maybe even God wasn't sure."

Bubble bubble, toil and trouble indeed. By now, you could use that egg for a handball. So, who wrote it? Dashiell Weinbaum? Edgar Rice Chandler? Harlan Spillane? Who?

Now, let's not always see the same hands. I'll give you a clue: it appeared in the Fall 1953 issue of *Tops in Science Fiction*. Of course, if you have the references on hand to look this up, you probably won't need to, you stfnal hipster, you.

Right you are. Ray Bradbury and Leigh Brackett in their one and only collaboration, "Lorelei of the Red Mist." Not Bradbury's first collab, mind you—that was "Pendulum" in the 11/41 *Super Science* with Henry Hasse—but we're not here to talk about him anyway. In any case, his contribution to their collaboration was the last half of the story after she left to work in Hollywood; the opening, noir to the max, was all Brackett.

Leigh Douglas Brackett was born December 7th, 1915, and was, by all reports, something of a tomboy. She was active and athletic (not to mention adventurous), playing pirates with her friends on the beach in California, and it's not too much of a stretch to assume they went at each other as cops/robbers and cowboys/Indians, too. An avid reader, she was given a copy of Burroughs's *The Gods of Mars*, and it was a literal (and literary) turning point: her life-long love of imaginary swashbuckling became an interplanetary one.

As is frequently the case with avid readers, Brackett began writing. Her first sale was in 1939 to *Astounding*, "Martian Quest" appearing in the February 1940 issue. Although she'd sell a handful of stories to Campbell in the next few years, she soon began appearing in the magazine she would be most associated with when *Planet Stories* ran "Stellar Region" in their Winter 1940 issue. (Something else life-changing happened that year, too: she met and befriended Edmond Hamilton; six years later, they were married.)

From the beginning, Leigh Brackett wrote tough. Not just hard-boiled, as in the excerpt above, but tough, like a smart Doberman. One with a gun. Not always, mind you; she could wax lyrical enough when the story required it, as in this passage from *The Sword of Rhiannon* (1953):

> Lean lithe men and women passed him in the shadowy streets, silent as cats except for the chime and the whisper of the tiny bells the women wear, a sound as delicate as rain, distillate of all the sweet wickedness of the world.

Makes you want to give it all up and go back to selling vinyl siding, doesn't it? But as dulcet and decadent as the above is, you can't deny that it's also... well, Tough.

Brackett is best know within the genre for her stories about Eric John Stark, the direct literary descendent of Burroughs's John Carter. Originally run in *Planet Stories*, they were published in book form (reportedly after revision by Hamilton) by Ace Books as part of their Doubles series.

However, her first books weren't fantasy at all, but mysteries. The first, *No Good From a Corpse* (Coward McCann 1944), would lead her into a very productive and lucrative career, but we'll get to that in a minute.

Actor George Sanders was credited with two novels, neither of which he wrote (nor read, in all probability). The first was ghosted by Craig Rice (who also ghosted mysteries by Gypsy Rose Lee) and Cleve Cartmill, and

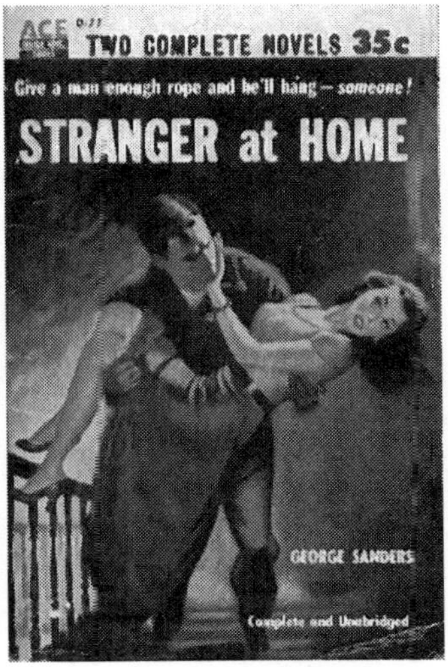

the second by Brackett. *Stranger At Home* was published in 1947 by Simon & Schuster as part of their "Inner Sanctum" series, and is dedicated by Sanders "To Leigh Brackett, whom I have never met." Nice enough of him, I suppose. It was later reprinted as an Ace Double with Stephen Marlowe's *Catch the Brass Ring*, which I assume he wrote by himself.

However, it was her first book that eventually brought her fortune, if not fame. As author and critic James Sallis wrote in the *Boston Globe*:

> It's 1944, and Howard Hawks has just hired William Faulkner to write the screenplay for Raymond Chandler's *The Big Sleep*. Thinking about who to bring on as collaborator, he remembers reading an outstanding hardboiled novel titled *No Good from a Corpse*. "Get me that Brackett guy," he tells an assistant. Surprised when an attractive young woman shows up, he hires her anyway, beginning a long relationship.

Hollywood being what it is, it didn't stop there. She wrote the script, it was passed around to the actors, and, again according to Sallis:

> When Humphrey Bogart got his copy of the script, feeling that some of his dialogue was too gentlemanly, went to Brackett to discuss it with her, he found that the parts he disliked had been written not by Brackett as he assumed but by Faulkner. The good stuff was hers.

That's *Tough*. Don't get me wrong, though, she did have her gentle side. When she and Hamilton moved to an old Ohio farmhouse in 1950, they had an ongoing problem with woodchucks which he decided to solve by means of a Sako .222 rifle. She wouldn't let him use it, explaining that she liked to watch the chucks at play while she was writing. "Needless to say," Hamilton wrote, "my fine high-powered rifle with its beautiful variable telescopic sight has never been used."

She was a lady as well, as author Robert Silverberg attests, saying, "Leigh was not only one of the best of the space-opera writers, whose style and plotting technique and way of handling character I studied with great care when I was starting out, but also a charming and gracious person." He goes on to illustrate his point:

> She also happened to be very conservative politically, which is at the core of one incident very typical of Leigh. It was 1964, when the Worldcon was in Oakland, and Leigh and Ed Hamilton and Harlan [Ellison] and our wives had gone out to dinner at some San Francisco restaurant. That summer was also the summer of the Goldwater-LBJ presidential race. Harlan, as far to the left then as he is now, started in on Goldwater at the dinner table, denouncing him as though he were Lucifer. Leigh listened to his tirade for a couple of minutes, and then said, very sweetly, with a pleasant smile, "Harlan, you ought to know that I'm a little old lady in tennis shoes"—which was not at all an accurate description of Leigh's physical self, but rather a code phrase then for a substantial band of Goldwater supporters. Harlan, who would not have wanted to give offense to Leigh for anything (she was one of his idols) shrank down in chagrin and muttered an apology. He said very little for the rest of the meal.

That certainly fits my definition of a Lady. Not only was she willing to spare Ellison the spectacle of slapping him down in public, she was good enough a writer in the first place—and enough of a gentleperson—that he was willing to accept her kind rebuke in the spirit in which it was offered. Silverberg continues:

> What was significant was the complete sweetness of her tone as she told Harlan to put a lid on it. Truly ladylike, which was amusing when you consider that Leigh was a broad-shouldered, athletic-looking woman with a fine two-fisted outlook on the world. 'Little old lady' indeed!

When I write these pieces, I make it a point to contact people who either knew the subject or at least had some kind of working relationship with them. Hard to do in some cases, like this one, when the subject has been gone for almost 30 years, but the point of those writers I touch on in Past Masters is that they've left a literary legacy of some sort, something that has outlived them, at least so far. So, Brackett having been a pioneering woman writer in a field dominated from top to bottom by men, I asked a number of women writers and editors, hoping that they'd share some insights about how Brackett had paved the way for the likes of McCaffrey and LeGuin, and thus themselves.

That ain't what I got. Perhaps I went to the wrong people, but most of what I got was noncommittal shrugging about how they'd liked her stuff as kids, but…

What I did get were, interestingly enough, accolades from men. Not surprising, I suppose. Brackett was a swashbuckler, not a gentle mother figure like Zenna Henderson (see last issue) or a strident feminist like Russ. She was what she was, and she wrote in a man's field so well that she stood out not because she was a woman—hell, most people thought Leigh was a man's name anyhow—but because she did it better than almost anyone else.

(I would have dearly loved to have been able to ask Catherine Moore about Brackett, as she and her husband Henry Kuttner were great friends of Hamilton and Brackett, but oh well.)

Author, editor and critic Barry Malzberg said: "[She] never got her true due. [It] was a hard and lonely thing to be a female scriptwriter in those times…and she made her way with panache and fury." Howard Hawks must have felt the same way; he used her a half a dozen times to write both gumshoe movies and westerns, and never second-guessed her. Some of the films he's best known for are ones she wrote: *The Big Sleep*, *Rio Bravo* and *Rio Lobo*, and *Hatari!*, which was kind of an African western (if you squint). In all, she would do 17 films and teleplays, including one taken from her own novel, *The Tiger Among Us*, winding up with what is widely considered the best of the Star Wars movies, *The Empire Strikes Back*. Laurence Kasdan may have finished it after her death in 1978, but Brackett put her indelible stamp on it.

Raymond Feist, a fantasist with deep roots in Hollywood, told me:

> I admired her because she did something that few of us do really well, operate in two different media. If she'd only written *The Big Sleep* with William Faulkner and Jules Furthman, she'd probably have been a footnote, but she got the job because Howard Hawks fell in love with her first novel…

Of Brackett's fiction, he says:

> …she wrote in the genre as well as anyone. Her Eric John Stark high-adventure stuff compares well with R. E. Howard's Solomon Kane and Burrough's Carter stuff, IMHO, though it's more "modern" circa 1950's. Her novel *The Long Tomorrow* is a fine example of post-nuclear stuff that ranks up there with Stewart's *Earth Abides* and Miller's *A Canticle for Leibowitz*…

Feist isn't alone in his praise for her best-known genre novel. No less a critic than Damon Knight waxed almost rhapsodic over it, calling it "…a startling performance from the gifted author of so much, but so entirely different, science-fantasy… Speculation as brilliantly sound as this no longer seems like speculation at all, but simple truth… as real, as intimately detailed and as warmly sympathetic as if the author herself had lived it."

Leigh Brackett died on March 18, 1978, three months or so after her 63rd birthday and only a year after burying her husband. She left behind a multitude of grieving fans and a legacy of finely-crafted stories, all of which I'm certain that she and her childhood pals would have loved to play out on the California sands.

The place to begin if you're not already a Brackett fan (and if not, why not?) is the well-chosen collection *The Best of Leigh Brackett*, edited and with an introduction by Edmond Hamilton. It's not so different from Brackett herself, being a broad-shouldered, athletic-looking book with a fine two-fisted outlook on her literary legacy. Bud sez, get into it.

(The following bibliography is necessarily incomplete, and as always, I welcome additions and corrections care of this site. C'mon, folks, make me look good.)

Short Fiction

"Martian Quest" (Feb. 1940 *Astounding*)
"The Treasure of Ptakuth" (Apr. 1940 *Astounding*)
"The Tapestry Gate" (Aug. 1940 *Strange Stories*)
"The Stellar Legion" (Winter 1940 *Planet*)
"Water Pirate" (Jan. 1941 *Super Science*)
"The Demons of Darkside" (Jan. 1941 *Startling*)
"Interplanetary Reporter" (May 1941 *Startling*)
"The Dragon-Queen of Jupiter" (Summer 1941 *Planet*)
"Lord of the Earthquake" (June 1941 *Science Fiction*)
"A World is Born" (July 1941 *Comet Stories*)
"No Man's Land in Space" (July 1941 *Amazing*)
"Retreat to the Stars" (Nov. 1941 *Astonishing*)
"The Sorcerer of Rhiannon" (Feb. 1942 *Astounding*)
"Child of the Green Light" (Feb. 1942 *Super Science*)
"Child of the Sun" (Feb. 1942 *Planet*)
"Out of the Sea" (June 1942 *Astonishing*)
"Cube from Space" (Aug. 1942 *Super Science*)
"Outpost on Io" (Nov. 1942 *Planet*)
"The Halfling" (Feb 1943 *Astonishing*)
"Citadel of Lost Ships" (Mar. 1943 *Planet*)
"The Blue Behemoth" (May 1943 *Planet*)
"Thralls of the Endless Night" (Fall 1943 *Planet*)
"The Veil of Astellar" (Spring 1944 *Thrilling Wonder*)
"The Jewel of Bas" (Spring 1944 *Planet*)
"Terror Out of Space" (Summer 1944 *Planet*)
"Shadow Over Mars" (Fall 1944 *Startling*)
"The Vanishing Venusians" (Spring 1945 *Planet*)
"Lorelei of the Red Mist" (Summer 1946 *Planet*, with Ray Bradbury)
"The Moon That Vanished" (Oct. 1948 *Thrilling Wonder*)
"The Beast-Jewel of Mars" (Winter 1948 *Planet*)
"Quest of the Starhope" (Apr. 1949 *Thrilling Wonder*)
"Sea-Kings of Mars" (June 1949 *Thrilling Wonder*)
"Queen of the Martian Catacombs" (Summer 1949 *Planet*)

"City of the Lost Ones" (Fall 1949 *Planet*, as "Enchantress of Venus")
"The Lake of the Gone Forever" (Oct. 1949 *Thrilling Wonder*)
"The Dancing Girl of Ganymede" (Feb. 1950 *Thrilling Wonder*)
"The Truants" (July 1950 *Startling*)
"The Citadel of Lost Ages" (Dec. 1950 *Thrilling Wonder*)
"Black Amazon of Mars" (Mar. 1951 *Planet*)
"The Starmen of Llyrdis" (Mar. 1951 *Startling*)
"The Woman from Altair" (July 1951 *Startling*)
"The Shadows" (Feb. 1952 *Startling*)
"The Last Days of Shandakor" (Apr. 1952 *Startling*)
"Shannach - The Last" (Nov. 1952 *Planet*)
"The Big Jump" (Feb. 1953 *Space Stories*)
"The Ark of Mars" (Sept. 1953 *Planet*)
"Teleportress of Alpha C" (Winter 1954 *Planet*)
"Mars Minus Bisha" (Jan. 1954 *Planet*)
"Runaway" (Spring 1954 *Startling*)
"The Tweener" (Feb. 1955 *F&SF*)
"Last Call from Sector 9G" (Summer 1955 *Planet*)
"The Queer Ones" (Mar. 1957 *Venture*)
"All the Colors of the Rainbow" (Nov. 1957 *Venture*)
"The Road to Sinharat" (May 1963 *Amazing*)
"Purple Priestess of the Mad Moon" (Oct. 1964 *F&SF*)
"Come Sing the Moons of Moravenn" (in *The Other Side of Tomorrow*, ed. Roger Elwood, Random 1973)
"How Bright the Stars" (in *Flame Tree Planet*, ed. Roger Elwood, Concordia 1973)
"Mommies and Daddies" (in *Crisis*, ed. Roger Elwood, Nelson 1974)
"Stark and the Star Kings" (in *Stark and the Star Kings*, Haffner 2005 with Edmond Hamilton)

As Editor

The Best from Planet Stories Vol. 1 (Del Rey 1975)
The Best of Edmond Hamilton (Del Rey 1977)

Nongenre Novels

No Good from a Corpse (Coward McCann 1944)
Stranger at Home (Simon & Schuster 1946, as by George Sanders)

An Eye For an Eye (Doubleday Crime Club 1957)
The Tiger Among Us (Doubleday Crime Club 1957)
Rio Bravo (Bantam 1959)
Follow the Free Wind (Doubleday 1963)
Silent Partner (Putnam 1969)

SF/Fantasy Novels

The Starmen (Gnome Press 1952)
The Sword of Rhiannon (Ace D-36 1953, bound with Howard's *Conan the Conqueror*)
The Long Tomorrow (Doubleday 1955)
The Big Jump (Ace D-103 1955, bound with Dick's *The Solar Lottery*)
The Nemesis of Terra (Ace F-123 1961, bound with Silverberg's *Collision Course*)
Alpha Centauri or Die! (Ace F-187 1963, bound with Wallis's *Legend of Lost Earth*)
The Secret of Sinharat (Ace M-101 1964, bound with Brackett's *People of the Talisman*)
The Ginger Star (Del Rey 1974)
The Hounds of Skaith (Del Rey 1974)
The Reavers of Skaith (Del Rey 1976)

Collections

The Coming of the Terrans (Ace G-669 1967)
The Halfling and Other Stories (Ace 31590 1973)
The Best of Leigh Brackett (Del Rey 1977)
Martian Quest: The Early Brackett (Haffner 2000)
Sea-Kings of Mars and Otherworldly Stories (Gollancz 2005, Vol. 46 of the Fantasy Masterworks series)

Screenplays and Teleplays

The Vampire's Ghost (1945, screenplay and story)
The Big Sleep (1946, screenplay)
Crime Doctor's Man Hunt (1946)
Rio Bravo (1959, screenplay)
Checkmate (one episode, "Face in the Window" 1960, story and teleplay)
Gold of the Seven Saints (1961)
13 West Street (1962, from her 1957 novel, *The Tiger Among Us*)

Hatari! (1962)
The Alfred Hitchcock Hour (2 episodes, "Terror at Northfield" and "Death of a Cop", both 1963)
Man's Favorite Sport? (1964, uncredited draft polish)
El Dorado (1966, screenplay)
Rio Lobo (1970)
The Long Goodbye (1973, screenplay)
Archer (1 episode, "The Body Beautiful", 1975)
The Rockford Files (1 episode, "The Four Pound Brick", 1975)
Star Wars: Episode V - The Empire Strikes Back (1980, screenplay, finished by Laurence Kasdan)

❑

Forest of Incandescent Bliss

I'M CONVINCED THAT it was not only necessary, but utterly inevitable, that SF would eventually produce writers who would transcend the genre, who would elevate it above its pulpish origins, who would stand up to the rest of Literature and say "You got nothing on *me*, yo." We know who they are, we've been reading them all our lives (if we've lived that long), but I'll mention some of their names here: Alfred Bester, Harlan Ellison, Ray Bradbury, Algis Budrys (before he was seduced by the Dark Side), Avram Davidson, William Kotzwinkle, Roger Zelazny, James Tiptree, Jr., Philip K. Dick (when he was On), Theodore Sturgeon (when he wasn't being Kilgore Trout), Ursula LeGuin. They tried to take Kurt Vonnegut from us, the bastards, and even convinced him he was Not Of This Earth, but those of us who read him in *Galaxy* and *Wonder Stories*—yes, I said *Wonder Stories*—know better, don't we?

And you know what? Most of these—check that, *all* of these—pale beside the finest writer the field has ever seen, the one against whom all others are never measured because it would be demonstrably unfair: Paul Myron Anthony Linebarger, known to his illustrious godfather (I'll get to it, don't worry) as Lin Bah Loh, or Forest of Incandescent Bliss, AKA Cordwainer Smith.

If I wanted to be all clever and post-modern, I'd deconstruct that pseudonym and tell you that "cord" not only refers to a woven strand, but a fabric made up of woven strands; that a "wain" is a wagon; and that a "smith" is a maker of things. I'd get one of those totally smug and supercilious little smiles on my mug and stretch those already-thin definitions to say something like "Cordwainer Smith wrote a wagon-load of intricately plaited and elaborately plotted stories." I might even get a grant.

But you don't need to pick apart the man's pen-name to know that. All you have to do is read any of the Instrumentality of Mankind stories, or his lone SF novel, *Norstrillia*, or, well, just about anything he wrote, really. But—and I'm not but about 12% facetious here—you *do* have to read him. There'll be a quiz even if I have to track you all down and come to your house.

Linebarger was destined for some kind of greatness. Although he was born in Milwaukee, of all places (his father wanted to ensure his status as natural citizen so he'd have his chance at the Presidency), he was raised in Europe and Asia. His father was legal advisor to Sun Yat Sen (Google it—I'll wait) and helped finance the 1911 Revolution, which is how little Paul became Sun's godson. In 1930, Linebarger himself negotiated a loan for China on his father's behalf. He was seventeen at the time. *Seventeen*. I know what I was doing at seventeen, and if I was negotiating for anything it was a lower price on a dime-bag or a better shot at second base.

But it gets better, really. Six years later, at a time in life when I was trying to stay awake during my 8:00am class in History of the Theater, he already had his Ph.D. in Political Science from some backwater college called Johns Hopkins. Then he started writing books instead of just editing his dad's, not to mention speaking six languages—none of them Klingon or Elvish. And you kids today think *you've* accomplished something when you've finished reading *Harry Potter and the Deathly Hallows*. It is, as they say, to laugh.

A little later, during WWII, he rose to the rank of colonel in Army Intelligence, but before that he did something that would have made Kimball Kinnison (Google it, kid) scratch his head and make Scooby-Doo noises: while working with the Operations and Planning Board, he...Ghod, I can't stand it...he created a profile for an intelligence operative in China that included a set of qualifications that could only be met by one man: Paul Anthony Myron Linebarger. Himself. AKA Cordwainer Smith. What *balls*.

Away he went to China as a lowly lieutenant; by the end of the war he'd be a major, and his experience led him to write the 1948 book, *Psychological Warfare*, still used as a text. He said in his introduction:

> This book is based on my five years of work, both as civilian expert and as Army officer, in American psychological warfare facilities—at every level from the Joint and Combined Chiefs of Staff planning phase down to the preparing of spot leaflets for the American forces in China. Con-

> sequently, I have…sought to incorporate those concepts and doctrines which found readiest acceptance among the men actually doing the job.

(Is it an accident that both Linebarger and Alice Sheldon, one of the few writers in or out of the field who even came close to his stylistic melisma, both worked in intelligence? I think the answer is far more complex than might be evident at first.)

That wasn't the first thing he published, even though he wouldn't "break into print" until 1950 in stfnal terms. Way back when he was fifteen years old, his first story, "War No. 81-Q" appeared in *The Adjutant*, the cadet corps publication of Central High School, Washington D. C., dated June 1928. It either appeared under the name "Karolman Junghar" or "Anthony Bearden," depending on whose scholarship you trust; my money's on Bearden, but I readily admit that I've never seen a copy of the original. As usual, I welcome correction (although I'll be grinding my teeth even as I thank you).

So what was this teen-age yarn about? I quote the description from Anthony R. Lewis's indispensable *Concordance to Cordwainer Smith* (3rd ed., NESFA Press 2000):

> The battle between America and Tibet for the Radiant Heat Monopoly. It was scheduled to take place from noon to 2p.m. on 5 January 2127 at Kerguelen. America won.

(Well, I should darned well hope so. Think of the ignominy if we'd lost. China would never let us hear the end of it.) Much later, the story would be significantly rewritten and published in NESFA's monumental *The Rediscovery of Man: The Complete Short Science Fiction of Cordwainer Smith*, edited by James Mann in 1993, and still available.

The years after the war brought several more novels from Duell, Sloane & Pearce: *Ria* in 1947, *Carola* a year later, both under the pseudonym Felix Forest (a nod to his Chinese name); and a third, *Atomsk*, under the name Carmichael Smith, in 1949. This is in addition to a number of books he wrote on China before the war, titles and exact dates unknown to me (hey, do I have to do everything for you guys? Ask around).

With all this going on, and a career as military advisor during the Korean conflict and to the British during their foray into Malaysia, not to mention being one of the founders of the Office of War Information, you'd

think his plate was pretty full. Well, apparently not, because however extraordinary Paul Anthony Myron Linebarger was, Cordwainer Smith passed him at a walk.

The January, 1950 issue of the little semi-prozine titled *Fantasy Book* and edited by William Crawford under the pseudonym of Garrett Ford was pretty un-(you should pardon the expression)Amazing; it was the sixth issue of an eight-issue run, ranging in size from bed-sheet (8.5x11.75") to several "digest" sizes, and the cover was in two colors only. As a fanzine, it was more than reasonable, but as a commercial venture, it was doomed.

The table of contents is about as impressive as the cover: trunk stories, mostly, including "The Little Man on the Subway" by Isaac Asimov and James MacCreigh (actually Fred Pohl), which had been gathering dust for a decade after being bounced by Campbell for *Unknown*. Oh, there were a couple of other names that were known at the time as well, such as Stanton Coblentz and Basil Wells (who had two stories in, the other as by Gene Ellerman), but the lead story by Asimov and "MacCreigh" paid only $10, so you can figure that *Fantasy Book* wasn't attracting A-list writers.

Nevertheless, amongst all that almost Gernsbackian dross was a definite gem: "Scanners Live in Vain" by the then-unknown Cordwainer Smith. Believe me, in 1950 there was *nothing* in the field like this story, nothing even remotely like it. Not even the nascent *F&SF* and *Galaxy* had published anything like it. In fact, it had more in kin with the *New Worlds* stories of a dozen years down the line than anything contemporary. Why Crawford, whose interests as publisher and editor tended towards pre-Campbell writers, chose this story is puzzling, but I'll hope to err on the Good side and assume it was because he recognized its merits.

If you haven't yet read this wonderful little pearl, you have ample opportunity to do so; here is a partial list of its anthology appearances:

Beyond the End of Time, ed. Frederik Pohl, Perma Books 1952
Science and Sorcery, ed. Garret Ford, FPCI 1953
You Will Never Be the Same, Evanston: Regency Books 1963
Science Fiction Hall of Fame Volume 1, ed. Robert Silverberg, Doubleday 1970
Survival Printout, ed. Total Effect, Vintage 1973
The Best of Cordwainer Smith, Ballantine 1975
Decade the 1950s, ed. Brian W. Aldiss & Harry Harrison, Macmillan UK 1976
First Voyages, ed. Damon Knight, Martin H. Greenberg & Joseph D. Olander, Avon 1981

In fact, the only Smith story with more reprint credits is "The Game of Rat and Dragon" (October 1955 *Galaxy*). Why? Well, "Game…" is better story, but "Scanners…" is no lightweight:

> Martel was angry. He did not even adjust his blood away from anger. He stamped across the room by judgment, not by sight. When he saw the table hit the floor, and could tell by the expression on Luci's face that the table must have made a loud crash, he looked down to see if his leg were broken. It was not. Scanner to the core, he had to scan himself. The action was reflex and automatic. The inventory included his legs, abdomen, Chestbox of instruments, hands, arms, face and back with the Mirror. Only then did Martel go back to being angry… "I tell you I must cranch. I have to cranch."

I won't spoil it for you by going into any further details, but I do expect you to find a copy in one of the dozen or so places it's been reprinted over the years and read it for yourself. Remember, when you do, that while it appeared at the beginning of the Korean Conflict, it had been conceived and written at least five years earlier. Think about that.

(In re-reading that passage above, it occurs to me that Smith cast Martel and the other Scanners as lepers. Victims of Hanson's Disease must constantly check themselves for injuries lest they let something go long enough for gangrene to set in, and the social aspects of trying to live with the disease are a strong analogue as well. I suspect that in the years he spent in the East, Linebarger saw quite a bit of it.)

Smith wouldn't poke his head above the horizon again until five years later with the aforesaid "The Game of Rat and Dragon," and would never be a terribly prolific writer; 29 stories and a bare handful of novels in sixteen years (not counting posthumous works) doesn't stack up well against Asimov or even any of the other Smiths (Doc, Clark Ashton, George O. or George H.), but as Spencer Tracy says of Katherine Heyburn in *Pat and Mike*, "Not much meat on her, but what's there is *cherce*."

And "cherce" it is, too. Smith was a mythmaker, a poet at heart. Even his titles arouse the imagination in ways few others had done before, or have done since: "No, No, Not Rogov!", "The Lady Who Sailed The Soul", "The Ballad of Lost C'Mell", "The Dead Lady Of Clown Town", "Golden The Ship Was - Oh! Oh! Oh!" Who else in the 1950s would use titles like that? Who else could even *conceive* of titles like that?

Not many people read "Scanners..." when it first came out, understandable considering the low circulation of the magazine it appeared in. But its reputation grew, and grew still more as it was anthologized, and it (along with Smith's subsequent wonderments) gradually but steadily began to influence a new generation of writers that included Harlan Ellison, Samuel Delaney, Roger Zelazny, Philip K. Dick, and a host of others. Indeed, his influence on what would be come known as the New Wave was substantial, which may have caused him some dismay considering his conservative politics.

So, who *was* this guy? I've told you a lot about him in earlier paragraphs, but at the time he was actively writing and publishing, Cordwainer Smith was the *only* name he was known by, and his real identity was a mystery. Robert Silverberg, in an article in *Amazing* as late as the mid-60s, mused:

> I think that Cordwainer Smith is a visitor from some remote period of the future, living among us perhaps as an exile from his own era or perhaps just as a tourist, and amusing himself by casting some of his knowledge of historical events into the form of science fiction.

All well and good, you might say, but the above bit of whimsy notwithstanding, answer the damn question, will ya? Okay, then, here's the word from Dr. Arthur Burns, who knew Linebarger while they were both teaching in the Department of Modern History at the Australian National University in 1957:

> [Linebarger] once said that Cordwainer Smith was a "pre-Cervantean"—the stories are like cycles of medieval legends, without the Aristotelian beginning-middle-and-end of classic tragedy....They are legendary cycles of the future, rather than future history, and were meant to be connected with and consistent with each other on the legendary and not the historiographic model.

Linebarger was also chronically ill; his stomach was bad enough that he had to drink dilute hydrochloric acid in order to digest food (and to those of you who're looking askance at this, I will add that my father did the same), and he spent much of his time confined to his bed. During these periods of inaction, he wrote SF, and the suffering he went through and the medical procedures he endured show through in most of them.

Composer Charles Ives and Dr. Linebarger had much in common. Both were experimentalists in their fields, both were willing to commit themselves fully to the project at hand, and neither of them was dependent on their art for their primary income. This last is vitally important in Cordwainer Smith's career, because had he felt the need to "tone down" his work in order to fit some editor's taste, stories like "Think Blue, Count Two" might never have been written, or, if they had, might have been significantly less than they are.

In a way, this is more than just fortunate for us; reading a Cordwainer Smith story isn't just the Grand Prize or the Gold Ring, it's winning the Pick Five with a single ticket bought on impulse. Smith's stories don't pay off the first time you read them, they declare new dividends each time you read them. I learned this myself as a kid reading "The Ballad of Lost C'Mell" for the first time in Conklin's *12 Great Classics of Science Fiction*. I finished the story, more than satisfied, but puzzled. Years later, I read it again and found that the story held more than I could ever have realized as an eleven year-old, and reading it again a week ago in preparing for this article showed me that it still had treasure to offer up.

There have been many attempts on the part of SF writers to create a massive framework in which their stories can fit. Some, like Gordon R. Dickson, begin with that in mind and write accordingly. Others come to the idea of a "future history" later in the game and then have to retro-fit, not always well (like Asimov). There's no shortage of broad canvases and vast reaches, either, if only in the work of Edmond Hamilton and Doc Smith.

But the Instrumentality of Mankind…! With all the wide-ranging breadth of China's history as his palette, he paints with broad but nuanced strokes. His mythology spans our present time (still the near future when written) to the year 16,000. It includes wars, expansions, the settlement of thousands of worlds, human life-spans of 400 years, men adapting themselves to hostile planets instead of vice versa, the rise of the Underpeople and the fall of the Lords; it may not have the crashing suns and giant vacuum tubes of the Interstellar Patrol or the Lensmen, but it has a brilliance and magnificence that marks it as unique:

> She was a girlygirl and they were true men, the lords of creation, but she pitted her wits against them and she won. It had never happened before, and it is sure never to happen again, but she did win. She was not even of human extraction. She was cat-derived….she won her tricks against the lawful and assembled Lords of the Instrumentality. [from "The Ballad of Lost C'Mell"]

In looking through Lewis's *Concordance*, I'm struck by the number of puns and neologisms Smith used to build his future: D'joan, the dog-derived character from "The Dead Lady of Clown Town" who was burned at the stake is based on Joan of Arc—Joan Dog/Jeanne D'Arc; C'Mell was named for one of the Linebarger's pets, Cat Melanie; the term "cranch" was taken from the name of an abandoned store in Linebarger's neighborhood. Smith's body of work is crowded with such.

Brian Ash, in *Who's Who in Science Fiction* (Taplinger 1976) says:

> Many of his stories verge on full-blown fantasy, steeped in legends of humanity originating ten millennia hence. They can be lyrical, bitter-sweet, elusive, surrealistic, vio-

> lent. Unlikely to appeal to the more technically-minded enthusiast, their haunting quality has nevertheless secured them a substantial following....

"Their haunting quality..." When I first read "The Ballad of Lost C'mell" back in my youth, it did, in fact, haunt me. I remembered her name, I remembered that silly song, I remembered her unrequited love for Lord Jestecost and the fact that, together, they waged successful revolution against the Instrumentality.

More than that, though, I was haunted by the language. I was haunted by the imagery, and the scope, and the sheer mythic *wonder* of it all. This was a story that sang to me then, even after the covers of the book were closed, and sings to me as much even now as AARP-fodder.

Paul Linebarger died on August 5th, 1966, leaving behind his loving wife, Genevieve, devoted fans, and a body of work that seems to have come from far above the plane of the ecliptic. There has never been a writer like him, in this or any other genre, and it is unlikely that we'll see his like again.

(I would like to thank Bruce Gillespie for his help in passing along to me material published in The Australian Review of SF.)

What follows is as complete a bibliography of first appearances as I can put together; the NESFA *Concordance* has a more complete one, and there are also on-line resources available, some listed below. I have omitted unpublished works, as I just don't know enough about them to feel justified in listing them, but they are mentioned in the *Concordance.*

Official Smith webpage, set up by Linebarger's daughter:
http://www.cordwainer-smith.com/
Mike Bennett's Illustrated Bibliography of Cordwainer Smith:
http://www.cordwainer-smith.com/CSBiblio/CSBiblio.htm
Wikipedia entry:
http://en.wikipedia.org/wiki/Cordwainer_Smith

Stories

"War No. 81-Q" – June 1928 *The Adjutant*
"Scanners Live In Vain" – January 1950 *Fantasy Book* (#6)
"The Game Of Rat And Dragon" – October 1955 *Galaxy*

"Mark Elf" – May 1957 *Saturn* (as "Mark XI")
"The Burning Of The Brain" – October 1958 *If – Worlds of Science Fiction*
"Western Science Is So Wonderful" – December 1958 *If—Worlds of Science Fiction*
"No, No, Not Rogov!" – February 1959 *If—Worlds of Science Fiction*
"Nancy" – March 1959 *Satellite Science Fiction* (as "The Nancy Routine")
"When The People Fell" – April 1959 *Galaxy*
"Golden The Ship Was – Oh! Oh! Oh!" – April 1959 *Amazing Science Fiction* (with Genevieve Linebarger)
"Angerhelm" – June 1959 *Star Science Fiction No. 6* (ed. Frederik Pohl, Ballantine)
"The Fife Of Bodhidharma" – June 1959 *Fantastic*
"The Lady Who Sailed The Soul" – April 1960 *Galaxy* (with Genevieve Linebarger)
"Alpha Ralpha Boulevard" – June 1961 *The Magazine of Fantasy & Science Fiction*
"Mother Hitton's Littul Kittons" – June 1961 *Galaxy*
"A Planet Named Shayol" – October 1961 *Galaxy*
"From Gustible's Planet" – July 1962 *Worlds of If Science Fiction*
"The Ballad of Lost C'Mell" – October 1962 *Galaxy*
"Think Blue, Count Two" – February 1963 *Galaxy*
"On The Gem Planet" – October 1963 *Galaxy*
"Drunkboat" – October 1963 *Amazing Stories Fact and Science Fiction*
"The Good Friends" – October 1963 *Worlds of Tomorrow*
"The Boy Who Bought Old Earth" – April 1964 *Galaxy*
"The Store Of Heart's Desire" – May 1964 *Worlds of If Science Fiction*
"The Crime And The Glory Of Commander Suzdal" – May 1964 *Amazing Stories Fact and Science Fiction*
"The Dead Lady Of Clown Town" – August 1964 *Galaxy*
"On The Storm Planet" – February 1965 *Galaxy*
"Three To A Given Star" – October 1965 *Galaxy*
"On The Sand Planet" – December 1965 *Amazing Stories*
"Under Old Earth" – February 1966 *Galaxy*

"Down To A Sunless Sea" – October 1975 *The Magazine of Fantasy & Science Fiction* (with Genevieve Linebarger, a posthumous collaboration)

"The Queen Of The Afternoon" – April 1978 *Galaxy* (with Genevieve Linebarger, a posthumous collaboration)

"The Colonel Came Back From Nothing-At-All" – *The Instrumentality Of Mankind*, Ballantine May 1979

"Himself In Anachron" – *The Rediscovery Of Man*, NESFA, 1993 (originally published in French in *Les Seigneurs de L'Instrumentalite*, ed. Jacques Goimbard, Presses Pocket, 1987

Books

You Will Never Be The Same – Regency, 1963

The Planet Buyer – Pyramid, October 1964

Space Lords – Pyramid, May 1965

Quest Of The Three Worlds – Ace, 1966

The Underpeople – Pyramid November, 1968

Under Old Earth and Other Explorations – Panther, 1970 (UK)

Stardreamer – Beagle Boxer, August 1971

Norstrilia – Ballantine, February 1975

The Best Of Cordwainer Smith – Ballantine, July 1975

The Instrumentality Of Mankind – Ballantine, May 1979

The Rediscovery Of Man – NESFA, 1993

❑

Piper at the Gates

Fans of H. Beam Piper (what few are left) are almost certainly aware of at least one salient aspect of his life: he killed himself. What nobody seems to be aware of is why or exactly when. What is known is that sometime between November 5th, 1964 (the date of the last entry in his diary) and either the 9th or the 11th (again, nobody knows for sure) when his body was discovered, Piper spread tarps on the floor and walls of his apartment and covered his furniture with drop cloths, took a .38 caliber revolver from his extensive collection of firearms, and fatally shot himself.

As to why... Well, it depends on who you ask. The story common in fandom when I was first active 30-35 years ago was that he was despondent over his "failed" career, unaware that his agent had died without telling him of several sales. Jerry Pournelle, a Piper enthusiast who wrote the introduction for the reprint of *Little Fuzzy*, blames it on that, as well as a messy divorce that caused him extreme financial setbacks. A well-known editor in the field also attributes it to the divorce but maintains that Piper killed himself in order to invalidate his life insurance policy, which would have paid his despised ex-wife a significant amount.

However all (or any) of that may be, it is largely irrelevant, especially when we come to consider the work rather than the man; after all, I come not to bury Piper, but to praise him. Irrelevant, and easy, too: it is, after all, speculation, and that can be done as easily sitting in a bar with a schooner between you and your listeners as it can here, or in a university auditorium.

The work… That's the hard part, really, because Piper was neither a sensational nor a sensationalist writer. He was a careful researcher, meticulous, and such writers are rarely as flashy or flamboyant as those of their colleagues who take chances (and blow it, as often as not).

Piper wasn't the swash-buckling blaster-blazing adventure writer that Brackett was; he didn't appeal to the wistfully nostalgic as Henderson did. His stories are subtle, painstakingly assembled, and as instructive as they are entertaining. To a fault sometimes, as Damon Knight remarked in his review of Piper's novella, "Uller's Uprising," one of three stories published in *The Petrified Planet* (Twayne 1952) by different authors based on a planetary profile created by Dr. John D. Clark:

> H. Beam Piper's "Uller's Uprising," hands-down the best of the three stories, is excellent writing largely wasted, for my taste, on a conventional native up-rising story—full of careful military-historical detail which I find no more bearable here than in a textbook.

Well, okay, but salt-grain that if you will, since Knight was as much curmudgeon as critic and felt that he had to find some fault in everything or he wasn't doing his job well. That same attention to detail was one of the aspects of Piper's work that our own editor-in-chief, William Sanders, respected:

> The first thing by him that I ever read was not SF but a mystery, *Murder in the Gunroom* (Knopf 1953). It wasn't terribly memorable as mysteries go, but I was tremendously impressed by his obvious knowledge of firearms… He always got the gun stuff right.

(As well he should, being a hoplophile with a collection of hundreds of weapons, as well as being a crack shot to boot.)

Piper's fiction falls primarily into two series: the Paratime Police stories (which include the Lord Kalvan yarns) and the Terran Federation, or the Fuzzy stories. It's the latter, for better or worse, that Piper's best known for.

Not that it's a bad series, not at all, but these days readers unfamiliar with the stories might be too put off by an unfortunate surface resemblance to George Lucas's Ewoks to take them with the seriousness they deserve. That the Fuzzies came first is immaterial; Lucas had a much better PR campaign.

The Federation stories concern a planet of…oh, let's face it, cute and cuddly-looking critters. Therein lies part of the integral conflict, since the humans don't take them any more seriously than you or I would. We'd be wrong, though, as were most of the humans in the first book, *Little Fuzzy* (not Piper's title, I hasten to point out—blame it on his editor at Avon) would be.

The premise is that these cuddly little dickenses, the dominant indigenous species of Zarathustra, are being exploited by the mining corporation that "runs" the planet, going as far as claiming that they aren't really intelligent, not "people." Piper spends much of the book proving that they are.

It's probably no coincidence that Piper conceived of and wrote this series at this time. The post-war years saw enormous changes in global politics, with indigenous peoples throwing off their colonial bosses seemingly right and left. Speculation once again, perhaps, but Piper didn't live in a vacuum, and he certainly wasn't the only writer around to have noticed and remarked on the phenomenon in their fiction. In true *ASF* tradition, though, the Fuzzy "revolution" is successful mostly because of benign human intervention.

In his lengthy treatise on the history and conceits of science fiction, *Trillion Year Spree*, Brian Aldiss says:

> Fuzzies could be seen as a symbol of conscience, of lost innocence, of unfallen humanity… But in Piper's novels they were also *sapient*—not merely animals to be slaughtered… The struggle to prove and then assert the sapience of these creatures lifts these books above their pulp elements, prefiguring genre concern for ecology and the sentience of whales and dolphins.

That is, of course, not *all* they are. Like most fantasy/SF writers, Piper used his aliens and their culture to make comments about US. His li'l critters live according to a philosophy he'd like humans to live by, a kind of pleasant, non-aggressive libertarianism that seems to permeate every aspect of Fuzzydom. Had he been the boisterous proponent of political libertarianism that, say, Neil Schulman is, or the advocate of personal libertarianism that Eric Frank Russell was, he might have ended up writing his Fuzzies as broadly as Dickson and Anderson did with their Hokas. It's evident, though, that he had little interest in his creations being seen as comic relief; he's holding up a mirror to us, all right, but it's not a fun-house mirror.

Those who love the Fuzzy stories seemingly can never get enough, or so publishers believe. Not quite 20 years after Piper's death, Ace commissioned several sequels, including one based on his notes completed by Michael Kurland, and two others by William Tuning and Ardath Mayhar. They also published *Fuzzies and Other People*, a complete Piper manuscript long believed lost (see bibliography for details).

The Paratime Police stories gave Piper a far more useful canvas against which to splash his stronger political opinions. Poul Anderson did this, too, of course, in his Time Patrol stories, but Piper occasionally crossed the line between story-telling and polemecizing.

Don't get me wrong; the stories are far more than just readable, and his sense of pacing and his careful, considered style prevents them from ever becoming shrill. If Piper does, from time to time, pontificate in order to make a point, he certainly wouldn't be the first author to do so, in *or* out of the field.

The idea of policing alternate time-streams wasn't new when Piper began his series, Sam Merwin having gotten there before him with his 1951 novel, *House of Many Worlds*, but with the publication of "Time Crime" in the February 1955 *Astounding*, Piper set the stage for his own take on the subject. Comparatively robust and aggressive, they were all but diametrically opposed to the pastoral Fuzzy yarns (of which Mary has many skeins…HAH! It's the *way* I tell 'em). Aldiss referred to them as "tough-jawed all-action," but Aldiss has his own axes to grind and is quick to point out what he considers flaws:

> Piper was very much an *Astounding* man, with his Paratime Police series….of a school of writers—mainly technophile—who didn't question the notion that Man was the best thing that had happened to the Universe, and hanging wasn't good enough for anyone who disagreed.

(If you have any granular NaCl left after reading the Knight quote back up there somewhere, snort it now; Aldiss is a brilliant writer and critic, but that doesn't prevent him from being bloviatious when his hobby-horse is a-rockin'.)

Lester del Rey, about as far from Aldiss's perspective as one could get and still be in the same pub, had this to say of the Paratime stories in his own examination of the genre, *The World of Science Fiction: The History of a Subculture*: "[Piper's] stories remain some of the best and most complicated examples of the idea of many time tracks together."

Piper's affinity for what is considered the typical *Astounding* template notwithstanding, he was immensely popular from the very beginning, winning first place in the Analytical Laboratory readers' poll with his first story, "Time and Again." (It pleases me no end to boast that Piper and I are the only two authors I know of so honored by the *ASF* readership, although the AnLab was a much different thing in '47.)

Stepping outside my role as objective historian for a moment, I think it necessary for me to put in a word for my favorite Piper novel, *Lone Star Planet* (also published as *A Planet For Texans* as half of an Ace Double with Norton's *Star Born*). I read this as a kid with no preconceived notions of libertarianism or politics in general. Well, aside from what I'd picked up by reading Heinlein juveniles, anyway.

I remember cackling out loud at the (to me, then) outrageous idea of a planet of "cows" as big as triceratopses (triceratopsi?) being herded by *tanks*. I damn near wet myself just because of that. The story itself is hardly slapstick, but the built-in humor is inescapable.

It was the first time I'd ever heard of H. L. Mencken, too, for all the good it did me; there was certainly no Mencken in my elementary school library, and I hadn't yet been granted access to the Big Peoples' books at the Roanoke Public Library. The book is based on Mencken's essay, "The Malevolent Jobholder," which in essence declares open season on political hacks, hangers-on, and pork-barrel riders, proclaiming loudly:

> ...that it shall be no longer *malum in se* for a citizen to pummel, cowhide, kick, gouge, cut, wound, bruise, maim, burn, club, bastinado, flay, or even lynch a [government] jobholder, and that it shall be *malum prohibitum* only to the extent that the punishment exceeds the jobholder's deserts.

In the novel, a low-level diplomat pisses off the wrong person and is posted to the Texan planet in hopes that he'll be assassinated, as his predecessor was. The plan is that when he's been offed by the locals, the Powers That Be can use it as an excuse to invade and conquer. Apparently, none of those Powers had ever met a Texan, and...well, much of a comparatively zany nature ensues. It's still in print, by the way, both dead-tree and electronical. Budzilla sez get into it.

Piper left us at age 60, hardly his dotage. Had his personal life not been in the mess it was; had his agent's files been as they should have been when *he* died; had communication between John Campbell and Piper not been interrupted by said agent's demise...well, I'm speculating again, and I'm not sure to what end. Would he have continued to write as he always had, sinking deeper and deeper into a libertarian morass and becoming more and more disputatious, as other writers have? Or would he have embraced what Aldiss calls "the revolution of style," and developed a less Campbellian approach to his stories? Moot, certainly.

At the end, what's left is a body of work which, although small, is nonetheless of a high quality. Say what you will about his politics, or his identity as an *Astounding/Analog* writer, his stories are as well-written as anyone's, and better than most. Writing of Piper in *The Encyclopedia of Science Fiction*, John Clute says:

> [Piper] was at his best when he applied an *ASF* [*Astounding Science Fiction*]-derived firmness of setting and plausibility of characterization to emotionally arousing adventure plots in which political agendas existed only as subtexts... it is probably wrong to think of HBP as a mouthpiece for [Campbell]: he was, (in the end tragically) his own man.

Brian Aldiss would seem to agree with this, his other comments notwithstanding:

> His was a literature of high organization and obscure knowledge; an auto-didact, Piper believed in the reconciliation of problems by logic, common sense or compromise—and, in the last resort, by justifiable force.

If you're not already familiar with him, H. (Henry or Horace—nobody seems to know even *that* for certain) Beam Piper is an author well worth seeking out, nor would you have to look far. Much of his work is in print in one format or another, and his biographer, John F. Carr, maintains an extensive website for Piper fans and scholars at http://www.hostigos.com. If you enjoy alternate worlds SF, or a lighter style of libertarianism than can usually be found, I urge you to look into Piper further. He, like all those I write about in these phosphoric pages, deserves your close attention.

(The following bibliography is almost certainly incomplete, and is offered here more as a guide than a definitive listing. There are other, far more up-to-date and inclusive bibliographies out there to be found; this one will get you started, though.)

Stories

"Time and Time Again" – April 1947 *Astounding*
"He Walked Around the Horses" – April 1948 *Astounding*
"Police Operation" – July 1948 *Astounding*
"The Mercenaries" – March 1950 *Astounding*
"Last Enemy" – August 1950 *Astounding*
"Flight from Tomorrow" – September/October 1950 *Future*
"Operation R.S.V.P." – January 1951 *Amazing*
"Dearest" – March 1951 *Weird Tales*
"Temple Trouble" – April 1951 *Astounding*
"Day of the Moron" – September 1951 *Astounding*
"Genesis" – September 1951*Future*
"Ullr Uprising" – in *The Petrified Planet*, ed. Theodore Pratt, Twayne 1952; February-March 1953 *Space SF* (abridged)
"Null-ABC" (with John J. McGuire) – February-March 1953 *Astounding*
"The Return" (with John J. McGuire) – January 1954 *Astounding*
"Time Crime" – February 1955 *Astounding*
"Omnilingual" – February 1957 *Astounding*
"Lone Star Planet" (with John J. McGuire) – March 1957 *Future*
"The Edge of the Knife" – May 1957 *Amazing*
"The Keeper" – July 1957 *Venture*
"Graveyard of Dreams" – February 1958 *Galaxy*
"Ministry of Disturbance" – December 1958 *Astounding*
"Hunter Patrol" (with John J. McGuire) – May 1959 *Amazing*
"Crossroads of Destiny" – July 1959 *Fantastic Universe*

"The Answer" - December 1959 *Fantastic Universe*
"Oomphel in the Sky" - November 1960 *Analog*
"Naudsonce" - January 1962 *Analog*
"A Slave Is a Slave" - April 1962 *Analog*
"Gunpowder God" - November 1964 *Analog*
"Down Styphon!" - November 1965 *Analog*
"Space Viking" - November 1962 - February 1963 *Analog*

Books

Murder in the Gunroom - Knopf 1953
Crisis in 2140 (with John J. McGuire) - Ace 1957 (double, with *Gunner Cade*)
A Planet for Texans (with John J. McGuire) - Ace 1958 (double, with *Star Born*)
Four Day Planet - Putnam 1961, Ace 1979 (with *Lone Star Planet*)
Little Fuzzy - Avon 1962, Ace 1981
Junkyard Planet - Putnam 1963
Space Viking - Ace 1963, Garland 1975, Ace 1981
The Cosmic Computer - Ace 1964 (retitling of *Junkyard Planet*)
The Other Human Race - Avon 1964
Lord Kalvan of Otherwhen - Ace 1965, Garland 1975, Ace 1981
Fuzzy Sapiens - Ace 1976
Lone Star Planet - Ace 1979 (retitling of *A Planet For* Texans, with *Four Day Planet*)
The Fuzzy Papers - SFBC 1977, Ace 1981
Federation - Ace 1981
When in the Course - Ace 1981
Empire - Ace 1981
Paratime - Ace 1981
First Cycle (with Michael Kurland) - Ace 1982
The Worlds of H. Beam Piper - Ace 1983
Uller Uprising - Ace 1983
Fuzzies and Other People - Ace 1984

❑

Still I Persist in Wondering

Always I have welcomed the sound of the night wind moving, as the leaves are passing on their secrets and sometimes falling, but falling lightly, easily, because their time to fall is come. Dressed in high colors, they fall to the day winds too this time of year, this autumn season. The smell of earth mold is spice on the tongue. I catch scent of apples ripening, windfalls rich-rotten pleasuring the yellow hornets. Rams and he-goats are mounting and crazy for it—O this time of year! They fall to the day winds echoing the sunlight, the good bright leaves, and that's no bad way to fall.

– from "The Night Wind"

Edgar Pangborn (1909-1976) was already 42 years old when his first SF story, "Angel's Egg," appeared in the June 1951 *Galaxy*, but don't think for a minute that he'd been twiddling his literary thumbs all that time. Nay, hence, and get that idea right outta your mind. By the time that famous story was published, he'd been a working pro for 21 years. Under the pseudonym Bruce Harrison, his first novel, *A-100: A Mystery Story*, was published by Dutton in 1930 when he was, himself, 21. He freelanced until he went into the Army Medical Corps in 1940, then took a two-year break from things authorial after WWII ended.

His time pre-1930 wasn't ill-spent, either. In fact, it had a significant impact on his later writing: he studied musical composition at Harvard (at the age of 15!), and later at the New England Conservatory, although he never got a degree from either institution. Whatever his music may (or may not) have been like I have no way of knowing, but the influence of rhythm, harmony, melisma and dynamics on his novels and stories is undeniable.

(I'll take this moment to mention that although Pangborn never really discussed his musical training, neither, apparently, did he give it up. 27 years after his death in 1976, a large number of his compositions were found in the attic of the house where he'd lived, including not only chamber music but symphonic works as well. There's a project underway to convert them to MIDI files and make them available for the listener. Get behind me in line.)

Pangborn was, first and foremost, a humanist. Not in the Campbellian way (as Eric Frank Russell and Christopher Anvil were, for example) with bright and crafty humans winning out over stupid, hide-bound aliens every time, but in the sense that his writing addresses human concerns and aspirations. Writing in *The New Encyclopedia of Science Fiction* (ed. James Gunn, Viking 1988), Edgar Chapman says of Pangborn, "In general Pangborn's SF is distinguished by an urbane and sometimes poetic style, depth of characterization, and a mature and compassionate humanism."

In *The Encyclopedia of Science Fiction* (St. Martin's Press 1993), co-editor John Clute more or less concurs, albeit with a mild caveat, when he writes of Pangborn's 1966 novel *The Judgment of Eve* which, he contends,

> ...represents the deepest of [Pangborn's] frequent descents into distinctly uneasy bombast. When, however, he was able to control himself—the early novels, most of *Davy*, and most of the stories in *Good Neighbors and Other Strangers* sidestep these pitfalls—the inherent though sometimes self-consciously rural decency of his view of life won through.

Like Clifford Simak, Pangborn was a pastoralist, but without Simak's occasionally awkward phrasing and with a broader literary palette with which to paint his portraits. In the headnote for Pangborn's "The Red Hills of Summer" in the anthology *Another Part of the Galaxy* (Fawcett 1966), editor Groff Conklin wrote:

> One of the reasons I am so fond of "Red Hills of Summer" is that—as in all of Edgar Pangborn's fiction, science or otherwise—the people are genuine human beings, vividly real. Pangborn's truly novelistic talent for character, which I think is a kind of artist's empathy for his puppets, is particularly well developed in this tale...

Conklin's comments echo those of Clute and Chapman, and with the authority not of the lit-crit, but of the guy who signs checks made out to the writer. He used three of Pangborn's stories over the years, including one—"Pick-Up for Olympus" in *The Supernatural Reader* (edited with wife Lucy, Lippincott 1953)—which was previously unpublished, one of only a half-dozen original stories that Conklin would buy in his 22-year career.

Nor was Conklin the only anthologist who valued Pangborn: Terry Carr gave us no fewer than four stories in his *Universe* series, including the exquisite "The Night Wind;" Roger Elwood published five, one each in his four excellent *Continuum* books and another in his singleton *Ten Tomorrows*; and this doesn't count the reprints.

What of Pangborn, the man? I've already said he was a serious musician, and that it had an enormous influence on his writing, but why did he drop it almost completely in favor of literature?

Well, his home and family environment may have had its effect as well. His mother, Georgia Wood Pangborn, was herself a writer of ghost stories for the slicks. His father, Harry Levi Pangborn, was not only an attorney, but an editor for *Webster's Dictionary*. As a kid, Pangborn and his sister, Mary, would write and illustrate their own storybooks, alone and with each other. Mary Pangborn is herself a published writer, so it was natural for him to turn to literature when it came time to choose a career.

Not that it was terribly distinguished at first. Pangborn himself considered most of what he wrote for the pulps (under a number of pseudonyms) hackwork, stuff he cranked out just to make a living. He did that for twenty years, off and on, until he created his first mature work, the aforementioned "Angel's Egg." This remarkable story seemingly came from nowhere. Pangborn simply wasn't known to the reading public *as* Pangborn, and his combination of style and subject matter was an unusually poetic one, even for *Galaxy*. It was very well received and has been reprinted at least a couple of dozen times since it first appeared in 1951. Even Damon Knight was impressed:

> Edgar Pangborn's first published science-fantasy story was a novelette… whose style and mood were perfectly suited to the story and its narrator—a gently loving old man who offers himself up, in a peculiarly moving kind of self-immolation, to an "angel" from another star. The style is leisurely and reflective; the mood is one of blended sorrow and delight.

One wonders what factors in his background might have molded Pangborn into the somewhat mournful, if optimistic, humanist he must have been to have created the body of work he left behind. Perhaps it was the home-schooling he received until age ten; perhaps it was his training on violin and piano. Maybe it was just a combination of the random arrangement of genetic material and life in New York City in the middle of the Progressive Era. The cause is academic; the result is wondrous and moving.

Like many another writer, especially in the SF/fantasy genre, Pangborn couldn't quite resist the temptation to write connected stories, which brings us to his best-known novel.

> *I'm Davy, who was king for a time. King of the Fools, and that calls for wisdom.*
>
> – *Davy*, first lines.

Now, Pangborn was far from the first writer, in or out of the genre proper, to speculate on what would happen after some cataclysmic event brought the Age of Modern Man to a screeching halt; Mary Shelley's *The Last Man* was published in 1826, eight years after that other book she wrote that I can never remember the title of. Nor did he write the only fine novel based on that idea. Walter Miller's *A Canticle for Liebowitz* is a classic example, as are George Stewart's *Earth Abides* and Pat Frank's *Alas, Babylon*. I could go on—the list is a long one—but you get the idea. "We all create worlds, and writers of projective fantasy are especially prone to let them grow up on paper," Pangborn wrote in his introduction to *Still I Persist in Wondering*, a collection of stories issued posthumously that are set in Davy's world. (As a writer of fiction myself, I can understand that and possibly even aspire to it, because it's a rich and fertile ground for almost any kind of treatment.)

Nor was he satisfied with writing only the one. *Judgment of Eve* and *The Company of Glory* would follow, as well as about a dozen stories, scattered throughout a future history that spans the late 20th Century (you remember back that far, right?) to 600 years from now.

An atomic war (the author himself, perhaps ironically, calls it a "twenty minute war") does what atomic wars do when left to themselves, and brings down Civilization-As-We-Know-It. Disease and plague spread, the population is reduced to the minimum number required for survival of the race, and a new Dark Age ensues.

Davy, the character, comes along 250 or so years later, born into a country divided into feudal enclaves. Reading and writing are taught, but material from before the war is forbidden except to the priests. Davy writes not in the current manner of the Church, nor in the common speech, but in what he calls "Old-Time style," because it's "...the only language I could have in common with you who may exist and one day read this."

The story itself is told as Davy looks back on his life and accomplishments, in a sort of melancholy wistfulness that briefly recalls (but doesn't ape) Bradbury's small-town ruminations.

And here my meager skills as a critic fail me, because Pangborn's prose is so lovely, so *human*, that it defies any attempt on my part to describe it adequately. In the long run, it would be simpler for me to hand you a copy of the book and watch as you read it.

This is true with his other work as well. Simak tried to capture the rural expression, Wellman found a similar voicing in the rhythms and cadences of his beloved mountain-folk, but Edgar Pangborn's words sing across the page like stones skipped across a quiet pond. Damon Knight, while apparently convinced that Pangborn's vision was clouded by what I might call a lack of cynicism, nevertheless paid him the high—if typically lit-crit—compliment of describing his prose style as "...very like the thing that Stapledon was always talking about and never quite managing to convey: the regretful, ironic, sorrowful, deeply joyous—and purblind—love of the world and all in it."

Although *Davy* is his best-known book, it would be a major error to ignore the others. The post-apocalyptic world of King Davy may be his most sustained work, but all the poetry and pastoral majesty are present in his first SF novel, *West of the Sun*, as well as *A Mirror for Observers*. The former tells the story of a small group of humans who crash their spaceship on a planet already populated by two dominant (but co-operative) species; when their rescue arrives, the six decide to remain on Lucifer and continue their Utopian society they built with the "natives."

In *A Mirror for Observers* (which won the International Fantasy Award in 1955), two Martians become involved in the life of an extraordinary human boy, Angelo Pontevecchio. Angelo is a genius, destined to play a role in Humanity's destiny, either as a major contributor to the mess Earth is in, or to help bring about its ultimate salvation and maturity. As is frequently the case with Pangborn, the two Martians are clearly delineated as Good and Evil; the latter, Abdicator Namir, is of the opinion that in order for the Martian race to survive, Humanity must die, and he sets about influencing Angelo to do just that. The other Martians, considering Namir to be a rogue and an outcast, send the Good One, Observer Elmis, to prevent it from happening.

This is an over-simplification, of course. Pangborn is nothing if not subtle and complex, with layers of subtext going on to conceal that the Mirror of the title is aimed square at Us and not just the society in his book. This is what almost every fiction writer does, especially those who write speculative fiction, but Pangborn's skill is quietly exceptional here, and throughout most of his writing.

One of the gauges of the effect a writer has on his or her colleagues is influence: not just how much, but *whom*. Peter Beagle has cited him on any number of occasions as a seminal inspiration, and his affection and respect for Pangborn were apparently reciprocated, as he became Pangborn's literary executor upon his death in 1976. No less a monster writer as Ursula K. Le Guin has stated that it was Pangborn who showed her that worthwhile science-fiction stories could be written at all. What a dismal place we would inhabit without *The Last Unicorn* and *The Dispossessed*, too.

When Pangborn died in 1976, he left behind a legacy far greater than the number of stories he wrote. He was witty, smart, and he loved people—and the *idea* of people - with a level of emotion that bordered on passion and which forgave folly. In his forward to *Still I Persist in Wondering*, a collection which he himself prepared before he died, he evoked all this with only a few (perhaps prophetic) words:

> ...[It] is comforting to reflect that in a universe of infinite universes, like ours, there must be a good many where things turned out more pleasantly—good Christ, there must even be one where Nixon wasn't re-elected!....It takes a bit of time to build a world....In a universe of infinite universes there must be one where you could keep at it for another fifty or sixty years, or until you got tired. With infinite royalties.

Amen, and so endeth the lesson. A fellow poet once remarked to me upon first reading *Davy* that it was a shame that Pangborn had never published poetry. He did, though. It's in nearly every line of his prose.

(As is the usual case, the following bibliography is limited in intent and almost certainly incomplete; as is also the usual case, I welcome corrections and additions.)

Stories

"Angel's Egg" – June 1951 *Galaxy*
"The Singing Stick" – ? 1952 *Ellery Queen's Mystery Magazine*
"Mrrrar!" – July 1953 *Ellery Queen's Mystery Magazine*; also as "Darius".
"Pick-up for Olympus" – *The Supernatural Reader*, ed. Groff & Lucy Conklin, Lippincott 1953
"The Music Master of Babylon" – November 1954 *Galaxy*
"Bottle Babe" – June 1956 *F&SF*
"The Red Hills of Summer" – September 1959 *F&SF*
"The Naked Man in the Elephant House" – December 1959 *Ellery Queen's Mystery Magazine*; appeared also as "The Ponsonby Case".
"The Wrens in Grampa's Whiskers" – April 1960 *F&SF*
"The Good Neighbors" – June 1960 *Galaxy*
"The Golden Horn" – February 1962 *F&SF*
"A War of No Consequence" – March 1962 F&SF
"Maxwell's Monkey" – October 1964 *Galaxy*
"Wogglebeast" – January 1965 *F&SF*
"A Better Mousehole" – October 1965 *Galaxy*
"Longtooth" – January 1970 *F&SF*
"Mount Charity" – *Universe 1*, ed. Terry Carr, Ace 1971

"Tiger Boy" – *Universe 2*, ed. Terry Carr, Ace 1972
"The Freshman Angle" – *Ten Tomorrows*, ed. Roger Elwood, Fawcett 1973
"My Brother Leopold" – *An Exaltation of Stars*, ed. Terry Carr, Simon & Schuster 1973
"The World Is a Sphere" – *Universe 3*, ed. Terry Carr, Random House 1973
"The Company of Glory" – serialized novel, August-October 1974 *Galaxy*
"The Children's Crusade" – *Continuum #1*, ed. Roger Elwood, Putnams 1974
"The Legend of Hombas" – *Continuum #2*, ed. Roger Elwood, Putnams 1974
"The Night Wind" – *Universe 5*, ed. Terry Carr, Random House 1974
"The Witches of Nupal" – *Continuum #3*, ed. Roger Elwood, Putnams 1974
"Harper Conan and Singer David" – *Tomorrow Today*, ed. George Zebrowski, Unity 1975
"Mam Sola's House" – *Continuum #4*, ed. Roger Elwood, Putnams 1975

Books

West of the Sun – Doubleday 1953, Dell 1966, Old Earth 2001
A Mirror for Observers – Doubleday 1954, Dell 1958, Old Earth 2004
Wilderness of Spring – Rinehart & Co. 1958
The Trial of Callista Blake – St. Martin's Press 1961, Dell 1963
Davy – St. Martin's Press 1964, Ballantine 1964, Old Earth 2004
The Judgment of Eve – Simon & Schuster 1966, Dell 1967

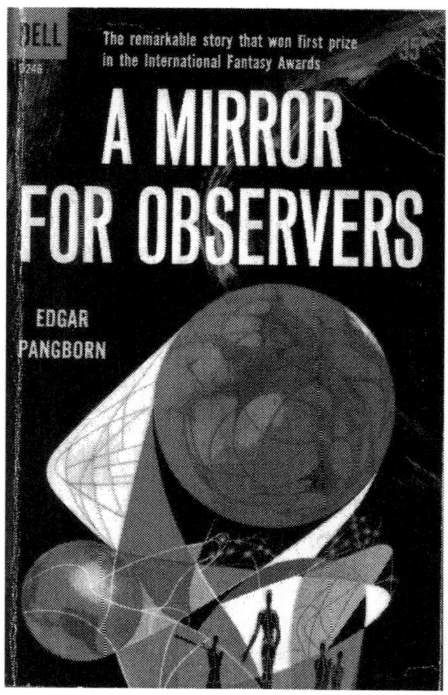

Good Neighbors and Other Strangers (collection) Macmillan 1972, Collier 1976
The Company of Glory – Pyramid 1975
Still I Persist In Wondering (collection) – Dell 1978

In addition, Pangborn left behind a number of unpublished stories and novels, including an erotic novel set in the "Davy" timeline titled *An Atlantean Night's Entertainment.* Phil Stephensen-Payne, raconteur, historian and bibliographer extraordinaire, was kind enough to alert me to that one, as well as the following:

"Amateur Snatch" – written in 1934 for *Detective Story Magazine.*
"Birth of a God" – "sold to Terry Carr for an anthology."
The Boss is Dead – a novel that may or may not have been published; the manuscript says "published in 1935/36" but no trace of it has yet been located.
Hurricane Hill – unpublished mystery novel.
Island of Departure – unpublished novel from the 1960s.
"The Life and the Clay" – His *Last Dangerous Visions* story.
Light Another Candle – Unpublished historical novel, written in the 1970s with his sister, Mary Pangborn.
Miranda – unpublished novel written in 1967.
Poor Devil – unpublished three act play.
The Training of Karen O'Reilly – unpublished novel.
The Voyage of the Fulmar – unpublished novel.

❑

It's Not the Length, It's What You Do With It

A FEW YEARS AGO AS TURTLES RECKON TIME, it became popular for 'net writers to write something called "flash" fiction, stories of fewer than a thousand words. Quick, in-your-face, and sharply pointed—or so flash writers fondly believed. Most of the time, they were obvious, tepid, overblown and, as Prof. F. Leghorn would have put it, about as sharp as a bowling ball. Bowling ball, that is.

And of course, the practitioners of said literary form considered themselves, quod erat demonstrandum, sine qua non (and non-compos mentis) *absolutely* on the Cutting Edge of Literature. After all, they were doing it online, right?

Booshwah. And again I say *boosh*-wah. Not even close. We can set aside for the moment the Drabble, a curious little literary object consisting of *exactly* 100 words (title included) created by the members of the SF association of Birmingham, England. They assembled at least two compilations of said shorties by their professional writer guests over the years, some of them not too shabby, considering. Hard to go wrong with names like Brunner, Aldiss and Ballard. I digress, though.

No, the short-short story has been around a lot longer than that, and has been collected in no fewer than a half-dozen anthologies over the years by such luminaries as Isaac Asimov, Groff Conklin, and Marty Greenberg.

What most of the flashistas don't seem to realize is that however fine they may whet what they consider the cutting edge, they're just grinding away at the back-strap with a rasp file. That razor-edge was honed to perfection years before by a master: Fredric Brown.

Fredric William Brown was born 102 years ago in Cincinnati. He matriculated at Hanover College in Indiana, and ended up spending a significant amount of time in Wisconsin working as a proofreader for the *Milwaukee Journal*, after the fashion of any number of genre writers, like Clifford Simak and Abraham Merritt, who learned how to put words in order as journalists.

Let me be frank. There's nothing terribly sensational or incredible about Brown, neither his fiction nor his life. He was born, he wrote some stuff, he died. Exactly the same could be said for dozens, if not hundreds, of writers, many of whom busted their humps to make a living as writers and ended up footnotes in a reference book, with little—if anything—in print after their deaths.

So what makes him different? Well, if you've read much of anything by him, you'd know the answer to that. For those of you who haven't, or who didn't get it on the first pass, here's my answer: he did what he did with an economy of words and an elegance of idea that only a handful of other writers can approach. Almost certainly, his work as a newspaperman taught him how, but he took it to the limit and made it not only his trademark, but he has become so identified with the short-short story that anyone daring to write that length will inevitably be compared to him—even if they've never heard of him, the poor dears. If you write about elves and rings, you're going to be compared to Tolkien; if you write military SF, you get smacked with Dickson (and more recently, Weber and/or Drake); if you go small at all, Brown takes the call.

And enough of *that*. It's true, though. Brown was capable of refining a story idea down to a couple of sentences, as is the case (in a way) with what is perhaps his best-known, if least-correctly remembered, story, "Knock," (originally published in the December 1948 *Thrilling Wonder Stories*) which begins:

> There is a sweet little horror story that is only two sentences long: "*The last man on Earth sat alone in a room. There was a knock on the door…*"

Many, many people (myself included until I began researching this article) are convinced that Brown wrote the shortest stand-alone SF/fantasy story ever with those two Italicized lines, but the reality is that, except for being quoted as such, they exist solely as part of a longer story. In the preface of *The Best Science Fiction Stories – 1949* (ed. Bleiler & Dikty, Fredrick Fell 1949), the editors say:

> ..."Knock" is based on the horror anecdote attributed to Thomas Bailey Aldrich—the last woman on earth hears a knock on her door... Well-known authors have dealt with the same theme before...but we wonder whether they would have had the courage to tell Brown's story of a middle-aged unromantic professor and an unwilling female.

In a way, it's a shame that Brown can't be credited with that two-liner. After all, it's the ultimate word in story-telling elegance, and that's his specialty. But I will state here and now that those two lines do not now, nor have they ever, constituted a "story" as I understand and practice it, and I suspect that I'll get little (if any) argument on the point. They do, however, make a pretty damn fine *hook* for a longer, and far more satisfying, yarn.

But how did he start? Not by writing SF, that's for sure. In fact, his first stories were apparently written for trade magazines like *The Michigan Well Driller* and *Excavating Engineer* from as early as 1936 (see the extensive biblio at the bottom of the page, and take a lunch), and he did a proofreaders' column, "The Proofreader's Page," in *American Printer* for the better part of a decade, but his first "real" sale was a mystery, "The Moon for a Nickel," in the March 1938 *Detective Story*. Throughout his career he was at least as well known (and for most of it, far better known) for his detective stories and novels. *The Fabulous Clipjoint*, published in 1947, won the Edgar for Best First Novel, and he never really turned away from the genre.

His first SF sale wasn't until 1941, with "Not Yet the End" in the Winter issue of *Captain Future*. It was an inauspicious beginning in the field, frankly, and showed little of the promise and wit of stories that came even a few years later. It certainly wasn't the confident and assured work that the next year's "Etaoin Shrdlu" would be, but cut the guy some slack. He made up for it pretty fast, and I do like it better than "The Moon for a Nickel."

Brown was equally adept at all the major pulpish genres, although his output of Westerns was less than that of his other stories. Nothing spectacular about that, of course, as anyone who wanted to make a living from writing in those days had to be able to write anything. But his heart wasn't really in sagebrush and gunfights, and after a while he limited himself to gumshoes, angels, and spaceships.

It's easy—way too easy—to look at Brown's body of work as "joke stories." All you have to do is read a half dozen and then assume all the rest are the same. That would be a huge mistake, though, as well as a slap in the face of a writer who produced a number of quite serious stories. Oh, there's plenty to laugh about in just about all of them, don't get me wrong. Fredric Brown was possessed of a lively wit and a gleeful imagination that could take him (and his readers) to some pretty bizarre places.

But read him with a little care, a little attention, and you'll find that although he was perfectly capable of making you snort milk out your nose (like all good baggy-pants comics), he was at the same time giving you plenty of Idea to consider and wonder at.

Take, for example, one of his most famous short-shorts, "Answer." In 222 words—barely one single manuscript page—Brown sets us up and then delivers a punch line that is so far from rubber chickens and Whoopee cushions that they're almost in another Einsteinian plane of existence. You might laugh, but it's a shaky kind of laugh, not a laugh engendered by pig's-bladders and big red noses. Wit, not slapstick, and yet those 200+ words are as famous—and as misattributed and misquoted—as anything ever published in the field.

(All right, all right, if you want to know what I'm talking about, it's in his collection *Angels and Spaceships*, published by Dutton in 1954. Wanna know something else about this little jewel? It was a toss-off, an after-thought. When he assembled the book, he decided to write nine vignettes to run alternately with the eight reprints. So he just whipped them out. Most of them, although nowhere near as notorious as "Answer," will smack you in the gob just as hard. You know, if you kids spent as much time hanging out in used bookstores instead of playing those damn videogames all day long, I wouldn't need to do this.)

The plain reality is that, as is true of very few of his contemporaries (and almost none of his successors), Brown wrote stories which eventually passed into stfnal legend. I just asked Mary, my Significant Other, if she knew the story about the Galactic civilization who hooked up all their computers and asked the question, "Is there a God?" She thought for a moment, then asked, "Wasn't that 'The Final Answer' by Asimov?" She was referring to Asimov's "The Last Question," of course, which is the story practically everybody mistakes for the Brown. But not only did the Brown story precede Asimov's by two years, Asimov took more than 4500 words more to tell *his* tale. I can tell you from my own experience that over the past 35+ years, I've heard those two stories conflated more than any other two in the genre (or outside of it, for that matter), and 99% of the time the last line of the Brown is misattributed to the Asimov. I'm sure that both gentlemen ground their teeth about that.

Fredric Brown did write a lot of short-short stories. *Nightmares and Geezenstacks* is full of them, and there are more scattered about hither and yon in various other collections. Don't overlook his longer works, though. His mystery novels are a blast, especially *The Screaming Mimi* (filmed in 1958 and starring Anita Ekberg and Gypsy Rose Lee), *Night of the Jabberwock* and *Mrs. Murphy's Underpants*, the title of which alone is reason enough to own.

His science fiction and fantasy novels, though…! The crazed (but controlled) madness of *Martians, Go Home!*, the recursive satire of *What Mad Universe*, in which the editor of a SF magazine is thrust into the bizarre and imaginary world of one of his readers; these are marvelous and intricately constructed books, filled with Brown's trademark dry wit, and are ultimately satisfying works that can be read and re-read for pleasure without effort.

Ah, but the exquisite and prescient *The Lights in the Sky are Stars* is where Brown outdoes himself. He managed, at a time when both the stfnal and mundane worlds were united behind the then-new Space Program, when those politicians and industrialists who supported it were seen as visionaries and their pronouncements seen as prophecies, Brown sat back, grinned and said, "Wanna bet?"

Lights was published in 1953, during Eisenhower's reign. There were plenty of stories out at the time—not to mention the decades before—in which space exploration was treated as the Brave New Future, as an epic struggle against all odds, as a heroic quest carried out by square jaws and snappy patter. And so it was considered by most of us, frankly (I still see it that way; I cry during the blast-off scene in *Apollo 13* and I still get teary thinking about Grissom, Chaffe and White).

But in 1953, Fredric Brown had the courage, the all-out *balls* to write a novel about space in which the politicians and industrialists used the space program to their own ends, with a hero clearly not of the hero type

(disabled and middle-aged), and—brace yourself—dares to show us an Earth in 1997 where the people are disillusioned with the whole thing. It is a romantic story, one in which its non-heroic protagonists are, at the end of the day, every bit as Heroic in their way as anyone Ed Hamilton or Doc Smith ever created.

What of Fredric Brown, the man, though? Well, I'll be honest. There isn't a whole lot written about him that I could get access to. A snippet here, a paragraph there, and the odd comment Brown made himself in this or that introduction. I know that he worked his day job as a proofer for years after he began selling regularly, just because he needed that steady paycheck to support his family.

I know from Fredrik Pohl's intro to Brown's "Hall of Mirrors" in *Assignment in Tomorrow* (Hanover House 1954) that he was "...a virtuoso on the Chinese Flute as well as on the typewriter..."; I know from long-time friend Robert Bloch's introduction to *The Best of Fredric Brown* that he was "Diminutive in stature, fine-boned, with delicate features partially obscured by horn-rimmed glasses and a wispy mustache..."; I know, from reading the various online references that he had a drinking problem which gave him significant difficulty later in life, that he liked cats, and that two of his biggest fans were (please sit down for this. No, I really mean it) were Ayn Rand and Mickey Spillane. Don't know about you, but it's hard for me to wrap my head around that.

Isaac Asimov (he of that *other* computer-God yarn) wrote this about his colleague:

> On December 4, 1948, there was a very pleasant Hydra Club meeting at Fletcher Pratt's place... Also present was Fredric Brown, a short, thin fellow who looked like a bookkeeper but who wrote excellent science-fiction short-shorts and amazingly good tough-guy detective novels... He was a chess buff and wanted badly to play me, even though I told him it was almost impossible for me to win....I had visited his apartment one time not long thereafter and he beat me rapidly in two games.

Brown made a number of friends in the field, not the least of whom was Mack Reynolds, a "red-diaper baby" whose father had run for president on the American Socialist Labor Party, and with whom Brown collaborated on a number of stories as well as a pretty damn good anthology, *Science Fiction Carnival*. Interestingly enough, he apparently didn't make friends with Damon Knight, seemingly slipping below the critic's radar; *In Search of Wonder* contains no mention of him.

When I mentioned to a gaggle of colleagues that I was doing a Past Masters bit on Fredric Brown, several of them admitted to a touch of confusion. Why him? He wasn't anything special, no innovator or creator of characters who have lived on long after he died. He didn't write best-sellers, he didn't win Nebulas and Hugos consistently or generate vast amounts of faanish adulation (although I maintain that he did his share of all that, just no more). Many of them made it clear that they thought his writing clumsy, or dated, or just not terribly good. Why *him*?

The glib answer is "It's my party and I'll cry if I want to." That's the glib answer, but it's not the best one, and it's as much a disservice to Brown as thinking he was nothing but a jumped-up class clown is.

The word "Master" isn't monolithic in definition. No, Fredric Brown wasn't the word-artist that, say, Alfred Bester was (although he clearly influenced Bester). He wasn't as adept at writing poetic prose as Zelazny or Delany. He didn't send planets crashing into suns like Hamilton, he didn't write intricately and complexly like Piper or Pangborn did.

But Fredric Brown was a Master Craftsman. There are damned few writers out there who wrote/write with as much facility, with as much economy. He wasn't flashy, he wasn't loud or showy or ostentatious. He didn't hide his considerable light under a barrel, mind you, but neither did he flaunt his talents; of course he didn't, that would have gotten in the way of the story.

Brown never let anything get in the way of the story. I'm convinced that this is one of the reasons why he wrote fewer novels than many of his contemporaries. Face it: a whole hell of a lot of novels out there, even the currently popular beach bricks, are short story ideas padded out to doorstop dimensions. Admit it, you've said the same thing to yourself more than once.

Fredric Brown, to state it simply and concisely, told the story and then he STOPPED. If it took 7500 words to tell the story, that was hunky-dory. If it took 222, then that's what it took. And look at the results: would

"Answer" have anywhere near the impact it does if he'd added more dialogue, exposition, or description? Not on your tintype, buckeroo.

Listen, flashers, assuming any of you are reading this (and props to you if you are), spend some time in the company of Brown and learn what can really be done with 1k words or fewer. And remember this: he wasn't trying to plow new ground, or prove a point, or be hip or any of that. He wasn't making jokes, or short-changing his readers (God, no!) or taking the easy way. He wrote the lengths he did not because it was The Newest Thing, but because he instinctively knew one of the toughest things any writer has to learn—it takes more skill to use less verbiage and still get the point across.

Word.

(What follows is a much simplified and abstracted version of the remarkably complete (and I do mean complete) bibliography of Fredric Brown compiled at great effort by Phil Stephenson-Payne, a tireless and dedicated bibliographer who makes my minor attempts look...well, minor. For my purposes here, I've left out poetry, non-fiction, and pretty much anything that isn't a novel, collection, or short-story. Any and all errors you see here are artifacts of my own unintentional biblio-clumsiness, so don't blame him. If you have any interest in seeing the complete mishigoss, *by all means contact me through HELIX SF and I'll put you in touch with Phil. Stories marked with an aserisk (*) are short-shorts. Collect the set.)*

1936

*"V.O.N. Munchdriller vacuum vengeance..." – *The Michigan Well Driller* Sep. 1936
"Business is Booming..." – *Excavating Engineer* Jan. 1936

1937

"We've Tried Everything!" – *Excavating Engineer* Feb. 1937
"Dear Boss..." (Letters of a Traveling Salesman to His Wife)" – *Independent Salesman* March 1937
"The Case of the Flying Cow, or How Did the Critter Get Into the Silo?" – *Feedstuffs* March 20, 1937
"But You Never Know" – *Excavating Engineer* April 1937
"The Case of the Stuttering Shoat" – *Feedstuffs* April 4, 1937
"The Case of the Haunted Haystack" – *Feedstuffs* May 15, 1937
"The Case of the Refrigerating Windmill" – *Feedstuffs* May 8, 1937

"The Case of Uncountable the Sheep" – *Feedstuffs* May Jun-1937
"The Worst is Yet to Come" – *Excavating Engineer* June 1937
"Something May Happen" – *Excavating Engineer* Aug. 1937
"Ernie and the Rescue on the Road, or The Case of the Missing Tacks" – *Feedstuffs* Oct. 16, 1937
"Ernie Catches up with Wily Willie or The Case of the Vanishing Duck" – *Feedstuffs* Oct. 9, 1937
"Ernie, Minister of Peace and Goodness, or the Case of the Multiplying Eggs" – *Feedstuffs* Oct. 2, 1937
"Wait and Pray" – *Excavating Engineer* Oct. 1937
"This Will Surprise You" – *Excavating Engineer* Dec. 1937

1938

*"V.O.N. Munchdriller does it the otter way!" – *The Michigan Well Driller* c. 1938-40
*"V.O.N. Munchdriller drills a portable well…" – *The Michigan Well Driller* c. 1938-40
*"V.O.N. Munchdriller fights fire with fizz…" – *The Michigan Well Driller* c. 1938-40
*"V.O.N. Munchdriller finds a cold answer to a hot problem" – *The Michigan Well Driller* c. 1938-40
*"V.O.N. Munchdriller gets water" – *The Michigan Well Driller* c. 1938-40
*"V.O.N. Munchdriller harnesses a thunderbolt" – *The Michigan Well Driller* c. 1938-40
*"V.O.N. Munchdriller Saves `Ozzie' From Digging Clear Down to China" – *The Michigan Well Driller* c. 1938-40
*"V.O.N. Munchdriller Sinks First Horizontal Well Known to History" – *The Michigan Well Driller* c. 1938-40
*"V.O.N. Munchdriller solves a problem" – *The Michigan Well Driller* c. 1938-40
"The Case of the Shrinking Stallion" – *Feedstuffs* Jan. 1, 1938
"The Case of the Wandering Scarecrow" – *Feedstuffs* Jan. 16, 1938
"Bear With Us" – *Excavating Engineer* Feb. 38
"The Case of the Apocryphal Ark" – *Feedstuffs* Feb. 19, 1938
"The Case of the Bewildering Barn" – *Feedstuffs* Feb. 5, 1938
"The Case of the Conjurer's Cat" – *Feedstuffs* March 26, 1938
"The Case of the Rebellious Rooster" – *Feedstuffs* April 2, 1938

"The Moon for a Nickel" – *Street & Smith's Detective Story Magazine* March 1938
"Hot Air Rises" – *Excavating Engineer* April 1938
"Nothing is Impossible" – *Excavating Engineer* June 1938
"Ernie Stops Shivering, or the Case of the Trackless Tractor" – *Feedstuffs* Sep. 24, 1938
"Tit for Tat, or the Case of the Purple Percheron" – *Feedstuffs* Sep. 4, 1938
"You Can't Get Brodway's Goat, or The Case of the Kidnapped Kid" – *Feedstuffs* Oct. 15, 1938

1939

"The Cheese on Stilts" – *Thrilling Detective* Jan.1939
"Blood of the Dragon" – *Variety Detective* Feb.1939
"There Are Bloodstains in the Alley" – *Detective Yarns* Feb.1939
"Murder at 10:15" – *Clues Detective Stories* May1939

1940

"Cause and Defect" – *The Inventor* March 1940
"The Case of the Bargain Butter" – *Feedstuffs* April 13, 1940
"Hex Marks the Spot" – *Excavating Engineer* May 1940
"Spice of Life!" – *The Coin Machine Review* May 1940
"The Case of the Rattled Robber" – *The Inventor* May 1940
"A Matter of Taste" – *The Layman's Magazine* June 1940
"Murder Draws a Crowd" – *Detective Fiction Weekly* July 27, 1940
"The Prehistoric Clue" – *Ten Detective Aces* July 1940
"Trouble in a Teacup" – *Detective Fiction Weekly* July 13, 1940
"Footprints on the Ceiling" – *Ten Detective Aces* Sep. 1940
"The Little Green Men" – *The Masked Detective* Fall 1940
"Town Wanted" – *Detective Fiction Weekly* Sep. 7, 1940
"Herbie Rides His Hunch" – *Detective Fiction Weekly* Oct. 19, 1940
"The Stranger from Trouble Valley" – *Western Short Stories* Jan. 1940
"The Strange Sisters Strange" – *Detective Fiction Weekly* Dec. 28, 1940

1941

"Fugitive Imposter" – *Ten Detective Aces* Jan. 1941
"Miracle on Vine Street" – *The Layman's Magazine* Jan. 1941
"The King Comes Home" – *Thrilling Detective* Jan. 1941
"The Sematic Crocodile" – *The Layman's Magazine* Feb. 1941

"Big-Top Doom" – *Ten Detective Aces* March 1941
"Life and Fire" – *Detective Fiction Weekly* Mar 22, 1941
"The Discontented Cows" – *G-Men Detective* March 1941
"Big-League Larceny" – *Ten Detective Aces* April 1941 (as by Jack Hobart)
"Client Unknown" – *The Phantom Detective* April 1941
"Selling Death Short" – *Ten Detective Aces* April 1941
"Your Name in Gold" – *The Phantom Detective* June 1941
"Here Comes the Hearse" – *10 Story Detective* July 1941 (as by Allen Morse)
"Six-Gun Song" – *10 Story Detective* July 1941
"Star-Spangled Night" – *Coronet* July 1941
"Wheels Across the Night" – *G-Men Detective* July 1941
"Armageddon" – *Unknown Worlds* Aug. 1941
"Little Boy Lost" – *Detective Fiction Weekly* Aug. 2, 1941
"Bullet for Bullet" – *Western Short Stories* Oct. 1941
"Listen to the Mocking Bird" – *G-Men Detective* Jan. 1941
"You'll End Up Burning!" – *Ten Detective Aces* Jan. 1941
*"Not Yet the End" – *Captain Future* Winter 1941
"Number Bug" – *Exciting Detective* Winter 1941
"Thirty Corpses Every Thursday" – *Detective Tales* Dec. 1941
"Trouble Comes Double" – *Popular Detective* Dec. 1941

1942

"Bloody Murder" – *Detective Fiction* Jan. 10, 1942
"Clue in Blue" – *Thrilling Mystery* Jan. 1942
"Death is a White Rabbit" – *Strange Detective Mysteries* Jan. 1942
"Twenty Gets You Plenty" – *G-Men Detective* Jan. 1942
"Etaoin Shrdlu" – *Unknown Worlds* Feb. 1942
"Little Apple Hard to Peel" – *Detective Tales* Feb. 1942
"Death in the Dark" – *Dime Mystery* March 1942
"Everything is Ducky" – *Excavating Engineer* March 1942
"Mad Dog!" – *Detective Book Magazine* Spring 1942
"Moon Over Murder" – *The Masked Detective* Spring 1942
"Pardon My Ghoulish Laughter" – *Strange Detective Mysteries* March 1942
"The Incredible Bomber" – *G-Men Detective* March 1942
"The Star Mouse" – *Planet Stories* Spring 1942
"Twice-Killed Corpse" – *Ten Detective Aces* March 1942

"Who Did I Murder?" – *Detective Short Stories* April 1942
"A Cat Walks" – *Street & Smith's Detective Story Magazine* April 1942
"Murder in Furs" – *Thrilling Detective* May 1942
"Suite for Flute and Tommy Gun" – *Street & Smith's Detective Story Magazine* June 1942
"Three-Corpse Parlay" – *Popular Detective* June 1942
"You'll Die Before Dawn" – *Mystery Magazine* July 1942
"A Date to Die" – *Strange Detective Mysteries* July 1942
"Red is the Hue of Hell" – *Strange Detective Mysteries* July 1942 (as by Felix Graham)
"Two Biers for Two" – *Clues Detective Stories* July 1942
"A Little White Lye" – *Ten Detective* Aces Sep. 1942
"Get Out of Town" – *Thrilling Detective* Sep. 1942
"Nothing Sinister" – *Mystery Magazine* Sep. 1942
"Runaround" – *Astounding* Sep. 1942 (as Starvation)
"Satan's Search Warrant" – *10 Story Detective* Sep. 1942
"The Men Who Went Nowhere" – *Dime Mystery* Sep. 1942
"The Numberless Shadows" – *Street & Smith's Detective Story Magazine* Sep. 1942
"Where There's Smoke" – *Black Book Detective* Sep. 1942
"Boner" – *Popular Detective* Oct. 1942
"Legacy of Murder" – *Exciting Mystery* Oct. 1942
"Murder Can Be Fun" – *Street & Smith Detective Story Magazine* Oct. 1942 (condensed, as "The Santa
Clause Murders"
"The New One" – *Unknown Worlds* Oct. 1942
"A Fine Night for Murder" – *Detective Tales* Jan. 1942
"Double Murder" – *Thrilling Detective* Jan. 1942 (as by John S. Endicott)
"Heil, Werewolf!" – *Dime Mystery* Jan. 1942 (as by Felix Graham)
"I'll See You at Midnight" – *Clues Detective* Stories Jan. 1942
"Satan One-and-a-Half" – *Dime Mystery* Jan. 1942
"The Monkey Angle" – *Thrilling Detective* Jan. 1942

1943

"A Lock of Satan's Hair" – *Dime Mystery* Jan. 1943
"The Spherical Ghoul" – *Thrilling Mystery* Jan. 1943
"The Wicked Flea" – *Ten Detective Aces* Jan. 1943

"Beware of the Dog" – *Ten Detective Aces* Feb. 1943 (as Hound of Hell)
"Death is a Noise" – *Popular Detective* Feb. 1943
"The Angelic Angleworm" – *Unknown Worlds* Feb. 1943
"The Hat Trick" – *Unknown Worlds* Feb. 1943 (as by Felix Graham)
"The Sleuth from Mars" – *Detective Tales* Feb. 1943
"A Change for the Hearse" – *New Detective Magazine* March 1943
"Encore for a Killer" – *Mystery Magazine* March 1943
"Handbook for Homicide" – *Detective Tales* March 1943
"Trial by Darkness" – *Clues Detective Stories* March 1943
"Cadavers Don't Make a Fifth Column" – *Detective Short Stories* April 1943
"Death of a Vampire" – *Strange Detective Mysteries* May 1943
"Death's Dark Angel" – *Thrilling Detective* May 1943
"Market for Murder" – *The Shadow* May 1943
"The Freak Show Murders" – *Mystery Magazine* May 1943
"Madman's Holiday" – *Street & Smith's Detective Story Magazine* July 1943
"The Corpse and the Candle" – *Dime Mystery* July 1943
"Tell 'Em, Pagliaccio!" – *Street & Smith's Detective Story Magazine* Sep. 1943
"Blue Murder" – *The Shadow* Sep. 1943
"Daymare" – Thrilling *Wonder Stories* Fall 1943
"The Geezenstacks" – *Weird Tales* Sep. 1943
"Whispering Death" – *Dime Mystery* Sep. 1943
"Death Insurance Payment" – *Ten Detective Aces* Oct. 1943
"Paradox Lost" – *Astounding* Oct. 1943
"The Motive Goes Round and Round" – *Thrilling Detective* Oct. 1943

1944

"Murder in Miniature" – *Street & Smith's Detective Story Magazine* Jan. 1944
"The Djinn Murder" – *Ellery Queen's Mystery Magazine* Jan. 1944
"The Ghost of Riley" – *Detective Tales* Feb. 1944
"And the Gods Laughed" – *Planet Stories* Spring 1944
"Nothing Sirius" – *Captain Future* Spring 1944
"The Devil's Woodwinds" – *Dime Mystery* March 1944
"Homicide Sanitarium" – *Thrilling Detective* May 1944
"The Yehudi Principle" – *Astounding* May 1944

"Arena" – *Astounding* June 1944
"The Jabberwocky Murders" – *Thrilling Mystery* Summer 1944
"Murder While You Wait" – *Ellery Queen's Mystery Magazine* July 1944
"The Ghost Breakers" – *Thrilling Detective* July 1944
"The Gibbering Night" – *Detective Tales* July 1944
"Mr. Smith Kicks the Bucket" – *Street & Smith's Detective Story Magazine* Aug. 1944 (as "The Bucket of Gems Case)
"To Slay a Man About a Dog!" – *Detective Tales* Sep. 1944
"A Matter of Death" – *Thrilling Detective* Jan. 1944

1945

"The Night the World Ended" – *Dime Mystery* Jan. 1945
"The Waveries" – *Astounding* Jan. 1945
"The Dangerous People" – *Dime Mystery* March 1945 (as "No Sanctuary")
"Compliments of a Fiend" – *Thrilling Detective* May 1945
"Murder in Ten Easy Lessons" – *Ten Detective Aces* May 1945 (as "Ten Tickets to Hades")
"Murder-on-the-Hudson" (with Bob Woehlke) – *Thrilling Detective* June 1945 (as by Bob Woehlke)
"Pi in the Sky" – *Thrilling Wonder Stories* Winter 1945

1946

"Dead Man's Indemnity" – *Mystery Book Magazine* April 1946
"Placet Is a Crazy Place" – *Astounding* May 1946
"The Song of the Dead" – *New Detective Magazine* July 1946
"Obit for Obie" – *Mystery Book Magazine* Oct. 1946
"Whistler's Murder" – *Street & Smith's Detective Story Magazine* Dec. 1946

1947

"Miss Darkness" – *Avon Detective Mysteries #3*, 1947
"A Voice Behind Him" – *Mystery Book Magazine* Jan. 1947
"Don't Look Behind You" – *Ellery Queen's Mystery Magazine* May 1947
"I'll Cut Your Throat Again, Kathleen" – *Mystery Book Magazine* Winter 1947

1948

"The Dead Ringer" – *Mystery Book Magazine* Spring 1948
"Four-Letter Word" – *Adventure* April 1948
"The Four Blind Men" – *Adventure* Sep. 1948
"The Laughing Butcher" – *Mystery Book Magazine* Fall 1948
"What Mad Universe" – *Startling Stories* Sep. 1948
"The Joke" – *Detective Tales* Oct. 1948 (as "If Looks Could Kill")
"Cry Silence" – *Black Mask* Jan. 1948
"Red, Hot and Hunted!" – *Detective Tales* Jan. 1948
*"Knock" – *Thrilling Wonder Stories* Dec. 1948

1949

"The Bloody Moonlight" – *2 Detective Mystery Novels* Winter 1949 (condensed)
"The Screaming Mimi" – *Mystery Book Magazine* Fall 1949 (condensed, as "The Deadly Weekend")
"This Way Out" – *Dime Mystery* Feb. 1949
"All Good Bems" – *Thrilling Wonder Stories* April 1949
"Mouse" – *Thrilling Wonder Stories* June 1949
"Murder and Matilda" – *Mystery Book Magazine* Summer 1949
"Come and Go Mad" – *Weird Tales* July 1949
"Last Curtain" – *New Detective Magazine* July 1949
"Crisis, 1999" – *Ellery Queen's Mystery Magazine* Aug. 1949
"Each Night He Died" – *Dime Mystery* Aug. 1949
"Letter to a Phoenix" – *Astounding* Aug. 1949
"The Cat from Siam" – *Popular Detective* Sep. 1949
"The House of Fear" – *New Detective Magazine* Sep. 1949
"Gateway to Darkness" – *Super Science Stories* Jan. 1949

1950

"Death and Nine Lives" – *Black Book Detective* Spring 1950
"The Case of the Dancing Sandwiches" – *Mystery Book Magazine* Summer 1950
"The Last Train" – *Weird Tales* Jan. 1950
"Blind Lead" – *Detective Tales* June 1950
"The Nose of Don Aristide" – *2 Detective Mystery Novels* Summer 1950
*"Vengeance Fleet" – *Super Science Stories* July 1950 (as "Vengeance, Unlimited")
"Entity Trap" – *Amazing Stories* Aug. 1950 (as "From These Ashes")

"Obedience" – *Super Science Stories* Sep. 1950 (as "The Undying Ones")
"Walk in the Shadows" – *Giant Detective* Fall 1950
"Gateway to Glory" – *Amazing Stories* Oct. 1950
"The Frownzly Florgels" – *Other Worlds* Oct. 1950
"The Last Martian" – *Galaxy* Oct. 1950
"Honeymoon in Hell" – *Galaxy* Jan. 1950
"Mitkey Rides Again" – *Planet Stories* Jan. 1950
"Six-Legged Svengali" (with Mack Reynolds) – *Worlds Beyond* Dec. 1950

1951

"Something Green"—*Space On My Hands*, 1951
"Dark Interlude (with Mack Reynolds)" – *Galaxy* Jan. 1951
"Man of Distinction" – *Thrilling Wonder Stories* Feb. 1951
"The Switcheroo" (with Mack Reynolds) – *Other Worlds* March 1951
"The Weapon" – *Astounding* April 1951
"Cartoonist (with Mack Reynolds)" – *Planet Stories* May 1951 (as "Garrigan's Bems")
"The Dome" – *Thrilling Wonder Stories* Aug. 1951
"A Word from Our Sponsor" – *Other Worlds* Sep. 1951
"The Gamblers (with Mack Reynolds)" – *Startling Stories* Jan. 1951
"The Hatchetman (with Mack Reynolds)" – *Amazing Stories* Dec. 1951

1952

"Me and Flapjack and the Martians" (with Mack Reynolds) – *Astounding* Dec. 1952

1953

"Madball" – *The Saint Detective Magazine* June-July 1953 (condensed, as "The Pickled Punks")
"Witness in the Dark" – *New Detective Magazine* June 1953 (as "See No Murder")
"The Wench is Dead" – *Manhunt Detective Story Monthly* July 1953
"Rustle of Wings" – *The Magazine of Fantasy & Science Fiction* Aug. 1953
"The Little Lamb" – *Manhunt* Aug.1953
"Hall of Mirrors" – *Galaxy* Dec. 1953

1954

*"Answer" – *Angels and Spaceships*
*"Daisies" – *Angels and Spaceships*
*"Pattern" – *Angels and Spaceships*
*"Politeness" – *Angels and Spaceships*
*"Preposterous" – *Angels and Spaceships*
*"Reconciliation" – *Angels and Spaceships*
*"Search" – *Angels and Spaceships*
*"Sentence" – *Angels and Spaceships*
*"Solipsist" – *Angels and Spaceships*
*"Experiment" – *Galaxy* Feb. 1954 (as part of "Two Timer")
*"Sentry" – *Galaxy* Feb. 1954 (as part of "Two Timer")
"Keep Out" – *Amazing Stories* March 1954
"Martians, Go Home!" – *Astounding* Sep. 1954
*"Naturally" – *Beyond Fantasy Fiction* Sep. 1954 (as part of "Double Whammy")
*"Voodoo" – *Beyond Fantasy Fiction* Sep. 1954 (as part of "Double Whammy")

1955

*"Blood" – *The Magazine of Fantasy & Science Fiction* Feb. 1955
*"Millennium" – *The Magazine of Fantasy & Science Fiction* March 1955
"Premiere of Murder" – *The Saint Detective Magazine* May 1955
*"Fatal Error" – *Ellery Queen's Mystery Magazine* June 1955 (as part of "Killers Three: the Perfect Crime")
*"Dead Letter" – *Ellery Queen's Mystery Magazine* July 1955 (as part of "Killers Three: the Perfect Crime")
*"The First Time Machine" – *Ellery Queen's Mystery Magazine* Sep. 1955 (as part of "Killers Three: the Perfect Crime")
*"Too Far" – *The Magazine of Fantasy & Science Fiction* Sep. 1955

1956

"The Lenient Beast" – *Manhunt* April 1956 (condensed, as "Line of Duty")

1957

"Murder Set to Music" – *The Saint Detective Magazine* Jan. 1957
*"Expedition" – *The Magazine of Fantasy & Science Fiction* Feb. 1957

"Happy Ending" (with Mack Reynolds) – *Fantastic Universe* Sep. 1957

1958

"One for the Road" – *The Saint Detective Magazine* Feb. 1958 (condensed, as "The Amy Waggoner Murder Case")
*"Unfortunately" – *The Magazine of Fantasy & Science Fiction* Oct. 1958

1959

"The Late Lamented" – *The Saint Mystery Magazine* Feb. 1959 (condensed)
*"Nasty" – *Playboy* April 1959
*"Rope Trick" – *Adam* May 1959
"Knock Three-One-Two" – *High Adventure* June 1959 (condensed, as "Night of the Psycho")

1960

*"Abominable" – *Dude* March 1960 (as part of Portfolio)
*"Bear Possibility" – *Dude* March 1960 (as part of Portfolio)
*"Recessional" – *Dude* March 1960 (as part of Portfolio)
"The Mind Thing (N)" – *Fantastic Universe* March 1960 (part 1 only; final issue of *FU*)
*"Rebound" – *Galaxy* April 1960 (as "The Power")
"Earthmen Bearing Gifts" – *Galaxy* June 1960
*"Granny's Birthday" – *Alfred Hitchcock's Mystery Magazine* June 1960
*"The House" – *Fantastic* Aug. 1960

1961

"Before She Kills" – *Ed McBains Mystery Book #3*, 1961
*"Bright Beard"—*Nightmares and Geezenstacks* (1961)
*"Cat Burglar" – *Nightmares and Geezenstacks* (1961)
*"Death on the Mountain" – *Nightmares and Geezenstacks* (1961)
*"Fish Story" – *Nightmares and Geezenstacks* (1961)
*"Horse Race" – *Nightmares and Geezenstacks* (1961)
*"Jaycee" – *Nightmares and Geezenstacks* (1961)
*"Nightmare in Green" – *Nightmares and Geezenstacks* (1961)
*"Nightmare in White" – *Nightmares and Geezenstacks* (1961)

*"Second Chance" – *Nightmares and Geezenstacks* (1961)
*"The Ring of Hans Carvel" (retold and somewhat modernized from the works of Rabelais) – *Nightmares and Geezenstacks* (1961)
*"Three Little Owls (A Fable)" – *Nightmares and Geezenstacks* (1961)
*"Great Lost Discoveries I" – Invisibility" – *Gent* Feb. 1961 (as part of "Three Part Invention")
*"Great Lost Discoveries II" – Invulnerability" – *Gent* Feb. 1961 (as part of "Three Part Invention")
*"Great Lost Discoveries III" – Immortality" – *Gent* Feb. 1961 (as part of "Three Part Invention")
*"Hobbyist" – *Playboy* May 1961 (as "The Hobbyist")
*"Nightmare in Blue" – *Dude* May 1961 (as part of "Five Nightmares")
*"Nightmare in Gray" – *Dude* May 1961 (as part of "Five Nightmares")
*"Nightmare in Red" – *Dude* May 1961 (as part of "Five Nightmares")
*"Nightmare in Yellow" – *Dude* May 1961 (as part of "Five Nightmares")
*"The End" – *Dude* May 1961 (as "Nightmare in Time", part of "Five Nightmares")
"The Short Happy Lives of Eustace Weaver I, II, & III" – *Ellery Queen's Mystery Magazine* June 1961 (as
"Of Time and Eustace Weaver")

1962

"Aelurophobe" – *Dude* Sep. 1962 (as Cattin' on the Couch)
"Puppet Show" – *Playboy* Jan. 1962

1963

"Double Standard" – *Playboy* April 1963
*"untitled ("At thirty, a woman…")" – *Rogue* April 1963
*"untitled ("Little Red Riding Hood…")" – *Rogue* April 1963
*"untitled ("Padriac jumped…")" – *Rogue* April 1963
*"untitled ("When, after a long…")" – *Rogue* April 1963
*"Mistake" – *Rogue* May 1963
*"untitled ("Awaiting electrocution, Clyde…")" – *Rogue* May 1963
*"untitled ("In a dream, Robert…")" – *Rogue* May 1963

*"untitled ("The tall homely man...")" – *Rogue* May 1963
*"untitled ("Ferdinand, because he had...")" – *Rogue* June 1963
*"untitled ("Gretchen took home...")" – *Rogue* June 1963
*"untitled ("Howard thought the perfect crime...")" – *Rogue* June 1963
*"untitled ("Madeleine woke in the night...")" – *Rogue* June 1963
*"untitled ("A duke, jostled...")" – *Rogue* July 1963
*"untitled ("Enraged by the failure...")" – *Rogue* July 1963
*"untitled ("In Czarist Russia,...")" – *Rogue* July 1963
*"untitled ("The once popular wishing well...")" – *Rogue* July 1963
"It Didn't Happen" – *Playboy* Oct. 1963
"Ten Percenter" – *Gent* Oct. 1963 (as "Tale of the Flesh Monger")
"The Missing Actor" – *The Saint Mystery Magazine* Jan. 1963

1964

"Why, Benny, Why?" – *Ellery Queen's Mystery M*agazine Jan. 1964

1965

"Eine Kleine Nachtmusik (with Carl Onspaugh)" – *The Magazine of Fantasy & Science Fiction* June 1965

1986

"How Tagrid Got There"—*Sex Life on the Planet Mars* (1986)

1987

"Brother Monster" (unfinished novel)—*Brother Monster* (1987)
"Mirror"—*Nightmare in Darkness* (1987)
*"Nightmare in Darkness" – *Nightmare in Darkness* (1987)
"The Screaming Mimi" (original ending) – *Nightmare in Darkness* (1987)

1990

"The Case of the Languid Lamb"—*The Water-Walker* (1990)
"The Case of the Rambling Rocks" – *The Water-Walker* (1990)
"The Water-Walker" – *The Water-Walker* (1990)

Unpublished Stories

"Callisto Deadline"
"Coming, Georgia"

"Day of the Ogre"
"Death Comes Creeping"
"Greengoods Hideout"
"Habeas Ex Corpus"
"Headstone for a Grave"
"House of Silence"
"Klepto Trouble"
"Long Term Contract"
"Mr. Tayama's Box"
"Murder Wears Red"
"Murder, or Something"
"Old Judge Lynch"
"On the Dotted Lion"
"Printers and the Flag"
"Raw Magic"
"Sing While You're Able"
"Sleeping Dogs"
"The Case of Joseph Clark"
"The Clutch of Morpheus"
"The Earring Gods"
"The Eyes Have It"
"The Lights"
"The Magic Lamp"
"The Phantom and the Flying Death"
"The Phantom Mortician"
"The Sheriff Lays an Egg"
"The Sinister Mr. Dexter"
"The Thought Bomb"
"This is the Forest Primeval"
"Three Days of Coro-roth"
"To Fill a Grave"

Novels and Collections

The Fabulous Clipjoint – Dutton, 1947
The Dead Ringer – Dutton, 1948
Murder Can Be Fun – Dutton, 1948
The Bloody Moonlight – Dutton, 1949
The Screaming Mimi – Dutton, 1949
What Mad Universe – Dutton, 1949

Compliments of a Fiend – Dutton, 1950
Here Comes a Candle – Dutton, 1950
Night of the Jabberwock – Dutton, 1950
The Case of the Dancing Sandwiches – Dell, 1951
Death Has Many Doors – Dutton, 1951
The Far Cry – Dutton, 1951
Space on my Hands – Shasta, 1951
The Deep End – Dutton, 1952
The Five-Day Nightmare – Dutton, 1952
We All Killed Grandma – Duton, 1952
Madball – Dell, 1953
Mostly Murder – Dutton, 1953
The Lights in the Sky are Stars – Dutton, 1953
Angels and Spaceships – Dutton, 1954
His Name was Death – Dutton, 1954
Martians, Go Home – Dutton, 1955
The Wench is Dead – Dutton, 1955
The Lenient Beast – Dutton, 1956
Rogue in Space – Dutton, 1957
Honeymoon In Hell – Bantam, 1958
The Office – Dutton, 1958
One for the Road – Dutton, 1958
Knock Three-One-Two – Dutton, 1959
The Late, Lamented – Dutton, 1959
The Mind Thing – Bantam, 1961
The Murderers – Dutton, 1961
Nightmares and Geezenstacks – Bantam, 1961
Mrs. Murphy's Underpants – Dutton, 1963
The Shaggy Dog and Other Murders – Dutton, 1963
Daymares – Lancer, 1968
Paradox Lost and Twelve Other Great Science Fiction Stories – Random, 1973
The Best of Fredric Brown – Nelson Doubleday (SFBC), 1976
The Best Short Stories of Fredric Brown – NEL, 1982
4 Novels – Zomba, 1983
Before She Kills – Dennis McMillan, 1984
Homicide Sanitarium – Dennis McMillan, 1984
Carnival of Crime: The Best Mystery Stories of Fredric Brown – Southern Illinois University Press, 1985

The Freak Show Murders – Dennis McMillan, 1985
Madman's Holiday – Dennis McMillan, 1985
Pardon My Ghoulish Laughter – Dennis McMillan, 1986
Red is the Hue of Hell – Dennis McMillan, 1986
Sex Life on the Planet Mars – Dennis McMillan, 1986
Thirty Corpses Every Thursday – Dennis McMillan, 1986
And the Gods Laughed – Phantasia Press, 1987
Brother Monster – Dennis McMillan, 1987
Nightmare In Darkness – Dennis McMillan, 1987
Selling Death Short – Dennis McMillan, 1988
Three-Corpse Parlay – Dennis McMillan, 1988
Who Was That Blonde I Saw You Kill Last Night? – Dennis McMillan, 1988
Whispering Death – Dennis McMillan, 1989
Happy Ending – Dennis McMillan, 1990
The Water-Walker – Dennis McMillan, 1990
The Gibbering Night – Dennis McMillan, 1991
The Pickled Punks – Dennis McMillan, 1991
From These Ashes: The Complete Short Fiction of Fredric Brown – NESFA Press, 2001
Hunter and Hunted: The Ed and Am Hunter Novels, Pt. 1 – Stewart Masters Publishing, 2002
Martians and Madness: The Complete Novels of Fredric Brown – NESFA Press, 2002
Mitkey Astromouse – Harlan Quist, 2003

❑

Cyril With an M (or, I'm As Kornbluth as Kansas in August

With this, my first installment of "Past Masters" for *Baen's Universe* (the eleventh overall, with the previous ten residing in the *Helix SF* archives if you're interested), I've reached something of a milestone. A small one, perhaps, but there it is nonetheless. As is customary with milestones, I'd like to pause here and take stock. Bear with me; I'll get to our primary subject anon.

Much as I loved (and still do love) *Helix*, *JBU* offers a larger readership, a venue which isn't struggling to establish itself, and a far more visible storefront from which I can operate. For my purposes, this is important.

My intent with "Past Masters" has always been to highlight the history of SF and fantasy, a topic which has long fascinated me and to which I've returned over and over, with this column and others as well. Specifically, the column has dealt with authors, and even more specifically, those authors who seemed to have slipped from the Mass Consciousness (as well as the mass market) because their work has been allowed to fall out of print—out of print, out of mind.

In some cases, this is hardly a tragedy (I won't mention names, lest I become inundated by letters of protest from the one or two others out there who remember them more fondly than I), but in many cases it's not only a tragedy but a travesty. If this were a Perfect Universe, for example, Alfred Bester would remain in print eternally, translated into as many languages as is necessary to ensure that every sentient entity on the face of the planet had a copy of his complete works. (I would add that his books and stories should by law be transmuted into any and all alien languages we may happen upon in the future, but no; boasting doesn't become us.)

Since I first began writing seriously about SF and fantasy, I've frequently found myself moaning and grousing that I really should have started doing this stuff 25 or more years ago, when more of the subjects were still above ground, willing (and able) to answer questions. The reality, of course, is that a quarter of a century ago I wasn't nearly the writer I am today; more important than that, though - not to mention more frustrating—is that 25 years ago, I wouldn't have had to write about Fredric Brown, or Zenna Henderson, or Cordwainer Smith, or all the others, because 25 years ago *they hadn't been forgotten.*

They were still in print in the mass market then, you see; they were being read not only by their old fans, but by legions of newer fans who either happened upon their books by accident or who were guided towards them by their friends. Their titles might not have sold like the then-current stars' did, but they sold steadily enough that publishers who were raking in the bucks on Delany and Zelazny and Dick and Haldeman were more than willing to settle for their Elders' slower—but still profitable—sales.

Oh, the small- and fan-presses try their best. NESFA, for example, makes a point of publishing well-edited and handsome volumes of older authors' complete short works, and keeping them in print as long as they can sell a few copies a year. This is more than commendable, it's remarkable, and I salute them.

But it's not the mass market, not by a long chalk, and try as I will to understand the pressures of Big Business and the Bottom Line, I can only do so intellectually. In my heart, I still grieve that I can't drive to Borders and buy a new copy of Richard Meredith's brilliant novel, *We All Died at Breakaway Station*, or Spinrad's wonderful collection, *The Last Hurrah of the Golden Horde.*

That I'm 25 years too late for definitive answers to many of the questions I'd love to ask my Elders (and Betters) is hard enough to bear. That those self-same Elders, pioneers in the field we come here to celebrate, are falling further and further away from the Mass Consciousness which once revered them is unacceptable. Thus, "Past Masters," as well as anything else on the general subject that I can get away with (and, hopefully, get paid for).

Anyway (as Mort Sahl would say), onward.

My subject this time around, Cyril M. Kornbluth, wasn't born with an M in his name. According to Frederik Pohl (who ought to know) he added it when he decided to write in collaboration with his wife, Mary.

Just how many of Kornbluth's fifty or so stories were, in fact, written that way I don't know; it's entirely possible that, like Henry Kuttner and his spouse Catherine L. Moore, the collaborations were subtle and indirect as often as they were active exchanges.

Kornbluth was born in 1923. He made his first bones at age 17, selling "Stepsons of Mars"—a collaboration with Richard Wilson under the pseudonym Ivar Towers—to Pohl's *Astonishing Stories* for the April, 1940 issue, and followed this with his first solo story, "King Cole of Pluto" (as by S. D. Gottesman) in the May, 1940 *Super Science*, also edited by Pohl.

If you're paying close attention, you should have noticed two things by now: first, that CMK wasn't at all adverse to using pseudonyms, both with others and by himself, and that he hung around with the baddest literary gang this side of the Algonquin Hotel, the Futurians.

I'm going to assume that you already know about the Futurians. If you don't, I suggest you Google them directly; without argument, they were the single most important group—fan or pro—in the early history of science fiction. I'm not exaggerating here, even a little bit. The Futurians produced a significant number of writers, editors, and agents, not to mention an equally significant number of feuds, dalliances, schisms, and lifelong friendships. Frankly, I suspect that it would be impossible to overestimate their influence on the burgeoning field of magazine science fiction, and they would continue to do so as individuals well into the 1970s.

(For those of you whose interest is piqued, allow me to point you to a couple of books written by those who were there: *The Way the Future Was* by Frederik Pohl, an indispensable personal history by one of the most important figures in SF, and *The Futurians* by Damon Knight, hardly a figure of lesser stature. Budzilla sez, get into 'em.)

Kornbluth was a good fit with the Futurians for all that he was in his mid-teens when he first began hanging around them. He was opinionated, brash, wry and witty, and boiling with the compulsion to contribute to science fiction, not just read it. And that he did, for all that his catalog isn't as extensive as many of his fellows'; 90 or so short stories, a dozen novels, much of it in collaboration with one or another writer (mostly Pohl, or another Futurian). Take a look at one single year in the biblio at the end of this installment: more than two dozen stories in 1941 alone, and in many cases, two stories in the same issue under different names. This, clearly, was a man trying to prove himself.

Numbers aren't everything, however. In fact, an author's prolificacy is meaningless in the long run if s/he has little of sum and substance to say;

look at Lionel Fanthorpe or Barbara Cartland. They certainly filled their editors' in-boxes, but how widely are they read now?

Kornbluth was all about sum and substance, crafting near-perfect little gems that could cut you to ribbons if you didn't handle them carefully. The contents of *The Best of C. M. Kornbluth* (ed. Frederik Pohl, Ballantine 1976) give the reader plenty of opportunities for such self-injury, all of them as rewarding as they are cynical, as entertaining as they are scornful.

No accident, this. In his introduction to the above, Pohl described his old friend as "a sardonic soul," and said his work "...relates to the essential hypocrisies and foolishnesses of mankind." Well, yeah. Even a brief examination of his stories—"The Marching Morons", "The Little Black Bag", and his novel *The Syndic* are typical—offer a particularly jaundiced view of the Great Unwashed.

This factor has a particular and peculiar effect on the reader: either you get it, and you have a really good time, or you don't—and you end up scratching your head and wondering what all the fuss is about. I'm serious about this; the reader who "gets" Kornbluth will more than once find him/herself snorting and saying, "Yeah, ain't *that* th' truth!"

That's a bit of an oversimplification, of course. Even if you don't agree with Kornbluth's amused contempt at the majority of the Human Race, his skill as a writer is engaging and admirable. I'm far less of a gleeful pessimist than he was, and he's always been one of my favorites.

Take one of his most famous stories, for example. If there is a typical Kornbluthian story, it is "The Marching Morons" (originally in the 4/51 *Galaxy*). It begins with a character sincerely near and dear to Kornbluth's heart, a potter. The opening scene works as well as it does primarily because Mary Kornbluth, his wife, was a potter and ceramicist, and the details are spot-on as a result.

The character isn't just any potter, though, I should point out. Not only is he skilled in shaping and glazing his wares, he's also an engineer/physicist, and almost certainly a half-dozen or more other brainy-mug specialties. So is the secretary of the man who ostensibly buys his pots, although the buyer himself is...well, a moron.

And that's the point of this gleefully dark little yarn. The human race has split into proto-Eloi and proto-Morlocks, with the (comparative) handful of brains actually running things while the morons take the credit and drive their noisy, flashy cars. All is well, until the potter—in search of mineral deposits to use in making glazes—digs up "Honest John" Barlow, a real estate mogul who went to the dentist for an impacted wisdom tooth (note the irony there) and was accidentally thrown into a state of suspended animation.

What was, in the past, an accident with no foreseeable solution turns out to be child's play for the non-morons of the future, and Barlow is awakened to find his old world gone to dust, and this new one faced with the Problem: what to do with the moronic portion of the population? What, indeed, and if you haven't yet read this nasty little tale, I won't spoil it for you; it's way more fun if you read it for yourself.

As I mentioned, Frederik Pohl knew Kornbluth from an early age, and the two men took to writing early on. He told me:

> I think Cyril wanted to be a writer at an age when most of us did, in his early teens. His first efforts, or at least the first I knew anything about, weren't stories. They were poems.

Pohl himself was no stranger to poetry, and in fact, his first professional publication was the verse "Elegy to a Dead Satellite: Luna", published in the October 1937 *Amazing* under the name Elton V. Andrews. The two youngsters acquired a book by one of Kornbluth's teachers which gave the rules for writing just about every type of poem there is and were determined to try their hand at all of them:

> We made a good start, actually writing haiku (we spelled it hokku), a villanelle, a sestina, two sonnets (one Petrarchian and one Shakespearian) and I think a couple of others. We bogged down when it came to the chant royale (the chant royale is HARD) and, like most of the other

> Futurians, we decided to try our luck with science fiction. At that time I think Cyril was maybe 14, and I three or four years later.

The plain truth is that there is precious little of the sympathetic in Kornbluth's work, and not a drop of sentimentality. There is, if you want it, plenty of bitterness, but that alone wouldn't mean much: if you look hard enough, there's no lack of acerbic wit out there in Fantasyland, even in those writers not particularly known for it. Bitterness by itself is just a bad taste; what makes Kornbluth's prose memorable and gratifying is the skill with which he expresses his bitterness, and that really is a rarity.

I'm talking about elegance here. Elegance of prose, more specifically. Not just an economy of words, although that can be part of it, but using the optimum word or phrase for the task at hand. I could give you example after example: Bradbury's "It was a pleasure to burn"; Vonnegut's "Billy Pilgrim was unstuck in time"; Cordwainer Smith's... well, take your pick.

Kornbluth is eat-up with elegance, it's there almost everywhere you look. Not necessarily poetry, mind you—despite his early experimentation, there's little of the poetic in his work—but there is, nevertheless, an elegance born of his innate (and integral) sardonicism. Consider this, from "The Marching Morons:"

> Lying twisted and broken under the acceleration, [he] realized that some things had not changed, that Jack Ketch was never asked to dinner however many shillings you paid him to do your dirty work, that murder will out, that crime pays only temporarily.
>
> The last thing he learned was that death is the end of pain.

Only Kornbluth could have expressed the death of a soulless and cynical character so elegantly, at least in the still mostly-Campbellian SF world of 1951. Perhaps it's just as valid, though, to say that only Kornbluth would have found it desirable to do so.

I said above that there was little if any poetry in his writing, but that's not strictly true across the board. Like all fine writers, Kornbluth defies attempts to stuff him into convenient pigeonholes, even mine. He did it rarely, he did it for specific and precise effect, and he did it without fanfare or flash, as in this from "The Remorseful" (from *Star Science Fiction Stories 2*, ed. Frederik Pohl, Ballantine 1953):

> It does not matter when it happened. This is because the Visitors were eternal; endless time stretched before them and behind, which mentions only two of the infinities that their "lives" included. Precisely when they arrived at a particular planetary system was to them the most trivial of irrelevancies. Eternity was theirs; eventually they would have arrived at all of them.

Lovely. Just lovely. No sentiment, nothing wistful or nostalgic or lugubrious; just a few lines of quiet prose admirably constructed to express a concept using the optimum words for the task at hand. Elegance.

What of the man behind this elegance, though? That's rather complicated, I'm afraid, and not a little unfortunate as well. Pohl, probably Kornbluth's closest friend and his frequent collaborator, is perhaps the least likely to express a negative estimation, even though he was lampooned severely in *Gunner Cade*,[1] which was written during one of their occasional rifts. He says in his introduction to *The Best of C. M. Kornbluth*:

> There is a character in the book who is pitifully corrupt and whiningly ineffectual. It is not an accident that the character's name is what Judy's first daughter called me when she was first learning to talk: Threadwick.

"Sardonic," indeed. Others weren't nearly so forgiving. In a letter to Isaac Asimov dated after Kornbluth's death, John W. Campbell said, "His anger against the ways of the culture he didn't fit too well produced cumulative bitterness in him."

Author and critic Barry Malzberg goes even further:

> Kornbluth's nastiness is remarked on by everyone who knew him at all. He was deeply embittered by his experience in the War and by his economic struggles after the War. Don Wollheim… told me, "Cyril was so bitter in his last year that you knew that either the world would have to go away or he would. There was no compromise possible."

(Wollheim himself was at least once a Kornbluth collaborator. The January 1953 *F&SF* contained "The Mask of Demeter," as by Cecil Corwin and Martin Pearson; Corwin was a frequent pseudonym of Kornbluth's, and Pearson was Wollheim. How the story—actually, a story fragment—came to be published at all is one of a number of deplorable incidents Kornbluth suffered during his short life. It was sold to Boucher and McComas not by either of the authors, or by Kornbluth's agent, the ever-present Pohl, but by an agent who had no rights to it.[2] Needless to say, Kornbluth knew nothing of it until it appeared, and found it extremely difficult to collect his due; all in all, it was just another brick in the wall.)

That such a body of work as Kornbluth left behind was written by a man so cynical and angry is remarkable, frankly. It puts him in a class with Anthony Burgess and Kurt Vonnegut, without their literary pretensions (don't forget that Vonnegut, for all his rejection of the genre, began his career selling to *Galaxy* and *Wonder Stories* like every other sci-fi hack he so despised).

His noteworthiness wasn't limited to his sour outlook, though. His stories may lack sentimentality, but they certainly don't lack humanity.

The titular object in "The Little Black Bag" transforms its finder, Dr. Full, from a shattered drunk into a man again capable of feeling something other than a desperate need for another bottle of wine, back into a physician with the firm intent to use the contents of the magic case to do once again what he had always done best: heal the sick. Simple bitterness wouldn't give an author the range to create that character and make him breathe; it takes a clear understanding of, as well as a real affection for, people.

Kornbluth himself might have been horrified to hear me say that, but nevertheless

I'm convinced that he had more love for his fellows than he was ever comfortable expressing, either in fiction or in person.

The exception to this was almost certainly his family. Clearly he and his wife Mary loved each other deeply; the year following his death, she assembled a slim anthology, *Science Fiction Showcase* (Doubleday 1959), containing stories by a number of his friends including Futurians Damon Knight, James Blish, and the ever-present Pohl, as well as Bradbury, Philip K. Dick, and Theodore Sturgeon among others as a tribute to her late husband. It is a quiet, but heart-felt little book, well worth the reading even now, a half-century later.

CMK was an infantryman in WWII, fighting in the Battle of the Bulge and winning the Bronze Star. However, his injuries stayed with him for the rest of his too-short life, adding yet another brick to that already daunting wall.

After the war, he went into journalism, working his way up to the position of editor of the Chicago office of Trans-Radio Press and busting his hump to find that elusive thing that all penny-a-word scriveners lusted for and few found: a regular paycheck as a writer. He went back to writing fiction full-time in 1951, producing almost all of his best-known work, including a number of novels both solo and in collaboration.

Although he was making better money than before, the memories of his days with the miss-meal cramps loomed like the Sword of Damocles over his head, and he looked for something within his range of skills. Pohl relates:

> Although Cyril was doing reasonably well in economic terms a writer's income come sin lumps of various sizes at irregular times and (w/ two kids) he felt the need of a more regular income. He was offered an assistant editor job on *F&SF*, which he liked a lot. (He was delighted with some of the pieces he passed along to Bob Mills, particularly Fritz Leiber's "The Silver Eggheads".)

Unfortunately, his involvement with the magazine was not fated to be a long one. Early in the spring of 1958, he was scheduled to meet with Mills in NYC. It had snowed heavily at his home in Levittown, and he rushed to shovel out his drive before running to the station to catch his train. He was struck by a heart attack on the platform, and died there, age 35.

His death came at an age when most writers are just beginning to hit their stride and create mature, lasting bodies of work. Considering the maturity and complexity of the stories and novels he left behind, it's humbling to contemplate what he could have produced given even another few decades. Not only was he popular with the readers, but with the critics as well. In his Hugo-winning history of science fiction, *Trillion Year Spree* (Atheneum 1986), Brian Aldiss calls Kornbluth's passing "…a minor disaster…"; of his erudition and (if I may repeat myself) elegance of language, Damon Knight said:

> Kornbluth must have been born with a lexicon in his mouth. Legend has it that once, when a motherly stranger bent over him in his perambulator and made the sounds that are usually made to babies, Kornbluth remarked, "Madame, I am not the child you think me."

The three books which make up the first two volumes of that most excellent collection, *The Science Fiction Hall of Fame* (eds. Robert Silverberg and Ben Bova, Doubleday 1970 and 1973), contain stories which were chosen by the members of the SFWA as being worthy of the Nebula had it existed when those stories were originally published. Although he died before the founding of the Science-Fiction and Fantasy Writers of America and thus would never win the Nebula, Cyril M. Kornbluth is represented twice therein with—what else?—"The Little Black Bag" and "The Marching Morons."

Summing up a remarkable author like Kornbluth in a few words is a difficult task, one best left (in this case, anyhow) to someone who knew him well, and whose understanding of the man and his work is far greater than mine could ever be, so I will leave you with the words with which Frederik Pohl ended his appreciation of his friend and colleague in *The Best of C. M. Kornbluth*:

> As a person he was what he was as a writer: bright, sardonic, and immensely rewarding. Cyril had a great deal to say, and he said it all tersely, wittily, and with grace. I do not think we shall soon see his like again.

Nor do I. If you are unfamiliar with this outstanding man's books and stories, I urge you to haunt the used bookstores and convention dealers' tables, and to assiduously pore over the offerings of the on-line booksellers for his titles. It will not be a waste of your time or money. Budzilla sez so.

(The following bibliography is, as usual, as complete as I can make it given the print and online resources to which I have access. Also as usual, I welcome any and all additions and corrections. Because of the number of collaborations and pseudonyms herein, I have opted to list all the stories together in chronological order rather than breaking it up. Just to keep my sanity, I have placed an arbitrary cut-off coinciding with the publication of The Best of C. M. Kornbluth, i.e. 1976. In addition to those listed below, he also used the pennames Earl Balons and Carl F. Burke. There are also at least another dozen and a half mystery stories I could find no citation for; as always, I invite enlightenment from my readers.)

Short Stories and Articles

"Stepsons of Mars" – April 1940 *Astonishing Stories* (w/ Richard Wilson, as by Ivar Towers)

"Hollow of the Moon" – May 1940 *Super Science Stories* (as by Gabriel Barclay)

"King Cole of Pluto" – May 1940 *Super Science Stories* (as by S. D. Gottesman)

"Before the Universe" – July 1940 *Super Science Stories* (w/ Frederik Pohl, as by S. D. Gottesman)

"Nova Midplane" – November 1940 *Super Science Stories* (w/ Frederik Pohl, as by S. D. Gottesman)

"Trouble in Time" – December 1940 *Astonishing Stories* (w/ Frederik Pohl, as by S. D. Gottesman)

"Vacant World" – January 1941 *Super Science Stories* (w/ Frederik Pohl and Dirk Wylie, under Wylie's name)

"Dead Center" – February 1941 *Stirring SF* (as by S. D. Gottesman)

"Thirteen O'Clock" – February 1941 *Stirring SF* (as by Cecil Corwin)

"Callistan Tomb" – Spring 1941 *SF Quarterly* (w/ Frederik Pohl, as by Paul Dennis Lavond

"The Psychological Regulator" – March 1941 *Comet Stories* (w/ E. Balter, Robert W. Lowndes, John Michel, and Wollheim, as by Arthur Cooke)

"The Martians Are Coming" – March 1941 *Cosmic Stories* (w/ Robert W. Lowndes, under Lowndes' name)

"New Directions" – March 1941 *Cosmic Stories* (article, as by Walter C. Davies)

"Return from M-15" – March 1941 *Cosmic Stories* (as by S. D. Gottesman)

"The Reversible Revolutions" – March 1941 *Cosmic Stories* (as by Cecil Corwin)

"Exiles of New Planet" – April 1941 *Astonishing Stories* (w/ Frederik Pohl, Robert W. Lowndes and Dirk Wylie, as by Paul Dennis Lavond)

"The Rocket of 1955" – April 1941 *Stirring SF* (as by Cecil Corwin)

"The Castle on the Outerplanet" – April 1941 *Stirring SF* (w/ Frederik Pohl and Robert W. Lowndes, as by S. D. Gottesman)

"A Prince of Pluto" – April 1941 *Future SF* (w/ Frederik Pohl, as by Paul Dennis Lavond)

"Best Friend" – May 1941 *Super Science Stories* (w/ Frederik Pohl, as by S. D. Gottesman)

"Dimension of Darkness" – May 1941 *Cosmic Stories* (as by S. D. Gottesman)

"No Place to Go" – May 1941 *Cosmic Stories* (as by Edward J. Bellin)

"What Sorghum Says" – May 1941 *Cosmic Stories* (as by Cecil Corwin)

"Forgotten Tongue" – June 1941 *Stirring SF* (as by Walter C. Davies)

"Kazam Collects" – June 1941 *Stirring SF* (as by S. D. Gottesman)

"Mr. Packer Goes to Hell" – June 1941 *Stirring SF* (as by Cecil Corwin)

"The Words of Guru" – June 1941 *Stirring SF* (as by Kenneth Falconer)

"Fire Power" – July 1941 *Cosmic Stories* (as by S. D. Gottesman)

"Interference – July 1941 *Cosmic Stories* (as by Walter C. Davies)

"The City in the Sofa" – July 1941 *Cosmic Stories* (as by Cecil Corwin)

"Mars-Tube" – September 1941 *Astonishing Stories* (w/ Frederik Pohl, as by S. D. Gottesman)

"Sir Mallory's Magnitude" – Winter 1941-42 *SF Quarterly* (as by S. D. Gottesman)

"Crisis!" – Spring 1942 *SF Quarterly* (as by Cecil Corwin)

"Einstein's Planetoid" - Spring 1942 *SF Quarterly* (w/ Frederik Pohl, Robert W. Lowndes and Dirk Wylie, as by Paul Dennis Lavond)

"The Embassy" – March 1942 *Astounding* (w/ Donald Wollheim, as by Martin Pearson)

"The Golden Road" – March 1942 *Stirring SF* (as by Cecil Corwin)
"Masquerade" – March 1942 *Stirring SF* (as by Kenneth Falconer)
"The Perfect Invasion" – March 1942 *Stirring SF* (as by S. D. Gottesman)
"The Core" – April 1942 *Future SF* (as by S. D. Gottesman)
"An Old Neptunian Custom" – August 1942 *Super Science Stories* (w/ Frederik Pohl, as by Scott Mariner)
"The Extrapolated Dimwit" – October 1942 *Future SF* (w/ Frederik Pohl and Robert W. Lowndes, as by S. D. Gottesman)
"Blood on the Campus" – June 1948 *Detective Story* (mystery)
"The Only Thing We Learn" – July 1949 *Startling Stories*
"The Little Black Bag" – July 1950 *Astounding*
"Iteration" – September/October 1950 *Future*
"The Silly Season" – Fall 1950 *F&SF*
"The Mindworm" – December 1950 *Worlds Beyond*
"Friend to Man" – Spring 1951 *Thrilling Wonder Stories*
"The Marching Morons" – April 1951 *Galaxy*
"Mars Child" – serial, May-July 1951 *Galaxy* (w/ Judith Merril, as by Cyril Judd)
"With These Hands" – December 1951 *Galaxy*
"That Share of Glory" – January 1952 *Astounding*
"Gunner Cade" – serial, March-May 1952 *Astounding* (w/ Judith Merril, as by Cyril Judd)
"The Luckiest Man in Denv" – June 1952 *Galaxy* (as by Simon Eisner)
"Gravy Planet" – serial, June-August 1952 *Galaxy* (w/ Frederik Pohl)
"Make Mine Mars" – November 1952 *SF Adventures*
"The Altar at Midnight" – November 1952 *Galaxy*
"The Goodly Creatures" – December 1952 *F&SF*
"The Mask of Demeter" – January 1953 *F&SF* (as by Cecil Corwin and Martin Pearson, pseuds. of Kornbluth and Donald Wollheim respectively)
"Time Bum" – January/February 1953 *Fantastic*
"Sea Change" – March 1953 *Dynamic SF* (w/ Judith Merril, as by Cyril Judd)
"The Adventurer" – May 1953 *Space SF*
"Dip Detail" – July 1953 *Private Eye* (mystery)
"The Meddlers" – September 1953 *SF Adventures*
"Everybody Knows Joe" – October/November 1953 *Future*

"The Syndic" – serial, December 1953-February 1954 *SF Adventures* (w/ Judith Merril, as by Cyril Judd)
"I Never Ast No Favors" – April 1954 *F&SF*
"Takeoff" – serial, April-June 1954 *New Worlds* (#22-24)
"Gladiator At Law" – serial, June-August 1954 *Galaxy* (w/ Frederik Pohl)
"Dominoes" – in *Star SF Stories*, ed. Frederik Pohl; Ballantine 16 (simul. h'back and p'back), 1953
"The Remorseful" – in *Star SF Stories #2*, ed. Frederik Pohl; Ballantine 55 (simul. h'back and p'back), 1954
"The Adventurers" – February 1955 *SF Quarterly*
"Gomez" – February 1955 *New Worlds* (#32)
"Not This August" – serial, May-June 1955 *MacLean's*
"The Cosmic Charge Account" – January 1956 *F&SF*
"The Engineer" – February 1956 *Infinity* (w/ Frederik Pohl)
"The Education of Tigress Macardle" – July 1957 *Venture*
"MS. Found In a Chinese Fortune Cookie" – July 1957 *F&SF*
"The Unfortunate Topologist" – verse, July 1957 *F&SF* (as by S. D. Gottesman)
"The Slave" – September 1957 *SF Adventures*
"The Last Man Left in the Bar" – October 1957 *Infinity*
"Wolfbane" – serial, October-November 1957 *Galaxy* (w/ Frederik Pohl)
"Requiem for a Scientist" – article, December 1957 *Fantastic Universe*
"Passion Pills" – in *A Mile Beyond the Moon*, Doubleday 1958 (h'back only)
"The Events Leading Down to the Tragedy" – January 1958 *F&SF*
"Virginia" – March 1958 *Venture*
"Reap the Dark Tide" – June 1958 *Venture*
"Theory of Rocketry" – July 1958 *F&SF*
"Two Dooms" – July 1958 *Venture*
"The Advent on Channel Twelve" – in *Star SF Stories #4*, ed. Frederik Pohl; Ballantine 272K, 1958
"Nightmare With Zeppelins" – December 1958 *Galaxy* (w/ Frederick Pohl)
"A Gentle Dying" – June 1961 *Galaxy* (w/ Frederik Pohl)
"The Quaker Cannon" – August 1961 *Astounding* (w/ Frederik Pohl)
"The World of Myrion Flowers" – October 1961 *F&SF* (w/ Frederik Pohl)

"Critical Mass" – February 1962 *Galaxy* (w/ Frederik Pohl)

Collections and Novels

Gunner Cade – w/ Judith Merril, as by Cyril Judd; Simon & Schuster 1952; Ace D-277, 1957

Naked Storm – as by Simon Eisner; Lion 109, 1952 (mystery)

Outpost Mars – w/ Judith Merril, as by Cyril Judd; Abelard, 1952; Dell 760, 1954

Half – as by Jordan Park; Lion 135, 1953 (mystery)

Takeoff – Doubleday, 1952; Pennant P15, 1953

Valerie – as by Jordan Park; Lion 176, 1953 (mystery)

Space Merchants - w/ Frederik Pohl; Ballantine 21 (simul. h'back and p'back), 1952

The Syndic – Doubleday, 1953; Bantam 1317, 1955

The Explorers – Ballantine 86, 1954 (coll.)

Search the Sky - w/ Frederik Pohl; Ballantine 61 (simul. h'back and p'back), 1954

Gladiator-at-Law – w/ Frederik Pohl; Ballantine 107 (simul. h'back and p'back), 1955

Mindworm and Other Stories – M. Joseph, 1955 (UK coll.)

A Town is Drowning – w/ Frederik Pohl; Ballantine 123 (simul. h'back and p'back), 1955

Not This August – Doubleday 1955; Bantam A1492, 1956

Presidential Year - w/ Frederik Pohl; Ballantine 144 (simul. h'back and p'back), 1955

Sorority House – w/ Frederik Pohl, as by Jordan Park; Lion Library 97, 1956 (lesbiana)

A Man of Cold Rages – as by Jordan Park; Pyramid G368, 1958 (mystery)

A Mile Beyond the Moon - Doubleday, 1958; McFadden 40-100, 1962 (coll.)

The Marching Morons - Ballantine 303K, 1959 (coll.)

Wolfbane - w/ Frederik Pohl; Ballantine 335K, 1959

The Wonder Effect - w/ Frederik Pohl; Ballantine F638, 1962 (coll.)

Best Science Fiction Stories – Faber, 1968 (UK coll.)

Thirteen O'Clock – ed. James Blish, Dell 8731, 1970 (coll.)

The Best of C. M. Kornbluth – SF Book Club, 1976; Ballantine 25461, 1976 (coll.)

In addition to the above, Pohl mentions two unpublished Kornbluth novels in his introduction to The Best of C. M. Kornbluth, *but cites only one title:* The Crater. *Again, if anyone out there knows what the other title is, I invite you to share with the class.*

Notes

1. By Kornbluth and Judith Merril writing as Cyril Judd, originally serialized in three parts beginning with the March 1952 *Astounding*, and published later the same year in book form by Simon & Schuster
2. Rumor has it that said agent was Wollheim himself; I have not been able to confirm this, and if it's true, there seems to be no evidence that DAW acted as agent—legit or otherwise—for anyone else except himself. I will point out, though, that the only reprint of "The Mask of Demeter" in an anthology was in Wollheim's *Prize Science Fiction*, published by McBride in 1953.

❑

A Kuttner Above the Rest (But Wait, There's Moore!)

I SET OUT THIS TIME AROUND TO COMPLAIN about how doing this was both a pleasure and a pain for me; the former because I enjoy doing it and the latter because I shouldn't have to. I was pretty clever about it, too. However, it all seemed a bit too familiar, so I went back to last issue's installment and realized that I'd already said all that in the first few paragraphs.

Oh, bother. Much as I might have wanted to reiterate my earlier thoughts (not to mention that cleverness again), I figure if I do that you'll all do what people at conventions do when I get to yakking about The Good Old Days: smile desperately, make encouraging noises, look at your watches and start edging out of the room.

So I'll simply point you back to the first page or so of "Cyril with an M" from last ish and we'll take it as written (again), shall we? Thank you.

This time around, I want to talk about a pair of writers, collaborators on the most basic level. So basic, in fact, that it's impossible to see where one ends and the other picks up, two writers who honestly and inarguably write as One. They had a profound impact on the field Back in the Day, not only on their readers but on other writers as well. They didn't always sign both their names to a particular story or novel, but nevertheless they insisted until the last that it was the way they'd always worked.

Over the years, there have only been a bare handful of husband-and-wife writing partners: Leigh Brackett and Edmond Hamilton for example, and I suspect that Knight and Wilhelm, or perhaps the original del Reys, at least tossed around story ideas and bounced ideas off each other. Closer to home (literally), although Mary and I aren't married, she is my harshest critic and vets every single thing I write, and I am a far better writer for it.

In the case of our subjects, though, it was well and truly collaboration, not just critiquing sessions around the dinner table.

Henry Kuttner (1914-58) started out as one of H. P. Lovecraft's fans and correspondents, selling first a poem ("Ballad of the Gods") to *Weird Tales* at the age of 22, and following it up the next month with his first story, "The Graveyard Rats." He didn't stay there long, though, finding eeriness and unnamable horrors less to his liking than drunken inventors, mutant hillbillies and other, less arcane and eldritch personalities.

Catherine L. Moore (1911-1987) was three years older than her Other Half, and beat him into print accordingly, with her signature tale of SF horror, "Shambleau," appearing in the November 1933 *Weird Tales*. This justly famous and still well-regarded yarn of interplanetary adventure features her most enduring character, Northwest Smith, and was the first in a series eventually published as *Shambleau and Others* (Gnome Press 1953) and *Northwest of Earth* (Gnome Press 1954); in her afterword to her final collection, *The Best of C. L. Moore* (ed. Lester del Rey, Del Rey 1975), she dispelled a myth about its initial appearance:

> This story was *not* rejected by every magazine in the field before it crept humbly to the doorstep of *Weird Tales*. My own perfectly clear memory tells me that I sent it first to *WT* because that was the only magazine of the type I knew well, and that an answering acceptance and a check for the (then) fabulous amount of $100 arrived almost by return mail.

The story was an immediate sensation, and not just with the readership. In a letter to Editor Farnsworth Wright, some guy named Lovecraft said:

> "Shambleau" is great stuff. It begins *magnificently*, on just the right note of terror, and with black intimations of the unknown. The subtle evil of the Entity, as suggested by the

> unexplained horror of the people is extremely powerful—and the description of the Thing itself when unmasked is no letdown.

And who should know better about black intimations and subtle evil than the Gentleman from Providence, am I right? His one complaint was "the conventional interplanetary setting;" frankly, given his somewhat Puritanical perspective, I'd have thought he would have objected to the title character's overt sexuality, but perhaps he'd become inured by all those Margaret Brundage covers.[1]

Both Gnome collections also included stories featuring Jirel of Joiry, one of the few successful female sword'n'sorcery characters in the field aside from Howard's Red Sonja. Interestingly enough, Moore saw a clear similarity between the Shambleau and Jirel, remarking on:

> ...[T]he close relationship the two women bear to one another. They set the keynote for a lot of my own (incessant) writing until I met and married Henry Kuttner. I realize now [in 1975] that, unconsciously, no doubt, both were versions of the self I'd like to have been.

Hey, nice work if you can get it, right? Even today, some 75 years later, those two debut tales are effective, readable, and memorable. How many other pulp yarns can you say that about? I'm amazed that the Moore story has never been filmed, especially in these days of readily-available CGI software. It would have been a natural for, say, the recent "Masters of Science Fiction" series, and would have been equally at home in either incarnation of *The Twilight Zone.*

The two writers met in 1938 and married in 1940; the only guests at their civil wedding were Kuttner's mother and artist Virgil Finlay and his wife. According to Sam Moskowitz in his essay on Kuttner in *Seekers of Tomorrow* (World 1967):

> Virgil paid the Justice of the Peace $10, bought the bride a dubonnet and soda, and the career of the most famous writing team in science-fiction was launched.

From then on, the pair collaborated on practically everything they published, even if only to say, "Nah, it's not your best work. Let's try it *this* way."

The same year they were married, something in the way of a Major Conflict was taking place in many places around the globe, and this led to a reader's catastrophe: a lot of John W. Campbell's regular writers headed into the fray. Kuttner and Moore, under their own names as well as a bunch of pseudonyms, tried their best to fill the gap, selling almost five dozen stories to *Astounding* during that period, some under their own names, but most under the pseudonym of Lewis Padgett.

Padgett was responsible for what is probably their best-known character series, the five "Galloway Gallagher" stories, later collected as *Robots Have No Tails* (Gnome Press 1952). The stories concern an eccentric inventor, a *vino savant* if you will, who is unable to work unless he's blind drunk; this frees up his subconscious, and the crazed Goldbergian devices begin piling up while he sings duets with himself. The stories are almost perfect Campbellian SF, lacking only stupid aliens to fill out the requirements. They date a little today, and some will find the humor rather heavy-handed, but they're still fun and worth reading. (I should note here that later in her life, Moore blamed these yarns solely on Kuttner; make of that what you will, I certainly have no trouble believing it.)

The same penname was used for another successful series for Campbell's *Astounding*, the five Baldy stories, collected as *Mutant* (Gnome Press 1953)[2]. In these stories, our Interwoven Pair explored the idea of sympathetic mutants undergoing persecution by normals, much as van Vogt did in his Jommy Cross novel, *Slan* (Arkham House 1951); the Kuttner/Moore stories are quite a bit more contemplative, however, far from the usual run of such things in both the literature and films.

Not content with taking mutants seriously, they threw caution to the winds and wrote the popular Hogben stories for *Thrilling Wonder*. Many writers have worked with the concept of mutated humans and their struggles to be accepted by normal humans (or their struggles to totally and utterly subjugate said normal humans), but only these two could—or would—cast them as hillbillies. And make it work.

There were other series as well, both by Kuttner alone and in collaboration with others, most notably Arthur K. Barnes; not all of these were SF/fantasy, as befit writers who were trying hard to make a living by writing whatever there was a market for. On in particular fascinates me, considering the time in which it was written: the Hollywood on the Moon stories, eight of them, written for *Thrilling Wonder* between 1939 and '41. To my knowledge, these stories have never been reprinted together under cover; perhaps that will change before mid-Century.

I could go on about the stories (and I will, given any opportunity, don't you doubt it for a minute) but my time here is better spent talking about the authors. The bibliography at the end will give you the chance to decide for yourself about the individual yarns they spun (assuming you take the time and effort to track them down, as precious little remains in print), and I hope you'll take advantage of it.

There have been, as I said, any number of collaborators in the field down through the years; Ray Bradbury's first story, for example, was a collab with fellow faan Henry Hasse, and Baen Books has created a collaborative cottage industry by teaming their established writers with younger ones. Any number of writers have cooperated to produce successful novels, both stand-alone and series (with, in many cases, a varying degree of activity from the more senior colleague), but not every literary partnership is Niven and Pournelle, not by a long chalk.

In the case of Kuttner and Moore, though, we have something unique, something splendid, something that transcends the mere trading back-and-forth of pages. Like a Transformer, K&M became greater than the sum of their particular parts when they joined forces, complete with chest-cannons and arm-lasers. No less a critic than Damon Knight commented that when they began writing together:

> ...two seemingly discordant talents merged. Kuttner's previous stories had been superficial and clever, well constructed but without much content or conviction; Moore had written moody fantasies, meaningful but a little thin....working together, they began to turn out stories in which the practical solidity of Kuttner's plots seemed to provide a vessel for Moore's poetic imagination.

Nor is he alone in this assessment. Fellow author and critic Barry Malzberg says:

> Their styles meshed totally...they were the greatest collaborative writers in the history of collaboration. Like Gilbert & Sullivan, Frazier & Ali, the 1978 Red Sox and Yankees they brought out the best in one another.

Taken individually, Kuttner was by far the more versatile of the pair. Nothing odd about that, of course, as most of the hard-core pulpsters wrote

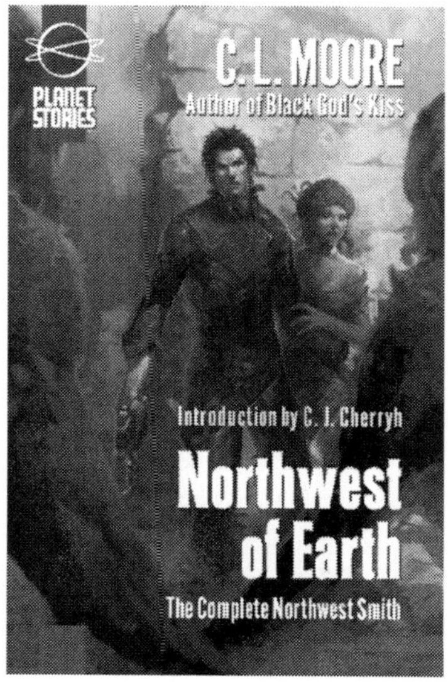

whatever they could get paid to: it's hard to imagine Murray Leinster writing westerns, but he did, just as Judith Merril wrote sports yarns. Neither of these remarkable writers placed work under as long a list of pseudonyms as Kuttner, though, which led to such faanish nonsense as the belief—still encountered today in the writings of past SF "historians" less inclined to, y'know, actually do research—that Jack Vance (Jack Vance!) was a Kuttner penname.

There was more to Kuttner than mere prolificacy, however. Along with Kornbluth, Bester, and a bare handful of others at that time in stfnal history, Henry Kuttner was capable of transcending the limitations of pulpery and creating something akin to art. There is a refinement to his prose, an elegance, that although missing in such toss-offs as the Gallagher stories, is present in practically all of his later work. Compare, if you will, "Graveyard Rats" to "Two-Handed Engine", and you'll see what I mean. The former is pure pulp fiction, a direct schmooze from Lovecraft (and intended to be nothing more than that, to be fair); the latter, a carefully constructed and beautifully written story by a master craftsman concerned with getting every word exactly right.

Moore, on the other hand, stayed mainly on the plain—by which I mean she stuck with what she did well; dark, moody adventure, rather the direct antithesis of Leigh Brackett's swashbuckling yarns. Moore's characters buckled few swashes, but held their own anyway, dragging themselves (or being dragged by more sober companions) grimly and broodingly away from Medusoid vampires and other CASmithian menaces.

This is not to say that she was any less a writer than her husband. Moore's solo work might not have had Kuttner's brilliance and immediate impact, but the panache with which she wove her stories leaves them sitting in the back of your mind, ready to ooze back into your forebrain yet again, immaculate and unforgettable.

Something happened, though, in the mid-50s: their output dropped to almost nothing. "Two-Handed Engine" appeared in the August 1955 *F&SF*, nine months later "Rite of Passage" ran in the same magazine, and Moore had a solo performance with "Song in a Minor Key" in *Fantastic Universe* for January of '57, but that was pretty much it.

This may not seem like much of a much, but bear in mind how productive they'd been in earlier years. Understand also that Henry Kuttner was a major influence on many other writers, not the least of whom was (wait for it)—Ray Bradbury. In fact, Malzberg makes the case (and makes it well) that Bradbury, who was a member of the LA chapter of the Science Fiction League (which later mutated into the LA SF Society, or LASFS, still going strong today) with Kuttner, aimed high and actually failed into his remarkable career:

> What he wanted desperately in the early 1940's was to sell to Campbell, become an ASF and UNKNOWN mainstay, etc. He didn't make it.... If Bradbury had *succeeded* in his [goal], if he had had what he wanted... he would have been Henry Kuttner.

I've addressed this before, in another time and place, and as then I will point to Bradbury's introduction to *The Best of Henry Kuttner* (Ballantine 1975), as evidence that Malzberg is correct in his assertion, presumptuous as it may seem to some at this point in time when Bradbury has been canonized by practically everybody and Kuttner forgotten by all. Bradbury himself says in that intro:

> It would be hard to guess the impact of these two stories ["The Twonky" and "Mimsy Were the Borogoves"] on other writers in the genre. But in all probability hundreds of imitations were written by struggling as well as by published authors. I count myself among them.

So what happened? Well, as has been the case with any number of other pulpsters who were unwilling to limit themselves to cheap paper and garish covers, Kuttner wanted more than the recognition of SF fandom, no matter how vociferous and adoring it might have been. When he couldn't get it, he simply dropped writing as a career and went back to school to obtain an advanced degree, which should surprise nobody familiar with his stories. Again, Malzberg:

> Kuttner's career was, I think, over... he was in the process of getting an MA in psychology at USC, he wanted to become (unsurprisingly) a shrink. His production had...shrunk to

> virtually nil, he had contracts with Harper's for mysteries but got someone else to write them… He had done his work.

And what of C. L. Moore? Why did she stop? Here, Malzberg admits to speculation, albeit based on his own knowledge and experience:

> She was also in school and her production was nil but I always suspected that this was more in deference to Henry and joint plans than to the issue of being burnt out. As we know, her second husband loathed SF and its denizens and wanted her to have nothing to do with it or writing.

(This last fact also prevented Moore from being honored by SFWA as their Grand Master before she died; how anyone could have objected to this is, frankly, beyond me. An honor is an honor, and even if one believes the source of said honor to be beneath them, simple civility and politeness would seem to demand that it be acknowledged. She did, however, serve as Guest of Honor at the 1981 WorldCon in Denver, so she hadn't been completely muted. But I digress.)

Henry Kuttner died in his sleep on the 3rd of February, 1958, most likely of a stroke. He never achieved his goal of becoming a clinical psychologist, and if he was disappointed in his body of work, few others were. He left behind an indelible mark, and even if he has been mostly forgotten now by readers[3], he continues to influence writers who aspire to his elegance and grace of style. Moskowitz said:

> Who was the real Henry Kuttner? We will never know. The man had discipline, technical brilliance, immense versatility, and ingenuity, and these betrayed him. Lured by opportunism, suffering from an acute sense of inadequacy, he refused to stand alone, but leaned on others for support: H. P. Lovecraft, Robert E. Howard, Stanley G. Weinbaum… and, of course, C. L. Moore.

Catherine Lucille Moore survived her first husband by almost three decades, although she wrote nothing besides the afterword to *The Best of C. L. Moore* (Ballantine 1975) in that time. She, too, left her signature on the stfnal broadside, and her stories and novels read as well today as they did when the ink was still damp.

Together and separately, they climbed from the slimes and ooze of *Weird Tales* to the heights of fantastic literature. There has never been their equal, and no one will come to make them obsolete.

I would like to thank William Contento for supplying me with his invaluable database, the *Science Fiction, Fantasy, & Weird Fiction Magazine Index: 1890-2007*, compiled by him and Stephen T. Miller. This remarkable index belongs in the reference library of anyone seriously interested in the history of fantastic literature.

(As is always the case with these bibliographies, especially when the author(s) are as prolific as Kuttner and Moore, I have been as complete as I can humanly be and still keep all my hair and fingernails. Also as always, I welcome any and all additions and corrections; just e-mail me care of this magazine. Please note that I have placed Kuttner ahead of Moore; nothing in the way of "value judgment" should be read into this, it's just the way the names fall alphabetically.)

Henry Kuttner Bibliography
Pseudonyms

Edward J. Bellin (house)
Paul Edmonds
Noel Gardner
Will Garth (house)
James Hall (house)
Keith Hammond
Hudson Hastings
Peter Horn (house)
Kelvin Kent
Robert O. Kenyon (house)
C. H. Liddell
K. H. Maepenn
Scott Morgan (house)
Lawrence O'Donnell
Lewis Padgett
C. K. M. Scanlon (house)
Woodrow Wilson Smith
Charles Stoddard

Novels

The Day He Died – Bantam 306, 1948, with C. L. Moore as by Lewis Padgett

Fury – Grossett & Dunlap, 1950, with C. L. Moore; reissued as *Destination: Infinity* in 1956 by Avon

The Well of the Worlds – Galaxy Novel #17, 1953 as by Lewis Padgett; Ace F-344, 1965 as by Kuttner

Beyond Earth's Gates – with C. L. Moore as by Lewis Padgett and Moore, Ace Double D-69, 1954, bound with Andre Norton's *Daybreak – 2250 A.D.*)

Valley of the Flame (Ace F-297, 1964)

Earth's Last CitaDel (Ace F-306, 1964, with C. L. Moore)

The Dark World (Ace F-327, 1965)

The Time Axis (Ace F-356, 1965)

The Creature from Beyond Infinity (Popular Library 60-2355, 1968)

The Mask of Circe (Ace 52075, 1971) with C. L. Moore

Collections

A Gnome There Was – Simon & Schuster 1950, as by Lewis Padgett

Tomorrow and Tomorrow and the Fairy Chessmen – Gnome Press 1951, with C. L. Moore

Robots Have No Tails – Gnome Press 1952, as by Lewis Padgett

Ahead of Time – Ballantine 1953, h'cover and paperback simultaneous

Mutant – Gnome Press 1953

Line to Tomorrow and Other Stories of Fantasy and Science Fiction – Bantam 1251, 1954, with C. L. Moore

No Boundaries – Ballantine 1955, h'cover and paperback simultaneous, with C. L. Moore

Bypass to Otherness – Ballantine 497K, 1961

Return to Otherness – Ballantine F619, 1962

The Best of Kuttner 1 – Mayflower 0547, 1965, UK

The Best of Kuttner 2 – Mayflower 0547, 1966, UK

The Best of Henry Kuttner – Nelson Doubleday 1975, through the SF Book Club; retitled *The Last Mimzy* and reissued by Del Rey in 2007

Clash by Night and Other Stories – Hamlyn 1980, with C. L. Moore, UK

Chessboard Planet and Other Stories – Hamlyn 1983, with C. L. Moore, UK

The Proud Robot – Hamlyn 1983, UK

Prince Raynor – Gryphon 1987, includes "Cursed Be the City" and "The CitaDel of Darkness"
Kuttner Times Three – Virgil Utter 1988, contains "The Old Army Game", "Bamboo Death", and "The Wolf of Aragon"
Secret of the Earth Star and Others – Borgo/Starmont 1991
Book of Iod – Chaosium 1995
Elak of Atlantis – Gryphon 1985
Detour to Otherness – Haffner Press 2002, with C. L. Moore
Thunder Jim Wade: The Complete Series – Altus Press, 2008

Omnibus

The Startling Worlds of Henry Kuttner – Popular Library/Questar 0445203285, 1986, with C. L. Moore. Includes "The Portal in the Picture", Valley of the Flame", and "The Dark World."
The Jungle – Tor Double 1991, with C. L. Moore, bound with David Drake's *Clash By Night*

Non-SF

The Brass Ring – Duell, Sloane and Pearce 1946, with C. L. Moore
The Day He Died – Duell, Sloane and Pearce 1947, with C. L. Moore
Man Drowning – Harper and Bros. 1952
The Murder of Ann Avery – Perma Books M-3058, 1956
The Murder of Eleanor Pope – Perma Books M-3046, 1956
Murder of a Mistress – Perma Books M-4082, 1957
Murder of a Wife – Perma Books M-4096, 1958

Short Fiction

"The Graveyard Rats" – March 1936 *Weird Tales*
"Bamboo Death" – June 1936 *Thrilling Mystery*
"The Secret of Kralitz" – October 1936 *Weird Tales*
"Coffins for Six" – December 1936 *Thrilling Mystery*, as by C. K. M. Scanlon
"It Walks by Night" – December 1936 *Weird Tales*
"The Faceless Fiend" – January 1937 *Thrilling Mystery*, as by K. H. Maepenn
"The Eater of Souls" – January 1937 *Weird Tales*
"I, the Vampire" – February 1937 *Weird Tales*
"We Are the Dead" – April 1937 *Weird Tales*
"The Salem Horror" – May 1937 *Weird Tales*

"The Black Kiss" – June 1937 *Weird Tales*, with Robert Bloch
"Raider of the Spaceways" – July 1937 *Weird Tales*
"The Jest of Droom-Avista" – August 1937 *Weird Tales*
"Terror on the Stage" – September 1937 *Thrilling Mystery*, as by K. H. Maepenn
"When the Earth Lived" – October 1937 *Thrilling Wonder Stories*
"Quest of the Starstone" – November 1937 *Weird Tales*, with C. L. Moore
"The Case of Herbert Thorp" – November 1937 *Weird Tales*
"The Bloodless Peril" – December 1937 *Thrilling Wonder Stories*, as by Will Garth
"Hands Across the Void" – December 1938 *Thrilling Wonder Stories*, as by Will Garth
"World's End" – February 1938 *Weird Tales*
"The Shadow on the Screen" – March 1938 *Weird Tales*
"Hollywood on the Moon" – April 1938 *Thrilling Wonder Stories*
"Thunder in the Dawn" – May 1938 *Weird Tales*
"Spawn of Dagon" – July 1938 *Weird Tales*
"The Disinherited" – August 1938 *Astounding SF*
"Doom World" – August 1938 *Thrilling Wonder Stories*
"Avengers of Space" – August 1938 Marvel *Science Stories*
"Dictator of the Americas" – August 1938 *Marvel Science Stories*, as by James Hall
"The Dark Heritage" – August 1938 *Marvel Science Stories*, as by Robert O. Kenyon
"Beyond the Phoenix" – October 1938 *Weird Tales*
"The Time Trap" – November 1938 *Marvel Science Stories*
"The Star Parade" – December 1938 *Thrilling Wonder Stories*
"Roman Holiday" – August 1939 *Thrilling Wonder Stories*, with Arthur K. Barnes as by Kelvin Kent
"The Invaders" – February 1939 *Strange Stories*, as by Keith Hammond
"The Frog" – February 1939 *Strange Stories*
"The Transgressor" – February 1939 *Weird Tales*
"The Bells of Horror" – April 1939 *Strange Stories*, as by Keith Hammond
"Hydra" – April 1939 *Weird Tales*
"Beyond Annihilation" – April 1939 *Thrilling Wonder Stories*
"Cursed Be the City" – April 1939 *Strange Stories*
"The Watcher at the Door" – May 1939 *Weird Tales*

"The Hunt" – June 1939 *Strange Stories*
"The Body and the Brain" – June 1939 *Strange Stories*, with Robert Bloch as by Keith Hammond
"'Telepathy Is News'" – June 1939 *Science Fiction*, as by Paul Edmonds
"The Misguided Halo" – August 1939 *Unknown*
"The CitaDel of Darkness" – August 1939 *Strange Stories*
"The Curse of the Crocodile" – August 1939 *Strange Stories*, with Bertram W. Williams
"The Energy Eaters" – October 1939 *Weird Tales*, with Arthur K. Barnes
"Towers of Death" – November 1939 *Weird Tales*
"The Grip of Death" – December 1939 *Strange Stories*, with Robert Bloch
"World's Pharaoh" – December 1939 *Thrilling Wonder Stories*, as by Kelvin Kent
"Suicide Squad" – December 1939 *Thrilling Wonder Stories*
"The Lifestone" – February 1940 *Astonishing*, as by Paul Edmonds
"When New York Vanished" – March 1940 *Super Science*
"All Is Illusion" – April 1940 *Unknown*
"Beauty and the Beast" – April 1940 *Thrilling Wonder Stories*
"Science Is Golden" – April 1940 *Thrilling Wonder Stories*, with Arthur K. Barnes as by Kelvin Kent
"The Seven Sleepers" – May 1940 *Thrilling Wonder Stories*, with Arthur K. Barnes
"50 Miles Down" – May 1940 *Fantastic Adventures*, as by Peter Horn
"The Shining Man" – May 1940 *Fantastic Adventures*, as by Noel Gardner
"Pegasus" – May-June 1940 *Famous Fantastic Mysteries*
"Dr. Cyclops" – June 1940 *Thrilling Wonder Stories*
"Room of Souls" – June 1940 *Strange Stories*, as by Keith Hammond
"Time to Kill" – June 1940 *Strange Stories*
"Improbability" – June 1940 *Astonishing*, as by Paul Edmonds
"The Mad Virus" – June 1940 *Science Fiction*, as by Paul Edmonds
"No Man's World" – August 1940 *Thrilling Wonder Stories*
"World Without Air" – August 1940 *Fantastic Adventures*
"The Comedy of Eras" – September 1940 *Thrilling Wonder Stories*
"The Elixir of Invisibility" – October 1940 *Fantastic Adventures*
"Man About Time" – October 1940 *Thrilling Wonder Stories*, as by Kelvin Kent

"The Uncanny Power of Edwin Cobalt" – October 1940 *Fantastic Adventures*, as by Noel Gardner
"Evil Galatea" – October 1940 *Super-Detective*, as by Paul Edmonds
"Reverse Atom" – November 1940 *Thrilling Wonder Stories*
"Threshold" – December 1940 *Unknown*
"The Devil We Know" – August 1941 *Unknown*
"Dragon Moon" – Jan. 1941 *Weird Tales*
"Remember Tomorrow" – January 1941 *Thrilling Wonder Stories*
"Hercules Muscles In" – February 1941 *Thrilling Wonder Stories*, as by Kelvin Kent
"The Land of Time to Come" – April 1941 *Thrilling Wonder Stories*
"The Touching-Point" – April 1941 *Stirring Science Stories*, as by Edward J. Bellin
"Tube to Nowhere" – June 1941 *Thrilling Wonder Stories*
"The Wolf of Aragon" – July 1941 *Thrilling Adventures*
"The Tree of Life" – September 1941 *Astonishing*, as by Paul Edmonds
"A Gnome There Was" – October 1941 *Unknown*, with C. L. Moore
"Chameleon Man" – November 1941 *Weird Tales*
"Red Gem of Mercury" – November 1941 *Super Science Stories*
"The Old Army Game" – November 1941 *Thrilling Adventures*
"Design for Dreaming" – February 1942 *Unknown*
"Silent Eden" – March 1942 *Startling Stories*
"Later Than You Think" – March 1942 *Fantastic Adventures*
"The Infinite Moment" – April 1942 *Thrilling Wonder Stories*
"Masquerade" – May 1942 *Weird Tales*
"Dames Is Poison" – June 1942 *Thrilling Wonder Stories*, as by Kelvin Kent
"False Dawn" – June 1942 *Thrilling Wonder Stories*
"The Crystal Circe" – June 1942 *Astonishing*
"Deadlock" – August 1942 *Astounding SF*, with C. L. Moore as by Lewis Padgett
"War-Gods of the Void" – Fall 1942 *Planet Stories*
"Secret of the Earth Star" – August 1942 *Amazing Stories*
"The Twonky" – September 1942 *Astounding SF*, with C. L. Moore as by Lewis Padgett
"Compliments of the Author" – October 1942 *Unknown*, with C. L. Moore
"Thunder in the Void" – October 1942 *Astonishing*

"We Guard the Black Planet!" – November 1942 *Super Science*
"Piggy Bank" – December 1942 *Astounding SF*, with C. L. Moore as by Lewis Padgett
"Too Many Cooks" – December 1942 *Thrilling Wonder Stories*
"Night of Gods" – December 1942 *Astonishing*, as by Paul Edmonds
"Nothing But Gingerbread Left" – Jan. 1943 *Astounding SF*
"Time Locker" – Jan. 1943 *Astounding SF*
"Wet Magic" – February 1943 *Unknown*
"Mimzy Were the Borogoves" – February 1943 *Astounding SF*, with C. L. Moore as by Lewis Padgett
"Soldiers of Space" – February 1943 *Astonishing*
"Probability Zero: Blue Ice" – February 1943 *Astounding SF*
"Shock" – March 1943 *Astounding SF*, with C. L. Moore as by Lewis Padgett
"Clash by Night" – March 1943 *Astounding SF*, with C. L. Moore as by Lawrence O'Donnell
"Under Your Spell" – March 1943 *Weird Tales*
"Open Secret" – April 1943 *Astounding SF*, with C. L. Moore as by Lewis Padgett
"No Greater Love" – April 1943 *Unknown*
"Probability Zero: Corpus Delicti" – April 1943 *Astounding SF*
"Volluswen" – April 1943 *Science Fiction*
"Better Than One" – Spring 1943 *Captain Future*
"Earth's Last CitaDel" – serial, April 1943 *Argosy*
"Ghost" – May 1943 *Astounding SF*
"Reader, I Hate You!" – May 1943 *Super Science*
"The World Is Mine" – June 1943 *Astounding SF* as by Lewis Padgett
"Problem in Ethics" – July 1943 *Science Fiction*
"Endowment Policy" – August 1943 *Astounding SF*, with C. L. Moore as by Lewis Padgett
"The Proud Robot" – October 1943 *Astounding SF* as by Lewis Padgett
"Crypt-City of the Deathless One" – Winter 1943 *Planet Stories*
"Gallegher Plus" – November 1943 *Astounding SF* as by Lewis Padgett
"The Iron Standard" – December 1943 *Astounding SF*, with C. L. Moore as by Lewis Padgett
"Music Hath Charms" – Winter 1943 *Startling Stories*
"To Dust Returneth" – Winter 1944 *Captain Future*
"Trophy" – Winter 1944 *Thrilling Wonder Stories*, as by Scott Morgan

"A God Named Kroo" – Winter 1944 *Thrilling Wonder Stories*

"The Children's Hour" – March 1944 *Astounding SF*) with C. L. Moore as by Lawrence O'Donnell

"The Black Sun Rises" – June 1944 *Super Science* (Canadian)

"The Eyes of Thar" – Fall 1944 *Planet Stories*

"Swing Your Lady" – Winter 1944 *Thrilling Wonder Stories*, as by Kelvin Kent

"Housing Problem" – October 1944 Charm

"When the Bough Breaks" – November 1944 *Astounding SF*, with C. L. Moore as by Lewis Padgett

"The Piper's Son" – February 1945 *Astounding SF*, with C. L. Moore as by Lewis Padgett

"Three Blind Mice" – June 1945 *Astounding SF*, with C. L. Moore as by Lewis Padgett

"The Lion and the Unicorn" – July 1945 *Astounding SF*, with C. L. Moore as by Lewis Padgett

"Beggars in Velvet" – December 1945 *Astounding SF*, with C. L. Moore as by Lewis Padgett

"Before I Wake…" – March 1945 *Famous Fantastic Mysteries*

"Baby Face" – Spring 1945 *Thrilling Wonder Stories*

"Percy the Pirate" – Summer 1945 *Thrilling Wonder Stories*

"Camouflage" – Sept. 1945 *Astounding SF*, with C. L. Moore as by Lewis Padgett

"What You Need" – October 1945 *Astounding SF*, with C. L. Moore as by Lewis Padgett

"Line to Tomorrow" – November 1945 *Astounding SF*, with C. L. Moore as by Lewis Padgett

"Sword of Tomorrow" – Fall 1945 *Thrilling Wonder Stories*

"The Fairy Chessmen" – January 1946 *Astounding SF*, with C. L. Moore as by Lewis Padgett

"This Is the House" – February 1946 *Astounding SF* as by Lawrence O'Donnell

"What Hath Me?" – Spring 1946 *Planet Stories*

"We Kill People" – March 1946 *Astounding SF*, with C. L. Moore as by Lewis Padgett

"The Dark Angel" – March 1946 *Startling Stories*

"Valley of the Flame" – March 1946 *Startling Stories* as by Keith Hammond

"The Cure" – May 1946 *Astounding SF*, with C. L. Moore as by Lewis Padgett
"The Dark World" – Summer 1946 Startling Stories
"Rain Check" – July 1946 *Astounding SF*, with C. L. Moore as by Lewis Padgett
"Absalom" – Fall 1946 *Startling Stories*
"The Little Things" – Fall 1946 *Thrilling Wonder Stories*
"Call Him Demon" – Fall 1946 *Thrilling Wonder Stories*, as by Keith Hammond
"Vintage Season" – September 1946 *Astounding SF*, with C. L. Moore as by Lawrence O'Donnell
"Time Enough" – December 1946 *Astounding SF*, with C. L. Moore as by Lewis Padgett
"I Am Eden" – December 1946 *Thrilling Wonder Stories*
"Tomorrow and Tomorrow" – serial, January-February 1947 *Astounding SF*, with C. L. Moore as by Lewis Padgett
"Juke-Box" – February 1947 *Thrilling Wonder Stories*, as by Woodrow Wilson Smith
"Trouble on Titan" – February 1947 *Thrilling Wonder Stories*
"Project" – April 1947 *Astounding SF*, with C. L. Moore as by Lewis Padgett
"Way of the Gods" – April 1947 *Thrilling Wonder Stories*
"Fury" – serial, May-July 1947 *Astounding SF*, with C. L. Moore as by Lawrence O'Donnell
"Jesting Pilot" – May 1947 *Astounding SF*, with C. L. Moore as by Lewis Padgett
"Lands of the Earthquake" – May 1947 *Startling Stories*
"The Big Night" – June 1947 *Thrilling Wonder Stories*, with C.L. Moore as by Hudson Hastings
"Dream's End" – July 1947 *Startling Stories*
"Atomic!" – August 1947 *Thrilling Wonder Stories*
"Dark Dawn" – August 1947 *Thrilling Wonder Stories*, as by Keith Hammond
"Noon" – August 1947 *Thrilling Wonder Stories*, with C. L. Moore as by Hudson Hastings
"Lord of the Storm" – September 1947 *Thrilling Wonder Stories*, as by Keith Hammond
"Exit the Professor" – October 1947 *Thrilling Wonder Stories*, with C. L. Moore

"Margin for Error" – November 1947 *Astounding SF*, with C. L. Moore as by Lewis Padgett
"The Power and the Glory" – December 1947 *Thrilling Wonder Stories*
"Don't Look Now" – March 1948 *Startling Stories*
"Pile of Trouble" – April 1948 *Thrilling Wonder Stories*
"The Mask of Circe" – May 1948 *Startling Stories*
"Ex Machina" – April 1948 *Astounding SF* as by Lewis Padgett
"Happy Ending" – August 1948 *Thrilling Wonder Stories*
"Private Eye" – January 1949 *Astounding SF*, with C. L. Moore as by Lewis Padgett
"The Time Axis" – January 1949 *Startling Stories*
"The Prisoner in the Skull" – February 1949 *Astounding SF*, with C. L. Moore as by Lewis Padgett
"See You Later" – June 1949 *Thrilling Wonder Stories*, with C. L. Moore
"Cold War" – October 1949 *Thrilling Wonder Stories*
"The Sky Is Falling" – Fall 1950 *Planet Stories*, with C. L. Moore as by C. H. Liddell
"Carry Me Home" – November 1950 *Planet Stories*, with C. L. Moore as by C. H. Liddell
"The Voice of the Lobster" – February 1950 *Thrilling Wonder Stories*
"As You Were" – August 1950 *Thrilling Wonder Stories*
"The Odyssey of Yiggar Throlg" – January 1951 *Startling Stories*, with C. L. Moore as by C. H. Liddell
"Android" – June 1951 *F&SF*, with C. L. Moore, also as Those Among Us as by C. H. Liddell
"We Shall Come Back" – November 1951 *SF Quarterly*, with C. L. Moore as by C. H. Liddell
"Golden Apple" – March 1951 *Famous Fantastic Mysteries*, with C. L. Moore as by C. H. Liddell
"Well of Worlds" – March 1952 *Startling Stories*, with C. L. Moore as by Lewis Padgett
"The Ego Machine" – May 1952 *Space SF*
"Humpty Dumpty" – September 1953 *Astounding SF*, with C. L. Moore as by Lewis Padgett
"By These Presents" – original, in *Ahead of Time*, Ballantine 1953
"Year Day" – original, in *Ahead of Time*, Ballantine 1953
"Satan Sends Flowers" – Jan/Feb 1953 *Fantastic*

"A Wild Surmise" - original with C. L. Moore, in *Star Science Fiction Stories #1*, ed. Frederik Pohl, Ballantine 1953

"The Visitors" - May 1953 *SF Quarterly*, with C. L. Moore as by C. H. Liddell

"Home Is the Hunter" - July 1953 *Galaxy*, with C. L. Moore

"Or Else" - August/Sept. 1953 *Amazing Stories*, with C. L. Moore

"Where the World Is Quiet" - May 1954 *Fantastic Universe*, as by C. H. Liddell

"Home There's No Returning" - original with C. L. Moore, in *No Boundaries*, Ballantine 1955

"Two-Handed Engine" - August 1955 *F&SF*, with C. L. Moore

"Rite of Passage" - May 1956 *F&SF*, with C. L. Moore

"Near Miss" - original, in *SF:58*, ed. Judith Merril, Gnome 1958

"A Cross of Centuries" - in *Star SF #4*, ed. Frederik Pohl, Ballantine 1958

"The Grab Bag" - Spring 1991 *Weird Tales*, with Robert Bloch

Poetry

"H.P.L." - September 1937 *Weird Tales*

"The Sunken Towers" - December 1936 *PHANTAGRAPH*

C. L. Moore Bibliography - See above for collaborative work with Kuttner

Pseudonyms

Hudson Hastings

Lawrence O'Donnell

Lewis Padgett

Novel

Doomsday Morning - Doubleday 1957

Collections

Judgment Night - Gnome Press 1952; Dell 1979; Red Jacket Press 2004

Shambleau and Others - Gnome Press 1953; Galaxy Novel #31, 1958; Consul 1961 - UK

Northwest of Earth - Gnome Press 1954

Jirel of Joiry – Paperback Library 1969; Ace 1996
The Best of C. L. Moore – Nelson Doubleday 1975, through the SF Book Club; Del Rey 1976; Ballantine 1980
Scarlet Dream – Grant 1981
Northwest Smith – Ace 1982; 1986
Black Scarlet Gods and Dreams – Gollancz 2002

Short Fiction

"Shambleau" – November 1933 *Weird Tales*
"Scarlet Dream" – May 1934 *Weird Tales*
"The Black God's Kiss" – October 1934 *Weird Tales*
"Black God's Shadow" – December 1934 *Weird Tales*
"Black Thirst" – April 1934 *Weird Tales*
"Dust of Gods" – August 1934 *Weird Tales*
"The Bright Illusion" – October 1934 *Astounding SF*
"Julhi" – March 1935 *Weird Tales*
"Nymph of Darkness" – April 1935 *Fantasy Magazine*, with Forrest J Ackerman
"Jirel Meets Magic" – July 1935 *Weird Tales*
"The Challenge from Beyond" – September 1935 *Fantasy Magazine*
"The Cold Gray God" – October 1935 *Weird Tales*
"Greater Glories" – September 1935 *Astounding SF*
"The Dark Land" – January 1936 *Weird Tales*
"Yvala" – February 1936 *Weird Tales*
"Lost Paradise" – July 1936 *Weird Tales*
"The Tree of Life" – October 1936 Weird Tales
"Tryst in Time" – December 1936 *Astounding SF*
"Werewoman" – *Leaves #2* 1938
"Hellsgarde" – April 1939 *Weird Tales*
"Miracle in Three Dimensions" – April 1939 *Strange Stories*
"Greater Than Gods" – July 1939 *Astounding SF*
"Song in a Minor Key" – February 1940 *Scienti-Snaps*
"Fruit of Knowledge" – October 1940 *Unknown*
"There Shall Be Darkness" – February 1942 *Astounding SF*
"Judgment Night" – August-September 1943 *Astounding SF*
"Doorway Into Time" – September 1943 *Famous Fantastic Mysteries*
"No Woman Born" – December 1944 *Astounding SF*
"The Code" – July 1945 *Astounding SF*, as by Lawrence O'Donnell
"Daemon" – October 1946 *Famous Fantastic Mysteries*

"Promised Land" – February 1950 *Astounding SF*, as by Lawrence O'Donnell
"Heir Apparent" – July 1950 *Astounding SF*, as by Lawrence O'Donnell
"Paradise Street" – September 1950 *Astounding SF*, as by Lawrence O'Donnell

Notes

1. Look her up at Wikipedia if you don't know the name. She was a revolutionary artist.
2. If you're not familiar with Gnome Press, there are plenty of online resources to educate you. Let me just say that Gnome, along with Fantasy Press, Arkham House and a few others, had an enormous effect on SF and fantasy, putting otherwise ephemeral magazine stories into permanent hardcover format long before the major houses even gave it a thought. Believe me, that's important.
3. Due, at least in part, to the reluctance of his agent to allow reprints for anything less than Hollywood money; if you think this is a joke, ask any of the dozen or more anthologists who have been frustrated by the agency's unwillingness to accept what everybody else's stories are going for and who demand thousands of dollars for a single short story.

❑

Let Me Be Frank
(or, Welcome to the Allamagoosa Russell-Palooza!)

> **Eric Frank Russell** (who heartily dislikes writing about himself) was born on January 6, 1905, at Sandhurst, Surrey, England… He says he is still dizzy from fighting his way through courses in chemistry, physics, building and steel construction, quantity surveying, mechanical draftsmanship, metallurgy and crystallography….He has a number of ambitions: (1) to become a social parasite; (2) to write a story with which he is still thoroughly satisfied one year later; (3) to entertain so many readers so well that some may have a momentary regret when they bury him; (4) to type with more than two fingers.

So Russell wrote of himself (like it or not) in the back cover copy of his 1954 Fantasy Press novel, *Deep Space*. "Age forty-seven, look like fifty-seven, feel like thirty-seven, act like twenty-seven, think like seven," he said a year earlier on the back of *Sentinels of Space* (Bourgey & Curl). "I think that is all anyone could possibly care about. Oh, yes—I fiddle around trying to write stories."

"Fiddle around," he says. Would that we all could "fiddle around" as well. Russell may have been ironically self-effacing up there, but the fact is he wrote a lot of terrific stories, including one that was so good that legend has it John W. Campbell had to create a magazine to fit around it. I'll get to that a little later, though.

Russell has already told us where and when he was born. I'll add that he was raised in Egypt, served honorably with the RAF in WWII, and worked as telephone operator, quantity surveyor and "draughtsman"; certainly the UK equivalent of cab-driving, encyclopedia salesman and fast-food man-

ager, all typical writers' jobs (it says here). He was a founding member of the British Interplanetary Society, which is where he first ran into people like Arthur C. Clarke. You know, the 2001 guy.

It was there in the Society that he found science fiction, and decided to "fiddle around" with it. In fact, his first attempt, a story titled "Eternal Re-Diffusion", was based on an idea given to him by one of the other founders, one Leslie J. Johnson. He sent it to what was then the pre-eminent SF magazine in the US (and thus, the world, this being the mid-'30s and all), Astounding Stories, as it was then known. The editor, F. Orlin Tremaine[1], bounced it as "too difficult" for his readers. Okay, that begs the question of what Campbell might have said, but he wasn't given a chance to decide, apparently. The story finally saw print in 1973 in a UK chapbook, *The Harbottle Fantasy Booklet #3*. Russell and Johnson did collaborate on a more successful yarn, "Seeker of To-Morrow" for the July, 1937 *Astounding*.

Russell's first sale was "The Saga of Pelican West", which appeared in the February issue of that year. His third story, "The Prr-r-eet", included a plot element given Russell by none other than the young (20 years old) Arthur C. Clarke. Russell shared the wealth, passing along to Clarke 10% of the amount Russell was paid, which amounted to about three dollars. This was Clarke's first stfnal income; Ghu alone knows what would have happened if it was only one dollar. Why, *Childhood's End* might have been written by Deutero Spartacus. Or Pel Torro.[2]

Before I get much further into this little laudatorium, I want to break with my usual practice and step off the dais to talk about my own personal feelings about Russell and his stories.

Long before I actually put pen to paper (yeah, I started out that way—didn't we all?) for the express purpose of telling stories I wouldn't get spanked for, I was reading pretty much everything I could find that called itself "science fiction." At the library, if it had a rocket or atom on the spine, it was *mine*, daddy-o, at least until it was due back. I honestly don't recall at this far remove where I first encountered Eric Frank Russell's work, but I can tell you when I first read it and said to myself, "I'm gonna do this some day!"

It was an Ace Double, D-313 in fact, which put Russell's *The Space Willies* back to back with a collection of six of his other stories, *Six Worlds Yonder*. I read the A-side first, oddly enough (I was far more accustomed to reading short stuff), and I don't think I put it down until Mom had called me the third time for dinner.[3] I was absolutely delighted by this yarn about a smart-ass human using his imagination to put one over on hide-bound aliens. So much so, in fact, that when I came to write my first salable story, I had Willies and Eustaces very much in mind. It sold, of course, to *Analog*, and I'd like to think that John Campbell would have liked it, even if he wouldn't have bought it.

When I got to the B-Side, I fell in love all over again with "Diabologic", and after reading "Into Your Tent I'll Creep", it was more than a week before I could look my dog in the eye. Is it any wonder I ended up writing for *Analog* a few decades after that? I think not, Bubba. It was an inevitability, because that one Double influenced my reading for a long, long time. It wasn't until *Dangerous Visions* came along that I began to look elsewhere.

I learned a lot from reading Russell, I did, even though it would be decades before I would put it to any real use. I learned about pacing, characterization, and that humor on the page requires exactly the same things that stand-up (well, in my case, class-clowning) does: timing, delivery, wit, and a memorable punch-line. I can point to others who influenced me as well[4]—Simak, Heinlein, Davidson, Knight—but it was Russell who put me on the path to writing for *Astounding*—pardon me, *Analog*.

But enough personal reminiscences. Let's get back to that legend I mentioned in the second paragraph, shall we? That magazine was *Unknown*, later *Unknown Worlds*, and the first issue (March 1939) contained Russell's justly famous "Sinister Barrier". Much has been said, both at the time and in subsequent years, of the claim that Street & Smith's decision to launch a new fantasy magazine as a companion to their very successful *Astounding Stories* was predicated on finding the perfect place to publish Russell's "Sinister Barrier". Stfnal legend tells us that Campbell, planning a fantasy magazine to go along with his harder SF monthly, had an "AHA!" moment and pegged *Unknown* to Russell's short novel.

Moskowitz, though, says this just isn't so[5]. Writing about Russell in his important collection of authorial essays, *Seekers of Tomorrow* (World

1967), he puts the whole thing up to coincidence, more or less:

> The origin of the magazine and the publication of the novel seemed too happy a wedding to be fortuitous. Nevertheless, it was.

Seems that Russell first submitted the story to Campbell in 1938 for *Astounding* under the title "Forbidden Acres". Campbell loved the first half but not the second, and sent it back to Russell for a rewrite. SaM continues:

> Russell… decided to rewrite the novel from end to end, utilizing as his technical model the Dan Fowler stories which ran in *G-Men*, a popular pulp magazine of the period. Campbell, on accepting the revision, openly admitted he was astonished that Russell, with his limited writing experience, had been able to do the difficult theme justice.

We'll get to that theme in a few, but first I want to add one vote in favor of legend, if I may. In the first volume of his two-volume autobiography, *In Memory Yet Green* (Doubleday 1979), Isaac Asimov writes of meeting Russell at a meeting of the Queens Science Fiction League in '39:

> *Unknown* was a magazine the like of which had never appeared before…
>
> Campbell had conceived of it precisely as a vehicle for *Sinister Barriers* [sic]…

Well, I'm sure the Good Doctor meant well[6], but the fact is that I can find no real confirmation that the above is the case, and a look at the foreword to the 1948 Fantasy Press edition of the full novel puts, I firmly believe, the final kibosh on the legend (much as I'd have loved it to be true). In dedicating the book in part to Campbell, Russell says "… for kicking me around until this story bore more resemblance to a story." Add to this the fact that, although there is a letter to Russell in *The John W. Campbell Letters Volume 1* (edited and compiled by Perry A. Chapdelaine, Sr., Tony Chapdelaine, and George Hay, AC Projects 1985), it dates from 1952; there is no mention of the story or its having been a factor in the creation and publication of *Unknown*, just a long argument with Russell about Charles Fort. And finally, Alan Dean Foster, in his glowing and laudatory introduction to *The Best of Eric Frank Russell* (Ballantine/Del Rey 1978), never once mentions it even as a legend. QED, I think we can put this one to bed.

Which leads us, William Nilliam, to the basic premise of this justly famous novel: we are property. Cows, if you will. Don't worry, I'll explain.

Charles Fort was a popular force in the late 19-teens through his death in 1932. He was heatedly debated, both in the field of science fiction and the Real World, and his "conclusions" were targets of both derision and reverence. This is not the place to delve too deeply into his "theories", but the Wikipedia entry under his name is both informative and, given the vagaries of both format and subject, reasonably accurate.

To put it concisely, Fort compiled odd-ball news stories, what newspaper folk refer to as "silly season" items: rains of fish and/or frogs, people disappearing without explanation, that sort of thing. I suspect he didn't really believe most of what he gleefully presented to an eager readership, but just enjoyed screwing with peoples' minds.

One thing he said, though, not only rang true with Russell, but Edmund Hamilton and several other authors in and out of the field (although Russell certainly got more mileage than most). As Russell said in the intro to the Fantasy Press edition:

> Charles Fort gave me what might well be the answer… Casually but devastatingly, he said, "*I think we're property.*" [Italics Russell's] And that is the plot of *Sinister Barrier*.

More specifically, we are the property of an unseen (unsee-able?) alien race that keeps us in an uproar, prevents a long-lasting peace, and in essence breeds us like cattle. For much the same reason we breed cattle, too.

I honestly don't know how much of Fort's blather Russell actually believed, either, but he was a long-time member of the Fortean Society, and I think it's reasonable to believe that he wasn't just in it for the plot ideas.

All that to give you a background for this very fine novel, and thanks for sticking around. *Sinister Barrier* begins, more or less, with those cows I mentioned a while ago in the form of a quote from one Peder Bjornson, a professor with funny eyes: "Swift death awaits the first cow that leads a revolt against milking", he says. Dunno about you, but it hooked me right away.

Seems that a lot of his fellow profs, all of whom have funny eyes[7], have been dropping like, well, pole-axed steers. An investigator, one Bill Graham (and didn't I get a kick out of *that* name in my Fillmore days), is sent to look into the deaths—he even witnesses one early on—and what he finds would have Charles Fort nodding his head up and down frantically and yelling, "See? See, I *told* you!" There is much ensuing paranoia involving iridescent blue globes flying about feeding off peoples' emotions, causing wars and strife so that their *à la carte* menu will have plenty of daily specials, desserts and those amber beverages we're all so fond of[8].

This is perhaps the best known of his novels, and deservedly so, but there's another book I constantly and consistently saw in the used bookshops[9] I used to haunt that's almost as well-known, if not more famous. That book, one of my own all-time favorites, is *Men, Martians and Machines.* A collection of stories about a man/robot named Jay Score (J20 in his robotic persona), this was not only my first introduction to aliens and humans working together (predating Star Trek by most of a decade), but also the first time to my knowledge that an African-American had been featured as ship's crewman (in this case the doctor). There was a reason for this in Russell's plot-line—apparently, no Negroes (as was then the respectful term) ever got space sick. Don't forget this was the early '40s, a time when the depiction of African-Americans in popular culture was still less than courteous, and an African-American as a serious character who did nothing in the way of either shucking or jiving was rare indeed, not to mention pretty cool. I don't necessarily think that Russell was trying to make a major point, or to showcase his (comparative) broad-mindedness; I just don't think he felt that a Negro had to be portrayed as a Steppin Fetchit caricature instead of a reasonable human being. If this be Libertarianism (or—say it softly!—Liberalism), then so be it.

Jay Score is a big, quiet man in the middle of a crew of characters who border on the wacky, and occasionally edge all the way into zany. One might even call them madcap, if one were inclined to do so. Most of them are human, but a few are Martians, and they're just as wacky/zany/madcap as the regular folk are.

Don't get the idea that they're all that two-dimensional, however. They're fun, and funny, but Russell's skill even in a series of yarns tossed off to make John Campbell laugh is evident, and if they don't exactly leap out of the story and dance around the room, they nevertheless work just fine on the page. I especially like the Martians, haughty and sarcastic, playing chess at every opportunity and complaining about the thick (to them) atmosphere, who still manage to get their work done and act just as heroically in defense of their non-tentacled shipmates as they do to protect themselves. Zany individuals the crew and officers may be—this is Russell, after all—but they are first and foremost a *crew*.

The book contains four stories, "Jay Score", "Mechanistra", "Symbiotica" and an original, "Mesmerica". I re-read this one at least once a year, with as much delight and amusement as I got from it the first time.

You shouldn't get the idea that Russell was all about cattle or provincial aliens, either. Perhaps my favorite EFR story, one that still lumps up my throat a little when I re-read it, is "Dear Devil" (May 1950 *Other Worlds*[10]). I honestly don't know why Campbell didn't take this one—it's certainly ASF-worthy—and I really don't know why Russell sent it to that most pulpish of the digests, *Other Worlds*. Leaving aside for the moment that *OW* seems lost in the '30s, the editor was none other than Ray Palmer, best known in the field for the Shaver Mystery (isn't Google wonderful?) and "fact articles" about flying saucers. However odd the match-up might seem at this remove, though, it was apparently just the thing for EFR; "Dear Devil" was his first for Palmer, but indubitably not his last. Perhaps the two men shared a Fortean connection. It's a definite possibility.

The story itself is, my own teary opinion aside, one of Russell's best, and deservedly one of his best-known. One could compare it to the famous axiom that clowns aspire to serious roles, but that's just a little too easy for me to be comfortable with. For all his puns and jokes and humor bordering on the bawdy—in *Trillion Year Spree*, Brian Aldiss refers to him as "[Campbell's] licensed jester" - Russell was no clown. His humor, broad as it may be, is satire (if not out-right parody), frequently of the one major thing other than Forteanasticness that inspired him to write: bureaucrats and the red-tape restraints which is their only reason for existence. According to Russell, that is.

Here, though, the humor is gentle, the satire moderated by honest sentiment. He chews no scenery, bangs no drums, constructs no bopamagilvies. He gives us a Martian poet, not a soldier with a steel rod up his fundament or a clever human ready to mess with said rod-butted soldier. Already, I'm intrigued. How many exploratory missions would NASA make with a poet onboard to "maintain morale by entertaining"?

The poet, Fander, asks to be left behind when the captain decides that the third stone from the Sun is dead and worthless. The captain reluctantly grants his request, and there the story really begins.

Fander finds people, of course, hiding in the ruins, "ragged, dirty, and no more than half grown." Children, almost feral, and almost certainly doomed. Under less capable hands, we could already be moving into the town square of Greater Maudlinity, but Russell is better than that.

"He lay within the cave, a ropy, knotted thing of glowing blue with enormous, bee-like eyes…" And tentacles, don't forget the tentacles. No wonder the first child who sees him cowers from him, calling him "Devil! Devil!" Little by little, the poet gains their trust by leaving food. Disaster is averted, not by massive Governmental action or by military intervention, but by the simple acts of kindness shown by this "Dear Devil" and the love and veneration shown him by his adopted charges.

What happens subsequently won't surprise anyone whose reading level is somewhere north of *Bambi*, but that isn't the point. In many cases, the greatest joy of the tour is not what you see as much as how the curator has arranged it. Here, the title says it all. If you want to know more, track down a copy of *The Best of Eric Frank Russell* or any other collection/anthology that contains the story (go to William Contento's invaluable *Index to Science Fiction Anthologies and Collections*, at http://users.ev1.net/~homeville/isfac/0start.htm to find out which ones). Trust me, how can you go wrong?

"Alamagoosa", *Deep Space*, *Wasp*, "Homo Saps", "The Hobbyist"… Y'know what? The truth, painful as it may be, is simple: I could go on for a lot longer than I already have about Russell and his work, to the point that most of you reading this would edge out of the room to escape. I make no apology for this—Russell is a writer well worth going on and on about. But even though space on the *Baen's Universe* site is for all intents and purposes endless, I owe it to my editors and you as well not to take a chance on running you off. Not to mention what I may owe Eric Frank Russell himself. There are numerous copies of his books out there to be had, either online or (preferably) at your local used bookshops or convention dealers' rooms, so take a tip from ol' Budzilla his own self and get into them. You'll have a good time, I promise.

(As is usually the case, although the list below is as complete as I can make it, I am more than happy to stand corrected on errors or omissions. Contact me care of this fine magazine and I'll fix it, and probably give you credit as well. I would like to thank fellow bibliophile and scholar/historian Phil Stephenson-Payne (http://www.philsp.com/pubindex.html#gcp) *for his enormous help in compiling the following bibliography.* Huzzah, *Phil!)*

Bibliography of Eric Frank Russell
Stories

"The Saga of Pelican West" – February 1937 *Astounding*
"The Great Radio Peril" – April 1937 *Astounding*
"The Prr-r-eet" – Winter 1937 *Tales of Wonder*, #1
"Seeker of Tomorrow" (with Leslie J. Johnson) – July 1937 *Astounding*; Johnson's name given as Leslie T.
"Mana" – December 1937 *Astounding*
"Egyptian Episode: The Rocket Plane and the Drug Traffickers" – 11/37 *Tales of Crime and Punishment*
"Poor Dead Fool" – January 1938 *Thrilling Detective* (aka "Murder Without Motive")
"The World's Eighth Wonder" – Sum 1938 *Tales of Wonder*
"Impulse" – September 1938 *Astounding* (aka "The Man From the Morgue" and "A Matter of Instinct")
"Shadow Man" – December 1938 *Fantasy*, #1 (aka "Invisible")
"Sinister Barrier" – March 1939 *Unknown*
"It's Hell to Be Shot" – *Mystery Stories* #15, 1939
"Vampire from the Void" – *Fantasy* #2, 1939
"Mightier Yet" – *Fantasy* #3, 1939
"Me and My Shadow" – February 1940 *Strange Stories*
"I, Spy!" – Fall 1940 *Tales of Wonder* (aka "Venturer of the Martian Mimics" and "Spiro")

"The Mechanical Mice" – January 1941 *Astounding* (as by Maurice G. Hugi, a real writer; Russell ghost-wrote the story)
"Jay Score" – May 1941 *Astounding*
"Seat of Oblivion" – November 1941 *Astounding*
"Homo Saps" – December 1941 (as by Webster Craig) *Astounding*
"With a Blunt Instrument" – December 1941 *Unknown*
"Mechanistria" – January 1942 *Astounding*
"Mr. Wisel's Secret" – February 1942 *Amazing* (aka "Wisel")
"Describe a Circle" – March 1942 *Astounding*
"The Kid from Kalamazoo" – August 1942 *Fantastic Adventures*
"Symbiotica" – October 1943 *Astounding*
"Controller" – March 1944 *Astounding*
"Resonance" – July 1945 *Astounding*
"Metamorphosite" – December 1946 *Astounding*
"The Timid Tiger" – February 1947 *Astounding*
"Relic" – April 1947 *Fantasy, The Magazine of Science Fiction* (aka "The Cosmic Relic")
"Hobbyist" – September 1947 *Astounding*
"Dreadful Sanctuary" – serial, June-August 1948 *Astounding*
"Displaced Person" – September 1948 *Weird Tales* (vignette)
"Muten" – October 1948 *Astounding* (as by Duncan H. Munro)
"The Ponderer" – November 1948 *Weird Tales*
"Late Night Final" – December 1948 *Astounding*
"The Big Shot" – January 1949 *Weird Tales*
"A Present from Joe" – February 1949 *Astounding*
"The Glass Eye" – March 1949 *Astounding*
"The Undecided" – April 1949 *Astounding*
"U-Turn" – April 1950 *Astounding* (as by Duncan H. Munro)
"Dear Devil" – May 1950 *Other Worlds*
"Exposure" – July 1950 *Astounding*
"The Rhythm of the Rats" – July 1950 *Weird Tales*
"First Person Singular" – October 1950 *Thrilling Wonder Stories*
"Follower" – November 1950 *Astounding*
"MacHinery" – December 1950 *Thrilling Wonder Stories*
"Test Piece" – March 1951 *Other Worlds*
"Afternoon of a Fahn" – April 1951 *Imagination* (aka "Rainbow's End")
"...And Then There Were None" – June 1951 *Astounding* (aka "Talisman")
"The Witness" – September 1951 *Other Worlds*

"Ultima Thule" – October 1951 *Astounding*
"The Illusionaries" – November 1951 *Planet Stories*
"The Star Watchers" – November 1951 *Startling Stories*
"The Big Dark" – January 1952 *World Youth*
"Second Genesis" – January 1952 *Blue Book Magazine*
"I'm a Stranger Here Myself" – March 1952 *Other Worlds*
"Fast Falls the Eventide" – May 1952 *Astounding*
"Take a Seat" – May 1952 *Startling Stories* (vignette)
"Dreamers of Space" – June 1952 *World Youth*
"I Am Nothing" – July 1952 *Astounding*
"Hell's Bells" – July 1952 *Weird Tales* (as by Duncan H. Munro; originally in March 1945 *Short Stories*, as "Bentley's Old London Djinn"; slightly modified for *Weird Tales*)
"The Sin of Hyacinth Peuch" – Fall 1952 *Fantastic*
"A Little Oil…" – October 1952 *Galaxy*
"Last Blast" – November 1952 *Astounding*
"The Timeless Ones" – November 1952 *Science Fiction Quarterly*
"Design for Great-Day" – January 1953 *Planet Stories* (aka "The Ultimate Invader")
"Somewhere a Voice" – January 1953 *Other Worlds*
"When the Sun Goes Down: A Fantasy of the 'Dark Ones'" – serial, April-June 1953 *World Youth*
"It's in the Blood" – June/July 1953 *Fantastic Universe*
"This One's on Me" – *Nebula* #4, 1953
"A Great Deal of Power" – August/September 1953 *Fantastic Universe* (aka "Boomerang")
"Postscript" – October 1953 *Science Fiction Plus* (aka "P.S.")
"Bitter End" – December 1953 *Science Fiction Plus*
"Sustained Pressure" – *Nebula* #6, December 1953
"Appointment at Noon" – March 1954 *Amazing*
"The Door" – March 1954 *Universe*
"Fly Away Peter" – April 1954 *Nebula*, #8
"Anything to Declare?" – April 1954 *Fantastic* (as by Naille Wilde)
"Weak Spot" – May 1954 *Astounding*
"I Hear You Calling" – November 1954 *Science-Fantasy*, #11
"The Courtship of 53 SHOTL 9 G" – December 1954 *Fantastic* (as by Naill Wilde)
"Mesmerica" – in *Men, Martians and Machines*, q.v.
"Nothing New" – January 1955 *Astounding*

"Diabologic" – March 1955 *Astounding*
"Allamagoosa" – May 1955 *Astounding*
"Tieline" – July 1955 *Astounding* (as by Duncan H. Munro)
"Proof" – July 1955 *Fantastic Universe*
"Saraband in C Sharp Major" – July 1955 *Science Fiction Stories*
"The Waitabits" – July 1955 *Astounding*
"Call Him Dead" – serial, August-October 1955 *Astounding*
"Heart's Desire" – September 1955 *Science-Fantasy*, #16 (contents page reads "Niall Wilde", story byline is "Nigel Wilde")(aka "A Divvil With the Women")
"Down, Rover, Down" – November 1955 *Nebula*, #14 (aka "The Case for Earth")
"Minor Ingredient" – March 1956 *Astounding*
"Legwork" – April 1956 *Astounding*
"Sole Solution" – April 1956 *Fantastic Universe* (vignette)
"Run, Little Men! – June 1956 *Famous Detective Stories*
"Plus X" – June 1956 *Astounding*
"Storm Warning" – July 1956 *Nebula*, #17
"Top Secret" – August 1956 *Astounding*
"Quiz Game" – September 1956 *Fantastic Universe*
"Fall Guy" – November 1956 *Fantastic Universe*
"Heav'n, Heav'n" – September 1956 *Future*, #30
"Nuisance Value" – January 1957 *Astounding*
"Love Story" – August 1957 *Astounding*
"Into Your Tent I'll Creep" – September 1957 *Astounding*
"Early Bird" – November 1957 *Science Fiction Stories*
"Brute Farce" – February 1958 *Astounding*
"Wasp" – serial, March-May 1958, *New Worlds*
"Basic Right" – April 1958 *Astounding*
"There's Always Tomorrow" – June 1958 *Fantastic Universe*
"Study in Still Life" – January 1959 *Astounding* (aka "Still Life")
"Now Inhale" – April 1959 *Astounding*
"The Army Comes to Venus" – May 1959 *Fantastic Universe* (reprint of "Sustained Pressure")
"Panic Button" – November 1959 *Astounding*
"Meeting on Kangshan" – March 1965 *If*
"Eternal Rediffusion" (with Leslie J. Johnson) – *Harbottle Fantasy Booklet* #3 1973

Articles

"Over the Border – September 1939 *Unknown*

"Spontaneous Frogation – July 1940 *Unknown*

"Asstronomy – July 1955 *New Worlds*

"And Still It Moves – June 1957 *Astounding*

"The Creeping Coffins of Barbados – in *Great World Mysteries*, Dobson 1957

"The Riddle of Levitation – in *Great World Mysteries*, Dobson 1957

"Satan's Footprints – in *Great World Mysteries*, Dobson 1957

"The Ship that Vanished – in *Great World Mysteries*, Dobson 1957

"The Case of the `Mary Celeste"' – in *Great World Mysteries*, Dobson 1957

"The Child of Nuremburg" – in *Great World Mysteries*, Dobson 1957

"Gadgets in the Sky" – in *Great World Mysteries*, Dobson 1957

"The Last of the Long-Ears" – in *Great World Mysteries*, Dobson 1957

"Ordeal by Fire" – in *Great World Mysteries*, Dobson 1957

"The Riddle of Levitation – in *Great World Mysteries*, Dobson 1957 as "The Mystery of Levitation" in *Great World Mysteries*

"Sea Monsters" – in *Great World Mysteries*, Dobson 1957

"The Ship that Vanished – in *Great World Mysteries*, Dobson 1957 as

"The Loss of the Waratah" in *Great World Mysteries*

"Stargazers – January 1959 *Amazing*, revision of "Asstronomy"

"The Vanishing Courier" – in *Great World Mysteries*, Dobson 1957

"Stargazers" – January 1959 *Amazing*

"...And Who the Pot?" – June 1959 *Amazing*

"A Many Legged Thing" – November 1959 *Fantastic Universe*

"A Trench and Two Holes" – November 1960 *New Worlds* (guest editorial)

Novels and Collections

Sinister Barrier – World's Work 1943 (UK); Fantasy Press 1948 (expanded from

Unknown appearance); Galaxy Novel 1, 1950

Dreadful Sanctuary – Fantasy Press 1951; Lancer 74-819, 1963

Sentinels from Space – Bourgey & Curl 1953; Ace Double D-44 (as *Sentinels of Space*, bound with *The Ultimate Invader*, ed. Donald Wollheim; Ace D-468, 1961)

The Ultimate Invader – Ace Double D-44 (bound with his *Sentinels of Space*)
Deep Space – Fantasy Press 1954; Bantam 1362, 1955
Men, Martians and Machines – Dobson 1955 (UK); Roy 1956; Berkley G148, 1958 (collection)
Three to Conquer – Avalon 1956; Ace Double D-215 (bound with Robert Moore Williams's *Doomsday Eve*)
Wasp – Avalon 1957; Perma Books M4120, 1959
The Space Willies – Ace Double D-315 (bound with his *Six Worlds Yonder*); Dobson 1959 UK) as *Next of Kin*
Six Worlds Yonder – Ace Double D-315 (bound with his *The Space Willies*) (collection)
Far Stars – Dobson 1961 (UK); Panther 1691, 1962; Goldmann 1962 (collection)
The Great Explosion – Dobson 1962 (UK); Torquil 1962; Pyramid F862
Dark Tides – Dobson 1962 (UK); Panther 1599, 1962 (UK)
With a Strange Device – Dobson 1964 (UK); Penguin 2358, 1965 (UK); Lancer 72-942,
1965 (as *The Mind Warpers*)
Somewhere a Voice – Dobson 1965 (UK); Ace F-398, 1966 (collection)
Like Nothing On Earth – Dobson 1975 (UK); Methuen , 1986 (collection)
The Best of Eric Frank Russell – Ballantine 0345277007, 1978
Next of Kin – Ballantine 345-32761-6, 1986
Design for Great-Day (with Alan Dean Foster) – Tor 1995
Major Ingredients: The Selected Short Fiction of Eric Frank Russell – NESFA Press 2000 (collection)
Entities: The Selected Novels of Eric Frank Russell – NESFA Press 2001
Darker Tides: The Weird Tales of Eric Frank Russell – Midnight House 2006]

Non-Fiction Books

Great World Mysteries – Dobson 1957
The Rabble Rousers – Regency Books RB317, 1963
The ABZ of Scouse – Scouse Press, 1966 (as by Linacre Lane)

Notes

1. Yes, Virginia, there *was* an *Astounding* editor before John Campbell. A couple, in fact: first, Harry Bates (of "Farewell to the Master" fame; you'll remember it as "The Day the Earth Stood Still," and I'm talking about the good one, youngster, not the recent crapola) edited the magazine for Clayton, then Tremaine came along when Street and Smith acquired it in 1933.
2. Google Robert Lionel Fanthorpe, cowboy. Interesting character.
3. If you've ever met me, you know there's ample proof that I've been late for *very* few meals in my life. This should tell you how engaged I was in this short novel, *n'est-ce pas*?
4. As opposed to those I *wish* I'd been influenced by, including Cordwainer Smith, Harlan Ellison and Alfred Bester. Whew!
5. Although much earlier in his treatise on pre- and post-War fandom, *The Immortal Storm* (ASFO Press, 1954), he apparently thought otherwise. In chapter XXXV of this important book, he mentions *Unknown* "…which John W. Campbell declared was being put out be sic Street & Smith solely because receipt of a sensational novel by Eric Frank Russell called for creation of an entirely new type of fantasy magazine." However, the gap of thirteen years between the two books might account for this seeming disparity—and SaM didn't say in the earlier book that he believed Campbell; he only reported what Campbell was supposed to have said.
6. Dr. Asimov might have had something of a blind spot where *Unknown* was concerned. In 1943, he sold a short story titled "Author! Author!" to Campbell for the magazine, which folded before it could be published. It was, in fact, the sixth story he had tried at *Unknown*, and the only one Campbell had accepted. It didn't see print until 1964, when D. R. Benson made it the lead in his second Pyramid anthology of stories from the magazine, *The Unknown Five*, more than 20 years later.
7. "Strangely protruding, strangely hard" it says here. No, really.
8. Not me, though. I prefer my beer to be root.
9. Along with Conklin's little hardcover-paperback, *A Galaxy of Science Fiction*, raggedy-ass copies of *The Martian Chronicles* and stacks of *The Andromeda Strain*.
10. I find it interesting in a weird kind of way that the cover date of this issue is the same cover date as the issue of *Astounding* which contained L. Ron Hubbard's first article on Dianetics; I wonder what Charles Fort would have made of this little juxtaposition. Coincidence? I think not.

❑

Murray Leinster's a Ten(ster),
or, Deal Out the Lincolns to William F. Jenkins

> It has long been my belief that science fiction is really the hope of the nation. I have been saying for years that our real trouble, in the States, is people smoking mild cigarettes, drinking pale beer, and running after blondes. But I have noticed that at this convention the brunettes among us have been pursued with real vigah and enthusiasm—and possibly a little more predacity than the blondes. This is a heartening thing to witness and it gives me great hope for the future of the United States because characters like you are real. [*Murray Leinster, from his Guest of Honor Speech at Discon, the 21st World Science Fiction Convention in 1963*]

Reading those words now, some forty-six years after he spoke them in front of the gathered fans and pros of the day, I wonder what he would have said had Murray Leinster (working name of William Fitzgerald Jenkins) been the Dean of something other than science fiction. After all, he wrote mysteries, and westerns, and romances (under the name Louisa Carter Lee), and had there been the same kind of fandom surrounding those genres, what might he have told them as Guest of Honor?

He wasn't Dean of Westerns, though, or even Romances. He was, for all his work in other areas, one of US; then, now and forever. Writing for whichever market would pay him wasn't an indication of hackery, mind you, it was quite a common thing in the days when almost every conceivable subject had its own pulp magazine.[1] Robert E. Howard, he of the cowboy hat and mighty-thewed barbarians, wrote boxing yarns, and even that other Dean of science fiction, Robert Heinlein, wrote teen confessions.

For Heinlein, though, writing anything other than SF was very much an aberration, and, in fact, it wasn't until after his death that those few stories were reprinted under his name. Leinster was a total pro; he edited his own anthology (*Great Stories of Science Fiction*, Random House 1951), unlike RAH who relied on Fred Pohl and Judith Merril to pick the stories for *Tomorrow, the Stars* (Doubleday 1952)[2]. If there was a market he could figure out a yarn for, he wrote it and sold it. This strikes me as a handy thing for a professional writer to be able to do.

William Fitzgerald Jenkins (aka Murray Leinster and a few others) was born in 1896, on June 16th, to be exact. I met him three quarters of a century later at a small convention in downtown Norfolk, Virginia called Dixieland Fancon. Also in attendance were Donald Wollheim, Wally Wood, Kelly Freas (in 1973, already Virginia's Con Guest in Residence), and a few others I don't recall.

My eyes, though, were on Leinster. Like most of those attending this never-to-be-repeated convention, I'd been reading his books and stories pretty much since I'd been reading SF. His stories had been frequently reprinted in those days, Groff Conklin alone having presented me with nineteen of them in various anthologies, and he was no stranger to the other anthologists, major and minor: Wollheim, Derleth, Bleiler & Dikty, Merril...he was a favorite of the editors, and therefore (and/or concurrently) a favorite of the readers.

How did this tiny little convention get the Dean? That's easy: he lived just down the road a piece in Gloucester. It's difficult even now for me to imagine one of the Giants living in my almost-backyard, but there he was, and remained, until his death in 1975.

I was barely even a faan back then. I had attended a number of comic conventions, but DFC was my first SF con, even if the guy running it was a comic artist rather than a writer, faan or pro. The idea of meeting and speaking with one of my heroes, therefore, was more than a little alien to me.

Will, on the other hand, was an old pro at this. He knew how *not* to embarrass or discourage a fanboy, a skill I was later to discover was common in most pros, but appallingly lacking in others. Above all else, Will Jenkins was a gentleman, jokes about brunettes being pursued with "vigah" notwithstanding.

It's difficult to pin down his first publication, although Sam Moskowitz, in *Seekers of Tomorrow* (World Publishing, 1967), makes a good case for it being while Jenkins was barely a teenager. This is confirmed by Jenkins himself in an interview published in the June 1972 issue of *Literary Sketches*, a small 'zine published by Mary Lewis Chapman in Williamsburg:

> Robert E. Lee is responsible for my being a writer....[O]ne morning I was in school...[and] they made a very tragic discovery. They found that it was Robert E. Lee's birthday and nobody had remembered it. So the Principal, of course, went into a panic and immediately sent messages to all the teachers that they were to read something to us pupils about Robert E. Lee and let us write a composition about him...I wrote a composition, I always loved long words, and I put some nice long words in it....[A] couple of weeks later the Virginian Pilot [the Norfolk Virginia daily] printed my composition....it made quite a stir and a Confederate veteran sent me a $5 bill.

Jenkins goes on to say that he took this money and bought the material for a glider:

> ...I took it down to the [Cape Henry] lighthouse... I jumped off the top of the lighthouse hill and glided down through the air and damn near broke my neck....I took a snapshot of myself and the glider and I sent it, with an account of my achievement, to a magazine called *Fly*—it was the first aviation magazine in the United States—and they sent me a $5 bill. That was $10 I'd made out of writing.

All this was in 1908 or '09, when Jenkins was a bright—if foolhardy—twelve or thirteen. I don't remember exactly what I was doing at age thirteen, but I can guarantee you it wasn't building and flying gliders, unless they were made from balsa wood and cost 10¢ down at the Woolworth's.[3]

He wanted to become a chemist. This ambition, unfortunately, spiraled down the Porcelain Facility of Fate when his father went broke and took a job at an auto dealership in Cleveland (yes, they had such things in 1909). Jenkins, at that time making $3.50 a week as an office boy, had "...a frantic frenzied horror of working for somebody else." So, out of school and with no hope whatever of going on to college to become a scientist, he began writing. At least, he began putting words on paper:

> I started about thirteen—every night I'd come home from the office and write 1,000 words and I did that everyday for a year, 360,000 [sic] words, and I tore it all up because it was lousy.

Eventually he began selling epigrams and filler material to *The Smart Set*, one of the most important magazines of the day, a dozen short pieces for another one of those Lincolns. So, he finally was a pro writer. How much of one? "The first year I was writing, and selling my stuff, I made the magnificent sum of $72."

It may have been 1913, but $72 at $5 a pop still didn't go very far, so he began trying his output on the pulps. His editors at *Smart Set*[4] had something of a problem with the Jenkins name being soiled by those nasty old nickel and dime pulps, so they gave him a bit of advice. In Jenkins's words:

> One day I was in…the office of this magazine, and I boasted to them that something that they had returned I had sold somewhere else. George Jean Nathan—it wasn't fair of him but I was 17 and I was flattered as hell—he asked me to save my name, Will Jenkins, for *Smart Set* and use a pen name for "inferior" magazines.

Thus was born Murray Leinster, a pseudonym concocted from family names. It wasn't too very long before he discovered that those "inferior" magazines paid Leinster far better than the more aristocratic *Smart Set* paid Jenkins, though, so he devoted his energies to pulpdom and let the slicks slide.

Jenkins began writing in the 'teens of the 20th Century, and was still writing and getting awards in his sixties. In 1962, two years after the appearance of his Ace novel *The Pirates of Zan* (originally serialized in *Astounding* as *The Pirates of Ersatz*, which title I like much better), he was (in the words of Sam Moskowitz) "…voted one of the six favorite *modern* writers of science fiction…" [emphasis SaM's]. His last story appeared in a 1966 issue of *Analog*, and a year later his last article appeared in the same magazine.

Jenkins was a lot like the great jazz saxophonist, Coleman Hawkins. I know that's an odd comparison, but stick around and you'll get it. The Hawk was a skilled musician who relied on his chops to make music instead of just memorizing licks. This, in large part, was a major reason why he was as successful during the post-war Bop period as he was during the Swing/Big Band era; that, and his clear understanding of what the Boppers were doing. He liked the renewed energy Bop brought to a moribund jazz world, and he was able to adapt his playing style to the growing sophistication of both the listeners and the other musicians. He may never have attained bull-goose Bophood, but he adapted quite easily and well to fronting small combos.

Given all that, it would be easy to take the parallel with Hawkins further by cleverly linking story with song, book with album and so on, but you're faced with that kind of lit-crit booshwah enough here on the Information Turnpike without my adding to it. The simple fact is that Jenkins and the Hawk blew damned great stuff, and a great solo or a great story are all you need to prove yourself to anyone who matters.

Eventually, about the time he was 21, his boss (Jenkins was, by this time, a junior bookkeeper at Prudential) became aware of his extracurricular activities and advised him that Prudential didn't like its employees to moonlight, so he'd have to stop. After admitting that he was, in fact, writing, Jenkins stood mute. He was then taken up on the mountain and shown the kingdoms of the Earth if he would only bow down. Well, okay, his manager offered him a couple extra bucks a week to spy on his fellow workers and report any who complained about the company. Fat chance: "I resigned on the spot and it was worth all the trouble…when that guy pulled that on me."

He'd wanted to be a chemist; instead, he became an inventor, maybe the next best thing. One of his inventions is still used today: a process of front-projecting images onto a background and actors instead of rear-projection (which prevents the camera from moving). Perhaps the most famous use of this technique was during the "Dawn of Man" part of the Kubrick/Clarke film, *2001: A Space Odyssey*.

Most of his inventions, though, were firmly embedded in the pages of his stories. The annual award for best alternative history work, The Sidewise, is named for his story in the June 1934 *Astounding*, "Sidewise in Time," which was later combined with six other stories and issued by Shasta in 1950 under the same title. The 1934 story isn't the first time stfnal writers had played with the idea of alternate worlds and timelines—*Wonder Stories* ran John Taine's "The Time Stream" in the December 1931 issue, and there was an *ad hoc* anthology of speculative essays edited by one Sir John Collings Squire in 1931 titled *If It Had Happened Otherwise* that included a piece on the American Civil War by no less a personage than Sir Winston Churchill—but let's face it, Jenkins/Leinster did it better than they did, and made it look *easy*. That for you, Sir Winston.

That wasn't his only literary invention, though. In "A Logic Named Joe" in the March '46 issue of *Astounding*, he basically rolled up his sleeves and invented the whole damned computer InterWeb thing without breaking a sweat. That for *you*, Al Gore.

It's difficult, at some forty-plus years' remove, to recall with any surety just where I first read a long-time favorite author. In my case, in fact, it's even more difficult, because most of my reading when I was in my preadolescence was in anthologies, which I saw not necessarily as collections of individual stories by individual writers, but as massive sources of days and days worth of anonymous reading, like television I could make up in my own head, if you will. I wasn't concerned at first with who wrote the words; I was too busy making pictures in my mind.

That changed at least a little when I checked Groff Conklin's *Adventures in Mutation* (Vanguard 1955) out of the library and read a disturbing little story titled "Skag With the Queer Head" by someone whose name I didn't learn to pronounce correctly until just before meeting him: our subject, Murray Leinster.

I was initially drawn to the author's name because one of my aunts married into the Murray family, and for a nine year-old kid, it doesn't take much more than that to make a connection.

But the story…! Imagine being nine, with a dog of your own, and reading this:

> When Deena had her puppies, she was attended by no less eminent a person than Dr. B. J. Danil, late Wharton Professor of Experimental Biology at Braddock University. For Deena was no ordinary dog. Neither she nor her mate, Skag. They were the only two dogs of their kind, in fact, in the whole world.

I'd read my share of "mad scientist" yarns, of course, as well as seen them on TV and in cartoons (remember the Superman cartoon with the giant flying robots? Now, *that* was a mad scientist!), but never before one in which he wasn't just a foil against which the Hero acted.

Or perhaps he was, if you accept that in this case the Hero is a genetically altered Malamute named Skag. For once, in all the stories I'd read up until then, science wasn't the salvation of anything, but rather the weapon wielded by an uncaring and unfeeling human against someone who should have been his Best Friend.

Skag and Deena are the results of experiments in giving animals intelligence on an almost human level, in this instance by forcing their heads to retain the same shape as a puppy's, even as it grows larger, thus increasing brain size and intellect. Nothing unusual about the idea of smart dogs; Simak used it in his City sequence, and Heinlein used it more than once. The difference here is that Skag and Deena know what's been done to them, understand the lack of compassion and humaneness in their tormentor, and are determined that the same things will not be done to their pups. They act heroically, if impassively, with little of the rage and contempt the doctor shows them, and in the end are left to themselves to raise their pups as simply dogs.

Leinster could have let it go at that, and still have created a pretty intense yarn, but that's all it would have been—a yarn. He was never content to take the easy out, though, and if Prof. Danil is a prick, the old geezer who brings his mail through the Alaskan Winter, Joe Timmins, isn't. He's human to the core, which means that he has nothing but respect and affection for Skag and Deena, and they reciprocate.

There are scenes throughout the story, short as it is, which point up Danil's intentions towards the pups, as well as his two original subjects, and it becomes very clear early on that they know exactly what's going on. At one point, as he tries to take one of the pups from Deena, she grabs his wrist in her teeth; as he pulls out a gun to kill her, Skag immobilizes his other arm. Then, in a key incident, the two dogs then argue in their own "language" over what to do next. Deena, protective of her offspring, wants to simply tear him up. Skag, knowing full well what would happen if she did, twists Damil's arm until he drops the gun. Skag then carries it off to the side, then stares at Danil until he slinks away.

I won't describe the final encounter except to say that what follows is inevitable, and disturbingly satisfying to a kid who could never stand cruelty to animals. It stuck in my mind for years after, and upon re-reading it for the first time in decades, I find it still as disturbing, if not as groundbreaking.

You can say that about much of Leinster's work, really. He wasn't so much a Cordwainer Smith as much as he was a Doc Smith. I hasten to add that I *do not* see this as pejorative in the least—not everyone sits comfortably on the cutting edge, but it don't mean they can't still be plenty sharp. Leinster never fails to entertain, never makes a wrong move, never ceases to amaze. His body of work isn't just long and broad, it's got depth. It isn't self-consciously literary, and he eschewed pretentiousness, I think, not from any deliberate decision but just because it didn't occur to him that it might serve the stories he wanted to tell.

I love my Cordwainerist stories, believe me I do, but I love my Docologist stuff just as much. I know gourmet writing when I taste it; whether the robust *Provençal* of Bester's "Fondly Fahrenheit" or the *nouvelle cuisine* of Zelazny's "A Rose for Ecclesiastes", fine dining is fine dining. On the other hand, sometimes you just want a plateful of chili, or a steak and baked, and that's where you'll find Leinster, complete with barbecue tongs and "Kiss the Cook!" apron. You know, comfort food, but without the pre-processed cheese.

In the utterly necessary *In Search of Wonder* (Advent 1957) author, editor and critic Damon Knight describes Leinster's writing in the novel *The Monster From Earth's End* as:

> [W]orkmanlike first-reader prose which has not changed much in the last thirty years....The short, simple sentences carry the story forward in a sort of spiral fashion: one foot forward, two feet back to cover the old ground again, then another small advance.

(Knight didn't really intend the above to be a compliment, but Ghu love him, he was a critic first and a reader second. Face it, most critics don't read for the same reason Joe Lunchpail does, they read in order to find ways of describing what they're reading in cleverly witty ways. The rest of us read to have a good time.)

Leinster's "carefully pedestrian prose" (Knight's phrase) suits his stories just fine and dandy. Like Englishman Eric Frank Russell (see last issue), Leinster liked to posit a puzzle and then solve it right in front of the reader. This made him a favorite of John Campbell's *Astounding* readership, of course, and he ended up writing more than fifty stories for the magazine from 1930 (before Campbell was editor) until 1966.

Perhaps his best known story for *Astounding*, if not his best known period, is "First Contact", which appeared in the May, 1945 issue. In a very real way, this is the archetypal Golden-Age, Campbellian yarn. Leinster posits a problem, one with far-reaching consequences: two starships meet in deep space, both of them strangers to the other. No matter how much each might wish for good relations, neither can take the chance of being followed back to their home world. What if the Stranger ship were crewed by the alien equivalents of Professor Moriarty, Genghis Khan, and Evil Lincoln, after all?

Most of the story is taken up with desperate speculation. How can We trust Them? What can We do to prove that They can trust Us? Is commerce and communication with another race worth the risk of annihilation? The debate rages in the human ship, while the two most important characters—Tommy Dort, a photographer in the observation staff of the human ship *Llanvabon*, and an alien crew member Dort calls Buck—get to know each other as well as circs allow, sending messages back and forth while their respective Captains sweat it out. One communiqué in response to the *Llanvabon*'s cautious message of hope for friendship says it all:

> Tommy said dispassionately: "He says, sir, 'That is all very well but is there any way for us to let each other go home alive? I would be happy to hear of such a way if you can contrive one. At the moment it seems to me that one of us must be killed.'"

Boo-yah. Now, *that's* a problem to be solved. The solution is a clever one, as befits a self-educated inventor. I won't reveal it here, for obvious reasons. I will say, though, that Jenkins/Leinster is at his best in this story, "workmanlike first-reader prose" and all. Not only is there plenty of shrewdness to go around twice or thrice, not only are the characters and situations easy to comprehend and identify with, but the author weaves his trademark wit and humor throughout. The relationship that grows between Tommy Dort and "Buck" is one of sympathy and mutual respect and interest; we could ask little more of our real First Contact than to have two such somewhere in the middle of it all.

But where did the writer we in the stfnal community came to know and love as Murray Leinster get *his* start? What was his first undeniably science-fictional story?

Let me give you a little more background first. Bear with me, I won't keep you waiting long. A long time ago, there was a weekly magazine called *The Argosy*. It published a lot of material—some 90k words per issue—and it was one of the most popular of the dime fiction periodicals. Leinster had been selling them what the editor (one Matthew White, Jr.; Leinster described him as "…a little man with snow white whiskers and a slight lisp…") called "Happy Village Stories," sentimental yarns much along the lines of those sappy paintings done by Thomas Kincaid, the *soi-disant* "Painter of Light."

As you might imagine, Leinster got a little tired of writing these, even though White bought all he could crank out. Finally, he turned one in with a note saying that he was done with them:

> …I finished a story and sent it to him and said, "No more Happy Village stories, for the time being, I'm writing a story that I call the RUNAWAY SKYSCRAPER…the opening sentence is—'The whole thing began when the clock on the Metropolitan Tower began to run backwards!'"…I got, by return mail, a letter—"Dear Murray, when you finish that story about the Runaway Skyscraper, let me see it at once." And I had to write the darn thing to keep him from finding out I was a liar.

The darn thing was published in the February 22, 1919 issue of *The Argosy*, and has seen few reprintings since. It was not, however his first SF/fantasy story to see print, as his "Oh, Aladdin!" ran not quite six weeks earlier.

It took a few years for him to get around to writing SF, in spite of the fact that he'd been reading it for a long time. It wasn't just because he was selling plenty of other things, although that was certainly a factor. No, it was something else entirely.

I've been reading SF and hanging with my stfnal peeps for more than forty years now, and I've noticed that there are two basic types of writers, no matter what the genre. There are those who read everything voraciously, constantly, and to the exclusion of practically all else, then wake up one day and say "Hell, *I* can write this stuff. What's Jules Ursula C. J.

'Doc' Heinellison del Rey van Tucker got that I *don't*?" and then they start cranking them out.

Then there are those who read everything voraciously, constantly, and to the exclusion of practically all else, then wake up one day and say, "Boy, I wish I could write like Cordwainer L. Sprague Isaac Poul O'Spinrad Aldiss, but I just don't know..."

Believe it or not, Will Jenkins was in that second category, at least at first:

> I had been reading science fiction and I loved it, but I didn't think I was smart enough to write it. But...when I had to do it, I got away with it... I was very much surprised to find that I could write this type that I had admired so much and loved so much.

Well, he made up for any lost time, believe me. Just look at the biblio at the end of this darn thing.

William Fitzgerald Jenkins's career as Murray Leinster lasted a long, long time. He was active, if not writing, until his death in 1975, just short of eighty years after he was born. He was a dyed-in-the-wool Southern Gentleman, generous with his time and advice to younger authors. In his recent (as I write this) collection of autobiographical sketches, *Other Spaces, Other Times* (Nonstop Press 2009), Robert Silverberg—no slouch himself when it comes to career spans—writes of meeting Jenkins in the *Astounding* offices in 1956. Jenkins was already sixty, Silverberg a svelte twenty-one (and three years away from being able to purchase Fiorello La Guardia's old digs), and was there to give John Campbell a new story, titled "Sourdough."

Campbell read the fourteen page manuscript then and there, as was his habit, then said (in Silverberg's words), "Something's wrong with the ending of this, but I'm not sure what. Will, would you mind taking a look?" and passed the 'script to the elder writer. Silverberg writes:

> Jenkins, the cagy old pro, skimmed swiftly through the story, nodded, indicated page twelve. "I see the problem," he said—to Campbell, not to me. And offered a dazzling rewrite suggestion, with which Campbell concurred. John pointed to the typewriter on his secretary's desk and instructed me to sit down and write a couple of new paragraphs right on the spot... Campbell bought the story ten minutes later.

Nor was Silverberg the only famous writer in the field to benefit from Jenkinsian counsel, as none other than that other Dean of Science Fiction, Robert Heinlein, wrote in a letter to his agent dated July 28, 1959 and subsequently published in *Grumbles From the Grave* (Del Rey 1989):

> ...I have always worked on the theory that there is always a market somewhere for a good story—a notion that Will Jenkins pounded into my head many years ago.

Heinlein mentions this elsewhere as well. In his essay "On the Writing of Speculative Fiction" written for the 1947 Fantasy Press non-fiction anthology *Of Worlds Beyond* (edited by Lloyd Arthur Eschbach), he writes:

> Several years ago Will F. Jenkins said to me, "I'll let you in on a little secret, Bob. *Any* story—science fiction, or otherwise—if it is well-written, can be sold to the slicks." Will himself has proved this....

Jenkins wrote a lot in his six-decade career, impressing even the normally sober and dignified L. Sprague de Camp. In his *Science Fiction Handbook* (Hermitage 1953), he wrote:

> He has been writing fiction ever since 1915, his total number of stories reaching the staggering total of over 1,300, and he is the author of over thirty books... Mr. Jenkins has written almost every kind of copy including westerns, detective stories, adventure stories, love stories, comic-book continuity, reports on scientific research, technical articles, and radio and television scripts.

While I'm quoting the famous in reference to our subject, let me add one more. I mentioned up at the top there that Jenkins/Leinster was a favorite of the anthologists, and this is true. He remains one of the most reprinted classic authors almost thirty-five years after his death. In his headnote to the aforementioned story "Skag With the Queer Head" reprinted in *Science Fiction Adventures in Mutation* (Vanguard 1955), editor Groff Conklin[5] wrote:

> The Leinster-Sturgeon race in the Conklin anthologies is now a "draw"; each man has appeared in all but one[6] of my sixteen published or about-to-be-published collections. It is true that in two anthologies Leinster turned up under his own name, Will Jenkins, but this does not spoil the record.

All told, Jenkins/Leinster would appear in nineteen of Conklin's forty-one anthologies, to Sturgeon's twenty-three, a very close second. Other editors would reprint his stories over and over, right up until the present. As the first Dean of the genre, he helped blaze the trail for all the other Golden-Age writers, and most of those who came later. Allen Steele, Catherine Asaro, the late Charles Sheffield, any who still write hard-science fiction, who pose and then solve sweeping problems that threaten our tiny little system, owe much to William Fitzgerald Jenkins, our own Murray Leinster.

(As usual, this bibliography is for initial appearances only, and necessarily concentrates primarily on his SF and fantasy. As Leinster/Jenkins was one of the most prolific authors in the field, a complete biblio is inevitably impossible—there are those far more assiduous than I who have worked for years to assemble one, I promise you, and they're still not finished. In any case, such a project would be far larger than even JBU would allow me, so rest assured that there's still plenty of work for you to do by sending me additions and/or corrections. I want to thank Phil Stephenson-Payne once again for his help with the below, as well as by William Contento and Stephen Miller and their invaluable Science Fiction, Fantasy, & Weird Fiction Magazine Index: 1890-2007. *If you're at all serious about studying or collecting classic SF and fantasy, you could do far worse than to purchase their index. Google them for details.*

William F. Jenkins/Murray Leinster Bibliography

(In the listings below, text in square brackets indicates a series.)

Short Fiction

"Love" – August 1915 *The Parisienne* (poem)
"Grooves" – October 12, 1918 *All-Story Weekly*
"Oh, Aladdin!" – January 11, 1919 *Argosy*
"The Runaway Skyscraper" – February 22, 1919 *Argosy* and *Railroad Man's Magazine*

"Footprints in the Snow" – June 7, 1919 *All-Story Weekly*
"A Thousand Degrees Below Zero" – July 15 1919 *Thrill Book* [Davis & Gerrold]
"The Silver Menace" – serial, September 1 & 15, 1919 *Thrill Book* [Davis & Gerrold]
"Juju" – October 15, 1919 *Thrill Book*
"The Mad Planet" – June 12, 1920 *Argosy* [Burl]
"The Red Dust" – April 2, 1921 *Argosy All-Story Weekly* [Burl]
"Nerve" – June 4, 1921 *Argosy All-Story Weekly*
"The Street of Magnificent Dreams" – August 5, 1922 *Argosy All-Story Weekly*
"The Oldest Story in the World" – August 1925 *Weird Tales*
"The Man Who Went Black" – March 1926 *Danger Trail* (as by Will F. Jenkins, also August 1931 *Jungle Stories* as by Will T. Jenkins, possibly a typo)
"The Seventh Bullet" – March 1926 *Danger Trail*
"The Man Who Didn't Shoot" – June 1926 *Danger Trail*
"The Strange People" – serial, March-May 1928 *Weird Tales*
"The Darkness on Fifth Avenue" – November 30 1929 *Argosy* [Hines]
"The City of the Blind" – December 28 1929 *Argosy* [Hines]
"The Murderer" – January 1930 *Weird Tales*
"Tanks" – January 1930 *Astounding*
"The Storm that Had to be Stopped" – March 1, 1930 *Argosy* [Hines]
"Murder Madness" – serial, May-August 1930 *Astounding*
"The Fifth-Dimension Catapult" – January 1931 *Astounding* [Tommy Reames]
"The Power Planet" – June 1931 *Amazing*
"Morale" – December 1931 *Astounding*
"The Racketeer Ray" – February 1932 *Amazing*
"Politics" – June 1932 *Amazing*
"The Fifth-Dimension Tube" – January 1933 *Astounding* [Tommy Reames]
"The Monsters" – January 1933 *Weird Tales*
"Borneo Devils" – February 1933 *Amazing*
"Invasion" – March 1933 *Astounding*
"The Body in the Taxi" – October 1933 *Black Bat Detective Mysteries* [*The Black Bat*]

"Beyond the Sphinxes' Cave" – November 1933 *Astounding*
"The Trouble on the Dude Ranch" – November 1933 *Black Bat Detective Mysteries* (as by Will F. Jenkins) [*The Black Bat*]
"The Coney Island Murder" – November 1933 *Black Bat Detective Mysteries* [*The Black Bat*]
"The Hollywood Murders" – December 1933 *Black Bat Detective Mysteries*
"The Maniac Murders" – February 1934 *Black Bat Detective Mysteries* [*The Black Bat*]
"Sidewise in Time" – June 1934 *Astounding*
"The Mole Pirate" – November 1934 *Astounding*
"Conquest of the Stars" – March 1935 *Astounding*
"Proxima Centauri" – March 1935 *Astounding* (aka "Conquest of the Stars")
"The Morrison Monument" – August 10, 1935 *Argosy*
"The Challenge from Beyond" – September 1935 *Fantasy Magazine* (this was a five-part round-robin story; the other authors, in order, were Stanley G. Weinbaum, Donald Wandrei, E. E. "Doc" Smith, and Harl Vincent [pseud. of Harold Vincent Schoepflin])
"The Fourth-Dimensional Demonstrator" – December 1935 *Astounding*
"The Incredible Invasion" – serial, August-December 1936 *Astounding*
"Side Bet" – July 31, 1937 *Colliers* (as by Will F. Jenkins)
"Wall of Fear" – ? 1937 *Colliers* (as by Will F. Jenkins)
"Swords and Mongols" – April 1939 *Golden Fleece*
"Friends" – December 25, 1940 *Short Stories*
"The Wabbler" – October 1942 *Astounding*
"Double for Murder" – November 1942 *Strange Detective Mysteries*
"Four Little Ships" – November 1942 *Astounding*
"'...If You Can Get It'" – November 1943 *Astounding*
"Plague" – February 1944 *Astounding*
"Trog" – June 1944 *Astounding*
"The Eternal Now" – Fall 1944 *Thrilling Wonder Stories*
"De Profundis" – Winter 1945 *Thrilling Wonder Stories*
"First Contact" – May 1945 *Astounding*
"The Ethical Equations" – June 1945 *Astounding*
"Things Pass By" – Summer 1945 *Thrilling Wonder Stories*
"Tight Place" – July 1945 *Astounding*

"Pipeline to Pluto" – August 1945 *Astounding*
"The Power" – September 1945 *Astounding*
"Incident on Calypso" – Fall 1945 *Startling Stories*
"Interference" – October 1945 *Astounding*
"The Disciplinary Circuit" – Winter 1946 *Thrilling Wonder Stories* [Kim Rendell]
"The Plants" – January 1946 *Astounding*
"Adapter" – March 1946 *Astounding*
"A Logic Named Joe" – March 1946 *Astounding* (as by Will F. Jenkins)
"Like Dups" – Spring 1946 *Thrilling Wonder Stories*
"Dead City" – Summer 1946 *Thrilling Wonder Stories*
"Pocket Universes" – Fall 1946 *Thrilling Wonder Stories*
"The End" – December 1946 *Thrilling Wonder Stories*
"Time to Die – January 1947 *Astounding*
"The Manless Worlds – February 1947 *Thrilling Wonder Stories* [Kim Rendell]
"The Laws of Chance – March 1947 *Startling Stories*
"Skit-Tree Planet – April 1947 *Thrilling Wonder Stories*
"The Gregory Circle" – April 1947 *Thrilling Wonder Stories* (as by William Fitzgerald) [Bud Gregory]
"From Beyond the Stars" – June 1947 *Thrilling Wonder Stories* (as by Will F. Jenkins)
"The Boomerang Circuit" – June 1947 *Thrilling Wonder Stories* [Kim Rendell]
"The Nameless Something" – June 1947 *Thrilling Wonder Stories* (as by William Fitzgerald) [Bud Gregory]
"Propagandist" – August 1947 *Astounding*
"The Deadly Dust" – August 1947 *Thrilling Wonder Stories* (as by William Fitzgerald) [Bud Gregory]
"The Day of the Deepies" – October 1947 *Famous Fantastic Mysteries*
"The Man in the Iron Cap" – November 1947 *Startling Stories*
"Planet of Sand" – February 1948 *Famous Fantastic Mysteries*
"The Seven Temporary Moons" – February 1948 *Thrilling Wonder Stories* (as by William Fitzgerald) [Bud Gregory]
"West Winterd" – March 1948 *Astounding*
"The Strange Case of John Kingman" – May 1948 *Astounding*
"Space-Can" – June 1948 *Thrilling Wonder Stories*
"The Night Before the End of the World" – August 1948 *Famous Fantastic Mysteries*

"The Devil of East Lupton, Vermont" – August 1948 *Thrilling Wonder Stories* (as by William Fitzgerald)
"Regulations" – August 1948 *Thrilling Wonder Stories*
"The Ghost Planet" – December 1948 *Thrilling Wonder Stories*
"The Story of Rod Cantrell" – January 1949 *Startling Stories* [Rod Cantrell]
"Assignment on Pasik" – February 1949 *Thrilling Wonder Stories* (as by William Fitzgerald)
"The Black Galaxy" – March 1949 *Startling Stories* [Rod Cantrell]
"The Lost Race" – April 1949 *Thrilling Wonder Stories*
"The Life-Work of Professor Muntz" – June 1949 *Thrilling Wonder Stories*
"Fury from Lilliput" – August 1949 *Thrilling Wonder Stories*
"Doomsday Deferred" – September 24 1949 *The Saturday Evening Post* (as by Will Jenkins, also as "The Soldado Ant")
"The Queen's Astrologer" – October 1949 *Thrilling Wonder Stories*
"The Other World" – November 1949 *Startling Stories*
"This Star Shall Be Free" – November 1949 *Super Science Stories*
"Cure for a Ylith" – November 1949 *Startling Stories* (as by William Fitzgerald)
"The Lonely Planet – December 1949 *Thrilling Wonder Stories*
"The Fear Planet" – January 1950 *Super Science Stories*
"Planet of the Small Men" – April 1950 *Thrilling Wonder Stories*
"Nobody Saw the Ship" – May/June 1950 *Future*
"Be Young Again!" – July/August 1950 *Future*
"Journey to Barkut" – serial (incomplete; the magazine folded before finishing), October 1950 (#7) and January 1951 (#8) *Fantasy Book*
"Historical Note" – February 1951 *Astounding*
"The Other Now" – March 1951 *Galaxy*
"Skag with the Queer Head" – August 1951 *Marvel Science Fiction*
"If You Was a Moklin" – September 1951 *Galaxy*
"Keyhole" – December 1951 *Thrilling Wonder Stories*
"The Gadget Had a Ghost" – June 1952 *Thrilling Wonder Stories*
"The Middle of the Week After Next" – August 1952 *Thrilling Wonder Stories*
"The Barrier" – September 1952 *Space Science Fiction*
"Overdrive" – January 1953 *Startling Stories*
"The Invaders" – April/May 1953 *Amazing*
"The Sentimentalists" – April 1953 *Galaxy*

"Dear Charles" – May 1953 *Fantastic Story Magazine* (as by William Fitzgerald)
"The Castaway" – June 1953 *Universe*
"Nightmare Planet" – June 1953 *Science Fiction Plus* [Burl]
"The Ship Was a Robot" – June 1953 *Thrilling Wonder Stories*
"The Jezebel" – October 1953 *Startling Stories*
"The Trans-Human" – December 1953 *Science Fiction Plus*
"Second Landing" – Winter 1954 *Thrilling Wonder Stories* [Canis Venatici]
"Fugitive from Space" – May 1954 *Amazing*
"The Amateur Alchemist" – Fall 1954 *Thrilling Wonder Stories*
"The Psionic Mousetrap" – March 1955 *Amazing*
"Sam, This Is You" – May 1955 *Galaxy*
"White Spot" – Summer 1955 *Startling Stories*
"Honeymoon on Dlecka" – July 1955 *Fantastic Universe*
"Scrimshaw" – September 1955 *Astounding*
"Nightmare World" – November 1955 *Science Fiction Monthly* (#4) [Burl]
"Sand Doom" – December 1955 *Astounding* [Colonial Survey]
"Exploration Team" – March 1956 *Astounding* [Colonial Survey]
"Critical Difference" – July 1956 *Astounding* [Colonial Survey]
"The Swamp Was Upside Down" – September 1956 *Astounding* [Colonial Survey]
"Women's Work" – November 1956 *Science Fiction Stories*
"Anthropological Note" – April 1957 *F&SF*
"Ribbon in the Sky" – June 1957 *Astounding* (Calhoun [Med Service])
"Med Service" – August 1957 *Astounding* (Calhoun [Med Service])
"The Grandfathers' War" – October 1957 *Astounding* (Calhoun [Med Service])
"The Machine That Saved the World" – December 1957 *Amazing*
"Short History of World War Three" – January 1958 *Astounding*
"The Strange Invasion" – April 1958 *Satellite*
"The Pirates of Ersatz" – serial, February-April 1959 *Astounding*
"The Aliens" – August 1959 *Astounding*
"Long Ago, Far Away" – September 1959 *Amazing*
"A Matter of Importance" – September 1959 *Astounding*
"Attention Saint Patrick" – January 1960 *Astounding*
"The Leader" – February 1960 *Astounding*
"Tyrants Need to Be Loved" – February 1960 *Fantastic*

"The Ambulance Made Two Trips" – April 1960 *Astounding*
"The Corianis Disaster" – May 1960 *Science Fiction Stories*
"The Covenant" – July 1960 *Fantastic*
"Doctor" – February 1961 *Galaxy*
"Pariah Planet" – July 1961 *Amazing* [Calhoun/Med Service]
"The Case of the Homocidal Robots" – August 1961 *F&SF*
"Planet of Dread" – May 1962 *Fantastic*
"Imbalance" – December 1962 *Fantastic*
"Third Planet" – April 1963 *Worlds of Tomorrow*
"The Hate Disease" – August 1963 *Analog* [Calhoun/Med Service]
"Manners and Customs of the Thrid" – September 1963 *If*
"Med Ship Man" – October 1963 *Galaxy* [Calhoun/Med Service]
"Lord of the Uffts" – February 1964 *Worlds of Tomorrow*
"*Spaceman*" – March, April 1964 *Analog*
"Plague on Kryder II" – December 1964 *Analog* (Calhoun [Med Service])
"*Killer Ship*" – October, December 1965 *Amazing*
"A Planet Like Heaven" – January 1966 *If*
"*Stopover in Space*" – June, August 1966 *Amazing*
"Quarantine World" – November 1966 *Analog* (Calhoun [Med Service])

Articles

"Why I Use a Pen Name" – October/November 1934 *Fantasy Magazine*
"Author, Author" – Spring 1949 *The Fanscient*
"Guest Editorial" – September 1952 *Startling Stories*
"Where Are Those Space-Ships?" – August 1953 *Startling Stories*
"To Build a Robot Brain" – April 1954 *Astounding*
"Labor of Love" – January 1956 *Astounding*
"Applied Science Fiction" – November 1967 *Analog*

Novels and Collections

Murder Madness – Brewer Warren 1931
Murder of the U.S.A. – Crown 1946; Newsstand 141, 1950 (as by Will F. Jenkins)
The Last Space Ship – Fredrick Fell, Inc. 1949; Galaxy SF Novel 25, 1955 [Kim Rendell] (coll. 3 stories)
Fight For Life – Crestwood Prize Science Fiction Novels 10, 1949 (digest-sized, orig. as "The Laws of Chance")

The Lonely Planet - Whitman 1950
The Plants - *American Science Fiction* nn, nd (but 1950) (Aust., bound with Robert Moore Williams' *Red Death of Mars*, orig. in the January 1946 *Astounding*)
Sidewise in Time - Shasta 1950 (coll. 6 stories)
Conquest of the Stars - *American Science Fiction* nn, nd (but 1951) (Aust.)
Space Platform - Shasta 1953; Pocket Books 920, 1953 [Joe Kenmore]
Space Tug - Shasta 1953; Pocket Books 1037, 1955 [Joe Kenmore]
The Unknown - *American Science Fiction* nn, nd (but 1953)(Aust.)
The Black Galaxy - Galaxy SF Novel 20, 1954 (orig. in the March 1949 *Startling*)
The Forgotten Planet - Gnome Press 1954; Ace D-146, 1956 (coll. 3 stories, bound with Lee Correy's *Contraband Rocket*)[Burl]
Gateway to Elsewhere - Ace D-53, 1954 (orig. as "Journey to Barkut" in the January 1952 *Astounding*, bound with A. E. van Vogt's *The Weapon Shops of Isher*)
The Brain Stealers - Ace D-79, 1954 (orig. as "The Man in the Iron Cap" in the November 1947 *Startling*, bound with Francis Rufus Bellamy's *Atta*)
Operation: Outer Space - Fantasy Press 1954; Golden SF Library, 1957
The Other Side of Here - Ace D-94, 1955 (expanded from "The Incredible Invasion", bound with A. E. van Vogt's *One Against Eternity*, orig. serialized in the August-December 1936 *Astounding*)
Colonial Survey - Gnome Press 1956; Avon T202, 1957 (as *The Planet Explorer*, fix-up of 4 stories)
City on the Moon - Avalon 1957; Ace D-277, 1958 (bound with *Men on the Moon*, ed. Donald A. Wollheim)[Joe Kenmore]
Out of This World - Avalon 1958 (coll. 3 stories, all as by William Fitzgerald)[Bud Gregory]
War With the Gizmos - Gold Medal s751, 1958 (orig. as "The Strange Invasion")
Four From Planet Five - Gold Medal s937, 1959 (orig. as "Long Ago, Far Away" in the September 1959 *Amazing*)
The Monster From Earth's End - Gold Medal s832, 1959)
Monsters and Such - Avon T345, 1959 (coll. 7 stories)
The Mutant Weapon - Ace D-403, 1959 (bound with his *The Pirates of Zan*, orig. as "Med Service" in the August 1957 *Astounding*) [Med Service]

The Pirates of Zan – Ace D-403, 1959 (bound with his *The Mutant Weapon*; orig. serialized as "The Pirates of Ersatz" in the February-April 1959 *Astounding*)[Med Service]

The Aliens – Berkley G-410, 1960 (coll. 5 stories)

Men Into Space – Berkley G461, 1960 (TV tie-in)

Twists in Time – Avon T389, 1960 (coll. 7 stories)

Creatures of the Abyss – Berkley G-549, 1961 (aka *The Listeners*)

This World is Taboo – Ace D525, 1961 (orig. as "Pariah Planet" in the July 1961 *Amazing*)[Med Service]

The Wailing Asteroid – Avon T483, 1961

Operation Terror – Berkley F694, 1962

Talents, Incorporated – Avon G1120, 1962

Doctor to the Stars – Pyramid F987, 1964 (coll. 3 stories)[Med Service]

The Greks Bring Gifts – Macfadden 50-224, 1964

Invaders of Space – Berkley F1022, 1964

Time Tunnel – Pyramid R1043, 1964 (TV tie-in)

The Other Side of Nowhere – Berkley F918, 1964 (orig. serialized as "Spaceman" in the March-April 1964 *Analog*)

The Duplicators – Ace F-275, 1964 (bound with Philip E. High's *No Truce With Terra*, orig. as "Lord of the Uffts" in the February 1964 *Worlds of Tomorrow*)

Get Off My World! – Belmont B50-676, 1966 (coll. 3 stories)

Space Captain – Ace M-135, 1965 (bound with Philip E. High's *The Mad Metropolis*, orig. serialized as *Killer Ship* in the October-December 1965 *Amazing*)

Tunnel Through Time – Westminster 1966

Checkpoint Lambda – Berkley F1263, 1967 (orig. serialized as *Stopover in Space* in the June-August 1966 *Amazing*)

Miners in the Sky – Avon G1310, 1967

S.O.S. From Three Worlds – Ace G-647, 1967 (coll. 3 stories)[Med Service]

The Space Gypsies – Avon G1318, 1967

The Time Tunnel – Pyramid R1522, 1967 (TV tie-in, not the same as earlier entry)

Timeslip! – Pyramid R1680, 1967 (TV tie-in)

A Murray Leinster Omnibus – Sidgwick Jackson 1968 (UK, reprints *Operation Terror*, *Checkpoint Lambda*, and *Invaders From Space*)

Land of the Giants – Pyramid X1846, 1968 (TV tie-in)
Land of the Giants 2: The Hot Spot – Pyramid 1921, 1969 (TV tie-in)
Land of the Giants 3: Unknown Danger – Pyramid 2105, 1969 (TV tie-in)
The Best of Murray Leinster – ed. Brian Davis, Corgi , 1976 (UK, coll. 10 stories, not connected with the following entry)
The Best of Murray Leinster – ed. John J. Pierce, Ballantine/Del Rey , 1978 (coll. 13 stories)
The Med Series – Ace , 1983 (coll. 5 stories)[Med Service]
First Contacts: The Essential Murray Leinster – ed. Joe Rico, NESFA 1998 (coll. 24 stories)
Med Ship – ed. Eric Flint and Guy Gordon, Baen , 2002 (coll. 8 stories)[Med Service]
Planets of Adventure – ed. Eric Flint and Guy Gordon, Baen , 2003 (coll. 12 stories)
A Logic Named Joe – ed. Eric Flint and Guy Gordon, Baen , 2005 (coll. 6 stories)
The Runaway Skyscraper and Other Tales from the Pulps – Wildside Press 2007 (coll. 8 stories)

Anthology

Great Stories of Science Fiction – Random House 1951

Non-SF

Her Desert Lover – Chelsea House 1925 (romance, as by Louisa Carter Lee)
Scalps – Brewer & Warren 1930 (mystery, aka *Wings of Chance*)
Love and Better: A Love Story – Chelsea House 1931 (romance, as by Louisa Carter Lee)
Murder Will Out – John Hamilton 1932 (mystery, as by Will F. Jenkins)
The Gamblin' Kid – A. L. Burt, 1933; (western, as by Will F. Jenkins)
Mexican Trail – A. L. Burt, 1933 (western, as by Will F. Jenkins)
Sword of Kings – John Long 1933 (adventure)
Fighting Horse Valley – King 1934 (western, as by Will F. Jenkins)
Outlaw Deputy – Harlequin 281, 19** (western)
Outlaw Sheriff – King 1934; The West in Action 1, 1948 (digest-size, western)

Guns Along the Western Trail – The West in Action 2, 1948 (digest-size, western)

Kid Deputy – Alfred H. King 1934; The West in Action 3, 1948 (digest-size, western, as by Will F. Jenkins, orig. serialized in the February-April 1928 *Triple-X Western*)

No Clues – Wright & Brown 1935 (mystery, as by Will F. Jenkins)

Murder in the Family – John Hamilton 1935 (mystery, as by Will F. Jenkins, orig. in the April 1934 *Complete Detective Novels*)

Black Sheep – Julian Messer 1936 (western, as Will F. Jenkins)

Guns for Achin – Wright & Brown, 1936 (western, as Will F. Jenkins, orig. in the November 1936 *Smashing Novels)*

Two-Gun Showdown – The West in Action 4, 1948 (digest-size, western)

Wanted Dead or Alive! – Quarter Books 25, 1949 (orig. serialized in the February-May 1929 *Triple-X Magazine*, aka *Outlaw Guns)*

Texas Gun Slinger – Star Books 1, 195* (digest-size, western, aka *Fighting Horse Valley*)

Outlaw Guns – Star Books 3, 195* (digest-size, western, aka *Wanted Dead or Alive!*)

Texas Gun Law – Quarter Books 23, 195* (digest-size, western, aka *Black Sheep*)

Dallas – Gold Medal 126, 1950 (as by Will F. Jenkins, western, movie tie-in)

Son of the Flying Y – Gold Medal 161, 1951 (western, as by Will F. Jenkins)

Cattle Rustlers – Ward Lock 1952 (western, as by Will F. Jenkins)

The Man Who Feared – Gateway 1942 (mystery, as by Will F. Jenkins); Hangman's House 4, 195* (digest-size, as by Will F. Jenkins)

Notes

1. Including, believe it or not, plutocracy. There was a magazine, titled *The Wizard,* which.featured an ongoing series of stories about one Cash Gorman. If that's not a blatant attempt to combine an MBA with barbarian badness, I don't know what is.
2. I wrote about these two books way back in December of 2004 in *SF Chronicle* #254 under the subtitle "The Deans' List(s).
3. I once jumped out of my treehouse with a toy parachute, but I was never dumb enough to tell anybody about it, much less take pictures.

4. H. L. Mencken and George Jean Nathan. I told you *Smart Set* was important.
5. Groff Conklin was certainly the most important anthologist of the 1950s and ‘60s, assembling forty-one anthos (among other projects) from 1946 until his death in 1968.
6. The antho Conklin speaks of in which neither Jenkins nor Leinster appear was 1954's *Science Fiction Thinking Machines*, published by Vanguard. It's funny; you'd have thought it would have been *The Supernatural Reader* or *Science Fiction Terror Tales*, fantasy and horror not being the author's specialty, but there it is.

❑

Merrily We Roll Along (or, That's Funny... You Don't Look Judith)

> **WONDER**—informed, thoughtful, purposeful wonder—is loose on the Earth again. And this is what "SF" means, what "science fiction" is: not gimmicks and gadgets, monsters and supermen, but trained wonderment—educated and disciplined imagination—a marvelous mirror for Modern Man and the world he is only beginning to make.—from the editor's introduction, *Fifth Annual of The Year's Best SF*, 1960.

JUDITH MERRIL WAS MID-WAY THROUGH her productive career at the time she wrote those words. I suspect that she came to her understanding of what SF was (to her, at least) early on, and I very much doubt she changed her mind about it as she grew older. It's as workable a definition as I've ever seen, especially in a concise fifty words, and she was as qualified to hold an opinion on the subject as anyone else on the SF scene.

I had cause to write about Our Current Subject a few years ago in another place. I was examining two of her early anthologies, ones that had shown her determination to look beyond the limits of genre publication for material, a trait that she would exhibit throughout her career. Here's what I said:

> ...[S]ome of the best anthologists were also some of the best writers. One only need mention Damon Knight, Robert Silverberg, Fred Pohl and August Derleth to make that particular case.
>
> Or you could just say "Judith Merril" and be done with it.

That is as true now as it was when I originally wrote it. What is also true is the fact—unfortunate, perhaps—that Merril is better remembered now as an anthologist than as a writer. This is unfair, however accurate it may be, because much of Merril's writing sits squarely in the top percentile of the field, and almost all of it is elegant and expressive. I'm not alone in this assessment; writing in James Gunn's *The New Encyclopedia of Science Fiction* (Viking 1988), Stephen Goldman wrote, "The sum of Merril's impact on science fiction is far greater than her output in the field." She produced memorable and important work in the genre both as a writer and as an anthologist, and in this issue's installment of Past Masters, we'll be examining both these aspects of her career.[1]

Born January 21, 1923 as Josephine Juliet Grossman—some sources cite her middle name as Judith, which she clearly preferred—Merril was a zealous Zionist at the advanced age of... ten. That's right, ten. When you were ten, did you even know who the Speaker of the House was? I sure as hell didn't. I barely knew that the veep was Lyndon Johnson, and might not have known that if it hadn't been for Earl Doud's First Family comedy albums.

She became disillusioned with it after the USSR signed a treaty with Hitler in '39, but not until after spending most of the preceding decade at Zionist summer camps(!) and reading the *Communist Manifesto*. She met her first husband, Dan Zissman, at—I hope you're sitting down for this one, cowboy—a Trotskyite Fourth of July picnic in Central Park. Gotta love New York. They married in 1940, when she was but 17.

Yup, even for science fiction, Judith Grossman was a weird kid. Of course, our Shared World is rife with weird kids, but she didn't just push the envelope, she shoved it off the cliff.

Zissman was a science fiction fan, and he introduced his new wife to it; she took to her new interest with the same passion with which she once denounced running-dog capitalists. He was drafted in 1942, the same year their daughter, Merril, was born.

Zissman's problem was that couldn't stop being a radical (at least in relation to the officers above him), and that and his record of having attempted to unionize a defense plant got him transferred from a cushy gig at the San Francisco radar school to Pearl Harbor.

Mother and daughter went back to New York and fell in with a bunch of political no-goodniks: the Futurian Society of New York. Yeah, those guys again. That connection, as was the case with any number of other pioneers in the field, changed everything.

Judith Zissman began hanging out with these unsavory characters, most of them radicals like herself ("radical" by WWII standards, that is, what with several of them also being members of the Communist Youth League), folk like Isaac Asimov, Fred Pohl, Damon Knight, James Blish, Donald Wollheim, Cyril Kornbluth, Robert "Doc" Lowndes, Hannes Bok, and Larry Shaw. Pretty serious list of names there, as you may have noticed.

(Face it, the Futurians were just about the most important and influential fan groups in the world, let alone NYC. They would write, edit, illustrate and/or publish an enormous amount of the SF written from the late 1930s until the end of the war. In fact, in one way or another, they would tend to dominate the field well into the 1960s-70s. Anyone who considers him/herself to be conversant with the history of SF in America and who underestimates the significance of this little group of faans to the development of modern speculative fiction is on dangerous conceptual ground. Who's your stfnal daddy? The Futurians, hoss, and make no mistake about it.[2])

Merril wasn't intimidated in the slightest by the seething political morass she found herself in, though. Remember that remarkable ten year-old? A dozen years sure as hell hadn't dimmed her lights. Future agent extraordinaire Virginia Kidd recalled those days in her introduction to *The Best of Judith Merril* (Warner 85058, 1976):

> Judith Merril was a revelation to me. I had never before known a politically conscious female… I had never known a woman who could outthink me as often as she could outtalk me—not always, but often enough so that I could as easily have disliked her as admired her… This is the best of Judith Merril for me: she knew a lot of the answers before most people realized that there might be, ought to be, questions.

All that added up to this: in 1945, Judith Grossman Zissman moved in with Kidd, adopted her daughter's given name as her professional surname, and Judith Merril sprang full-blown from her own brow. Of such uncanny chains of events are our beloved legends often born, *n'cest pas*?

All this hanging out with SF writers/editors/illustrators/faans had its inevitable effect, and Merril plunged over the edge of the precipice and began working as a researcher and ghostwriter for the Scott Meredith

Agency and also writing on her own. Not SF, or fantasy, mind you, but a genre which was at the time one of the most popular and to which almost every one of our Old Favorites contributed at one time or another: the Sports pulps. Under pseudonyms like "Eric Thorstein" and "Ernest Hamilton," she sold a number of yarns to magazines like *Sports Leader*, *Sports Short Stories*, and *Sports Fiction*. Using the same pen-names she also wrote filler material for some of the Western pulps.

Her first sale wasn't science fiction, fantasy, or even football, however, but a mystery, "No Heart for Murder," to Futurian "Doc" Lowndes (she'd workshopped the story through the group) for the July 1945 issue of *Crack Detective Magazine*. A few months later, "The 'Crank' Case" appeared in the same magazine. Both were published under her married name, Judy Zissman. However, although they were her first actual sales, neither was her first publication. In 1939, a story titled "The Golden Fleece" appeared in something called *The Tower* as by Judith Grossman; I have no direct evidence of this, but given her age at the time—sixteen—I suspect it was a high school literary magazine.

None of this really mattered except that it was the beginning of an important career. She didn't stomp on the stfnal Terra until the June 1948 issue of Astounding hit the stands and the SF-reading world was confronted by one of the most moving and chilling stories Campbell would ever publish: "That Only a Mother."

On the assumption that a good percentage of you reading this haven't yet had the, er, pleasure, I won't spoil this disturbing little story for you. I will go so far as to mention that it involves radiation and motherhood. For me, it's more than enough proof that Campbell was a far more able and discerning editor that he's frequently given credit for these days; there's precious little of the problem/solution, smart Terran/dumb alien story he's often blamed for in this one.

The story behind the story is an interesting one, if you're anything like the process-tweak that I am. She ran the story through the Meredith Agency first—in those days, agents were happy to get ten percent of two cents a word—and it was read by Arnold Hano, who was chief reader at the time. He said:

> Scott had received her story, "[That] Only a Mother", and he tossed it to me to see if it was marketable. I read it and went crazy over it. He sent it out to Collier's ... and it bounced back with a weird comment that the editor nev-

er wanted to see another story by this writer… "

As I said in that other, earlier article, Hano's recollection isn't dead-on. In *Better to Have Loved: The Life of Judith Merril* (*Between the Lines* 2002, completed from Merril's notes by her grand-daughter, Emily Pohl-Weary), the *Collier's* rejection is reproduced. The text is clear; the editor who bounced the story was, to say the least, appalled by the subject matter, but concludes by saying that she would "like very much to see more of this author's work."

Whatever his recollections might be, Hano championed the story. When *Collier's* bounced it, he sent it back to Scott Meredith with a note that said (in part), "If you don't get $1,000 for this you ought to quit."

After the war, Arnold Hano went on to become managing editor at Bantam Books (under Ian Ballantine), still fairly new after a 1945 start-up. Bantam wanted to create a mystery line, and Hano immediately suggested Merril. Not content with making her wear the snap-brim Fedora, they asked her to wear their space helmet too, and put her in charge of their SF line.

She did a hell of a job, and within three years had assembled and delivered her very first SF anthology: *Shot in the Dark*, Bantam 751. Her lengthy dedication is dated September, 1949; the book itself is copyright 1950.

Looking at the cover, you'd never know it was science-fiction or fantasy. An exotic woman stares intently at the reader, décolletage visible but discreet, her raven hair combed straight back over her head in a vicious widow's peak. From the lower left, we see a man's hand pointing an automatic pistol directly at her, light glinting off the muzzle. Pretty damned hard-boiled, I'd say, barring the lack of a trench-coat. The only things that give it away are fairly subtle (for 1940s pulp fiction covers, anyhow): a misty, ringed planet behind her in the upper right, a spectral cat floating at her right shoulder, and her decidedly pointed ears.

The text at the top promises "A different kind of mystery thrill!", which must have amused many of the authors within—Heinlein, Sturgeon, Leinster, Asimov, and Tenn among others. Why the odd presentation? Well, as much as Bantam trusted Merril to do a good job, they just weren't sure about this science-fiction thing, so they packaged the book as a mystery, as much as was possible. I have to admit that it's a lovely little thing, colors far more muted than you'd expect from pulp fiction, and the contents are just terrific. I won't list them here (much as I'd like to), but you can check it out at William Contento's *Index to Science Fiction Anthologies and Collections, Combined Edition*, located at http://www.philsp.com/homeville/ISFAC/0start.htm, along with any other anthology or collection you want to dig into.

This first book was well-received (no matter the mixed message the art and blurbs gave the reader), selling out quickly and eventually going through several printings. It would lead directly to invitations to do other, more extensive anthologies.

However, before it did, Doubleday published her first novel, *A Shadow on the Hearth*, also in 1950. One of the first novels to deal with the aftermath of atomic war, it's still one of the best. As with "Only a Mother," it deals with a woman coping with the horrors and dangers of life after a nuclear war, although the wife and mother in the novel is far more adaptive and capable than the mother in the earlier story. She is caught where no post-WWII housewife would have wanted to be—alone with her daughters while her husband desperately tries to get back home from the city.

In the hands of a lesser writer (dare I say a male one?), *Shadow* could have been merely a blatant exercise in ham-handed satire: June Cleaver, in pearls and apron, meets the Fallout Monster and gives it what-for; or, worse, merely a disaster novel concerned only with blasted landscapes and ludicrous stereotypes. Instead, we're given a strong, resolute woman who belies categorization as a weak, indulged suburban hausfrau, tackling not only the perils of radiation and life without amenities, but the horny and determined guy next door. As a story of atomic awareness, it is perhaps dated; as a character study of strength found through adversity, it's still a solid and rewarding read. Thus began the literary career of one of the most important writers, anthologists and critics in the field. Her footprint may not have been huge, but she cast a long and lingering shadow. As Spencer Tracy said of Katherine Hepburn in "Babe," "There ain't much meat on her, but what's there is cherce."

As good as her first novel is, though, her next solo long-form effort was, well, let's just say problematic. *The Tomorrow People* was published in 1960 by Pyramid Books as a paperback original. The story, taken by itself, is fine: Johnny Wendt is disheartened by his experiences on Mars, experiences he can't even talk about, but which involve a fellow spaceman's disappearance on the Red Planet. His girlfriend, Lisa, wants to help him, but is unable to penetrate the psychological wall he's built around himself. Worse, there are pages missing from the ship's log, which creates even more (and not terribly compelling) complications.

There are other characters, including the psychiatrist who's trying to "cure" Johnny while being hopelessly in love with Lisa (as is every other male in the book) and a gaggle of military and political cyphers who all have their own agendas.

For whatever reason, here Merril doesn't seem to be as involved with her characters as elsewhere. There's an overall flatness, the characters are less developed, and there's little to engage the emotions of the reader. That, perhaps, is not the worst of the book's faults, sorry to say.

Judith Merril was many things, most of them admirable and commendable, but she was no scientist. For most of her work, this isn't really a drawback. Her stories deal not so much with technology as with her characters attempts to cope with it, and by and large this was a successful tack for her.

In *The Tomorrow People*, though, she somehow managed to have a helicopter work on the moon. Our moon, the one with no discernable atmosphere. She'd have done as well to write in a glider, frankly, and for many (myself included, which says as much about me as it does the book), this failure to stick to fact makes it difficult to enjoy the story. I mean, you'd expect this sort of thing from, say, Pel Torro, but not the author of "Dead Center." It's much like the Hollywood convention of having a private eye empty a .45 automatic pistol at a criminal only to have the gun click several times as it goes dry; that ain't the way the technology works, and those who are aware of it trip over the silliness and lose interest.

Damon Knight, that most erudite of stfnal critics (as well as fellow Futurian/Hydra), set aside his very real affection for the author and in his collection of reviews and essays, *In Search of Wonder*, published by Advent in 1956 wrote:

> What is objectionable in the book is its lack of any internal discipline, either in the writing or the thinking. Under the crisp surface it is soft and saccharine: wherever you bite it, custard dribbles out.
>
> Is this the "woman's viewpoint"? I don't believe it; I think it is the woman's-magazine viewpoint, from which God preserve us.

After *Shadow* was published, she assembled and produced two hardcover anthologies: *Beyond Human Ken* and *Beyond the Barriers of Space and Time* for Random House in 1952 and '54 respectively. Now, the first of these two powerhouse books was pretty well centered on the genre magazines of the time; only one of the stories, Stephen Vincent Benet's "The Angel Was a Yankee," came from an outsider periodical, namely the October 1940 *McCalls*, of all places. The others were gleaned from the Usual Suspects, except for a single original from Laurence Manning, "Good-Bye, Ilha!".

In *Beyond the Barriers*, however, she would further develop her penchant for looking outside the stfnal box, choosing stories from *Esquire*, *New Yorker*, *Saturday Evening Post*, and a vintage Agatha Christie story, "The Last Séance," from the November 1926 *Ghost Stories*.[3]

As much as I love this hefty pair of hardbacks, Merril's really revolutionary works were to come not long after; before we get to those, we'll take time to consider her own distinct perspective on the rightly-beloved "year's best SF/fantasy" trope.

The first book to pass judgment on the best SF stories of the year was put together by the "team" of Everett F. Bleiler and Thaddeus E. Dikty and was published by Frederick Fell in 1949 under the title *The Best Science Fiction Stories: 1949*. It may seem a bit presumptuous to issue a book of the year's best in the same year it titularly covers, but "1949" refers only to the year the book came out; the stories themselves ran in '48. Bleiler and Dikty would continue their series together until 1954, and Dikty would carry it on for another two years alone.

In the meantime, Donald Wollheim would create *Prize Science Fiction* for McBride in 1953 as the first in a series of year's best, but a disagreement with the publisher cancelled that project at the very beginning.

Merril would do her first annual retrospective in 1957 with *SF:57 The Year's Best Science Fiction* for Gnome Press. Like the B&D book, it covered not the year in the title but the one previous, and unlike the other series (which stayed pretty close to home, stfnally) it presented the reader with a number of stories from non-genre publications like *The London Observer*, *Playboy*, *Esquire* and *Harper's*. Again, we see not just a willingness on the part of the editor to look in the corners, but a determination to do so and to do so well.

Merril poured herself into this endeavor with enthusiasm and skill. Her association with the Futurians (and later, the Hydras) and her marriage to Frederik Pohl (from 1949-53) would provide her not only with a broad knowledge of literature but contacts throughout the publishing world. This would make it even easier to seek out the beyond-the-pale stories and other material she would present to the readers in the dozen volumes of her year's best series, and give her the insight and courage to offer such off-the-wall choices as cartoons (by Fleischer, Walt Kelly and others), articles, and verse. No one else would have the balls to spread their nets that far until Harry Harrison and Brian Aldiss inaugurated their *Best SF* series in 1967.

You wouldn't think this was so much of a much until you realize that Merril's visionary concept of what constituted "Best" indicated a perspective of science fiction far in advance of practically every other anthologist at the time, by a good ten years at least. She demonstrated this perspective in other ways as well: she was instrumental in creating the seminal Milford Conferences with fellow authors/critics Damon Knight and James Blish in 1956, which would lead directly to the founding of the Science Fiction and Fantasy Writers of America in 1965. Her image of speculative literature as a vital and essential part of all fiction led her to create a body of anthological work that transcends the Gernsbackian roots of the genre and anticipates the revolution of the mid- to late sixties. Over the years the series was active, you can see the contents moving gradually—if doggedly—away from the merely traditional and towards the decidedly experimental. This would culminate in two very remarkable books.

The first was the final volume of her year's best series, titled simply *SF12*. Thirty individual pieces (the other volumes ran from eleven to thirty-six), half of them from Outsider sources, including four poems from then-Fug Tuli Kupferberg and another verse from Tom Disch. From within the field, she chose stories by Kit Reed, Ballard, Bob Shaw, Aldiss, Lafferty, and Delany (as well as others), but the prizes here are the names that I'd wager the average SF reader knew only by reputation, if at all: Tommaso Landolfi, Donald Barthelme, John Updike, William Burroughs(!), Henri Michaux, and Gunther Grass, author of *The Tin Drum*. What on earth must have gone through the heads of teen-age Boomers as they read their way through this madness? I know I was seriously challenged by the contents of this hefty book at the age of sixteen, but—and here's the vital factor at work—I trusted Judith Merril to hand me readable and engaging work.

Oh, believe me, I didn't know what to make of Grass, or Barthelme, and I'd only just learned of Burroughs and hadn't yet read any, but how cool was it that she included poetry by a member of the Fugs?[4] At the time, I was the only person I knew who'd ever even heard of the Fugs, let alone listened to any of their albums. And here was this woman, this Judith Merril, this old adult person (she was forty-five at the time. "Old.") who not only knew about them but wanted to publish poetry by one of them. Yow.

I'm not joking. This book was, as I look back on it now, a turning point for me. It prepared me for new literature the way that listening to John Cage and Karlheinz Stockhausen prepared me for avant-garde music. Had it not been for this book, and her next one, I would never have been able to fathom *Dangerous Visions* and its follow-up a few years later. I doubt that I'm alone in this regard, either, as I still sell as many copies of *SF12* as I can get my hands on, mostly to people my age or a bit older, eager to relive the experience or to introduce it to their kids/grandkids.

As important as *SF12* was, though, it pales beside her next anthology, the hideously titled *England Swings SF*.[5]

In the year this anthology was published, John Brunner won the Hugo for his mosaic novel *Stand on Zanzibar*; Robert Silverberg won for his novella "Nightwings"; Harlan Ellison for the short story "The Beast that Shouted Love at the Heart of the World"; and Poul Anderson walked away with the rocket for his novelette "The Sharing of the Flesh."

Things were changing. Only a few years before, Heinlein had won for *The Moon is a Harsh Mistress*, with Jack Vance and Larry Niven taking the short fiction awards. Both writers and readers were becoming more erudite, eschewing "space opera" and looking for more mature and complex stories. Ellison's ground-breaking anthology, *Dangerous Visions*, lit the way for a revolution of sorts and the spotlight was on experimentation in both concepts and techniques. To many, it was a rude and objectionable intrusion into their comfortable world of time machines, robots and spaceships, and there was an enormous amount of ink spilled both in decrying and defending what quickly became known as the New Wave. Where did it come from, this wholesale transformation of genre from pulp to sophistication?

Good question.[6] The Milford Conferences, organized as I said before by Knight, Blish and Merril, certainly pre-dated and foreshadowed the mid-60s madness, but in its own way the work that resulted was fairly conservative—at least in relation to what would be done a few years later in England.

The history of the UK magazine *New Worlds* deserves far more space than I'm able to give it here, but I'll hit a few high spots. It was begun in 1946 as the continuation of a pre-WWII fanzine edited by John Carnell, who remained at the helm until 1964 when Michael Moorcock took over. Carnell was certainly no slouch as an editor (his anthology series, *New Writings in SF* lasted for twenty-one volumes under his guidance and showcased many new writers), but it was Moorcock who twisted the beast's tail and let it fly.

New Worlds spearheaded what would soon become known as the New Wave,[7] and fostered the early careers of many of the "movement"'s stars: Josephine Saxton, J. G. Ballard, Thomas Disch, Keith Roberts, Charles Platt, Chris Priest and Brian Aldiss were only a few of the authors who saw key work published there. Harlan Ellison's Nebula-winning "A Boy and His Dog" saw its first publication in *New Worlds*.

Merril, who was living in London at the time, was very impressed by what she read there and in a few other UK magazines, and she was determined to make the best of it available to US readers. Thus was born one of the most important anthologies of the 1960s, and one which would confound, frustrate and even infuriate more traditional SF fans and pros.

England Swings SF, for all the cheesiness of the title, was a vital and necessary exploration of what science fiction could be if authors were left unfettered to write what and as they wanted. Yes, much of the experimentation was influenced by non-genre writers from much earlier in the century, but most of those writers were largely unknown at the time to all but academic readers. I'm not going to spend a lot of time defending it—Ghu knows there was a lot of very bad writing issued as "New Wave"—but as an evolutionary step in the development of science fiction as literature, it was absolutely crucial.

So, what of the book? It is, in a word, brilliant. Forget the arguments in the fanzines and prozines of the day, ignore the pronouncements the pundits issued vilifying their Opponents, and never mind the knee-jerk cries of "Blasphemy!" heard from the Old Guard. Here is the only thing that matters: story. Story, plain and simple. Or, in the case of much of the contents of this book, rich and complex.

See, it doesn't matter how many typographic tricks or oddball formats you use, if you don't have much of anything to say. If you don't engage the readers' emotions and intellect, you can use all the fonts and page designs you want and the reader won't get past page three. Catch the reader up in the web of your story, though, and they'll be willing to forgive anything unusual, especially if it enhances their experience.

Merril, writer/editor/critic that she was, knew this, and she skimmed the cream for *England Swings SF*. Don't underestimate this substantial little book, you're going to be challenged even today by many of the stories herein. That speaks to the value of the work, and all I can say is that you'll be rewarded for the effort.

I'm going to drop any pretense at objectivity at this point and tell you my initial reaction to one of the stories, specifically Ballard's "The Assassination of John Fitzgerald Kennedy Considered as a Downhill Motor Race."[8]

I hated it. I despised it, I railed against it and I hocked metaphorical lugies at it and its author. On those occasions when I spoke of the New Wave to others, this was the story I pointed to as exemplar of how wrong-headed the "movement" was.

But… it haunted me. It provoked me, yeah, and it pissed me off (for me, the Kennedy assassination was as sacred as the Crucifixion—and I wasn't alone), but I couldn't get it out of my head. I re-read it. Then I re-read it again. It still angered me, but I was beginning to understand that it was supposed to. This wasn't some English snob snorting derisively at my dead president, it was an intellectual examination of the events that occurred in Dallas and the people involved. The very intellectualism of it was awash in emotion, and it carried me along like a rip-tide. It is an inspired and virtuoso performance, one I still find painful to observe, for all that I now recognize that it must be read over and over to get its full impact.

Another striking story is Pamela Zoline's "The Heat Death of the Universe," about which I have written elsewhere; I can do worse, I suppose, than to quote myself:

> Its format is experimental, a sort of by-the-numbers timeline of a woman going mad. Little by little, Zoline deftly shows us piece by piece how entropy is realized directly and specifically in the life of one Sarah Boyle. Although I recall a number of faans and pros alike decrying this story (and others like it) as unreadable and even as "anti-literature" (in the sense of matter/anti-matter), the proof of any pudding is how it tastes after 40 years in the fridge, and to me this one is still pretty yummy.

The constraints of a deadline prevent me from going into further detail of this fascinating book, but it is readily available online. If you're curious, drop the few bucks the Ace paperback will set you back and devote some time and thought to it.

Although Merril hung with both Futurians and Hydras, and even married one or two, she didn't choose to collaborate with any of them except Fred Pohl (one story, "Big Man With the Girls" in the March, 1953 *Future* as by James McCreigh) and Cyril Kornbluth,[9] with whom she wrote two novels, *Gunner Cade* (1952) and *Outpost Mars* (also 1952), and the story "Sea Change," all as by Cyril Judd.

Both novels are good but not outstanding; the reason for that may be the simple fact that Kornbluth had not yet written a novel on his own and wouldn't until he wrote *Takeoff* (also 1952).[10] Merril had, but only the one. I suspect that they perhaps hadn't gotten their long-form chops yet. It could also be that Merril just plain didn't work well with others, as I'm unaware of any other confirmed collabs. I can also readily imagine potential ego-clashes between two equally talented—and self-confident—authors.

As you look over the bibliography below, don't be fooled by the low numbers. Judith Merril was no Murray Leinster as far as quantity is concerned, but she was just as skilled a story-teller and, from a purely literary standpoint, more so. I say this as a long-time Leinster fan, too. It's all about story, y'all, and if Leinster had his inventiveness, Merril was eat up with erudition. Ain't nothing but a thing.

Merril moved to Canada for political reasons in 1968, telling Robert Fulford (editor of *Saturday Night*, a Canadian magazine):

My feeling was that in Canada I could at least offer some usefulness or assistance to some of the guys who had come [to avoid the draft]—who didn't have the choices I had...

This began yet another phase of her remarkable career, one which echoed her life-long love of books and learning, and to which she devoted not only an enormous amount of time, but her personal holdings as well.

In 1970, she donated her extensive SF/fantasy collection to the Toronto Public Library to create the Merril Collection of Science Fiction, Speculation and Fantasy, known until 1990 as the "Spaced Out Library." Why the change? I asked Collection Head Lorna Toolis:

> The name was changed in 1990 to honour Judith, over her strenuous objections. The Friends [of the Merril Collection] were also acting upon advice from the Chairman of the Library Board, who gently told them that the Library Board was finding it difficult to get funding from City Council for the Spaced Out Library because the '60s were long gone, and cute wasn't traveling well.

Subsequent donations from others has built up a reference collection of more than 70,000 books (including a complete set of Arkham House) and 25,000 magazines. Altogether, there are 1700 graphic novels, 6000 non-fiction books about SF/fantasy, and 500 gaming-related material. The rest are novels and anthologies.

Sort of makes what you and I have on our shelves pretty limited, right? Never fear, though; if you find yourself in Toronto, you can make use of the Merril Collection for your masters thesis or just a few hours' reading. The books no longer circulate, but it's worth the trip just to fondle Leah Bodine Drake's *A Hornbook for Witches* (Arkham 1950), of which there are only a few hundred copies. I'm not sure I'd ever leave the place once I got in.

Looking back at what I've written, I realize that there's much left out. Can't help that, really, as I have neither time nor space for the book-length examination that Merril deserves. Back up there near the beginning I mentioned the autobiographical book that Emily Pohl-Weary assembled from Merril's notes, but as valuable as that volume is, there are flaws in it. Don't blame grand-daughter Pohl-Weary for that, as I suspect that the notes left behind by Merril were as casually slap-dash as those for her reviews for *F&SF*.

Judith Merril was named SFWA's Author Emeritus for 1997, and although I attended the Nebula Awards that year in Kansas City, Merril was unable to be there due to illness. I had been looking forward to meeting her and telling her how much I enjoyed her work, both as fictioneer and anthologist, and I regret that I was never able to do so.

She passed on September 12, 1997, leaving behind a legacy perhaps less broad than others', but as deep as anyone's.

(As is always the case, the following bibliography is as complete as I can reasonably make it given time and resources. There is much missing in the Non-Fiction/Criticism section, especially that material published in Japan; that material is available elsewhere on the Web.)

A Bibliography of Judith Merril

Novels

Shadow on the Hearth – Doubleday, 1950

The Tomorrow People – Pyramid G502, 1960

Gunner Cade – (with C. M. Kornbluth, as by Cyril Judd, originally serialized in the March-May 1952 *Astounding*) Simon & Schuster, 1952; Ace Double D-227, 1958 (bound with Crisis in 2140 by Piper and McGuire)

Outpost Mars – (with C. M. Kornbluth, as by Cyril Judd, originally serialized as "Mars Child" in the May-July 1951 *Galaxy*) Abelard, New York, 1952; Dell 760, 1953; Beacon 312, 1961 (revised, as *Sin in Space*)

Short Story Collections and Novellas

Out of Bounds – Pyramid G-499, 1960

Daughters of Earth – Gollancz 1968; Dell 01705, 1970

Survival Ship – Kakabeka, 1974

The Best of Judith Merril – Warner, 1976

Daughters of Earth and Other Stories – McClelland & Stewart, 1985

Short Stories

"The Golden Fleece" – The Tower, 1939; reprinted in *Bakka Magazine* #6, 1977 (as by Judith Grossman)

"No Heart for Murder" – July 1945 *Crack Detective Stories* (as by Judy Zissman)
"The 'Crank' Case" – January 1946 *Crack Detective Stories* (as by Judy Zissman)
"Horsethief Hero" – December 1947 *Blue Ribbon Western* (article, as by Judy Zissman)
"Five Men Don't Make a Team" – Winter 1947 *Big Book Sports* (as by Ernest Hamilton)
"Pass for Arabella" – December 1947 *Double Action Western* (as by Ernest Hamilton)
"Strike 'im Out" – December 1947 *Western Action* (as by Eric Thorstein)
"Section Gang" – January 1948 *Complete Cowboy* (as by Ernest Hamilton)
"That Only a Mother" – June 1948 *Astounding*
"Squaw Fever" – January 1948 *Blue Ribbon Western* (as by Eric Thorstein)
"Dry Dust" – February 1948 *Double Action Western* (as by Eric Thorstein)
"Goldplated Greenhorns" – February 1948 *Double Action Western* (as by Ernest Hamilton)
"Five Men and Fate" – March 1948 *Sports Short Stories* (as by Ernest Hamilton)
"Golfer's Girl" – *Toronto Star Weekly*, 1949
"Death is the Penalty" – January 1949 *Astounding*
"Outlaw, Ride for Me!" – January 1950 *Real Western Romances* (as by Eric Thorstein)
"Barrier of Dread" – July/August 1950 *Future*
"Survival Ship" – January 1951 *Worlds Beyond*
"A Woman's Work is Never Done!" – March 1951 *Future*
"Mars Child" – serial, May-July 1951 *Galaxy*
"Gunner Cade" – serial, March-May 1952 *Astounding* (with C. M. Kornbluth, as by Cyril Judd)
"Whoever you Are" – December 1952 *Startling*
"Hero's Way" – November 1952 *Space*
"A Little Knowledge" – February 1953 *Science Fiction Quarterly*
"Big Man With The Girls" – March 1953 *Future* (with Frederik Pohl, as by James McCreigh)

"Sea Change" – March 1953 *Dynamic Science Fiction* (with C. M. Kornbluth, as by Cyril Judd)
"So Proudly We Hail" – in *Star SF Stories*, ed. Frederik Pohl, Ballantine 16, 1953
"Daughters of Earth" – in *The Petrified Planet*, ed. John Ciardi, Twayne, 1953
"Stormy Weather" – Summer 1954 *Startling*
"Rain Check" – May 1954 *Science Fiction Adventures*
"Peeping Tom" – Spring 1954 *Startling Stories*
"Connection Completed" – November 1954 *Universe*
"Dead Center" – November 1954 *F&SF*
"Project Nursemaid" – October 1955 *F&SF*
"Pioneer Stock" – January 1955 *Fantastic Universe*
"Exile from Space" – November 1956 *Fantastic Universe*
"Homecalling" – November 1956 *Science Fiction Stories*
"The Lady was a Tramp" – March 1957 *Venture* (as by Rose Sharon)
"Woman of the World" – January 1957 *Venture* (as by Rose Sharon)
"Wish Upon a Star" – December 1958 *F&SF*
"Death Cannot Wither" – February 1959 *F&SF* (with Algis S. Budrys?)
"The Deep Down Dragon" – August 1961 *Galaxy*
"One Death to a Customer" – June 1961 *Saint Mystery Magazine*
"Shrine of Temptation" – April 1962 *Fantastic*
"Muted Hunger" – October 1963 *Saint Mystery Magazine*
"The Lonely" – October 1963 *Worlds of Tomorrow*
"One Does Not (Have to) Equal Empty" – January 1967 *New Worlds*
"In the Land of Unblind" – October 1974 *F&SF*

Anthologies (Edited by Merril)

Shot in the Dark – Bantam 751, 1950.
Beyond Human Ken – Random House 1952; Bantam P56, 1954 (edited, as *Selections From Beyond Human Ken*)
Beyond the Barriers of Space and Time – Random House 1954
Human? – Lion 205, 1954
Galaxy of Ghouls – Lion Library LL25, 1955; Pyramid G-397, 1959 (as *Off the Beaten Orbit*)
SF: The Year's Greatest Science Fiction and Fantasy – Gnome 1956; Dell B103, 1956

SF:'57: The Year's Greatest Science Fiction and Fantasy – Gnome 1957; Dell B110, 1957 (as *SF: The Year's Greatest Science-Fiction and Fantasy, Second Annual Volume*)
SF:'58: The Year's Greatest Science Fiction and Fantasy – Gnome 1958; Dell B119, 1958 (as *SF: The Year's Greatest Science-Fiction and Fantasy, Third Annual Volume*)
SF:'59: The Year's Greatest Science Fiction and Fantasy (Gnome 1959; Dell B129, 1959 (as *SF: The Year's Greatest Science-Fiction and Fantasy, Fourth Annual Volume*)
Fifth Annual of the Year's Best S-F – Simon & Schuster 1960; Dell F118, 1961 (as *The Year's Best S-F, Fifth Annual Edition*)
Sixth Annual of the Year's Best S-F – Simon & Schuster 1961; Dell 9772, 1962 (as *6th Annual Edition, The Year's Best S-F*)
Seventh Annual of the Year's Best S-F – Simon & Schuster 1962; Dell 9773, 1963 (as *7th Annual Edition, The Year's Best S-F*)
Eighth Annual of the Year's Best S-F – Simon & Schuster 1963; Dell 9774, 1964 (as *8th Annual Edition, The Year's Best S-F*)
Ninth Annual of the Year's Best S-F – Simon & Schuster 1964; Dell 9775, 1965 (as *9th Annual Edition, The Year's Best S-F*)
Tenth Annual of the Year's Best S-F – Delacorte 1965; Dell 8611, 1966 (as *10th Annual Edition, The Year's Best S-F*)
Eleventh Annual of the Year's Best S-F – Delacorte 1966; Dell 2241, 1967(as *11th Annual Edition, The Year's Best S-F*)
SF: The Best of the Best – Delacorte 1967
SF12 – Delacorte, Aug '68; Dell 7815 1969
England Swings SF – Doubleday 1968; Ace 20670, 1968
Tesseracts – Press Porcepic 1985.

Non-Fiction/Criticism

Merril supplied book reviews for *F&SF* from March, 1965 until February, 1969; these were frequently turned in on whatever scraps of paper she had at hand rather than typed.

She also wrote a two-part critical piece titled "What Do You Mean, Science? Fiction?" for the journal of the Science Fiction Conference in the Modern Language Association, Extrapolation, edited by Thomas Clareson. It is still used in academic SF courses by many colleges and universities.

In addition, she wrote introductions and headnotes for her own books, as well as intros for others.

"Mars – New World Waiting" – August 1951 *Marvel Science Fiction*
"The Hydra Club" – November, 1951 *Marvel Science Fiction*
"Theodore Sturgeon" – September 1962 *F&SF*
"Japan: Hai!" – in *OSFIC* #24, 1970.
"Science: Myth Tomorrow, Magic Yesterday" – February 1972 *Issues & Events*
"Basil Tomatoes a la Ipsy Wipsy" – in *Cooking Out Of This World*, ed. Anne McCaffrey, Ballantine 1973
"The Three Futures of Eve" – September 11, 1976 *The Canadian*
"Close Encounters of a Monstrous Kind" – May 6, 1978 *Weekend Magazine*
"Beverly Glen Copeland" – *Canadian Women's Studies*, 1978.
"Questions Unasked, Issues Unaddressed" – *Perspectives On Natural Resources – Symposium II*, ed. Page, Sir Sandford Fleming College, 1979.
"The Future of Happiness" – January 1979 *Chatelaine*
"Jamaica: A View from the Beach" – April 1981 *Departures*
"The Crazies are Dying" – September 25, 1986 *NOW*
"Public Disservice" – *Quill and Quire*, 1994.
"Message to Some Martians" – *Visions of Mars*, CD Rom, Virtual Reality Laboratories, Inc., 1994
Better to Have Loved: The Life of Judith Merril – comp. by Emily Pohl-Weary, *Between the Lines* 2002

Poetry (1973-85)

"Auction Pit" – in *Survival Ship*, Kakabeka, 1974
"In the Land of Unblind" – *F&SF*, 1974
"Space is Sparse" – *Daughters of Earth and Other Stories*, McClelland & Stewart, 1985
"Woomers" – Unpublished; written for a poetry reading at Harbourfront Benefit for Pages Bookstore in 1985.

Notes

1. Well, I mean I will. You can look over my shoulder if you want, just don't chew so damn loud. And quit humming.
2. There's plenty of ink out there about this fascinating group, but in my own decidedly unhumble opinion the two best references are Frederik Pohl's *The Way the Future Was* (Del Rey 1978) and Damon Knight's *The Futurians* (John Day 1977). Copies are available online for cheap enough that you can satisfy your curiosity without having to forfeit your daily latté.

3. I'll say little more of these two wonderful (and full-of-wonder) books, as I covered them pretty thoroughly several years ago in a column subtitled "Two Steps Beyond" published in the Fall, 2006 *SFWA Bulletin*. Back issues are available from the SFWA website.
4. Haven't you Googled 'em yet, youngster? Do so. While you're at it, check out Frank Zappa and the Holy Modal Rounders, too. Primus ain't got nothing on those guys.
5. Not her choice, as I understand it. Put the blame on Larry Ashmeade at Doubleday, who wanted to capitalize on the popularity of the Roger Miller hit. Bleah.
6. As if I'd ask a dumb one.
7. Merril is credited with coining the term. I can't say for certain that she did, but I've found no evidence that anyone else used it prior to her in referring to the revolutionary fiction it came to describe.
8. I trust I'm not stealing Ballard's thunder by noting that his primary influence—aside from the assassination itself—was Alfred Jarry's "The Crucifixion Considered as an Uphill Bicycle Race". Jarry was influential in other areas as well, vis. Pere Ubu, the late '70s experimental band formed by David Thomas who took the name from Jarry's play, *Ubu Roi*.
9. See "Cyril With an M (or I'm As Kornbluth as Kansas in August)" a couple of issues ago.
10. Clearly Kornbluth was pretty busy in 1952, wouldn't you say?

❑

In a Klass By Himself (or, Tops On a Scale of One to Tenn)

I NEVER MET PHIL KLASS FACE-TO-FACE, which (it goes without saying) means I never met his alter ego, William Tenn. Unless you define "meet" as "encounter", in which case I met him during the Golden Age of SF: i.e., when I was about ten years old.

I don't recall which specific Tenn story was my first, but it may very well have been either his very first story, "Alexander the Bait" (which I would have read in Groff Conklin's *Omnibus of Science Fiction*, Crown 1952) or "Child's Play", his second story, reprinted by Conklin in *A Treasury of Science Fiction*, published by Crown four years earlier.

Not that it matters, really, since I was an ardent fan of William Tenn from whenever I first ran across him. I recall clearly the plans I had for my weekly pay when I was sixteen and delivering papers in the hills around Roanoke. I had a long list of albums (Mothers of Invention, Electric Prunes, Yardbirds and other soft-rock hits) and books I wanted to buy, and among them was the lovely little matched six-volume set of William Tenn stories that Ballantine brought out in 1968. I had to get them one at a time, as they came out, but I was proud of that little row of books and I showed them off to my other SF-reading friends.

Those original copies were lost in one move or another, but I've subsequently acquired another set, all in fine condition, and I *still* show them off to people, given the slightest encouragement. It doesn't bother me in the least that two of them—*Of All Possible Worlds* and *The Human Angle*—weren't first editions in that set, since I've also managed to track down perfectly nice copies of those originals as well; that the other four are, in fact, original publications is just icing on an already tasty cake.

Phil Klass (not to be mistaken, of course, for the UFO-debunker of the same name) didn't leave an extensive *oeuvre*, but what's there is, in the words of Spencer Tracy, "cherce". He wasn't a particularly poetic writer, although he came close from time to time, nor did he show the elegance of prose that Cordwainer Smith or Alfred Bester so often gave their readers.

What he had, and had by the bagful, was humanity. Oh, don't get me wrong, there's plenty of the Marx Brothers in his stuff, but just as often there's more than a hint of Charlie Chaplin. Klass could make you laugh out loud, but there was always an undercurrent of compassion in his writing that made you engage with his characters all that much more.

This is more important than you might think, and far more difficult than almost anyone understands. Humor depends on a number of things in able to work. In order for it to work, and to work well, they *all* have to be kept in the air at once. Timing, delivery, concept, build-up, gag: when one of these falls flat, they all fall flat, and nobody but another humorist can say that the others might still have come off. *Nothing* is less funny than something which is supposed to be hilarious—and isn't.

Phil Klass understood this at his core, and although his stories might not be Shecky Hackett/stand-up comic funny, they're still funny as hell. Stories, I should point out, aren't the correct vehicle for stand-up humor—the few times it's been tried by various writers, it's fallen even flatter than a CD-ROM in a punch-press—but they're a perfect vehicle for a funny situation, and here is where Klass shone.

In one of his first "2,000 Year-Old Man" routines with Carl Reiner, Mel Brooks defined humor thusly: "Tragedy is when I have a hangnail, comedy is when you step into an open manhole and die." This is a little black-and-white, but it's accurate enough as a general rule of thumb for us to work with. Let's face it—"America's Funniest Home Videos" wouldn't have stayed on the air for twenty years had it not been for this particular rule, nor would the Three Stooges still set newer and newer generations of kids howling in front of their after-school TVs.[1]

(Well, okay, we could debate that for a long time without actually coming to anything resembling a consensus about anything except that Mel Brooks and Carl Reiner are as funny as two adult human males can get.)

But comedy isn't the same thing as humor. Comedy is of-the-moment, here and now, and fast as a fat guy in a top hat and tails slipping on the ice. Humor (especially satire, Klass's forté) is extended, lingering, sustained; humor is the funny story, comedy is the punchline.

Phil Klass was all about the sustained humor of satire. Never satisfied with mere punchlines, he took us through the whole process of funny, spinning out his yarns bit by bit, injecting cross-cultural humor as required by his stories' concepts. Klass was Jewish, so naturally the humor in his work is predominately so. However, it isn't exclusively Jewish—Klass is just as adept at finding universal ways to make us laugh as he is at the ethnic stuff. But his cultural roots (as well as influences as widely diverse as Bernard Malamud and Sholem Asch) are evident even in those stories which occur far enough into the future that (let's face it) there would be very few people speaking in traditional Yiddish cadences.

Doesn't matter. Science Fiction isn't ever about the future, even when it's set there; it's about the Now, and part of the effectiveness of his humor was the juxtaposition of, say, the archetypal equivalent of a Brooklyn candy store owner in, say, a colony on Venus. Other writers tried to use this trope and failed at it. Klass could make it work because that's the way it worked for him. He knew funny, and was one of the lucky handful of writers who could actually get it right on paper.

Klass was no mere Borscht Belt *tummeler*, though, nor was he a one-trick pony, however good that trick might be. Satire is easy to find in SF, especially in the first decade or so of both *Galaxy* and *F&SF*: Kornbluth, Kuttner, Goulart, Brown, and Sheckley were only a few of the authors whose wry takes on subjects like television, psychiatry and advertising kept H. L. Gold and Boucher & McComas supplied throughout the 1950s and '60s.

But Phil Klass offered more than just lampoons of popular cultural icons, he gave the reader a sense of humanity, without which satire is mostly just, well, punchlines. He honestly liked people, and even though he was more than conscious of their foibles and frailties, he firmly believed in their kindnesses and empathy.

In one of my personal favorites, "On Venus, Have We Got a Rabbi" (written for *Wandering Stars*, ed. Jack Dann, Harper 1974), Klass (as Tenn, of course—when I speak of one, I also mean the other) tells of a problem of Talmudic proportions: aliens want to become Jews.

So what? you might ask. Well, leaving aside the fact that Jews don't proselytize, there are traditional aspects of Judaism—mostly what makes a Jew a Jew and what doesn't—that have been part of history since the very first yarmulke appeared on the very first *kopf*. How can an alien, a Bulba at that, be a Jew?

Why not? you might again ask. There's a reason, hence the conflict that must be resolved here: Bulbas are not just aliens—the blue people from Aldeberan are aliens, and they're Jews—they're *inhuman* aliens. They're described in the story as "...brown pillows, all wrinkled and twisted, with some big gray spots on this side and on that side, and out of each gray spot is growing a short gray tentacle."

The problem here isn't that they're different, it's that they're *too* different. "A Jew can be blue," the protagonist tells his son, "...and a Jew can be tall or short. He can even be deaf from birth like those Jews from Canopus, Sirius, wherever they come from. But a Jew has to have arms and legs. He has to have a face with eyes, a nose, a mouth. It seems to me that's not too much to ask."

Milchik, the narrator, is not the only one who is opposed to the Bulbas calling themselves Jews, this is a controversy that threatens the whole colony's well-being.

The solution is both properly Talmudic and properly science-fictional, and in resolving the conflict Klass shows us that even brown, cockroachy pillows can be endowed with a Human-ness that transcends their non-humanity. It's a warm, funny, compassionate story that leaves the reader with a feeling of deep satisfaction. That it was written a good seven years after his last published story is testament to Klass's aptitude, and a refutation of the old saw that those who can't, teach.

Didn't I mention that before? Phil Klass had a day job, from 1966 on, teaching writing and matters stfnal at Penn State. I can only imagine what it must have been like to sit in his classroom; his likable personality and communication skills must surely have enabled him to reach and influence his students over the years.

A day job was necessary, since Klass's period of greatest output was during a time when many SF/fantasy magazines were disappearing, some almost overnight. He didn't write the long form, at least not much. His only two books-published-as-novels were *A Lamp for Medusa* (originally "Medusa Was a Lady!") and *Of Men and Monsters* (originally "The Men in the Walls"), and both stories were actually novellas, not full-length novels.

In James Gunn's *The New Encyclopedia of Science Fiction* (Viking 1988), Brian Stableford wrote this about Klass:

> Tenn's strength as a writer lies in the sensitivity that allowed him to identify and dramatize the pathetic as well as the comic aspects of his ironic situations, giving stories such as "Down Among the Dead Men" (1954) and "Time Waits for Winthrop" (1957) an unusually poignant dimension.

I can't argue with that. "Poignant" is quite a well-chosen word here, in fact, especially in regard to the first story Stableford mentions, an atypically nasty little tale about a prolonged war and the technology that enables those fighting it to constantly repair and restore wounded—dead!—soldiers and return them to the fight. No candy-store ethnic humor here, no gags, no laughs; there's satire a-plenty, but it's dark, grim, bitter. It's a quietly brilliant story, told with subtlety and elegance. I wish Klass had written more like it, if only to silence those who would dismiss him as just another gagster.[2] Damon Knight had some uncharacteristically nice things to say about an earlier story in his review of Robert Heinlein's[3] one-off anthology, *Tomorrow, the Stars* in his collection of criticism, *In Search of Wonder* (Advent: Publishers 1957), a story which doesn't even appear in the book he's reviewing:

> ..."Liberation of Earth (*Future*, May 1953)—the funniest story [Tenn's] ever written, and about as equivocal as a punch in the solar plexus...If I'm right, it merely proves what needs no proof, that Tenn is another artist who won't stop till he's had the last word.

This truly funny story wasn't reprinted until 1968, when it was included in the Ballantine collection *Of All Possible Worlds*, but has been reprinted several times since. I urge you to seek it out.

"Down Among the Dead Men" and "Time Waits for Winthrop" came from H. L. Gold's *Galaxy*, the magazine where Klass found his greatest editorial welcome and most appreciative readership. From his first sale to Gold in 1951 until his last (to Frederik Pohl) in 1963, fully half of his output appeared in what was at the time the most important challenger to Campbell's *Astounding.*

Klass and *Galaxy* were matched perfectly. Satire was the magazine's strong suit, as I've said, and Klass's skill at sending up almost anything without betraying even a hint of contempt made him a favorite. *Galaxy* also gave him a platform for his more serious work, without which he might have never been able to stretch his wings as he did with "...Dead Men".

In all, Phil Klass published sixty-three stories from his first in 1946 to his last in 1993, a double handful of articles, and edited two anthologies, one of them in collaboration with Donald E. Westlake. I wrote an article about his SF anthology[4], and when it appeared, he actually called to thank me. He was so certain that he'd been completely forgotten—when Mary answered the phone, he introduced himself somewhat forlornly and was both surprised and moved when she immediately responded that she knew his work and had read his stories.[5]

We talked for more than an hour, about the book and his own stories, his career, other writers[6] and just Stuff. I found him to be bright, personable, funny as hell, and grateful that I'd thought his book was worth writing about. It led to other conversations, phone and e-mail, and a promise that he would approach the editor of the *SFWA Bulletin* about the possibility of writing a series of articles about his career.

Alas, his health intervened, and it never came to pass. However, his work speaks loudly and clearly on its own, appealing to any reader who is searching for wit and wisdom, for both pathos and joy, for meaning. I heartily recommend the three volumes of his fiction and non-fiction published by NESFA and listed at the end of the bibliography below. There are damned few authors whose (nearly) complete works can be had in three hefty volumes, and even fewer whose (nearly) complete works contain almost no filler. I can think of little else more worth your time and money.

(As usual, this biblio represents initial appearances only, and is almost certainly incomplete. By all means, if you have additions or corrections, feel free to let me know. Seriously. I want this to be as accurate as possible.)

A Bibliography of William Tenn

Short Stories

"Sonnet" – ? 1935 *Cargoes* (poem)
"Anecdote" – ? 1939 *Apprentice* (vignette)
"The Apotheosis of John Chillicothe" – ? 1939 *Apprentice*
"Eleven P.M." – ? 1939 *Apprentice* (vignette)
"Incident Gourmandien" – ? 1939 *Apprentice* (vignette)
"Alexander the Bait" – May 1946 *Astounding*
"Child's Play" – March 1947 *Astounding*
"Mistress Sary" – May 1947 *Weird Tales*
"Errand Boy" – June 1947 *Astounding*
"Me, Myself, and I" – Winter 1947 *Planet Stories* (as by Kenneth Putnam)
"The House Dutiful" – April 1948 *Astounding*
"Dud" – April 1948 *Thrilling Wonder Stories* (as by Kenneth Putnam)
"Confusion Cargo" – Spring 1948 *Planet Stories* (as by Kenneth Putnam)
"Consulate" – June 1948 *Thrilling Wonder Stories*
"The Ionian Cycle" – August 1948 *Thrilling Wonder Stories*
"Brooklyn Project" – Fall 1948 *Planet Stories*
"The Human Angle" – October 1948 *Famous Fantastic Mysteries*
"The ReMarchkable Flirgleflip" – May 1950 *Fantastic Adventures*
"The Puzzle of Priipiirii" – July 1950 *Out of This World Adventures*
"The Last Bounce" – September 1950 *Fantastic Adventures*
"Null-P" – January 1951 *Worlds Beyond*
"The Quick and the Bomb" – Spring 1951 *Suspense Magazine*
"Betelgeuse Bridge" – April 1951 *Galaxy*
"Hallock's Madness" – May 1951 *Marvel Science Stories*
"A Matter of Frequency" – May 1951 *Science Fiction Quarterly*
"Venus Is a Man's World" – July 1951 *Galaxy*
"Everybody Loves Irving Bommer" – August 1951 *Fantastic Adventures*
"The Jester" – August 1951 *Thrilling Wonder Stories*

"Medusa Was a Lady!" – October 1951 *Fantastic Adventures*
"'Will You Walk a Little Faster'" – November 1951 *Marvel Science Fiction*
"Firewater" – February 1952 *Astounding*
"Ricardo's Virus" – March 1953 *Planet Stories*
"Liberation of Earth" – May 1953 *Future*
"The Custodian" – November 1953 *If*
"Project Hush" – February 1954 *Galaxy*
"The Tenants" – April 1954 *F&SF*
"Down Among the Dead Men" – June 1954 *Galaxy*
"Party of the Two Parts" – August 1954 *Galaxy*
"The Servant Problem" – April 1955 *Galaxy*
"The Flat-Eyed Monster" – August 1955 *Galaxy*
"The Discovery of Morniel Mathaway" – October 1955 *Galaxy*
"The Sickness" – November 1955 *Infinity Science Fiction*
"Murdering Myra"—November 1955 *Suspect Detective Stories*
"Wednesday's Child" – January 1956 *Fantastic Universe*
"Time in Advance" – August 1956 *Galaxy*
"She Only Goes Out at Night" – October 1956 *Fantastic Universe*
"Of All Possible Worlds" – December 1956 *Galaxy*
"Time Waits for Winthrop" – August 1957 *Galaxy*
"The Dark Star" – September 1957 *Galaxy*
"Sanctuary" – December 1957 *Galaxy*
"Eastward Ho!" – October 1958 *F&SF*
"Lisbon Cubed" – October 1958 *Galaxy*
"The Malted Milk Monster" – August 1959 *Galaxy*
"The Men in the Walls" – October 1963 *Galaxy*
"Bernie the Faust" – November 1963 *Playboy*
"The Masculinist Revolt" – August 1965 *F&SF*
"My Mother was a Witch"—August 1966 *P.S.*
"The Lemon-Green Spaghetti-Loud Dynamite-Dribble Day"—January 1967 *Cavalier*
"The Last Bounce"—April 1967 *Amazing*
"The Remarkable Firgleflip"—July 1967 *Fantastic*
"On Venus, Have We Got a Rabbi"—in *Wandering Stars*, ed. Jack Dann, 1974
"There Were People on Bikini There Were People on Attu" – *The Best of Omni Science Fiction* #5, 1983
"The Girl with Some Kind of Past. And George." – Oct. 1993 *Asimov's*

Articles

"7 Out of 10 Astrogators Choose Venus! – *Marvel Science Fiction* August 1951

"The Fiction in Science Fiction – *Science Fiction Adventures* March 1954

"The Frank Merriwell Compulsion or Winning the Championship the Hard Way" – April 1963 *Rogue*

"The Student Rebel: Then and Now" – June 1966 *P.S.*

"The Bugmaster" – ? 1968 *True* (also as "Mr. Eavesdropper")

"Jazz Then, Musicology Now – *F&SF* May 1972

"An Innocent in Time: Mark Twain in King Arthur's Court"—December 1974 *Extrapolation*

"From a Cave Deep in Stuyvesant Town—A Memoir of Galaxy's Most Creative Years" - in *Galaxy: Thirty Years of Innovative Science Fiction*, ed. Frederik Pohl, Joseph D. Olander & Martin H. Greenberg, Playboy Press 1980

"'The Lady Automaton' by E. E. Kellett: A Pygmalion Source?" – in *Shaw: The Annual of Bernard Shaw Studies 1982*, Pennsylvania State University Press 1982

"It Didn't Come from Outer Space" – in *The Digital Deli*, ed. Steve Ditlea, Workman 1984

"The Enormous Toothache" – ? 1985 *Stories*

"What's Wrong with My Daughter?" – ? 1992 *The Reader's Digest* (as by Philip Klass)

"Constantinople" – *U.S. Catholic*, 1994

"Curiosities: Dr. Arnoldi, by Tiffany Thayer, 1934" – *F&SF* August 1998

"Author Emeritus Speech: Given Here Without the Gestures, Intonations and Pauses Which Made It Moderately Funny in the First Place" – *he Bulletin of the Science Fiction and Fantasy Writers of America #143*, 1999

"Welles or Wells: The First Invasion from Mars" – *Synergy SF: New Science Fiction*, ed. George Zebrowski, Gale Group/Five Star 2004; revised from an earlier version in *The New York Review of Books* 1988 as by Philip Klass

Novels/Collections

Of All Possible Worlds—Ballantine 99, 1955 (collects 7 stories)

The Human Angle—Ballantine 159, 1956 (collects 8 stories)

Time in Advance—Bantam A1786, 1958 (collects 4 stories)

A Lamp For Medusa—Belmont B60-077, 1968 (a Belmont Double, bound with Dave van Arnam's *The Players of Hell*)
Of Men and Monsters—Ballantine U6131, 1968
The Seven Sexes—Ballantine U6134, 1968 (collects 8 stories)
The Square Root of Man—Ballantine U6132, 1968 (collects 9 stories)
The Wooden Stars—Ballantine U6133, 1968 (collects 11 stories)
Immodest Proposals: The Complete SF of William Tenn, Vol. 1—NESFA Press, 2001 (collects 33 stories)
Here Comes Civilization: The Complete SF ofWilliam Tenn, Vol. 2—NESFA Press, 2001 (collects 27 stories and 1 article)
Dancing Naked: The Unexpurgated William Tenn—NESFA Press, 2004 (collects 36 non-fiction essays and articles)

Anthologies

Children of Wonder—Simon & Schuster 1953 (collects 19 stories and 1 poem)
Once Against the Law—with Donald E. Westlake, MacMillan 1968 (collects 22 mystery stories

Notes

1. Frankly, all that's different now from when I was a kid is that my great-nephews are watching Larry, Moe and Curly on DVD instead of Channel 13. They still run around the house afterwards yelling "WUBWUBWUBWUB!" and calling each other "knuckleheads" while their mothers despair and their sisters think they're idiots. So did mine, so did mine, and so it goes.
2. Well, okay. If he had written more "serious" stories, I'd also have had a lot more really good reading, but that would be pampering myself.
3. Actually, Frederik Pohl and Judith Merril did most of the work; Heinlein wrote the intro and approved their choices.
4. *Children of Wonder*, in case you're unaware (it appeared in paperback as *Outsiders: Children of Wonder).*
5. "Of *course* I know who you are!" she said when he introduced himself, and she later told me that he almost cried.
6. He mentioned that he used to sell copies of the anthology to a bookshop in the Village, and one day as he was going in, a young Bob Dylan was coming out of the folk club upstairs. They spoke for a while, and Klass's recollection was of an intense but friendly young man who expressed an interest in his work as a writer.

❑

A Logic Named Clement
(or, Open the Pod Bay Doors, Hal)

> His work has from the first been characterized by the complexity and compelling interest of the scientific (or at any rate scientifically literate) ideas which dominate each story.
> – John Clute, writing in *The Encyclopedia of Science Fiction* (St. Martin's 1993)

THAT'S HAL CLEMENT, ALL RIGHT. Even when I was a kid, we knew when we picked up a new Clement story or book that we were going to be challenged—those of us who weren't already science geeks, anyway.

Not that he was utterly abstruse, mind you. You had to know your stuff, or at least have access to a science teacher who didn't mind answering questions about "sci fi", but there was plenty of story in there to be had, even if the ideas were most important.

Of course, this endeared him to John Campbell and the readers of *Astounding/Analog* (where most of his stories appeared) for years, but he never had trouble finding an audience wherever he went.

Several years ago, I was asked by a friend to speak to a group of middle-school faans who had decided to form a science fiction club at their school. I found them curious, enthusiastic, and eager to have anything new to read after finishing the most recent Harry Potter book. I read my own stories to them (set in their home town, which is the reason I was approached in the first place), answered their questions, and at the end, presented them with two grocery bags filled with old classic SF paperbacks: old Groff Conklin anthologies I had duplicates of, Asimov, Bradbury and Laumer collections, a few volumes of the Del Rey *Best of...* series, and whatever else I had around the house I thought they'd like (and wouldn't get them in trouble with their folks).

I still hear from some of them once in a while, and by far the author many of them are most grateful for having been introduced to is Hal Clement. Which is as it should have been; these were good, smart and clever kids, ready to delve into the ideas and concepts that Clement, a teacher himself, was keen to impart. It was a match made, well, if not in heaven then certainly above the plane of the ecliptic.

> "Look," he explained it all to me once. "A writer is a man who makes his living writing. I make my living teaching. So I'm not a writer."
>
> – Lester del Rey, quoting the author in his introduction to *The Best of Hal Clement* (Del Rey 1979)

That's a characteristically low-key self-appraisal, of course, and one could debate it all day, but why argue with the man? He knew his priorities, and his students and scouts came before publishers and editors with their eye-shades and cheap cigars. This is not to say that he didn't have a handle on how good he really was as a writer, however, as editor and publisher (sans shades and cigars) Warren Lapine recalls:

> The most interesting thing I ever heard him say about his own writing was (and I'm paraphrasing here) that he (Harry) had an ego every bit as big as Isaac's (Asimov) and that he (Harry) was as good a writer as Isaac, but that Isaac had a much better press agent.

Harry Clement Stubbs was born in Somervile, Massachusetts on May 30, 1922. He got his B. S. in Astronomy from Harvard(!) when he was 21(!!), and four years later got his Masters in Education from Boston U. He also did grad work in chemistry.

During WWII, he co-piloted B-24s for the Army Air Force, flying 33 combat missions in the ETO with the 8th. In the early 1950s he was recalled as a tech instructor at the special weapons school at Sandia. He taught science[1] at the Milton Academy in Cambridge, Mass. until his retirement, and if that wasn't enough, he was an avid scoutmaster the whole time.

In his spare time, he was the epitome of the hard-science SF writer, the one that all SF fans pointed to when asked who paid the most stringent attention to the laws of physics when writing about aliens, humans and other planets. *In his spare time*, I repeat. He did it better than anybody else at the time (and for a long time after), he was a telling and righteous influence on Sheffield, Asaro, Benford, and all the other hard-science writers who came after him, and he did all that when he *wasn't* teaching kids astronomy or chemistry or how to tie knots.

Do this for me. Look all the way down at the bottom of this article at the bibliography. Go ahead, I'll wait here and finish my root beer.

Did you notice something? I sure as hell did: as influential as Hal Clement was, as important as he was as a yarn-spinner, as much as his name was bandied about for, oh, five decades or so as one of the giants, he built it all on the basis of a little over fifty stories and about a dozen books. *In his spare time.* Doesn't that just suck?

No, it doesn't. It is, in fact, remarkable as hell. He was a remarkable individual, was Harry Clement Stubbs, and his work bears that out. He didn't cheat, he didn't fudge the numbers, and he didn't keep his eyes closed when he speculated. That wasn't what Clement was about, not at all. He was about making the story fit the science, not the other way around. Science was a suit he put on, it's what he *was*, and if the story had to work around the physics, it didn't work at all. Oh, he got it wrong once in a rare while, but when he did, you can bet that every pro in a labcoat had it wrong at the time, too. Nonetheless, science was never the trimmings in a Clement story, it was the whole turkey.

He sold his first story to—as should surprise none of you reading this—John Campbell's *Astounding*. "Proof" appeared in the June, 1942 issue, and if it didn't quite raise a fuss, it was the camel's nose, and *Astounding* was the tent. How could Campbell have possibly resisted a story featuring aliens who lived inside a *star*:

> They had evolved far down near the solar core, where pressures and temperatures were such that matter existed in the "collapsed" state characteristic of the entire mass of white dwarf stars.... The race had evolved to the point where no material appendages were needed. Projected beams and fields of force were their limbs, powered by the annihilation of some of their own neutron substance.

O, my little droogies, your faithful narrator would love to have been a fly on the wall of the Street and Smith offices *that* afternoon. Of his fifty-plus stories, no fewer than twenty appeared in *Astounding/Analog*, with his last story gracing the pages of the January 2000 issue. That's a span of 58 years, a record few can even come close to.

> Hal Clement's second story, "Impediment," was a carefully thought out account of the landing of a space ship near the Arctic Circle and its discovery by one man.... The story was interesting on an intellectual level, as are all Clement's later works, but cold emotionally.
>
> – Alva Rogers, in *A Requiem for Astounding* (Advent 1964)

Therein lies the focus of much of the criticism of Clement's writing, from the beginning right up until the end. Clement had the reputation for being the Mr. Spock of (real) science fiction, eschewing sentiment and emotions and stressing ideas over character. Well, yeah, but science is all about ideas, is it not? It's when you bring people into the mix that science gets all screwed up and messy and before you know it there are giant flying robots knocking off banks and cackling madmen in lab coats firing funny-colored rays at World Capitols and making Superman choose between London and Lois Lane. Right?

Okay, I'm exaggerating for effect. Clement's characters are perfectly acceptable as characters; just don't expect them to cry or rave or even laugh more than is necessary to get the point across. In his world, characters exist to serve the idea, not the other way around. Damon Knight noted this in his examination of Clement's best (and best-known) story, *Mission of Gravity*:

> [Clement's] failings are a certain emotional blandness—no Clement character ever gets excited—and a low romantic quotient: where [Raymond] Gallun's monsters are alien and humanly sympathetic at the same time...Clement's often fail to convince simply because they're too human: more so, in fact, than some of the human characters.

Nevertheless, Knight doesn't stint his praise for the book, calling it "...the most back-breaking job of research ever undertaken to buttress a science fiction story. Moreover," he continues, "the result is worth the trouble." And boy-howdy, is it ever. This is the one book that is invariably mentioned whenever fans get together with other fans and talk about hard SF. When articles on the topic are written, or panels/workshops on hard science fiction are conducted by faans and pros alike, *Mission of Gravity* is the one title that is either praised or castigated as the ultimate case in point.

Allow me to elaborate on that Rogers quote above, if you will. As I write this, Mary (my harshest critic and Boon Companion, Feeder of Cats and Painter on Fabrics) has read over the first draft of this little piece and has admonished me for my apparent dispassion towards my Subject. As is usually the case, she is correct, but don't tell her I said that or I'll never hear the end of it, okay?

But she's right, I'm not terribly passionate about Clement's work, for all that I've read it over and over throughout the years and eagerly grabbed stories and books I didn't already have for my personal library. There's a reason for this.

Let me be absolutely clear about it: Hal Clement is not a writer who engages the emotions. To the contrary, Clement's work appeals almost entirely to the intellect. Is this a bad thing? I think not, for many good reasons, but here's the best—Wonder is as much an object of the mind as it is the heart, perhaps more so. I'm not talking about the wonder of a rainbow here, but the Wonder of what makes that rainbow appear where before there was none.

There are plenty of very fine writers who address the emotions, in one way or another or to one degree or another. Harlan Ellison, Zenna Henderson, Edgar Pangborn, and Barry Malzberg are only a bare few whose works tweak, tap or tear at the heart. They excel at it, and their work is effective and affecting.

Hal Clement didn't play that. His interest was not in pulling strings or pushing buttons (well, not emotional ones anyway) but in taking hold of the mind and shaking it until that mind is a quivering lump of *Wow!* To that end, he created worlds and people—human and otherwise—who exemplify the very best of science fiction, accent on the first word. This is not an easy thing to do.

I'm no scientist, I can tell you that: when I write a story that includes a specific bit of physics or chemistry or astronomy, I get out my phone list or e-mail address book and start asking those who know better than I. I am in awe of those who don't need to do that, and trust me, Harry Clement Stubbs was *awesome*. He had his speculative ducks in a row before he ever put paper in his typewriter, and it really does show.

Mesklin, the planet on which *Mission of Gravity* takes place, is the original Discworld.[2] During its formation, it spun so fast that the sphere flattened, and as a result, gravity is just *all* outta whack; a gentle three times Earth normal at the equator, but a he-man challenging *700*g at the poles. Talk about needing orthotics.

Clement figured out all the accessories for a planet like this, from weather patterns to how life would have evolved (intelligent centipedes), and I can tell you for certain that he enjoyed every single minute of it. Believe me, there are those of us for whom research is an evening's entertainment, whether its figuring out the biota of an alien planet or studying up on those who do.

It is a wonderful book, and by that I mean one filled with wonder, not just a terrific read. A landmark in the field, its impact on those who read it and loved it stretches far beyond the bookstore or library shelves and further on into aerospace technology and even NASA. In a way, it really does represent science fiction just the way the Know-Nothings think it does when they point at it. They're right, of course, but for all the wrong reasons.

Mission wasn't his first book, though. Before that came *Needle* and *Iceworld*. The former came about as a result of a statement John Campbell made to Clement in hopes that the author would do just what he did: write a story to prove him wrong.

Campbell, let's face it, had all kinds of ideas for his own stories, and until he took over the reins of *Astounding* back in 1937 he did pretty well with them. Being an editor, unfortunately, means that your own career as a writer has to suffer to one degree or another, and Campbell's screeched almost to a halt; he published little fiction after taking over the *Astounding* post, and that in other magazines.

But there were all these ideas he had, see, and if he couldn't write 'em he sure as hell didn't see why somebody else couldn't. So, he would frequently toss an outrageous question or comment to one of "his" writers, and they quickly learned that he loved to be proven wrong, especially in his own magazine[3].

Ergo, *Needle*. In a letter to the author dated April 12, 1953[4], Campbell said, "Once upon a time I told you 'Science Fiction detective stories don't work—you can't write a good one.' So you proved that I was wrong in that, and wrote *Needle*."

High praise, *nicht wahr*? Of course, even higher praise followed in the form of checks from every editor he submitted to (in his spare time), so that even if he still listed "educator" on his QV, his hobby was plenty lucrative.

As an educator, kids were important to Clement. It shows in his writing: the protagonist of his first novel, *Needle*, is a teen-aged boy working with an alien symbiote detective to track down another symbiote, wherever on Earth it is, hence, a needle in an Earthstack; *Close to Critical* offers an Earthican robot on a heavy-gravity planet called Tenebra raising native children Earthishly, and his rescue of human children who have crashed there. Don't think that these are kids' stories, although kids can certainly enjoy them. Like another educator/writer, Zenna Henderson, Clement was writing *about* children, not down to them. They were important in his life, ergo they were present in his fiction.

A significant percentage of his short fiction has been anthologized and/or collected over the years, seven stories alone between 1951 and '54. One of these, "Critical Factor", was commissioned by Frederik Pohl for his *Star Science Fiction* original anthologies and appeared in the second volume of that inestimable series in 1953. This was not the last time Clement would contribute an original story to an anthology, either. Twenty-three years later he would give Judy-Lynn del Rey "Stuck With It" for the second volume of *that* inestimable series, *Stellar SF*.

Both stories bear the clear and unmistakable imprint of our beloved science teacher, for all that they don't bear resemblances to each other elsewise. Each has a primary concept used as a pivotal element around which Clement weaves his story, and both show the author's keen talent at presenting, and then (cleverly) solving, a problem based on that concept.

Sounds cold and rigid, don't it? Well, it isn't. Clement might have been all about the science, but he was also all about the story. Anybody can take an idea and hang words on it with a beginning, middle and end[5] and call it a "story", but it takes a real *storyteller* to do it right.

Clement worked well with others on a social level, but only collaborated once in his career. In 1956, the magazine *Satellite* appeared with the promise of "...a complete science fiction novel in every issue", much as *Startling* had done a decade and change before. Sam Merwin, Jr., edited the first two (digest) issues, then left. Before he did, however, he added some 10k words to a story Clement wrote entirely from an alien viewpoint by inserting alternating chapters from a human perspective. It was published in the February, 1957 issue as "Planet for Plunder". As SF historian and critic Mike Ashley writes in his utterly necessary *Transformations: Vol. 2, History of the Science Fiction Magazine, 1950-70* (Liverpool University Press 2005):

> Clement was asked if he could pad the story out to novel length. Clement had neither the time nor the desire to do so but, with his agreement, the story was revised.... It was never published in book form in this version, but the original novella, "Planetfall", was eventually printed in Robert Hoskins' anthology *Strange Tomorrows* in 1972.

Ashley doesn't hesitate to cast a critical eye over the unfortunate result of this "collaboration", either, saying it "...added nothing new to the story and virtually killed it for the way Clement had planned and plotted it. In fact it's an object lesson in how to ruin a good story."

In the last years of his life, Clement suffered from diabetes. I recall a panel at a local convention[6] in 2002 at which he sat to be interviewed by another writer/historian, Paul Dellinger, and myself. At one point, as the afternoon went on, Clement began repeating himself, slurring his words and misunderstanding questions. He caught our expressions, reached into his pocket and unfolded a bag of plain M&Ms. Carefully counting out a precise number of the little candies, he popped them into his mouth and chewed. Within moments, he was sharp again, energetic and right on top of us.

It was a typically Clementian thing to do, of course. He could never stand being fuzzy or confused, either in his writing or his daily life, and his interface with the world had to be just so. That he was "medicating" himself with candy-coated chocolate that melts in your mouth (not in your hand) instead of prescription drugs was just another clue to his meticulous approach to everything, fiction included. Why spend money on pills you can barely pronounce when you can get the same effect from shopping at any 7-11 candy aisle?

"Meticulous", he says… Paul and I asked him a number of process-oriented questions that afternoon, and he remembers a comment Clement made which clearly exemplifies his habitual pains-taking, one I had since forgotten:

> He did stories by writing scenes on index cards, and only when he had sufficient numbers of those would he begin actually writing the story.

Between 1994 and 1999, he wrote six stories for the DNA magazine *Harsh Mistress* (later *Absolute Magnitude*). *HM/AM* was, for the duration of its publication, a periodical that bubbled just under the level of its principal competitors, each issue threatening to burst through the floor and out-sell the older and more established markets. So, how did it rate an almost regular appearance by one of the Major League Hall of Famers? Editor and publisher Warren Lapine met Clement at Not Just Another Con in 1993, found him to be (as usual) very approachable, and, er, approached him:

> At that point our first issue wasn't even out, but I asked him if we could get a story from him. He gave a noncommittal answer and I figured that was that. A few months later I was at another convention….I was literally telling a new would-be writer that he could not just hand me a manuscript at a con and expect me to consider it when Harry walked up to me and said, "Here's the story you asked for," and handed it to me on a five-inch floppy. I, of course, said "Thank you!" and then amended what I had been saying to the new writer to, "You can't hand me a manuscript at a con and expect me to consider it unless you're Hal Clement…"

That story was "Sortie", and it appeared *sixteen years* after his previous one. Why so long? Well, first of all, it wasn't as if Clement didn't have other things to do; recall, if you will, that his career as an author was pursued in his spare time. Lapine asked him why he'd stopped, and "…he told me it was because people had stopped asking him for stories." Unwilling to let that one go, and because "Sortie" was deliberately unresolved, Lapine urged him to write a sequel to tie up loose ends. Clement replied that he could do that, but that it might take two or three stories. "I was okay with that," Lapine says, "I told him 'Of course' and he wrote three more stories that ended up as the novel *Half Life*."

Harry Clement Stubbs left us on October 29th, 2003, at the age of eighty-three. He went quietly in his sleep, and perhaps he's somewhere still dreaming, file cards in hand and papers to be corrected stacked neatly by his elbow. The body of work he left behind isn't as extensive as many, but it's as rich and intricate as any. He left a large footprint on the Terra, and unlike all too many of his colleagues, his stories read as well now as they ever did. Warren Lapine praises him highly, saying "Harry was the nicest and easiest person I've ever worked with. I can't remember a single tense moment with him…I don't think he ever said an unkind word about anyone."

He was a fascinating man to talk to, filled with stories and facts, and above all, *Ideas*. His absence leaves a void that can never be filled by another.

(As usual, this bibliography is as complete as I can make it given my resources, and is limited to first publications except where the same story was published under two or more titles. Also as usual, I welcome and all corrections and additions; c'mon, folks, keep me honest.)

Bibliography of Hal Clement

Short Stories

"Proof" – June 1942 *Astounding*
"Impediment" – August 1942 *Astounding*
"Probability Zero: Avenue of Escape" – November 1942 *Astounding*
"Attitude" – September 1943 *Astounding*
"Technical Error" – January 1944 *Astounding*
"Trojan Fall" – June 1944 *Astounding*
"Uncommon Sense" – September 1945 *Astounding* [Laird Cunningham]
"Cold Front" – July 1946 *Astounding*
"Assumption Unjustified" – October 1946 *Astounding*
"Answer" – April 1947 *Astounding*
"Fireproof" – March 1949 *Astounding*
"Needle" – serial, May, June 1949 *Astounding* [Robert Kinnaird]

"Iceworld" – October-December 1951 *Astounding*
"Halo" – October 1952 *Galaxy*
"Critical Factor" – in *Star Science Fiction Stories No. 2*, ed. Frederik Pohl, Ballantine 55, 1953
"Mission of Gravity" – serial, April-July 1953 *Astounding* [Mesklin]
"Ground" – December 1953 *Science Fiction Adventures*
"Dust Rag" – September 1956 *Astounding*
"Planet for Plunder" – February 1957 *Satellite* (with Sam Merwin, Jr.)
"Close to Critical" – serial, May-July 1958 *Astounding* [Easy Rich]
"The Lunar Lichen" – February 1960 *Future*
"Sunspot" – November 1960 *Analog*
"The Green World" – May 1963 *If*
"Hot Planet" – August 1963 *Galaxy*
"Raindrop" – May 1965 *If*
"The Foundling Stars" – August 1966 *If*
"The Mechanic" – September 1966 *Analog*
"Ocean on Top" – serial, October-December 1967 *If*
"Bulge" – September 1968 *If*
"Star Light" – serial, June-September 1970 *Analog* [Mesklin; Easy Rich]
"Lecture Demonstration" – in *Astounding: John W. Campbell Memorial Anthology*, ed. Harry Harrison, Random House 1973
"The Logical Life" – in *Stellar 1*, ed. Judy-Lynn del Rey, Ballantine
"Mistaken for Granted" – January/February 1974 *Worlds of If*
"Longline" – in *Faster Than Light*, ed. George Zebrowski and Jack Dann, Harper & Row 1976
"A Question of Guilt" – in *The Year's Best Horror Stories IV*, ed. Gerald W. Page, DAW 1976
"Stuck With It" – in *Stellar 2*, ed. Judy-Lynn del Rey, Ballantine 1976
"Seasoning" – September/October 1978 *Asimov's* [Medea]
"Sortie" – Spring/Summer 1994 *Harsh Mistress*
"Settlement" – Fall/Winter 1994 *Absolute Magnitude*
"Seismic Sidetrack" – Spring 1995 *Absolute Magnitude*
"Simile" – Summer 1995 *Absolute Magnitude*
"Oh, Natural" – Spring 1998 *Absolute Magnitude*
"Exchange Rate" – Winter 1999 *Absolute Magnitude*
"Under" – January 2000 *Analog* [Mesklin]

Articles and Essays

"Whirligig World" – June 1953 *Astounding*

"Gravity Insufficient" – November 1961 *Analog*

"Atoms and Opinions" – *Galileo* #2 1976

"Introduction to 'Proof'" – Spring 1977 *Unearth*

"Science" – (column) Winter 1977 – Winter 1979 *Unearth*

"Red World 2" – *Galileo* #11 1979

"On the Tenth of Apollo 11" – July 1979 *Galileo*

"Voyager 2" – November 1979 *Galileo*

"Pretty Pictures" – *Event Horizon* #2 1980

"The Home System" – October 1986 *Aboriginal SF*

"Essay: Whatever Happened to the Science in Science Fiction?" – September 1993 *Science Fiction Age*

"Only Once" – Spring 1994 *Fractal*

"Ardent Thuria, Chilly Cluros: Seeing, and Seeing From, Low Orbiting Satellites" – Fall 1994 *Mindsparks*

Novels and Collections

Needle – Doubleday 1950; also as *From Outer Space*, Avon T175, 1957

Iceworld – Gnome Press 1953; Lancer 75-128, 1967

Mission of Gravity – Doubleday 1954; Galaxy Novel 33, 1958; Pyramid F786, 1962

Ranger Boys in Space – Page 1956 (YA)

Cycle of Fire – Ballantine (hc), 200 (pb), 1957 (simultaneous publication)

Close to Critical – Ballantine U2215, 1964

Natives of Space – Ballantine U2235, 1965 (collects three novellas)

Small Changes – Doubleday 1969; also as *Space Lash*, Dell 8039, 1969

Star Light – Ballantine BB 2361, 1971

Ocean On Top – DAW 57, 1973

Through the Eye of a Needle – Ballantine 25850, 1978

The Best of Hal Clement – Del Rey 27689, 1979

The Nitrogen Fix – Ace 1980

Intuit – NESFA Press 1987 (for Boskone, limited to 820 copies)

Still River – Del Rey 1987

Half Life – Tor 1999

The Essential Hal Clement, Vol. 1: Trio for Sliderule and Typewriter – NESFA Press 1999
The Essential Hal Clement, Vol. 2: Music of Many Spheres – NESFA Press 2000
The Essential Hal Clement, Vol. 3: Variations On a Theme By Sir Isaac Newton – NESFA Press 2000
Heavy Planet – Tor 2002 (Mesklin)
Noise – Tor 2003

Anthology

First Flights to the Moon – Doubleday 1970 (Note: *The Encyclopedia of Science Fiction* [compiled by John Clute and Peter Nichols, St. Martin's 1993] indicates that this is a non-fiction anthology, but it is all fiction.)

Notes

1. Can you imagine your science teacher writing science fiction? How cool is *that*? I don't know about you, cowboy, but I'd have been over the moon about it. Nyuk-nyuk.
2. I honestly have no idea if Sir Terry Pratchett had read *Mission* before he wrote *Strata*, his first novel about a flat planet (and unconnected with the Discworld books), but he may very well have done.
3. Except about psionics, Dianetics, and the Dean Drive. He got really cranky about those.
4. This is the same year that Asimov's response to that statement, *The Caves of Steel*, was published. In another magazine. Hey, Campbell didn't always get his way.
5. Urk. Considering some of the workshops I've been in over the years, perhaps that statement is a bit of a stretch.
6. SheVaCon, held in Roanoke, Virginia. Clement was a frequent guest.

❑

A Martian? Odd, I See
(or, a Taste of Milwaukee's Finest)

"There was a racket like a flock of crows eating a bunch of canaries—whistles, cackles, caws, trills, and what have you. I rounded a clump of stumps, and there was Tweel!"

"Tweel?" said Harrison, and "Tveel?" said Leroy and Putz.

"That freak ostrich," explained the narrator. "At least, Tweel is as near as I can pronounce it without sputtering. He called it something like 'Trrrweerrll!.'"

"What was he doing?" asked the Captain.

"He was being eaten! And squealing, of course, as any one would."

WELL, I CERTAINLY WOULD. That's from the first few pages of "A Martian Odyssey" by Stanley Graumen Weinbaum, originally published in the July 1934 *Wonder Stories*. A year and a half later, Weinbaum died of throat cancer. In between, he published a dozen more stories, including "Valley of Dreams",[1] which also featured "Trrrweerrll," his enduring (and endearing) ostrich-like alien. More would come later, bringing the total to twenty-seven shorts; he would publish only one novel during his short life,[2] *The Lady Dances*, and that as a newspaper serial under the pen-name Marge Stanley. Again, a few more would follow his death, but clearly his métier was the short form. The root of this is simple, if crass: short work was easier to sell to the pulps than long, and this was the middle of the Great Depression.

So what's the big deal, anyway? Just another dead writer, hacking away at pulpish bug-eyes, right?

No. Not by a long shot. Weinbaum wasn't prolific, but he did something no other SF writer had done before him: he created an alien that really was, y'know, *alien*. Prior to Trrrweerrll (or Tweel, or Tveel, depending on whether or not you're a Putz)[3]—and for quite a long time afterwards, in the case of less adventuresome writers—most aliens tended to be thinly disguised humans in rubber suits with the zippers plainly visible. And funny hats; can't ignore those funny hats.

There was a reason for this, above and beyond a lack of imagination on the part of half-cent-a-pop wordsters more concerned with the rent and groceries than creativity: aliens are frequently used as fun-house mirrors of human frailties, foibles and foolishments. A good reason, don't get me wrong; but suitable more for allegory and/or satire than nutzenbolts science fiction. Some are still doing it, to greater or lesser effect, depending on the madness of their skills.

Skill was something Weinbaum had. Don't get me wrong, there are plenty of rough edges in his work, but he was a consummate story teller, and that's of far more use than mere smooth prose. As you may have noticed, storytelling is a thing I value quite highly, and also something I keep separate from grammar and spelling. I can forgive quite a bit of the latter if the former is strong enough.

Stanley G. was born in Kentucky in 1902, or 1900, depending on which unassailable reference you use for research. His family moved to Milwaukee, and he attended the U. of Wisc where he studied chemistry. He did not, however, graduate; stories differ, but the one I hear the most concerns his having taken an exam for another student on a bet and getting caught. Hey, I did worse stuff than that, I kicked in my dean's door once. Or twice.

But this made it even harder for him to make a living for himself and his wife, Margaret. So, he started knocking out witty, eminently readable yarns, exactly the sort of thing editors wanted. Believe me, as much as editors love to say they want the cutting-edge, the cold actuality is that the majority of their readers want stuff that they can, in effect, fall through without hitting the sides—i.e., stories that are fun to read without making their skulls sweat. That Weinbaum's were also damn good stories, written so well that they still work after three-quarters of a century, is both beside the point and tribute to his innate sense of what makes a narrative *work*.

This is not to say that he was the only pulpster who transcended the medium: C. L. Moore, Leigh Brackett, Manly Wade Wellman, and Clifford Simak certainly did, among others. Weinbaum, however, managed to do it in eighteen short months, and almost from the very beginning. One gauge of his skill is the fact that when Robert Silverberg went to the membership of SFWA to assemble the first volume of *The Science Fiction Hall of Fame*, the earliest story they chose was "A Martian Odyssey" and it received the next to the highest number of votes. This means more than you might think on first consideration. The contents weren't just picked to fill a book, but to present to the world those stories published before 1965 that were of Nebula quality, as determined by the very people who would have awarded that honor had it existed at the time.

(Useless, if inevitable, speculation on my part: what could Weinbaum have turned out, had he lived long enough to become aware of Alfred Bester [who debuted with "The Broken Axiom", 1939]? Or Robert Heinlein ["Life-Line", also 1939]? Or, for that matter, Cordwainer Smith ["Scanners Live in Vain", 1950]? Would he have gone with it, producing better and more venturesome work? Or would he have been daunted, writing less and less before fading from the scene entirely? I would like to think the former, but whatever the case, I'd be grateful for the extra Weinbaum.)

Isaac Asimov was highly impressed by Weinbaum (which should tell you a lot), even though he missed reading that monumental first story when it originally appeared. In his introduction to *The Best of Stanley G. Weinbaum*, he said:

> ["A Martian Odyssey"] had the effect on the field of an exploding grenade. With this single story, Weinbaum was instantly recognized as the world's best living science fic-

> tion writer, and at once almost every writer in the field tried to imitate him.

The Good Doctor didn't confine his comments to just that book, however. When he reprinted the story in his most excellent anthology *Where Do We Go From Here?*[4] (Doubleday 1971), he commented in his end-note:

> It was not just the realism of his alien other-world creatures, but it was his light and easy style, a far cry from the creakiness of the writing of most of the s.f. authors of the early thirties.

That would be a big ten-four, stfnal good buddy. Reading some of the Gernsbackian science fiction of the period (no matter where it was published) is a bit more than a minor chore; characters are tissue-thin, plots contrived and unbelievable, and dialogue filled with clumsy "As you know, Borm-123K, here in the Future we..." tropes. Stanley Weinbaum, practically all by himself, changed all that. The other writers in the field had to run damn fast to catch up.

Asimov wasn't alone, either. Praise for Weinbaum's style came from the most...well, *eldritch* places. In his introduction to the 1962 Lancer collection, *A Martian Odyssey*, Sam Moskowitz quotes none other than the Gentleman from Providence, H. P. Lovecraft:

> Somehow he had the imagination to envisage wholly alien situations and psychologies and entities, to devise consistent events from wholly alien motives and to refrain from the cheap dramatics in which almost all adventure-pulpists wallow.

Maybe *you're* inclined to argue with the father of The Great Lord Cthulhu, but I'm sure as hell not, so deal.

What makes the story even more remarkable is that it preceded and anticipated the Campbellian Age of SF. Campbell is famous for giving his authors story ideas, frequently passing out the same suggestion to multiple writers and thus getting utterly different takes on that single germ. One legendary dictum would seem to fit Weinbaum's first story perfectly: "Write me a creature that thinks as well as a man, or better than a man, but not *like* a man." Weinbaum, who predated Campbell's tenure at *Astounding*, would seem to have been prophetic in fulfilling that request.

Everything Weinbaum wrote is measured against "A Martian Odyssey," which is, perhaps, unfortunate. Nothing unusual about this, of course; everything Asimov wrote for a couple of decades was compared to "Nightfall," and I'm sure that Richard Matheson is weary of everything he wrote being weighed against "Born of Man and Woman."

In Weinbaum's case, though, it's even more unfair because he didn't live long enough to accumulate a body of work that would outshine his initial foray into the field. Damn shame, that, because there's enough shine on his other stories to light up a total eclipse.

The fact is that Asimov, who wouldn't publish his first story ("Marooned Off Vesta" in the March, 1939 *Amazing*) until four years after Weinbaum's death, didn't see any of Weinbaum's stories until he broke into *Astounding* with "Flight On Titan" in the January, 1935 issue. He had this to say in his head note to Weinbaum's "The Parasite Planet" in his anthology, *Before the Golden Age* (Doubleday 1974):

> I liked it ["Flight On Titan"], of course, but "The Parasite Planet," in the very next issue, was what hit me with the force of a pile driver and turned me instantly into a Weinbaum idolater.

I'll mention one more Asimovian riff and then shut the hell up about him. He posits in his intro to *The Best of Stanley G. Weinbaum* that the early history of science fiction was illuminated by three supernovae, stories which succeeded in "...altering the nature of science fiction and converting every other writer into an imitator"; the first being Edward Elmer "Doc" Smith's collaborative[5] first story, a serialized novel beginning in the August, 1928 *Amazing* titled *The Skylark of Space*, and the third being Robert Anson Heinlein's debut in the August, 1939 *Astounding* with "Life-Line."

Need I say that the second super-nova was Weinbaum's inaugural foray into scientifiction? I didn't think so.

> "So what's happened to Kyra Zelas, by some mad twist I don't understand, is that her adaptive powers have been increased to an extreme. She adapts instantly to her environment; when sun strikes her, she tans at once, and in shade she fades immediately. In sunlight her hair and eyes are those of a

> tropical race; in shadow, those of a Northerner. And—good Lord, I see it now—when she was faced with danger there in the courtroom, faced by a jury and judge who were men, she adapted to that! She met that danger, not only by changed appearance, but by a beauty so great, that she couldn't have been convicted!" He paused. "But how? How?"

That's a quote from "The Adaptive Ultimate", originally published in the November 1935 *Astounding* under the pen-name John Jessell. Now, I'm going to be honest here. This ain't the best-written tale I've ever read, not even close. It's not even Stanley G.'s best. But there a decent story hiding in there, and it's worth the minor hassle of coping with a little clumsy phrasing and awkward syntax. I've seen infinitely worse in a couple of decades of sitting in on convention workshops and writers' groups (not mine, of course—my guys are terrific).

The conceit is fairly simple, and echoes the sort of super-science yarn Hugo Gernsback got all sweaty over. A physician fiddles around with putrefied fruit-flies and creates a serum that he claims will cure anything. He and his buddy, another doctor, inject a dying woman with the serum, and, whaddaya know, it *works*.

Too well, as it turns out. See, she *adapts*. Instantly, and to anything and everything in her environment. And so it goes.

There are, of course, unforeseen circumstances, but there wouldn't be much of a story if there weren't. Said circs verge on the tragic, but there's love in the air and in the end, lessons are learned by all and sundry, and a sort of normality is restored.

As I said, it's a better-than-fair story, but there are lumps and ridges where there shouldn't be. For example: "Somehow it angered him that she should be so beautiful and at the same time deadly with an inhuman deadliness." Yeah, that's lumpy prose. Nevertheless, the story is well worth reading, if you can bear in mind the context: 1935 pulp fiction. Believe me, there's worse out there.

> "Bah! Would you mention them in the same breath with the name of van Manderpootz? A pack of jackals, eating the crumbs of ideas that drop from my feast of thoughts! Had you gone back into the last century, now—had you mentioned Einstein and de Sitter—there, perhaps, are names worthy to rank with or just below) van Manderpootz!"

That's from one of my favorite Weinbaums, "The Worlds of If", which originally ran in the August '35 *Wonder Stories*. It's a good enough introduction to Prof. Haskel van Manderpootz (jeeze, I love Weinbaum's character names! I mean, if you're gonna be slapstick about it, go ahead and leap over the top, right?), Stanley G.'s entry in the Mad (or at least quirky) Scientist rodeo.

As you might have gathered from the quote above, the Prof isn't shy. Of course, he's convinced that he has no reason to be, as viewpoint character Dixon Wells describes:

> It seems he'd transferred to N.Y.U. as head of the department of Newer Physics—that is, of Relativity. He deserved it; the old chap was a genius if ever there was one…

The premise with this one is almost recursive—van Manderpootz invents a "What If" machine, the subjunctivisor, which shows What Might Have Been just like his fellow crazed scientist Hubert Farnsworth's[6]. Based on the (equally fictitious) "Horsten psychomat," one plugs oneself into the machine, watches the blobs of color floating across the screen, twiddles a dial, and… well, it's a pulp story, and it doesn't have to make much sense. Just sit back and enjoy the story and forget the science for once, okay? Just like a Robert Sheckley story.

The problem is, our friend Wells is habitually late for everything, so no matter what the subjunctivisor shows him might happen, he manages to blow it. Gee, none of *us* have ever done that, have we?

There are three van Manderpootz stories, and they're all fun to read, something I'm finding rarer and rarer these days. I suppose I could make the case that van Manderpootz was a precursor to such later characters as Henry Kuttner's Gallegher,

Nelson Bond's Lancelot Biggs, or Sterling Lanier's Brigadier Ffellowes. Problem is, none of them are practitioners of insane-o-science. They're certainly all quirky as hell, though, and even van Manderpootz has his literary ancestor in the person of Arthur Conan Doyle's Professor Challenger.

Weinbaum wasn't the only writer in the Milwaukee area. Robert Bloch, Ray Palmer (editor of *Amazing* and flying saucer maven), Roger Sherman Hoar (who wrote as Ralph Milne Farley), Fredric Brown and a few others banded together as the Milwaukee Fictioneers, mostly to party hearty, but also to critique each other and talk shop. Weinbaum was a member in excellent standing, and upon his death, they arranged to have Conrad Ruppert, fan and printer, produce a memorial volume titled *Dawn of Flame*. Published in an edition of 250 copies, there were two versions: the first one with an introduction by Palmer, to which Weinbaum's widow objected; there were only five copies of this version issued. The second, far more plentiful (if you can use that term with any book limited to 250 copies) version replaces the Palmer intro with one by fellow Fictioneer Lawrence Keating.

The book, as you can imagine, sells for a significant sum when offered at all. A search of eBay turns up no sales of the title in the past year, but long-time bookseller and bibliophile Lloyd Currey recently sold a copy for $2,500. In 35 years of collecting and selling SF/fantasy books, I've only seen one copy myself, and that one came from Ruppert's own library. The book itself is interesting, as Ruppert primarily printed and bound bibles. Thus *Dawn of Flame* is bound in limp leather with the title and author's name stamped in gold on the cover and spine.

Bloch, the youngest[7] and later the best known Fictioneer, was not just an admirer *a la* Asimov, but a friend as well. In his afterword to *The Best of Stanley G. Weinbaum*, he wrote about those meetings where the members would read aloud from works in progress and, they hoped, benefit from the comments of the others:

> ...Stanley Weinbaum told his tales almost as well in person as in print. He had a true storyteller's presence and dramatic delivery, and he seemed to enjoy the reactions of his audience... [His] questions usually concerned characterizations—ways to build credibility in his nonhumans as well as his humans.

Later in his reminiscence, Bloch praised Weinbaum's skill at building that credibility:

> This, of course, was Stanley Weinbaum's greatest contribution to science fiction. He introduced empathy to the field. In an era of rising racial, religious and nationalistic discord... Weinbaum somehow found the courage and creativity to present—without plea or preachment—the case for brotherhood.

Indeed, the relationship between Jarvis and Tweel (however you choose to spell and/or pronounce it) is clearly one of equals. Jarvis might be amused by Tweel's actions, but he takes his companion in adversity seriously and gives him his props to the other humans.

Let me close this out by expanding on the first sentence of that last paragraph. People read for various reasons, both individually and overall. Speaking personally, I read for enlightenment, for knowledge, for entertainment. And, since I was just a kid reading about cats in hats and off-color breakfast foods, just for the *fun* of it all.

It's simple, really. If I'm having fun, if I'm enjoying what I'm reading, it matters less if the prose isn't elegant or the style is less than blank iambic pentameter. Don't get me wrong, now, I'm as big a fan of lobster thermidor and oysters Rockefeller as the next gourmet, but there are plenty of times when what I really want is a chicken-salad sandwich with American cheese, toasted, and a frosty mug of IBC root beer.

Cordwainer Smith, Harlan Ellison, James Tiptree, Jr.: they weren't just wordsmiths or craftsmen; they set out to create art. By and large, in my less-than-humble opinion, they succeeded. Stanley Grauman Weinbaum wasn't about art, he was about having a good time; and passing that good time along to his readers was his ultimate goal. Hey, I may know a lot about art, but I know what I like, too, and I like Weinbaum. Give him a chance, and I think you will, too.

(I know I keep on about this, but for those of us who take bibliographic matters seriously, well, we take them very *seriously. So if you have additions or corrections to the biblio below, please* do *take the time and effort to let me know care of this magazine so I don't look like a putz.)*

A Stanley G. Weinbaum Bibliography

Novels

The Lady Dances – King-Features Syndicate 1933
The New Adam – Ziff-Davis, 1939
The Black Flame – Fantasy Press, 1948
The Dark Other (aka *The Mad Brain*) – Fantasy Publishing Co., 1950
The Black Flame (restored) – Tachyon Publishing, 1997

Short stories

"A Martian Odyssey" – July 1934 *Wonder*
"Valley of Dreams" – November 1934 *Wonder*
"Flight on Titan" – January 1935 *Astounding*
"Parasite Planet" – February 1935 *Astounding*
"The Lotus Eaters" – April 1935 *Astounding*
"Pygmalion's Spectacles" – June 1935 *Wonder*
"The Worlds of If" – August 1935 *Wonder*
"The Challenge From Beyond" – September 1935 *Fantasy Magazine* (round robin, Weinbaum wrote the opening 800+ words)
"The Ideal" – September 1935 *Wonder*
"The Planet of Doubt" – October 1935 *Astounding*
"The Adaptive Ultimate" – Nov 1935 *Astounding* (as by John Jessel)
"The Red Peri" – November 1935 *Astounding*
"The Mad Moon" – December 1935 *Astounding*

Posthumous publications

"The Point of View" – January 1936 *Wonder*
"Smothered Seas" – January 1936 *Astounding*
"Yellow Slaves" – February 1936 *True Gang Life* (with Roger Sherman Hoar, as by Ralph Milne Farley)
"Redemption Cairn" – March 1936 *Astounding*
"The Circle of Zero" – August 1936 *Thrilling Wonder*
"Proteus Island" – August 1936 *Astounding*
"Graph" – September 1936 *Fantasy Magazine*
"The Brink of Infinity" – December 1936 *Thrilling Wonder*
"Shifting Seas" – April 1937 *Amazing*
"Revolution of 1950" – serial, October-November 1938 *Amazing* (with Roger Sherman Hoar, as by Ralph Milne Farley)
"Tidal Moon" – December 1938 *Thrilling Wonder* (with Helen Weinbaum, his sister)

"The Black Flame" – January 1939 *Startling*
"Dawn of Flame" – June 1939 *Thrilling Wonder*
"Green Glow of Death" – July 1957 *Crack Detective and Mystery Stories*
"The King's Watch", Posthumous Press, 1994

Collections of stories and poetry

Dawn of Flame: The Stanley G. Weinbaum Memorial Volume—Milwaukee Fictioneers (Conrad H. Ruppert), 1936
A Martian Odyssey and Others – Fantasy Press, 1949
The Red Peri – Fantasy Press, 1952
A Martian Odyssey and Other Classics of Science Fiction—Lancer 74-808, 1962
The Best of Stanley G. Weinbaum – Ballantine, 1974
A Martian Odyssey and Other Science Fiction Tales – Hyperion Press, 1974
Lunaria and Other Poems – The Strange Publishing Company, 1988
The Black Heart – Leonaur Publishing, 2006
Interplanetary Odyssey – Leonaur Publishing, 2006
Other Earths – Leonaur Publishing, 2006
Strange Genius – Leonaur Publishing, 2006

Notes

1. In the November '34 *Wonder.*
2. He had written two more, but they remained unpublished until after his death. This makes Weinbaum one of the very few writers, in or out of the field, whose posthumous output exceeded their life-time credits.
3. That, I say, that's a *joke,* son. Mary tells me I should let you all know about these more often, her words being "give them fair warning."
4. A title I hope to cover at another time, and in another place.
5. With Mrs. Lee Hawkins Garby, wife of Dr. Carl DeWitt Garby, a classmate of Smith's at the U of Idaho. Like you'll remember *that.*
6. You do watch *Futurama*, don't you? Coulda been worse, too, it coulda been the FingLonger.
7. He was invited to join the Fictioneers at age eighteen after they saw a newspaper article about his selling "The Feast in the Abbey" and "The Secret of the Tomb" to *Weird Tales* in 1935.

Secret Crocodiles and Strange Doings

(or, Sometimes the Magic *Really* Works)

> Gilford Gadberry had a contempt for dawns badly done. He knew how blatant and stylized the outdoor world can be in its pristine moments: the contrived shagginess of grass, the stupidity of trees, the falsity of flowers, the oafishness of the birds and their inept melody. These scratched the smooth surface of his soul. "Bad work, very bad work," Gadberry would opine, for he was an artist.
>
> – R. A. Lafferty, "Seven Story Dream"

WITH YOUR INDULGENCE, I would like to preface this installment of "Past Masters" with some clarification, tinged perhaps with just a *soupcon* of justification. It bears on the subject at hand, so I hope you'll grant me a moment before I plunge headlong into my customary mix of enlightenment and entertainment. Grab a root-beer, if you've a mind to.

Although most of these columns include some critical elements, I am not, as I've said here and elsewhere, principally a Critic, interested only in the literary aspects of my subjects. Rather, I'm a biographer and historian—a biorian?—and my purview is above all the individual who created the work, and the significant personal characteristics that infused their work. This can place me in an uncomfortable position at times, but if I always opted for comfort over reality, little of what I (and the few others who walk alongside) did would be of value aside from the mere satisfaction of someone else's passing curiosity.

I am also no freer from my own prejudices and intolerance than anyone else who treads the skin of this particular oblate spheroid, and although I do try very hard to prevent that small-mindedness from affecting how I address my subjects, it is frequently difficult to clearly see where the line is. My bad; I am, as the three damn cats habitually remind me, only human.

So. As I broach the discomfiting components of this essay, bear in mind that I have an obligation to be honest, and that I will do my very best to be so with fairness. I would expect no less from anyone writing about me.[1] Onward.

Our subject this time around was a complex and complicated man, and that makes writing about him a knotty task. There are no easy conclusions to be made (or at least none with any validity), and few opportunities to be glib at his expense, so I won't even try. Lafferty made it impossible for anyone to pigeonhole him as either a stylist or a human being, whether deliberately or unintentionally, and no two readers are likely to agree about him or his writing on anything other than a very general level.

Like his work, Lafferty was multi-layered. He had a self-deprecating sense of humor that served as a buffer for many of the people with whom he worked and interacted. When I met him at the 1976 worldcon, MidAmeriCon in Kansas City, I was introduced to him by Jerry Pournelle. At the time, I was still suffering under the misapprehension that Lafferty was around the same age as the other New Wavers that I'd classed him with, and I was totally unprepared for the reality that he was already in is 60s and looked like what he was: a retired electrical engineer. Me being super-fast on my feet and always ready with a witty comment, I responded to the intro by saying something pithy like "*You're* R. A. *Lafferty*?!" He chuckled and shook his head, saying "Naw, I just stole his badge," and walked away laughing. Not for the first time was I faced with having to alter my mental construct of someone I knew only from their work.

It's easy to see why I was confused. Nobody ever wrote—or will ever write—quite like Lafferty. I'm not at all certain that the literature could hold two such, in fact. This is, I think, a blessing, as I'd hate for it to blow up or deliquesce or something. Sticky.

Lafferty wasn't a science fiction writer, regardless of the section of the bookstore in which his titles may have appeared; rather, he was a mad fantasist, a maker of mythologies, a Wizard of Oddities.

In addition, though, there were facets of his personality—facets which informed and influenced his writing—which will be difficult for me to write about. Write about them I must, however, as journalistic objectivity prevents me from washing over them without mention. Bear with me, please.

Three primary things made Lafferty the brilliant writer he was, inevitably and indubitably. The first, and foremost, was his unfaltering and dogmatic Catholicism. I have heard a rumor, still floating around, that Lafferty had six female sibs, all of whom took the veil. His sisters were all Sisters, in other words. This is untrue; so far as I know, although he had five siblings, none were nuns. In fact, he lived with his sister, Anna, until his death.

Nothing odd about SF/fantasy writers being religious, of course. C. S. Lewis made an entire career out of it, as you probably already know. Tenets of the Church of Latter-Day Saints infuse the work of Orson Scott Card, and we won't even mention L. Ron Hubbard.[2] The number of stories and novels offering speculative takes on various religious ideas is legion (heh), and include some of the best-known and well-regarded works in the field: Miller's *A Canticle for Leibowitz*, Simak's "The Creator," del Rey's "For I Am a Jealous People", and Michael Moorcock's *Behold, the Man* not the least of them.

Second, and not far behind, were his staunchly conservative political views, which caused friction between him and fellow writers and convention committees more than once. It's not inconceivable that he and the Tea Party could have been friendly, although I suspect he valued intellect far more than most of those who considered Sarah Palin a viable candidate for high office.[3]

Right-Wing politics aren't at all rare in the field of science fiction. During the Viet Nam War, for instance, Judith Merril and Kate Wilhelm arranged for an anti-war full-page ad to appear in *Galaxy*, signed by those who opposed the war. Word apparently got out before it appeared, and they were prevailed upon to make it a "fair and balanced" ad to include those SF writers who favored our involvement. On the "pro-war" side, along with John W. Campbell and Robert Heinlein (and a number of others, some quite surprising) was R. A. Lafferty. This came as a surprise to many readers who associated him with the New Wave, which had a reputation for being liberal and pacifistic (at least where South-East Asia was concerned).

The combination of those first two aspects of Lafferty's mindset separated him from a significant number of his readers, who were unaware of his far-right-of-center rigidity for the most part. Organized fandom was less oblivious, with convention encounters written up in fanzines and whispered about at dead-dog parties. Fandom has always represented the smallest number of people in the field's readership, so effectively nobody really knew much of anything about this Lafferty guy.

Noted fan Guy Lillian, whose excellent fanzine *Challenger* has been nominated a remarkable fourteen times (so far) for the Hugo, wrote of his response to Lafferty's novel *Past Master* in his introduction to his publication of Lafferty's guest of honor speech at the 1979 DeepSouth-Con:

> I'll never forget my reaction to Lafferty's tale of Thomas More on the golden planet Astrobe… "Ah," I said. "I have found my boy." What I meant was that I had found a writer who—though a rock-ribbed conservative—spoke to a scrawny Berkeley hippie used to being generously teargassed every spring. I'd found a poetic spirit who invested science fiction with madness and tragedy and laughter.

The third facet, however, is where the difficulty really lies. In his off-hours at conventions, Ray Lafferty drank heavily. It was not an isolated or occasional thing, either. When speaking to his colleagues, his fans, and those professionals in the field with whom he worked, the one unifying comment I heard across the board (after his genius as a writer) concerned his serious alcohol use. I do *not* raise this issue to demean the man, or to denigrate him or his skills with pen and paper, but it a key fact of heavy alcohol use is that it unavoidably permeates every facet of the drinker's life.[4]

In this, of course, he was far from alone; as a species, writers are notorious sots, and the literary world is crowded with fables of overindulgence and subsequent debauchery. As a gopher at a Star-Trek convention some thirty-five years ago, I was assigned the task of following one such author around in order to smooth over the ruffled feathers he left in his wake. It was almost a full-time job. Thus, I can no more ignore Lafferty's tendency to imbibe socially than I could Zenna Henderson's Mormon childhood or Horace Gold's agoraphobia. Those things had enormous influence on their work, as Lafferty's personality traits had on his.

How did it affect his writing? I asked Mike Resnick, who knew Lafferty well, and he told me this:

> There were a number of people… who thought he was the most brilliant short story writer in the field. But his novelettes weren't as good, and except for "Space Chanty" his novellas were unexceptional, and his novels were for the most

> part mediocre. I blame his drinking for this. If he could grind out a story in one or two sittings, he could be brilliant. But if a novel took him 50 writing sessions, you get the feeling that each day he had to refresh his memory of what the hell he wanted to do, how he wanted to say it, etc.

Lafferty is no longer with us to be interviewed, but extensive reading of his writings shows an arch bitterness. Again, this is nothing unusual for a writer, even in the field of science fiction/fantasy. Cyril M. Kornbluth, for example, was flat-out *eat up* with bitterness.

However, whereas Kornbluth's acrimony was directed at his fellow man (you only have to read a few random pages of "The Marching Morons" to see this; hell, the title alone is a flashing neon sign), Lafferty seems to have internalized his bitterness, perhaps as an inevitable product of his alcohol use in conflict with his doctrinaire Catholicism. Robert Silverberg, who published a number of Lafferty's stories, said this:

> He was clearly a very troubled man, and he clearly drank much too much at conventions, and no doubt was extremely lonely. But he could be a charming guy… and anyone who knew his work—brilliant, of course—would instantly be aware of the disconnect between the work and the unhappy figure we saw at conventions and know that something very sad was involved.

I have said that our subject was both complex and complicated, and there is more to Lafferty that just the above. If I'm duty-bound to mention his politics, religion and alcohol use, I'm equally bound to shine a light on other, more positive factors of his character. Lafferty was capable of great warmth and generosity, and many people I spoke to, both faan and pro, were forthcoming about their positive encounters. The aforementioned (and eloquent) Guy Lillian told me this:

> If, in the pursuit of accurate reporting, you insist on dwelling on Ray's flaws, mention also the love and loyalty he engendered in fans who knew him, who took care of him when he was incapacitated, because they appreciated that they were dealing with a genius with great depths of humor and sadness… and the strongest Catholicism of

> anyone in the field. He expressed these things exquisitely through his incredible gift, with humility and verve, and was loved for it. After St. LouisCon [the 27th WorldCon in 1969], where he first appeared to fandom... a 20-year-old boy I know - myself - wrote him a fan letter. He sent me back a page of gratitude, affection and wisdom I still cherish. I have never known a finer soul.

And, come on. It's the Twenty-First Century. What was once something to be desperately hidden under a rock is now so commonly spoken of that they hardly even do after-school specials about it anymore. In our next installment, we'll jump into this multifaceted man's equally convoluted and intricate work. See you then.

Raphael Aloysius Lafferty was born November 7, 1914, in Iowa, but before he entered school his family moved to Oklahoma. He spent most of his life in Tulsa, working twin jobs as an electrician and a newspaper writer before enlisting in the Army in 1942. He served in the Pacific, leaving the Army as a Staff Sergeant in '46. He never married, but lived with a sister, Anna.[5]

Little of this would seem to have led him to a life as a fictioneer, let alone one who would turn the stfnal world on its literary ear, but that's what he did.

For me, it began with the July/August, 1971 *If*. I had just finished part two of Farmer's *The Fabulous Riverboat* and was looking forward to "Occam's Scalpel" by Theodore Sturgeon, when I decided to take a break and read one of the other stories in that issue. I had a choice between "Arnten of Ultima Thule" by Avram Davidson (one of my favorite writers), a story by an author I'd never heard of ("To Seek Another" by James A. Gotaas, to my knowledge the physicist's only fiction), and a story by R. A. Lafferty, of whom I had heard but at the time had not read.[6]

It was "Boomer Flats," and it blindsided me. I'd never read anything quite like it, with its utterly unEarthly-but-of-the-earth characters ("The Comet was a long gray-bearded man (in fact, comet means a star with a beard) and small pieces were always falling off him.") The story still knocks me out, and is one I always recommend to those who haven't read Lafferty.

It's magic. Not "magic realism," whatever that may mean, but just full-on, bull-goose *magic*. I read it with my eyes wide and my mouth agape. It was not the last time Lafferty would have that effect on me.

I'm not alone in that assessment, either. No less a critic than Brian Aldiss, in his important history of the field, *Trillion Year Spree* (with David Wingrove, Avon 1988), said this: "Hard to categorize other than as [a] conjuror—[a] singer of strange, sometimes acutely humorous songs—[is] R. A. Lafferty…" I think that's a perfect description of Lafferty as written by someone far more knowledgeable and qualified than I.

I frankly didn't know where this story had come from. Being who I was at the time, my initial thought was "Wow, I bet this guy has done a lot of acid!" Little did I know.

Of course, it was an honest mistake; a lot of the imagery, the detail, the sheer atmosphere of Lafferty's work is almost hallucinatory in nature. The idea that someone could have created "Boomer Flats" without having dropped a lot of Orange Sunshine[7] never even occurred to me.

Acid was the last thing R. A. Lafferty would have downed, considering his religious and political views. No, all that dream-like stuff came straight out of his own unenhanced imagination, and that's almost scary. Phil Farmer, yes; Harlan Ellison, certainly. Lafferty, however, was almost 60 years old when that story ran, and although age isn't an absolute barrier to trippy fantasy, it's the way to bet.

After that startling encounter, I began seeking out all the Lafferty I could find. Not all of it was as brilliant as that first mind-blowing tale, but it was all just as unEarthly. This wasn't science fiction as we usually think of it. No fancy hardware, high-concept technology or plot-points turning on an astrophysical dime here. Nor was it what Bradbury and Nelson Bond used to call "science fantasy," although it comes close in some ways. Lafferty's work stands apart—not necessarily above, but undeniably apart—from his colleagues'. You can't even hold it in the same (metaphorical) hand without your fingers wanting to bend in strange directions they weren't designed for. He was *sui generis*, was Lafferty, and there were plenty of readers who scratched their heads and called his stories unfathomable, but oh, the mythological impact of those stories!

In tune with Mike Resnick's words above, I find that Lafferty's longer works don't read quite as well. That's me, not him, and it's just as much a commentary on my own flaws as it is on anything of his. I think he was more comfortable at shorter lengths, and I certainly understand that. The kind of elliptical worldview in which he worked would have been terribly difficult to sustain for 50 thousand words or more, and readers could have found the effort of keeping up with it daunting.

Luckily there is plenty of short-form Lafferty out there to be read and wondered at: he published more than 250 short stories between 1959 and 1997, many of them in the original anthology series that were prevalent throughout the '70s.

Of his novel-length works, the most cohesive is probably *Past Master* (Ace 1968), the fifth of Terry Carr's Science Fiction Specials and Lafferty's first novel. Something of a stfnal *roman à clef*, it features the historical Sir Thomas More transported to the planet Astrobe a thousand years after the year of his death (but before his death took place).

Astrobe, once a utopia, is declining so irrevocably that it may mean the end of the human race. Not a good thing, they realize—hence the use of a time machine to bring in the Boss. Well, it seemed to be a good idea at the time, but they didn't anticipate the fact that he is a *sixteenth-century* dude with all the concomitant limitations, not to mention a mind very much of his own.

Honest mistake, really. After all, he did coin the word "utopia". See, they figured he'd fix everything up and be all gosh-wow about being in the future, and they could handle him. Yeah, not so much - this is, after all, Sir Thomas More we're talking about here, described in Wikipedia as:

> ...lawyer, social philosopher, author, statesman, and noted Renaissance humanist. He was an important councilor to Henry VIII of England and, for three years toward the end of his life, Lord Chancellor. He is recognized as a saint within the Catholic Church and is commemorated by the Church of England as a "Reformation martyr".

Does that sound to you like a guy who would sit up and bark if you waved a Beggin' Strip™ over his head? It doesn't hurt that this isn't the Lord Chancellor's first experience with time travelers, and he takes it all in stride. He finds allies—not all of them human—and enemies too; ones who are prepared to off themselves and take the Human Race with them.

Much of what ensues comes out of Lafferty's heart-felt opinion that More's 1516 novel *Utopia* (written completely in Latin, how cool is that?) was a satire. Fair enough—More did use the book as a way of commenting on the mess that Europe was in at the time, and that's what satirists do. If More didn't choose to wear a funny hat or do an impression of Buddy

Hackett while writing it, well, that just means it wasn't intended to be a *Mad Magazine* strip. Satire doesn't always have to be fronted by Alfred E. Neuman, you know.

Ace books, edited at the time by both Donald Wollheim and Terry Carr, devoted a great deal of paper and ink to Lafferty. Carr published three of Lafferty's titles as part of his Science Fiction Specials, and Wollheim bought his *Space Chantey* for the Doubles series.

This illustrates the dichotomy of Lafferty's work in the late '60s and early '70s: was he a New Wave writer, or wasn't he? Carr's support of the New Wave, both as a critic and as an editor, was well-known. But wasn't Donald Wollheim a hide-bound traditionalist?

Not really. Sure, he was a Futurian, a pulp writer and editor, and the Ace Double line included a lot of stories pulled directly from the pulps, but it shouldn't be forgotten that he was an early proponent of Philip K. Dick, Margaret St. Clair, Jack Vance and John Brunner among others, none of whom can easily be considered old-fashioned by any means.

Did I say "dichotomy"? I could have as easily said "schizoid." The positive response to Lafferty's work came almost exclusively from the stfnal Counter-Culture, which fact must have alternatively caused the writer both amusement and frustration. One wonders if, while reading some fan's rave review of one of his books or stories Lafferty ever sat back, shook his head ruefully and said "Boy, if they only knew."

At this remove, it hardly matters whether he accepted his endorsement by the New Wave reluctantly or not. I'm fairly certain that when those quarterly royalty payments came in the mail he didn't waste much time trying to figure out which percentage came from Those Damned Hippies.

Lafferty was smart enough and realistic enough (despite his stylistic extravagance) to understand that readership is readership. If anything, he courted the antiestablishment audience by selling to such New Wave-friendly markets as Damon Knight's *Orbit*, Carr's *Universe*, Silverberg's *New Dimensions* and other non-traditional venues[8].

There was a problem with his being identified with the New Wave, though: when the Wave broke and went back out to sea, it left him without much of a context. He continued with the original anthologies, staying in both *Orbit* and *Universe* almost to the bitter end, but aside from a few other anthology appearances and a few stories in *F&SF* and *Asimov's*, the rest of his writing came out in collections published by small presses, primarily Corroboree and Chris Drumm.

In the late 1970s it was all too common to see Lafferty's hardcover collections, published earlier in the decade by Scribner, sitting in piles on chain store remainder tables and selling for $1.99. He wasn't alone, of course, but while a number of other authors weren't adversely affected by Scribner's decision to thrift out their mid-list, Lafferty's career never recovered. Of his sixteen novel-length books, half were published in the decade 1968-77. The other eight were spread out over almost twenty years, and only one—1983's *Annals of Klepsis*—was published by a major house, Ace. The others were, like his later collections, produced by small presses. His last novel was *Sindbad: The 13th Voyage* (Broken Mirrors 1989) and his last short story, "The Emperor's Shoestrings," appeared in a 1997 anthology published by a gaming company.

As a used-book seller, I can say that there is still a readership for the work of R. A. Lafferty, one that crosses age boundaries and appeals to people who have never even heard of the New Wave. I find this both reassuring and enriching, as his books—even the ones Scribner so blithely dumped—command good prices. Many of his titles have been reissued by publishers like Wildside, presenting them before an audience for whom his work is a new wonder, as well as making it possible for his "hippie" fans to read him again.

There is one more exceptional aspect to Raphael Aloysius Lafferty's career as a writer, one that I'm not sure has a parallel, and that is the disposition of his literary estate. As I write this, his estate has been auctioned off by the family to the highest bidder. No announcement has as yet been made, so I'm not about to reveal the high bidder, but from what I know it will be in good hands.

This singular circumstance arises from two main factors: first and foremost, Lafferty (coming as he did from a strongly Catholic family) had a *lot* of heirs, among then not only his sister(s), but nephews, nieces, great-nephews and great-nieces. Aside from the numbers, they are almost certainly scattered around the country, making it difficult for decisions to be made with the participation and input of all.

The second reason stems from the cold reality that the small press, however enthusiastic and well-intentioned, has very little money to pay its authors. They rarely pay advances of more than a few hundred dollars, and royalties are limited not only by the relatively low print runs (less of a problem with PoD) but by a lack of major-house distribution channels. Face it; small press publishers may love what they do, but there just ain't a whole lot of money in it and never has been.

Add these two factors together and what you get is a bunch of checks for a bare few dollars being written and sent out to a hundred or more family members; it hardly seems worth the trouble, but honorable publishers have to do it.

As a result, the family offered the entire estate, print and film rights included, for a one-time payment to be divided equally. Only the passage of time will show if this was a wise move, but chances are that it will at the very least simplify things for the family. That is, of course, the whole point of a literary estate.

Literary estate… There's more to an author's literary property than just his/her published works, and whereas Lafferty was heavily published, not everything has seen print. Mike Resnick had this to say about a visit he made to Lafferty's digs in the mid-1980s:

> When I visited his house down in Oklahoma, I opened the guest closet to hang up my coat—and saw a 3-foot-high pile of manuscripts. He told me they were his unsold books, he had just turned 70, and he wasn't writing another word until Virginia (Kidd, his agent) sold all of these. She found a little press up in Minnesota, but she never did sell them all. She used to cry on my shoulder that she and I and four dozen others thought he was one of the greatest short story

> writers alive... but she couldn't find 10,000 people to buy his paperbacks or even 500 to buy his signed, numbered hardcovers.

Editor and anthologist Jonathan Strahan agrees, telling me "There's certainly a LOT of unpublished work. About 16 novels and something like 80 short stories."

I would very much like to think that, once the Lafferty estate is settled and a new agent found to represent it, many of the unpublished stories and novels will be made available to an eager (if unfairly small) readership.

"Sui generis" was the term I used back up there a ways, but there's actually more to it than that. I can think of only two other writers in the field who even approach him stylistically, and then only marginally; their only real resemblance is that all three seem to come from places the rest of us only find in dreams.

The other two are Cordwainer Smith and James Tiptree, Jr. I hasten to point out that the resemblance is all relative—they are alike mostly because they're so utterly different from everyone else.

Look at the language they use, though, even in just what they chose for titles: "Thus We Frustrate Charlemagne", "Entire and Perfect Chrysolite", "Nor Limestone Islands", "The World as Will and Wallpaper" by Lafferty; "Golden the Ship Was—Oh! Oh! Oh!", "The Dead Lady of Clown Town", "No, No, Not Rogov!", "The Game of Rat and Dragon" by Smith; "All the Kinds of Yes", "Her Smoke Rose Up Forever", "Love is the Plan the Plan is Death", "Your Faces, O My Sisters! Your Faces Filled of Light!" by Tiptree.

These are titles beyond the poetic, they spill over into the mythopoetic, and the stories they stand for are the work of myth-makers, no matter that the three are so very different from each other in concept and execution. They were also almost certainly triametrically opposed politically as well, but that's only to be expected.

R. A. Lafferty left us a magnificent body of work, stories that cry and wail and laugh and bray. They come from, and take their readers to, places few others could even conceive of, let alone limn with the skill and richness that he wielded. Already middle-aged when he sold his first, he laid down a road paved with bright, deadpan madness for us to walk, mouths agape and eyes wide with wonder and trepidation; after all, he's taking us to worlds never seen before, and we can't know what's around that corner until the page is turned.

He was a writer of shining, bedazzling stories made all the richer by his flaws. Would that we all could employ our own imperfections so superbly.

(This bibliography is deliberately incomplete, as R. A. Lafferty wrote poetry extensively, and in the interests of space, I have omitted them here. I would like to thank Jonathan Strahan for his invaluable help in compiling this bibliography.)

Bibliography of Raphael Aloysius Lafferty

Short Fiction

"The Wagons" – Spring 1959 *New Mexico Quarterly Review*
"Day of the Glacier" – January 1960 *Science Fiction Stories*
"Through Other Eyes" – February 1960 *Future Science Fiction #47*
"Other Side of the Moon" – March 1960 *Husk Magazine*
"Saturday You Die" – Spring 1960 *Artesian Magazine*
"Long Teeth" – August 1960 *Keyhole Mystery Magazine*
"Adam Had Three Brothers" – Fall 1960 *New Mexico Quarterly Review*
"The Ugly Sea" – Fall 1960 *The Literary Review*
"The Six Fingers of Time" – September 1960 *If*
"Beautiful Dreamer" – September 1960 *Shock*
"McGonigal's Worm" – November 1960 *If*
"Snuffles" – December 1960 *Galaxy*
"Try to Remember" – December 1960/January 1961 *Collage Magazine*
"The Polite People of Pudibundia" – January 1961 *If*
"In the Garden" – March 1961 *If*
"All the People" – April 1961 *Galaxy*
"The Weirdest World" – June 1961 *Galaxy*
"Aloys" – August 1961 *Galaxy*
"Rainbird" – December 1961 *Galaxy*
"Seven-Day Terror" – March 1962 *Galaxy*
"Dream" – June 1962 *Galaxy* (aka "Dreamworld")
"Sodom and Gomorrah, Texas" – December 1962 *Galaxy*
"The Transcendent Tigers" – February 1964 *Worlds of Tomorrow*
"Name of the Snake" – April 1964 *Worlds of Tomorrow*
"What's the Name of That Town?" – October 1964 *Galaxy*

"Mad Man" – October 1964 *If*
"Pig in a Pokey" – December 1964 *If*
"The Man With the Speckled Eyes" – December 1964 *F&SF*
"The Pani Planet" – January 1965 *Worlds of Tomorrow*
"Slow Tuesday Night" – April 1965 *Galaxy*
"Guesting Time" – May 1965 *If*
"In Our Block" – July 1965 *If*
"Hog-Belly Honey" – September 1965 *F&SF*
"Nine Hundred Grandmothers" – February 1966 *If*
"Golden Trabant" – May 1966 *If*
"Among the Hairy Earthmen" – August 1966 *Galaxy*
"Narrow Valley" – September 1966 *F&SF*
"Primary Education of the Camiroi" – December 1966 *Galaxy*
"The Man Who Never Was" – Summer 1967 *Magazine of Horror*
"The Hole on the Corner" – in *Orbit* 2, ed. Damon Knight, Putnam 1967
"Thus We Frustrate Charlemagne" – February 1967 *Galaxy*
"Polity and Custom of the Camiroi" – June 1967 *Galaxy*
"Ginny Wrapped in the Sun" – August 1967 *Galaxy*
"Land of the Great Horses" – in *Dangerous* Visions, ed. Harlan Ellison, Doubleday 1967
"Camels and Dromedaries, Clem" – October 1967 *F&SF*
"The Ultimate Creature" – November 1967 *Magazine of Horror*
"One at a Time" – in *Orbit* 4, ed. Damon Knight, Putnam 1968
"Maybe Jones and the City" – *The Third Foundation* #80 1968
"How They Gave It Back" - February1968 *Galaxy*
"McGruder's Marvels" – July 1968 *Galaxy*
"This Grand Carcass" – November 1968 *Amazing* (aka "This Grand Carcass Yet")
"Cliffs That Laughed" – March 1969 *Magazine of Horror*
"Configuration of the North Shore" – in *Orbit* 5, ed. Damon Knight, Putnam 1969
"Frog on the Mountain" – in *Nine Hundred Grandmothers*, Ace 58050, 1970 (Science Fiction Special)
"Entire and Perfect Chrysolite" – in *Orbit* 6, ed. Damon Knight, Putnam 1970
"Hands of the Man" – in *Infinity One*, ed. Robert Hoskins, Lancer 75-108, 1970
"Ride a Tin Can" – April 1970 *If*

"Continued on Next Rock" – in *Orbit* 7, ed. Damon Knight, Putnam 1970
"Old Foot Forgot" – in *Orbit* 7, ed. Damon Knight, Putnam 1970
"The All-At-Once Man – July 1970 *Galaxy*
"About a Secret Crocodile" – August/September 1970 *Galaxy*
"Interurban Queen" – in *Orbit* 8, ed. Damon Knight, Putnam 1970
"All Pieces of a River Shore" – in *Orbit 8*, ed. Damon Knight, Putnam 1970
"The Cliff Climbers" – in *Quark/1*, ed. Samuel R. Delany and Marilyn Hacker, Paperback Library 66-480, 1970
"Condillac's Statue, or Wrens in His Head" – in *Alchemy and Academe,* ed. Anne McCaffrey, Doubleday 1970
"Been a Long, Long Time" – December 1970 *Fantastic*
"Sky" – in *New Dimensions 1: Fourteen Original Science Fiction* Stories, ed. Robert Silverberg, Doubleday 1971
"Nor Limestone Islands" – in *Universe 1*, ed. Terry Carr, Ace 84600, 1971
"When All the Lands Pour Out Again" – in *Orbit* 9, ed. Damon Knight, Putnam 1971
"Groaning Hinges of the World" – in *The Ruins of Earth*, ed. Thomas M. Disch, Putnam 1971
"The Man Underneath" – January/February 1971 *If*
"Encased in Ancient Rind" – in *Quark/3*, ed. Samuel R. Delany and Marilyn Hacker, Paperback Library 66593 1971 (aka "Incased in Ancient Rind")
"Enfant Terrible" – June 1971 *Ellery Queen Mystery Magazine*
"All But the Words" – July/August 1971 *Galaxy*
"Boomer Flats" – July/August 1971 *If*
"Ishmael Into the Barrens" – in *Four Futures*, ed. Robert Silverberg, Hawthorn 1971
"Bubbles When They Burst" – November/December 1971 *Galaxy*
"World Abounding" – December 1971 *F&SF*
"Eurema's Dam" – in *New Dimensions II: Eleven Original Science Fiction Stories*, ed. Robert Silverberg, Doubleday 1972
"And Walk Now Gently Through the Fire" – in *And Walk Now Gently Through the Fire and Other Science Fiction Stories*, ed. Roger Elwood, Chilton 1972
"Once on Aranea" – in *Strange Doings*, Scribner's 1972
"A Special Condition in Summit City" – in *Universe 2*, ed. Terry Carr, Ace 84601, 1972

"Dorg" – in *Orbit 10*, ed. Damon Knight, Putnam 1972
"Rang Dang Kaloof" – February 1972 *Playboy*
"In Outraged Stone" – in *Frontiers 1: Tomorrow's Alternatives*, ed. Roger Elwood, MacMillan 1973
"The Ungodly Mice of Doctor Drakos" – in *Ringing Changes*, Ace 1973
"The Wooly World of Barnaby Sheen" – in *Ringing Changes*, Ace 1973
"Four Sides of Infinity" – in *Frontiers 2: The New Mind*, ed. Roger Elwood, MacMillan 1973 (consists of four related stories: "The Ungodly Mice of Doctor Drakos", "The Two-Headed Lion of Cris Benedetti", "The Hellaceous Rocket of Harry O'Donovan", and "The Wooly World of Barnaby Sheen."
"Barnaby's Clock" – in *Showcase*, ed. Roger Elwood, Harper & Row 1973
"Scorner's Seat" – in *Saving Worlds*, ed. Roger Elwood and Virginia Kidd, Doubleday 1973
"Symposium" – in *Omega*, ed. Roger Elwood, Walker 1973
"Mud Violet" – in *Demon Kind*, ed. Roger Elwood, Avon 14886, 1973
"Parthen" – May/June 1973 *Galaxy*
"Ghost in the Corn Crib" – June 1973 *Haunt of Horror*
"The World as Will and Wallpaper" – in *Future City*, ed. Roger Elwood, Trident 1973
"Seven Story Dream" – July 1973 *Alfred Hitchcock's Mystery Magazine*
"Days of Grass, Days of Straw" – in *New Dimensions 3*, ed. Robert Silverberg, Nelson Doubleday 1973 (Science Fiction Book Club original)
"By the Seashore" – November 1973 *Galaxy*
"And Name My Name" – in *Orbit 13*, ed. Damon Knight, Berkley/Putnam 1974
"The Most Forgetable Story in the World" – in *Long Night of Waiting and Other Stories*, ed. Roger Elwood, Aurora Publishers 1974
"Flaming Ducks and Giant Bread" – in *Orbit 15*, ed. Damon Knight, Harper & Row 1974
"The Man with the Aura" – *Witchcraft and Sorcery* #10, 1974 (aka "Tom O'Shanty's Aura")
"And Mad Undancing Bears" – in *The Berserkers*, ed. Roger Elwood, Trident 1974

"And Read the Flesh Between the Lines" – in *Universe 4*, ed. Terry Carr, Random 1974

"Royal Licorice" – in *Orbit 14*, ed. Damon Knight, Harper & Row 1974

"Rivers of Damascus" – February 1974 *Galaxy*

"Endangered Species" – May 1974 *Galaxy*

"Mr. Hamadryad" – in *Stellar 1*, ed. Judy-Lynn del Rey, Ballantine 1974

"Animal Fair" – in *New Dimensions IV*, ed. Robert Silverberg, Signet 1974

"For All Poor Folks at Picketwire" – in *Epoch*, ed. Roger Elwood and Robert Silverberg, Berkley/Putnam 1975

"Or Little Ducks Each Day" – in *Dystopian Visions*, ed. Roger Elwood, Prentice-Hall 1975

"The Skinny People of Leptophlebo Street" – in *Orbit 16*, ed. Damon Knight, Harper & Row 1975

"Great Day in the Morning" – in *Orbit 17*, ed. Damon Knight, Harper & Row 1975

"Heart Grow Fonder" – in *Future Corruption*, ed. Roger Elwood, Warner Paperback Library 1975

"Three Shadows of the Wolf" – March 1975 *F&SF*

"Old Halloweens on the Guna Slopes" – August 1975 *Fantastic* (aka "Men Who Knew Everything")

"From the Thunder Colt's Mouth" – in *In the Wake of Man*, ed. Roger Elwood, Bobbs-Merril 1975

"Puddle on the Floor" – in *New Constellations: An Anthology of Tomorrow's Mythologies*, ed. Thomas M. Disch and Charles Naylor, Harper & Row 1976

"Fog in My Throat" – in *Superhorror*, ed. Ramsey Campbell, W. H. Allen 1976

"Cabrito" – in *Funnyfingers & Cabrito*, Pendragon Press 1976

"Funnyfingers" – in *Funnyfingers and Cabrito*, Pendragon Press 1976

"Horns on Their Heads" – published as a chapbook by Pendragon Press, 1976

"Smoe and the Implicit Clay" – in *Future Power*, ed. Jack Dann and Gardner Dozois, Random 1976

"Love Affair With Ten Thousand Springs" – Summer 1976 *Odyssey*

"The Hand with One Hundred Fingers" – in *Orbit 18*, ed. Damon Knight, Harper & Row 1976

"Oh Tell Me Will It Freeze Tonight" – in *Frights*, ed. Kirby McCauley, St. Martin's 1976

"Assault on Fat Mountain" – in *Beyond Time*, ed. Sandra Ley, Pocket 1976

"Berryhill" – December 1976 *Whispers* (#9)

"Where Have You Been, Sandaliotis?" – in *Apocalypses*, Pinnacle 1977

"Oh, Those Trepidatious Eyes!" – *Algol* #28, 1977

"Brain Fever Season" – in *Universe 7*, ed. Terry Carr, Doubleday 1977

"Thou Whited Wall" – January 1977 *F&SF*

"Fall of Pebble-Stones" – in *Orbit 19*, ed. Damon Knight, Harper & Row 1977

"Bequest of Wings" – in *Rooms of Paradise*, ed. Lee Harding, Quartet Books 1978 (Australia)

"Selenium Ghosts of the Eighteen Seventies" – in *Universe 8*, ed. Terry Carr, Doubleday 1978

"Bright Coins in Never-Ending Stream" – in *Orbit 20*, ed. Damon Knight, Harper & Row 1978

"Splinters" – in *Shadows*, ed. Charles L. Grant, Doubleday 1978

"Quiz Ship Loose" – in *Chrysalis 2*, ed. Roy Torgeson, Zebra Books 1978

"The Man Who Walked Through Cracks" – in *Chrysalis 3*, ed. Roy Torgeson, Zebra Books 1978

"Bright Flightways" - in *Chrysalis 3*, ed. Roy Torgeson, Zebra Books 1978

"Oh Tell Me It Will Freeze Tonight" – in *Frights 1*, ed. Kirby McCauly, Sphere 1979 (UK)

"St. Poleander's Eve" – in *Chrysalis 4*, ed. Roy Torgeson, Zebra Books 1979

"Almost Perfect" – in *Who Done It?*, ed. Isaac Asimov and Alice Laurence, Houghton Mifflin 1980

"The Funny Face Murders" – in *New Terrors 2*, ed. Ramsey Campbell, Pan 1980 (UK)

"And All the Skies Are Full of Fish" – in *Universe 10*, ed. Terry Carr, Doubleday 1980

"Lord Torpedo Lord Gyroscope" – in *The Berkley Showcase: New Writings in Science Fiction and Fantasy, Vol. 2*, ed. John Silbersack and Victoria Schochet, Berkley 1980

"The Forty-Seventh Island" – in *Basilisk*, ed. Ellen Kushner, Ace 1980

"The Only Tune That He Could Play" – in *Orbit 21*, ed. Damon Knight, Harper & Row 1980

"Crocodile" – in *Chrysalis 8*, ed. Roy Torgeson, Doubleday 1980

"Bank and Shoal of Time" – in *A Spadeful of Spacetime*, ed. Fred Saberhagen, Ace 1981

"New People" – March 1981 *Isaac Asimov's Science Fiction Magazine*

"In Deepest Glass: An Informal History of Stained Glass Windows" – in *The Berkley Showcase: New Writings in Science Fiction and Fantasy, Vol. 4*, ed. John Silbersack and Victoria Schochet, Berkley 1981

"You Can't Go Back" – September 1981 *Isaac Asimov's Science Fiction Magazine*

"Golden Gate" – in *Golden Gate and Other Stories*, Corroboree 1982

"One-Eyed Mocking-Bird" – in *Golden Gate and Other Stories*, Corroboree 1982

"Marsilia V" – in *Golden Gate and Other Stories*, Corroboree 1982

"Make Sure the Eyes Are Big Enough" – in *Golden Gate and Other Stories*, Corroboree 1982

"Tongues of the Matagorda" – in *Golden Gate and Other Stories*, Corroboree 1982

"The Boding Itch" – in *Golden Gate and Other Stories*, Corroboree 1982

"Great Tom Fool or The Conundrum of the Calais Customhouse Coffers" – in *Speculations*, ed. Isaac Asimov and Alice Laurence, Houghton-Mifflin 1982

"Thieving Bear Planet" – in *Universe 12*, ed. Terry Carr, Doubleday 1982

"Square and Above Board" – October 1982 *F&SF*

"Calamities of Last Pauper" – *Fantasy Book #6*, November 1982

"Ifrit" – in *Perpetual Light*, ed. Alan Ryan, Warner Books 1982

"Company in the Wings" – in *Heart of Stone, Dear and Other Stories*, Chris Drumm 1983

"Haruspex" – in *Heart of Stone, Dear and Other Stories*, Chris Drumm 1983

"Heart of Stone, Dear" – in *Heart of Stone, Dear and Other Stories*, Chris Drumm 1983

"The End of Outward" – in *Heart of Stone, Dear and Other Stories*, Chris Drumm 1983

"And You Did Not Wail" – in *Heart of Stone, Dear and Other Stories*, Chris Drumm 1983
"What Big Tears the Dinosaur's" – in *Through Elegant Eyes*, Corroboree 1983
"Unique Adventure Gone" – in *Snake in His Bosom and Other Stories*, Chris Drumm 1983
"Snake in His Bosom" – in *Snake in His Bosom and Other Stories*, Chris Drumm 1983
"Posterior Analytics" – in *Snake in His Bosom and Other Stories*, Chris Drumm 1983
"Pleasures and Palaces" – in *Snake in His Bosom and Other Stories*, Chris Drumm 1983
"Jack Bang's Eyes" – in *Snake in His Bosom and Other Stories*, Chris Drumm 1983
"Bird-Master" – in *Four Stories*, Chris Drumm 1983
"Faith Sufficient" – in *Four Stories*, Chris Drumm 1983
"In the Turpentine Trees" – in *Four Stories*, Chris Drumm 1983
"The Last Astronomer" – in *Four Stories*, Chris Drumm 1983
"Pine Castle" – September 1983 *Amazing*
"And Some in Velvet Gowns" – in *Ringing Changes*, Ace 1984
"The Doggone Highly Scientific Door" – in *Ringing Changes*, Ace 1984
"Oh Whatta You Do When the Well Runs Dry?" – in *Ringing Changes*, Ace 1984
"Two For Four Ninety-Five" – in *The Man Who Made Models and Other Stories*, Chris Drumm 1984
"Of Laughter and the Love of Friends" – in *The Man Who Made Models and Other Stories*, Chris Drumm 1984
"The Effigy Histories" – in *The Man Who Made Models and Other Stories*, Chris Drumm 1984
"I'll See It Done and Then I'll Die" – in *The Man Who Made Models and Other Stories*, Chris Drumm 1984
"The Man Who Made Models" – in *The Man Who Made Models and Other Stories*, Chris Drumm 1984
"The Ninety-Ninth Cubicle" – Fall 1984 *Weird Tales* (aka "99th Cubicle")
"John Salt" – in *Slippery and Other Stories*, Chris Drumm 1985
"All Hollow Though You Be" – in *Slippery and Other Stories*, Chris Drumm 1985
"Ewe Lamb" – in *Slippery and Other Stories*, Chris Drumm 1985

"Slippery" – in *Slippery and Other Stories*, Chris Drumm 1985
"Magazine Section" – July 1985 *Amazing*
"Flaming-Arrow" – in *Magic in Ithkar*, ed. Andre Norton and Robert Adams, Tor 1985
"Junkyard Thoughts" – February 1986 *Isaac Asimov's Science Fiction Magazine*
"Inventions Bright and New" – May 1986 *Isaac Asimov's Science Fiction Magazine*
"Something Rich and Strange" – July 1986 *Isaac Asimov's Science Fiction Magazine*
"Along the San Pennatus Fault" July 1986 *Amazing*
"Gray Ghost: A Reminiscence" – in *Serpent's Egg*, Morrigan Publcations 1987
"Strange Skies" – published as a chapbook by United Mythologies Press, 1988
"The Story of Little Briar-Rose, A Scholarly Study" – in *East of Laughter*, Morrigan 1988
"Task Force Fifty-Eight and One Half" – in *The Early Lafferty*, United Mythologies Press 1988
"Rain Mountain" – in *The Early Lafferty*, United Mythologies Press 1988
"Le Hot Sport" – in *Terry's Universe*, ed. Beth Meacham, Tor 1988
"The Man Who Lost His Magic" – in *The Elliptical Grave*, United Mythologies Press 1989
"Holy Woman" – in *Dotty*, United Mythologies Press 1990
"Maleficent Morning" – in *The Early Lafferty II*, United Mythologies Press 1990
"Apocryphal Passage of the Last Night of Count Finnegan On Galveston Island" – in *Episodes of the Argo*, United Mythologies Press 1990
"The Casey Machine" – in *Episodes of the Argo*, United Mythologies Press 1990
"Episodes of the Argo" – in *Episodes of the Argo*, United Mythologies Press 1990
"Buckets Full of Brains" – in *Mischief Malicious (And Murder Most Strange)*, United Mythologies Press 1991
"Hound Dog's Ear" – *Strange Plasma* #4, 1991
"Anamnesis" – published as a chapbook by United Mythologies Press, 1992

"Oh Happy Double-Jointed Tongues! By Major Audifax O'Hanlon (unretired)" – *Boomer Flats Gazette 2*, United Mythologies Press 1993

"Rainy Day in Halicarnassus" – in *Betcha Can't Read Just One*, ed. Alan Dean Foster and Martin H. Greenberg, Ace 1994

"I Don't Care Who Keeps the Cows" – Autumn 1994 *Crank!* (#4)

"Happening in Chosky Bottoms" – in *Amazing Stories: The Anthologies*, ed. Kim Mohan, Tor 1995

"Goldfish" – Summer 1996 *Crank!* (#7; originally sold to *Haunt of Horror* and scheduled to appear in the October 1973 issue, but the magazine folded before publication)

"The Emperor's Shoestrings" – in *Destination Unknown*, ed. Peter Crowther, White Wolf 1997

"There'll Always Be Another Me" – in *Alchemy #1*, 2003

Non-Ficton

"That Moon Plaque" – in *Men on the Moon*, ed. Donald A. Wollheim, Ace 1969

It's Down the Slippery Cellar Stairs – Chris Drumm 1984 (collects 13 essays; Borgo Press reissued this two years later, and again in 1995 with two added essays)

True Believers – United Mythologies Press 1989

Novels

Past Master – Ace H-54, 1968 (Ace Science Fiction Special)

Space Chantey – Ace H-56, 1968 (Ace Double, bound with *Pity About Earth* by Ernest Hill)

The Reefs of Earth – Berkley Medallion X1528, 1968

Fourth Mansions – Ace 24590, 1969 (Ace Science Fiction Special)

Arrive at Easterwine: The Autobiography of a Ktistec Machine – Scribner's 1971

The Fall of Rome – Doubleday 1971 (historical, aka *Alaric: The Day the World Ended*, from United Mythologies Press, 1993

The Flame is Green – Walker 1971 (Book One of the Coscuin Chronicles)

The Devil is Dead – Avon V2406, 1971 (part one of *The Devil is Dead* trilogy)

Okla Hannali – Doubleday 1972 (historical)

Not to Mention Camels – Bobbs-Merril 1976

Apocalypses – Pinnacle 1977 (collects two short novels, *Where Have You Been,*
Sandaliotis? and *The Three Armageddons of Enniscorthy Sweeney*)
Archipelago – Manuscript Press 1979 (part two of *The Devil is Dead* trilogy)
Aurelia – Donning/Starblaze 1982
Annals of Klepsis – Ace 1983
Half a Sky – Corroboree 1984 (Book Two of the Coscuin Chronicles)
Serpent's Egg – Morrigan Publications 1987
East of Laughter – Morrigan Publications 1988
How Many Miles to Babylon – United Mythologies Press 1989
The Elliptical Grave – United Mythologies Press 1989
Dotty – United Mythologies Press 1990
More Than Melchisedech – United Mythologies Press 1992 (novel issued in three separate parts in the same year: *Tales of Chicago, Tales of Midnight*, and *Argo*; *More Than Melchisedech* is, itself, the third part of *The Devil is Dead* trilogy. Well, I did say that Lafferty was "complex and complicated," didn't I?)
Sindbad: The 13th Voyage – Broken Mirrors 1999

Collections

Nine Hundred Grandmothers – Ace 58050 1970 (Ace Science Fiction Special, collects 21 stories)
Strange Doings – Scribner's 1972 (collects 16 stories)
Does Anyone Else Have Something Further to Add? – Scribner's 1974 (collects 16 stories)
Funnyfingers & Cabrito – Pendragon Press 1976 (collects 2 stories)
Golden Gate and Other Stories – Corroboree 1982 (collects 16 stories and 6 illustrations)
Among the Hairy Earthmen – Hayakawa 1982 (Japanese, number of stories unknown)
Four Stories – Chris Drumm 1983 (Drumm Booklet #7, collects 4 stories)
Laughing Kelly and Other Verses – Chris Drumm 1983 (Drumm Booklet #11, collects 9 poems)
Heart of Stone, Dear and Other Stories – Chris Drumm 1983 (Drumm Booklet #12, collects 5 stories)

Snake in His Bosom and Other Stories - Chris Drumm 1983 (Drumm Booklet #13, collects 5 stories)

Through Elegant Eyes: Stories of Austro and the Men Who Know Everything - Corroboree 1983 (collects 12 stories and 1 illustration)

Ringing Changes - Ace 1984 (originally published in the Netherlands as *Dagen van Gras, Dagen van Stro* [*Days of Grass, Days of Straw*], Meulenhoff #144, 1979)

The Man Who Made Models and Other Stories - Chris Drumm 1984 (Drumm Booklet #18, collects 5 stories)

Le Livre d'Or de la Science-Fiction: R. A. Lafferty - Presses Pocket 1984 (French, collects 19 stories plus essay by the editor and a bibliography)

Slippery and Other Stories - Chris Drumm 1985 (Drumm Booklet #19, collects 4 stories and 1 poem)

Promontory Goats - United Mythologies Press 1988 (contents unknown)

The Back Door of History - United Mythologies Press 1988 (collects 6 stories)

The Early Lafferty - United Mythologies Press 1988 (collects 6 stories)

The Early Lafferty II - United Mythologies Press 1990 (collects 6 stories and introduction by Darrell Schweitzer)

Episodes of the Argo - United Mythologies Press 1990 (collects 3 stories and introduction by Gene Wolfe)

Lafferty in Orbit - Broken Mirrors Press 1991 (collects 19 stories and introduction by Damon Knight)

Mischief Malicious (And Murder Most Strange) - United Mythologies Press 1991 (collects 11 stories and illustration)

Iron Tears - Edgewood Press 1992 (collects 15 stories and introduction by Michael Swanwick)

A Lafferty Reader - Hayakawa 1993 (Japanese, edited and translated by Hisashi Asakura, number of stories unknown)

Notes

1. Yeah, as if.
2. *PLEASE.*
3. I sometimes wonder what Barry Goldwater or William F. Buckley, Jr. would have made of the current crop of conservatives. Bird houses, maybe.

4. Let me hasten to add here that none of the persons I spoke to about Lafferty indicated that he drank in anything other than social situations; face it, an electrical engineer who showed up plastered all the time wouldn't keep his job long, and wouldn't do it well even if he did. But conventions are public, if limited, venues, so I cannot treat it as a secret.
5. Legend has it that Lafferty had five sisters, all of whom "took the veil." I have no confirmation of this from anyone, and offer it only as an aside.
6. I was still working my way through Harlan Ellison's landmark *Dangerous Visions* (Doubleday 1967), but hadn't yet gotten to Lafferty's "Land of the Great Horses."
7. All while listening, of course, to Pink Floyd or Bubble Puppy or the 13th Floor Elevators, any of those feedbacky psychedelic bands. Or maybe Lothar and the Hand People.
8. He sold a good deal to Roger Elwood, too, but Elwood was hardly a discriminating editor; he was, at the time, one of the top markets for short fiction and as a result bought from just about everybody.

❑

City Slickers, Country Bumpkins, Ants, Robots and Mutants

(I Think That's Everybody... Oh Yeah, There's Goblins, to Say Nothing of the Banshee)

> It was a place without a single feature of the space-time matrix that he knew. It was a place where nothing yet had happened - an utter emptiness. There was neither light nor dark: there was nothing here but emptiness. There had never been anything in this place, nor was anything ever intended to occupy this place.
>
> – *Time is the Simplest Thing*, 1961

Not a word of that reads as though it was written by an old-fashioned, Mid-Western newspaperman, but it was. It may not be poetry, exactly, but as prose it's effective as hell. It's to-the-point without being terse; it paints a clear, if other-worldly picture; and it sets up the concept of the novel with a minimum of what my old junior high English teacher used to call "Who shot John."

So I guess it *is* the writing of an old-fashioned, Mid-Western newspaperman after all: Clifford Simak, to be exact.

When I was young, oh so much younger than today, I read my first Simak book: *City*, in its original Ace edition. I was bowled over—quietly, gently, but bowled over anyway. I had never before read a story about characters with *my name*.

That sold me on the book, but the stories paid for themselves. Once I got over the shock of seeing "Webster" in a book that wasn't about Dan-

iel or Noah, I leaned forward and began listening to the story Simak was telling me, and I was hooked.

Here was wonder, but not the thrilling wonder of vast galactic empires, technological super-science or mile-long spaceships. This was wonder that could have happened next door to me. You can't imagine how cool that is when you're 12. The Universe is impressive as hell, but next door is *real.*

Simak wasn't all that interested in exploring the Universe, see. What he was interested in was exploring Man. Not extraordinary men, either, just your average Joe Lunchpail with everyday problems, like hyper-intelligent mutants and ants who build their own civilizations. Oh, and talking dogs.

Of such elements are the stories which comprise the *City* sequence made. There's more than that, of course; for all the simplicity of the prose, Simak's stories aren't at all simple.

What they are is bucolic. Where many, if not most, SF authors at the time concentrated on urban yarns, placed either here or on other planets, Simak took a page from his youth in small-town Wisconsin and saw the potential for setting his fantastica among…folks. Mountain men, country folk, old-timers, and farmers, and not a rube or redneck in the lot, except where it served the tale he was telling. He might include a bumpkin or a village idiot now and then, but there was a reason for their presence, usually a pivotal one.

It's interesting to compare one pastoral fantasist with another: Ray Bradbury was also a small-town mid-Westerner, another stfnal scrivener whose stories didn't depend on intricate descriptions of hardware, but it's hard to imagine two more disparate writers. Although the work of both men seems deceptively uncomplicated, Bradbury's prose is that of a poet (he did write poetry extensively, and lovely stuff it is, too); Simak's is, as I indicated above, journalistic—right down to the lack of contractions. That used to drive me nuts when I was younger.

So why are they so different, text-wise? Leaving aside the crass and obvious fact that they're two very different people, there's one detail that might have had a clear effect. Bradbury's family moved to Los Angeles when he was a young teen-ager; Simak stayed in the Middle all his life. Of course, that's not the whole story, not by a long chalk, but it's a salient point nevertheless.

Clifford Donald Simak was born in Millville, Wisconsin in the late summer of 1904. He matriculated at the Madison campus of the University of Wisconsin, got married at the age of 25, and at 35 he hooked up with the *Minneapolis Star* (which later merged with the *Minneapolis Tribune* to become *The Star-Tribune*), where he stayed for the next 37 years until he retired from the newspaper business. He didn't stop writing, though, just because he stopped yelling "HOLD THE FRONT PAGE, I GOT A *SCOOP*!" on a daily basis. His last novel, *Highway of Eternity* (Del Rey, 1986) was published just two years before his death in 1988.

His first story, "The World of the Red Sun," appeared in the December 1931 issue of *Wonder Stories* (edited by Hugo Gernsback); Simak not only "sold" the story (Gernsback was notorious for not paying for stuff unless threatened by a lawsuit, so I'm unsure if he saw a check), but actually made the cover. That's pretty rare for a newbie.

The story was good enough for Isaac Asimov to reprint in his first *Before the Golden Age* anthology (Doubleday 1974), and in his head-note has this to say:

> During 1931… I began to retell the stories I had read… I well remember sitting at the curb in front of the junior high school with anywhere from two to ten youngsters listening attentively…[a]nd the specific story that I most vividly recall telling was "The World of the Red Sun," by Clifford D. Simak…

Considering the radio programs and movies around in the early '30s that Asimov could have been rapping to his peeps, that's pretty high praise.

Nevertheless, although this story was his first appearance, it was not the first one accepted. According to Sam Moskowitz in *Seekers of Tomorrow* (World Publishing, 1965) Simak's first story, "The Cubes of Ganymede," was submitted to T. O'Connor Sloane at *Amazing*. Sloane kept it for two years before accepting it (without payment); its subsequent publication was announced in the fan press, but another *three* years would pass without the story seeing print before Sloane ultimately rejected it, citing changes in SF trends. The story has never been published, and is assumed to be lost.

I looked into this as best I could with all the principals in the ground, and there's nothing to say that this isn't the gospel truth. Author, editor and all-around stfnally brilliant guy Robert Silverberg remarked:

> Sloane was legendary for his slowness to read and then to publish and finally to pay for stories. The writers of the Thirties nicknamed him "T. Oh Come On Slow One." So the Simak tale is probably true…

And, of course, once I elicited a quote from the inestimable AgBerg, I find final confirmation from Simak himself in an interview with the equally inestimable Darrell Schweitzer published in the February, 1980 *Amazing*:

> I sold my first story, but it was never published because *Amazing* sent it back after holding it for five years and said it was somewhat outdated.

So that, he said as he symbolically wiped the dust off his hands in clichéd dismissal, would seem to be *that*. Simak does sort of indicate above that he was paid, but he may just have been feeling kind.

Of course, the field is rife with horror stories about editors who hold on to stories without paying for, publishing or rejecting them, but Sloane was apparently their patron saint. So my money is on SaM this time around.

Traumatic as hell, and lesser man might have given up the whole thing as a bad job, never again writing for the vagaries of pulp editors. And, well, Simak did, at least for a few years. His only appearance between 1932's "The Asteroid of Gold" (November *Wonder Stories*) and 1938's "Rule 18" (his second sale to *Astounding*, for the July issue) was the publication of "The Creator," a novelette which ran in the March/April, 1935 *Marvel Tales*,[1] and that may have been sold a good deal earlier.

"The Creator" was a what-the-hell story, an item that Simak almost certainly intended as a "so long and thank you very little" gesture. The pulps hadn't been terribly good to him, let's face it, and by and large they weren't whatcha call yer great literature. A good deal of what was published by the editors was, frankly, filler. There might be a couple or three good yarns in any given issue, but a lot of the rest was cranked out by pro hacks in an afternoon, more or less. Editors had to fill pages to keep both their readers and their advertisers happy, and many of them (at the time, anyway) were convinced that their readers wouldn't know schlock from Shinola if it leapt up and gnawed them on the fundament.

This wasn't a very heartening prospect for a young and eager wordsmith determined to be a good writer, and so, secure in the knowledge that he had a day-job, Simak sat down and pounded out his stfnal fare-thee-well.

Only it didn't end up being that. This was the Thirties, see, and stories which questioned the very existence of the Judeo-Christian God were, shall we say, uncommon. It managed to blow a lot of minds (not to mention honking a lot of people off) even though Crawford's little semi-pro magazine didn't have a circulation above a few hundred. C'mon, this is a story that states categorically that the Universe wasn't created by God, but by Some Other Guy. A really big Some Other Guy, but not the old white man with the long flowing beard and robes that Michelangelo painted on that ceiling.

The story's influence wasn't just felt among the seated-on-the-subway readers, but also by a young fan who would make a name for himself (in more than one way), namely Lester del Rey[2]. Moskowitz says:

> …[I]n the efforts of his relatively more mature years no influence is as evident as that of Clifford D. Simak, who made an enduring impression on del Rey with "The Creator"… in which the universe is said to be the experiment of a creator of macrocosmic size rather than the handiwork of God.

No argument; if nothing else, that influence can be seen in one of del Rey's finest stories, "For I Am a Jealous People!", published in Pohl's *Star Short Novels* (Ballantine 1954), a good two decades after the daring Simak.

You may ask why I'm spending so much time and wordage on what is, after all, an early short story. There are a couple of reasons, aside from the fact that despite its place in the Simakian chronology it's still a pretty good read. The first is what I alluded to above when I called it "his stfnal fare-thee-well."

When someone creative is waving goodbye to an arena in which they'd hoped to work, especially after the experience Simak had, the temptation is to pull out all the stops and write a "Toccata and Fugue in D-Minor" instead of just another pedestrian prelude. In a very real way, this is what Simak did, throwing caution to the wind and tackling a subject nobody else had, at least not in the American pulps. It was so much a "dangerous vision," in fact, that fandom—both organized and casual—was still arguing about it ten years later. Not a lot, perhaps, but enough that Crawford was willing to issue that 500-copy chapbook.

The second reason is the clear indication that "The Creator" didn't just influence Lester Alvarez Et Cetera del Rey; it influenced Clifford Donald Simak as well. Religion is a theme he would return to a number of times in his career, always with the interest any good newsman would show an important and absorbing subject, but without the presumption that he knew The Answer. Frankly, I think his story-sense would have suffered from a strong commitment one way or the other, as it would have limited his ability to address more far-ranging religious concepts. Like our universe having been created by Some Other Guy.

It was also his first book—or, more technically, his first separate publication. Although it was a very short run, as things go, it was something other than a cheap pulp copy or tear-sheets for him to hold, and that means something.

So, why did Simak stay? Why didn't he, as planned, turn his writerly energies back to covering local/regional news for a large daily? Because something—and someone—very important happened around the time he was watching Science Fiction recede in his rear-view: John W. Campbell took over the reins of Street & Smith's stfnal flagship, *Astounding*, and all of a sudden not only was the door opened wider to newer and more controversial[3] subject matter, but there was finally a SF pulp editor who cared how good the stories were *as stories*. That's why.

Of course, there had been editors around who wanted good, literate stories from their writers, and who knew that their readers wouldn't be satisfied with less. Donald Kennicott of *Blue Book*, for one, bought stories from such high-quality authors as Nelson Bond, Philip Wylie, Booth Tarkington, and some guy named Heinlein; Farnsworth Wright and Dorothy McIlwraith kept *Weird Tales* from descending into a third-rate *Terror Tales*; and over on the other side of the Big Drink, the tenures of Newman Flower and Clarence Winchester at the helm of the UK's *Story-Teller* saw the publication of such low-brows as Chesterton, Hodgson, Wells and Kipling.[4]

However, periodicals, whether slick or pulp, were never intended to have permanence; as a rule, even the longer stories the pulpsters wrote ended up in their readers' trash cans (with a few exceptions, of course). The major houses flat out refused to believe that there was a market for science fiction between hard covers, and the mass market paperback was still a decade away. There were a few collections and anthologies, but book publication was almost the sole property of the fan-presses (Arkham House, most notably, although there were others) until the end of WWII.

Simak himself didn't see hardcover book publication until Gnome Press brought out *Cosmic Engineers* in its second year, 1950. Originally serialized in Campbell's *Astounding* in early 1939, it's… well, it's a product of its time, is what it is. Don't get me wrong, it's perfectly readable even today, but as is the case with a lot of pulp writing, the dialogue is a bit dated. Not on the level of "Say, what kind of mug are you, gettin' all sappy over some dame?", perhaps, but dated it is.

The story itself has echoes of Doc Smith and Edmond Hamilton; it seems that two universes—one of them ours—are on a collision course, and we have to work with some of the inhabitants of the other one to avoid said celestial fender-bender. It's a first novel, no doubt about it, and sentimental as I am about it, I wouldn't recommend it as a Simakian starting place. However, there was far better to come, and plenty of it.

> Mr. Simak, I realize that you have done almost everything in newspaper work from printer's devil to publisher… but I know also that you have spent much of the past half century either on the beat, in the slot, or on the rim—then have gone home and written highly effective fiction that same day. *How* did you do it?
>
> – Robert Heinlein, in a letter congratulating Simak on being named SFWA's 1977 Grand Master

Heinlein goes on to say that the question is rhetorical: "…I would be incapable of understanding the answer and would continue to be amazed."

Simak was the third recipient of SFWA's Damon Knight Memorial Grand Master Award, following Jack Williamson in 1976 and Heinlein himself in '75. He won his share of other awards as well: the 1953 International Fantasy Award for *City*; Hugos in 1959 (for his novelette "The Big Front Yard"), 1964 (for his novel *Way Station*), and 1981 (for "Grotto of the Dancing Deer," which incidentally also won the Nebula, Locus and AnLab Awards for Best Short Story); and three or four other ones including the Bram Stoker Lifetime Achievement Award in '88 along with Fritz Leiber and Frank Belknap Long.

Think about that for a minute. The Horror Writers of America (HWA), who give out the Stokers, define the Lifetime award as "Presented periodically to an individual whose work has substantially influenced the horror genre." Note the other two recipients that year, Leiber and Long, both fine writers of fantasy, both dark and not. Simak, though?

It's not simple, as befits a deceptively intricate writer. Although Simak is known for his rural characters and settings, there's more there than meets the stfnal eye. Author, editor and critic Barry Malzberg (who penned the introduction for the Simak collection *Physician to the Universe*) says:

> Simak had an odd, tormented streak; try "Second Childhood"... from early *Galaxy*. *Why Call Them Back From Heaven?* is a quasi-zombie novel. Simak is now mislabeled as a gentle pastoralist, the codgers' farmer in the dell, but take another look.

That's Simak's rep all right, and in the main it's accurate enough. Look, though, at just the titles of many of his novels and stories: *They Walked Like Men*, *The Werewolf Principle*, *Cemetery World*; "Hellhounds of the Cosmos", "Bathe Your Bearings in Blood!", "A Death in the House", "The Thing in the Stone". Any of those could have been titles written by one of the Lovecraft Circle.

As for the stories themselves, yeah, Simak had his dark side and no mistake. One of my favorites, an obscure little tale originally published in the March '41 *Astounding* as "Masquerade" and subsequently reprinted by Donald Wollheim as "Operation Mercury" in the *Tales of Outer Space* side of his only Ace Double double anthology[5] (if you'll excuse the necessary clumsiness), concerns two races alien to each other—humans and Mercurians—who would like to find a basis of cooperation, but can't. There's no great conflict, no hatred, but neither is there any foundation for friendship. The story, aside from a scene where the energy-based Mercurians dance wildly to the bluegrass fiddling of a human crewman called "Old Creepy,"

is melancholy, almost tragic. It might not seem so in the colder light of 2011, but 70 years ago this was pretty dark—especially for *ASF*[6].

For that matter, read his 1951 story, "Good Night, Mr. James" (also published as "Night of the Puudly" in the UK and adapted—badly—as an episode of *The Outer Limits* titled "The Duplicate Man"). This is a profoundly human story, far darker and more layered than "Masquerade." It involves an illegal clone, a vicious and intelligent alien called a puudly, and a tragic case of mistaken identity. There's no Yankee trader ready to take advantage of vacationing out-of-towners here, no hillbillies, just the quiet devastation of a human life. Twice.

Even the darkness, though, is tinged with compassion. There is a scene in *Goblin Reservation* in which the viewpoint character, Peter Maxwell, makes an unpleasant choice based to a large degree on practicality, but also out of a sense of the right thing to do, the Human thing to do. One of the few banshees left in the world is dying, alone and despised. Out of duty, other are holding a wake, but no one but Maxwell will simply sit with it as it dies, company in its last moments:

> He walked slowly across the intervening space and stopped a few feet from the tree. The black cloud moved restlessly, like a cloud of slowly roiling smoke.
>
> "You are the Banshee?" Maxwell asked the tree.
>
> "You've come too late," the Banshee said, "if you wish to talk with me."
>
> "I did not come to talk," said Maxwell. "I came to sit with you."
>
> "Sit then," the Banshee said. "It will not be for long… The others did not come," the Banshee said. "I thought, at first, they might. For a moment I thought they might forget and come. There need be no distinction among us

> now. We stand as one, all beaten to the selfsame level. But the old conventions are not broken yet. The old-time customs hold."
>
> "I talked with the goblins," Maxwell told him. "They hold a wake for you. The O'Toole is grieving and drinking to blunt the edge of grief."
>
> "You are not of my people," the Banshee said. "You intrude upon me. Yet you say you come to sit with me. How does it happen that you do this?"
>
> Maxwell lied. He could do nothing else. He could not, he told himself, tell this dying thing he had come for information.

It would have been perfectly easy for Maxwell to pretend to care for this dying entity, or to reflect its own abhorrence of the human race; it wouldn't have cared, and nobody else was around to see. But no, despite his primary reason for being there (read the book to find out, you will *not* regret it), he still could not bring himself to effectively slap the banshee across its face. That might be the human thing to do, but it wouldn't be Human.

Let me elaborate on that, with your kind indulgence. From a purely practical standpoint, Maxwell would be justified in asking the dying thing (it's an alien, not a Terran creature of the fantastic) what it knows about the novel's Mysteries, including how his Other Self had died. He goes there, in fact, with that intention in mind and is frustrated by the creature's unwillingness to give him the answers he needs. No one would have been angry; no one would have blamed him had he tried to somehow force the banshee to tell him.

He doesn't, though. Instead, he asks the entity if there's anything he can do to make its passing easier, and as it becomes more talkative, tells it "You should conserve your strength." There's no badgering, no harrying of the dying energy-being, not even anger until, with its last "breath," it becomes recalcitrant and refuses to tell him anything. Instead, he sits with it as any human might sit with a dying stranger; so that even the most inhuman, unlikeable life form, one with no emotional connection with (and nothing but a mild contempt for) Humanity would not have to die alone and ignored.

That simple gesture of compassion is a touchstone of Simak's perception of what Mankind means, and the scene one of his most eloquent expressions of how a good man responds to the Darkness surrounding him.

You know something? I'm almost 4000 words into a column that generally runs no more than 2200, and I am nowhere *near* being done talking about this writer. Not only that, but I have another seven pages of bibliography to present you.

You guys know me by now, and you know I can wax as loquacious as the next guy (assuming the next guy is as long-winded as I am), but Simak (not pronounced "SY-mak" as I said it as a kid, or even "Sih-mak" as I have since then, but "SIH-mik") was quite a significant influence on my own fiction, and I've read and enjoyed almost all of his books and stories. I hope I can pass along at least some of my enthusiasm to you, the readers, but in any case please bear with me; I'll take a look at a couple more of my favorites and then return you to your regular Grantvillian pursuits.

> A million years ago there had been no river here and in a million years to come there might be no river—but in a million years from now there would be, if not Man, at least a caring thing. And that was the secret of the universe, Enoch told himself—a thing that went on caring.
>
> (From *Way Station*)

Not many writers are capable of summing up Humanity and its place in the cosmos. Many try throughout their careers to do so, devoting reams of paper to the task, always falling short. Poets, novelists, playwrights, essayists; all have done their level best to define the Human Condition, seeking and creating complexities, looking in the darkest corners of their souls to find the one identifying characteristic that separates Man from, say, Plant.

Clifford Simak did it in fewer than 60 words. *That's* what.

Way Station is Simak at his best, combining that pastoral gentility he's so well known for with a subtle, but deep-rooted melancholia that makes Ray Bradbury look a little like Ohio Express[7] lyrics.

Enoch Wallace didn't die in the War Between the States. Instead, he was chosen by aliens to tend the Terran depot of an intergalactic transport system, which has remained hidden from prying Terran eyes until now, when the Gummint notices that he's still, y'know, alive, which makes them curious. This is made worse when the body of an alien is disinterred by a Gummint man. There were already plenty of questions being asked—you can't be 100+ years old and not attract some attention—and things get a little uncomfortable.

Wallace is something of a loner, as are many of Simak's people. Not entirely, but since he's more than a century old, that kinda precludes his palling around with the local bowling team. He does have some "human" companions, but are they ghosts? They may as well be, but actually they're projections of long-dead friends who eventually leave him. The locals are more protective of him than suspicious, but his loneliness is a necessary adjunct of his "job." His best friend, in fact, is Ulysses, the alien who recruited him to begin with. There is a girl though; mute, deaf, and possessed of certain…talents, she is the only one of her redneck family who wouldn't sell the other members for a jug o' moonshine.

The crisis (all good stories have some kind of crisis, or they ain't stories) comes when Wallace, an intelligent man with access to other-worldly science, determines irrefutably that Earth is headed for an unavoidable atomic conflagration. The ultimate outcome is…but no, that would be telling.

Artificial longevity, aliens, intergalactic teleportation, and there's even some virtual reality (a la Bradbury's "The Veldt") as well. Those are the science fictional elements, and most any of Simak's contemporaries could have woven a pretty good yarn from them. Hell, Asimov alone could have kicked it out of the park.

Trouble is that Asimov, however erudite and visionary, had a tendency to create thin, almost wooden characters. In a very real way, his people were there to handle the hardware, to hold it up in front of the reader and (in effect) say, "See? Isn't this cool?"?

Simak was never satisfied with just the technology. For him, that meant nothing without the human component. He was a *rara avis* in the world of Science Fiction, at least for his time - an author for whom Character was just as important as Idea. There are lots and lots of ideas out there to be marveled at, believe me: time dilation and relativity, artificial intelligence, alien-human compatibility, magic rings/swords/books, smart-alecky kids who do wizardry, and so on.

Good fiction, though, demands a story not just about hardware or weird beasties but how those concepts affect—and are affected by—humans. Just plain folks. That's what Simak excelled at. Don't get me wrong; you can't take the fantastical element out of his stories without losing the humanity, too. *Way Station* would fall apart without the artificial longevity, aliens, intergalactic teleportation and so on against which Simak cast his characters, no doubt about it, but at the same time without the people there would be little for the hardware to do.

This really is rarer than you might think. There are plenty of SF writers who are, as we say, idea driven, and more than a few who are character driven. Those who can do both at the same time, seamlessly, are exceptional. Simak leads that pack, in mine own (not-so-)humble opinion.

There's more to it, although for almost anyone else that would be plenty. Simak's stories, long- or short-form, are laced with wit. Not just humor, for all that there's plenty of it to be found (there's something really comical, if slightly surreal, about Mercurian energy beings frenetically square-dancing to Old Creepy's fiddlin'), but *wit*; i.e., skill at engaging the reader and giving his characters depth and breadth. He doesn't resort to giving them funny hats like so many others do, but instead creates richness and intensity that elevates him away from the level of mere pulp.

In *Goblin Reservation* (Putnam 1968), for example, he gives us a well-educated Neanderthal named Alley-Oop, alien bad guys who run around on wheels instead of feet, an android saber-tooth, William Shakespeare in the flesh, and a ghost (just called Ghost) with whom the late playwright pals around. Ghost knows he's a ghost, but doesn't remember just whom he is a ghost of. You get the idea. Well into the story, Ghost suddenly recalls that he is the spirit of…Willy the Shake, himself. Both of them are more than a little freaked out, understandably, and take off running and screaming.

It's not over yet, however. During the magnificent *dénouement* of this wonder-filled book, when superb chaos reigns and the truly magical egg is hatching, we see Shakespeare and his own ghost, reconciled and again friends, dancing together in a moment of pure enchantment. My god, what a *book* this is.

> [W]hat I recall is meeting Cliff Simak [at Chicon II, the 1952 world convention]… There, sitting with him in a Chicago hotel room, sipping a little good whiskey and talking about ourselves and our worlds, I really got to know and love him. The writers of good science fiction are nearly always bright and interesting and likable, but Cliff has a genuine humanity, something calmly wise and warm that is all his own.

No less a stfnal personage than Jack Williamson wrote that about our subject in his memoir, *Wonder's Child: My Life in Science Fiction* (Blue Jay 1984), and I think it sums up Simak's gift elegantly. "Calmly wise and warm" isn't just a richly-deserved paean but a goal, a challenge.

From a personal perspective, I can cite Clifford D. Simak as a major influence on my own writing. Without "The Big Front Yard" and "Idiot's Crusade" (among others) there would be no Gentleman Mechanic from Central Garage, Virginia, no hobos in space, and precious little else of a fictional nature from Yours Truly. Once of the great disappointments of my life is that I was never able to find a copy of the first edition of *City* (which is, after all, a history of the Webster family) for him to sign.

Still, the legacy he left for me and countless other reader/writers in the field is for all practical purposes incalculable. One of the greatest compliments I've ever been paid as a bookseller was when a young college-aged customer returned to my table this past year at a local convention and said, "Last year you suggested I buy *Way Station*. I'll buy anything else you suggest." I take only a small part of the credit for that, much as it made me beam for a couple of hours. The calmly wise and warm Clifford Simak deserves it all. I'll give the last word to a critic and commentator far more articulate than I, Barry Malzberg, himself a humanist of great warmth and skill:

> Simak's work is already buried, but he knew that was inevitable and all of it is informed by wonder in the face of oblivion. What a great writer and more importantly: what a good man.

(As usual, the bibliography below is as complete as I can make it, and I welcome additions and corrections. For Novels and Collections, "hc" designates hardcover and "pb", paperback. UK editions are listed in a similar fashion. My thanks to Phil Stephensen-Payne and Scott Henderson for their expert help in compiling this monster.)

Short Stories

"The World of the Red Sun" – December 1931 *Wonder Stories*
"The Voice in the Void" – Spring 1932 *Wonder Stories Quarterly*
"Mutiny on Mercury" – March 1932 *Wonder Stories*
"Hellhounds of the Cosmos" – June 1932 *Astounding Stories*
"The Asteroid of Gold" – November 1932 *Wonder Stories*
"The Creator" – March/April 1935 *Marvel Tales* (Volume 1, #4)
"Rule 18" – July 1938 *Astounding Science-Fiction*
"Hunger Death" – October 1938 *Astounding Science-Fiction*
"Reunion on Ganymede" – November 1938 *Astounding Science-Fiction*

"The Loot of Time" – December 1938 *Thrilling Wonder Stories* (Plagiarized as "S.O.S in Time" by Australian "writer" Durham Keith Garton under the pseudonym "Durham Keys" in the October 1950 issue of the Australian magazine, *Thrills Incorporated.*)

"Cosmic Engineers" – serial, February-March-April 1939 *Astounding Science-Fiction*

"Madness from Mars" – April 1939 *Thrilling Wonder Stories*

"Hermit of Mars" – June 1939 *Astounding Science-Fiction*

"The Space-Beasts" – April 1940 *Astonishing Science Fiction*

"Rim of the Deep" – May 1940 *Astounding Science-Fiction*

"Clerical Error" – August 1940 *Astounding Science-Fiction*

"Sunspot Purge" – November 1940 *Astounding Science-Fiction*

"Masquerade" – March 1941 *Astounding Science-Fiction* (AKA "Operation Mercury")

"Earth for Inspiration" – April 1941 *Thrilling Wonder Stories*

"Spaceship in a Flask" – July 1941 *Astounding Science-Fiction*

"The Street That Wasn't There" – w/Carl Jacobi, July 1941 *Comet* (AKA "The Lost Street")

"Tools" – July 1942 *Astounding Science-Fiction*

"A Bomb for No. 10 Downing" – September 1942 *Sky Fighters* (non-SF)

"Shadow of Life" – March 1943 *Astounding Science-Fiction*

"A Hero Must Not Die" – June 1943 *Sky Raiders* (non-SF)

"Hunch" – July 1943 *Astounding Science-Fiction*

"Infiltration" – July 1943 *Science Fiction Stories*

"Green Flight, Out!" – Fall 1943 *Army-Navy Flying Stories* (non-SF)

"Guns on Guadalcanal" – Fall 1943 *Air War* (non-SF)

"Message from Mars" – Fall 1943 *Planet Stories*

"Ogre" – January 1944 *Astounding Science Fiction*

"Lobby" – April 1944 *Astounding Science Fiction*

"Smoke Killer" – May 1944 *Lariat Story Magazine* (non-SF)

"City" – May 1944 *Astounding Science Fiction*

"Mr. Meek – Musketeer" – Summer 1944 *Planet Stories*

"Cactus Colts" – July 1944 *Lariat Story Magazine* (non-SF)

"Huddling Place" – July 1944 *Astounding Science Fiction* (Chosen by SFWA for *The Science Fiction Hall of Fame Vol. 1*)

"Mr. Meek Plays Polo" – Fall 1944 *Planet Stories*

"Trail City's Hot-Lead Crusaders" – September 1944 *New Western* (non-SF)

"Census" – September 1944 *Astounding Science Fiction*
"The Gravestone Rebels Ride by Night!" – October 1944 *Big Book Western Magazine* (non-SF)
"War is Personal" – Winter 1945 *Army-Navy Flying Stories* (non-SF)
"Desertion" – November 1944 *Astounding Science Fiction*
"The Fighting Doc of Bushwack Basin" – November 1944 *.44 Western Magazine* (non-SF)
"The Reformation of Hangman's Gulch" – December 1944 *Big Book Western Magazine* (non-SF)
"Way for the Hangtown Rebel!" – May 1945 *Ace High Western Stories* (non-SF)
"Good Nesters are Dead Nesters" – July 1945 *.44 Western Magazine* (non-SF)
"The Hangnoose Army Rides to Town" – September 1945 *Ace High* (non-SF)
"Barb Wire Brings Bullets" – November 1945 *Ace High Western Stories* (non-SF)
"The Gunsmoke Drummer Sells a War" – January 1946 *Ace High Western Stories* (non-SF)
"No More Hides and Tallow" – March 1946 *Lariat Stories* (non-SF)
"When it's Hangnoose Time in Hell" – April 1946 *.44 Western Magazine* (non-SF)
"Paradise" – June 1946 *Astounding Science Fiction*
"Hobbies" – November 1946 *Astounding Science Fiction*
"Aesop" – December 1947 *Astounding Science Fiction*
"Eternity Lost" – July 1949 *Astounding Science Fiction*
"Limiting Factor" - November 1949 *Startling Stories*
"The Call from Beyond" – May 1950 *Super Science Stories*
"Seven Came Back" – October 1950 *Amazing Stories* (AKA "Mirage")
"Time Quarry" – serial, October-November-December 1950 *Galaxy Science Fiction* (Title was changed to *Time and Again* when published as a novel)
"Bathe Your Bearings in Blood!" – December 1950 *Amazing Stories* (AKA "Skirmish")
"The Trouble with Ants" – January 1951 *Fantastic Adventures* (AKA "The Simple Way")
"Second Childhood" – February 1951 *Galaxy Science Fiction*
"Good Night, Mr. James" – March 1951 *Galaxy Science Fiction* (AKA "The Duplicate Man" and "The Night of the Puudly"[UK only])

“You'll Never Go Home Again” – July 1951 *Fantastic Adventures* (AKA “Beachhead”)
“Courtesy” – August 1951 *Astounding Science Fiction*
“The Fence” – September 1952 *Space Science Fiction*
“Gunsmoke Interlude” – October 1952 *Ten Story Western* (non-SF)
“Ring Around the Sun” – serial, December 1952-January-February 1953 *Galaxy Science Fiction*
“…And The Truth Shall Make You Free” – March 1953 *Future Science Fiction* (AKA
“The Answers”)
“Retrograde Evolution” – April 1953 *Science Fiction Plus*
“Junkyard” – May 1953 *Galaxy Science Fiction*
“Kindergarten” – July 1953 *Galaxy Science Fiction*
“Spacebred Generations” – August 1953 *Science Fiction Plus* (AKA “Target Generation”)
“The Questing of Foster Adams” – August/September 1953 *Fantastic Universe*
“Worrywart” – September 1953 *Galaxy Science Fiction*
“Shadow Show” – November 1953 *Fantasy & Science Fiction*
“Contraption” – in *Star Science Fiction Stories*, ed. Frederik Pohl, Ballantine 16, 1953
“Immigrant” – March 1954 *Astounding Science Fiction*
“Neighbor” – June 1954 *Astounding Science Fiction*
“Green Thumb” – July 1954 *Galaxy Science Fiction*
“Dusty Zebra” – September 1954 *Galaxy Science Fiction*
“Idiot's Crusade” – October 1954 *Galaxy Science Fiction*
“How-2” – November 1954 *Galaxy Science Fiction*
“Project Mastodon” – March 1955 *Galaxy Science Fiction*
“Full Cycle” – November 1955 *Science Fiction Stories*
“The Spaceman's Van Gogh” – March 1956 *Science Fiction Stories*
“Drop Dead” – July 1956 *Galaxy Science Fiction*
“So Bright the Vision” – August 1956 *Fantastic Universe*
“Honorable Opponent” – August 1956 *Galaxy Science Fiction*
“Galactic Chest” – September 1956 *Science Fiction Stories*
“Jackpot” – October 1956 *Galaxy Science Fiction*
“Worlds Without End” – Winter 1956/57 *Future* (#31)
“Operation Stinky” – April 1957 *Galaxy Science Fiction*
“Founding Father” – May 1957 *Galaxy Science Fiction*
“Lulu” – June 1957 *Galaxy Science Fiction*

"Shadow World" – September 1957 *Galaxy Science Fiction*
"Death Scene" – October 1957 *Infinity Science Fiction*
"Carbon Copy" – December 1957 *Galaxy Science Fiction*
"Nine Lives" – December 1957 *Short Stories*
"The World That Couldn't Be" – January 1958 *Galaxy Science Fiction*
"Leg. Forst." – April 1958 *Infinity Science Fiction*
"The Sitters" – April 1958 *Galaxy Science Fiction*
"The Money Tree" – July 1958 *Venture Science Fiction*
"The Civilization Game" – November 1958 *Galaxy Magazine*
"The Big Front Yard" – October 1958 *Astounding Science Fiction* (Winner, 1959 Hugo award for best novelette, and chosen by SFWA for *The Science Fiction Hall of Fame Vol. 2b*)
"Installment Plan" – February 1959 *Galaxy Magazine*
"No Life of Their Own" – August 1959 *Galaxy Magazine*
"A Death in the House" – October 1959 *Galaxy Magazine*
"Final Gentleman" – January 1960 *Fantasy & Science Fiction*
"Crying Jag" – February 1960 *Galaxy Magazine*
"All the Traps of Earth" – March 1960 *Fantasy & Science Fiction*
"Gleaners" – March 1960 *If*
"Condition of Employment" – April 1960 *Galaxy Magazine*
"The Golden Bugs" – June 1960 *Fantasy & Science Fiction*
"The Trouble with Tycho" – October 1960 *Amazing*
"Shotgun Cure" – January 1961 *Fantasy & Science Fiction*
"Horrible Example" – March 1961 *Analog Science Fact-Fiction*
"The Fisherman" – serial, April-May-June-July 1961 *Analog Science Fact-Fiction* (Title was changed to *Time is the Simplest Thing* when published as a novel)
"The Shipshape Miracle" – January 1963 *If*
"Day of Truce" – February 1963 *Galaxy Magazine*
"Physician to the Universe" – March 1963 *Fantastic Science Fiction*
"A Pipeline to Destiny" – *HKLPLOD* #4, Summer 1963 (unfinished story in a fanzine published by Michael McInerney)
"Here Gather the Stars" – serial, June-August 1963 *Galaxy Magazine* (Title was changed to *Way Station* when published as a novel)
"New Folk's Home" – July 1963 *Analog Science Fact-Fiction*
"Over the River and Through the Woods" – May 1965 *Amazing Stories*
"Small Deer" – October 1965 *Galaxy Magazine*
"The Goblin Reservation" – serial, April-June 1968 *Galaxy Science Fiction*

"Buckets of Diamonds" – April 1969 *Galaxy Science Fiction*
"I Am Crying All Inside" – August 1969 *Galaxy Science Fiction*
"The Thing in the Stone" – March 1970 *If*
"Reality Doll" – Spring 1971 *Worlds of Fantasy* (was expanded to novel length as *Destiny Doll*)
"The Autumn Land" – October 1971 *Fantasy & Science Fiction*
"To Walk a City's Street" – in *Infinity #3*, ed. Robert Hoskins, Lancer 1972
"The Observer" – May 1972 *Analog Science Fiction-Science Fact*
"Cemetery World" – serial, November-December 1972-January 1973 *Analog Science Fiction-Science Fact*
"Construction Shack" – January/February 1973 *Worlds of If*
"Our Children's Children" – serial, May/June-July/August 1973 *Worlds of If*
"Epilog" – in *Astounding*, ed. Harry Harrison, Random House 1973
"UNIVAC: 2200" – in *Frontiers 1: Tomorrow's Alternatives*, ed. Roger Elwood, MacMillan 1973
"The Marathon Photograph" – in *Threads of Time*, ed. Robert Silverberg, Thomas Nelson 1974
"The Birch Clump Cylinder" – in *Stellar #1*, ed. Judy-Lynn del Rey, Ballantine/DelRey 1974
"The Ghost of a Model T" – in *Epoch*, ed. Roger Elwood and Robert Silverberg, Berkley 1975
"Senior Citizen" – October 1975 *Fantasy & Science Fiction*
"Unsilent Spring" – (w/Richard Simak) in *Stellar #2*, ed. Judy-Lynn del Rey, Ballantine 1976
"Auk House" – in *Stellar #3*, ed. Judy-Lynn del Rey, Ballantine/Del Rey 1977
"Brother" – October 1977 *Fantasy & Science Fiction*
"Party Line" – November/December 1978 *Destinies*
"The Visitors" – serial, October-November-December 1979 *Analog Science Fiction-Science Fact*
"Grotto of the Dancing Deer" – April 1980 *Analog Science Fiction-Science Fact* (Winner, 1981 Hugo, Nebula, Analytical Laboratory and Locus awards)
"The Whistling Well" – in *Dark Forces*, ed. Kirby McCauley, Viking 1980
"Byte Your Tongue!" – in *Stellar #6*, ed. Judy-Lynn del Rey, Ballantine 1981

Novels

The Creator – originally in March/April 1935 *Marvel Tales*; first separate publication was as a chapbook in 1946 by William Crawford, and reprinted again in September 1981 by Locus Press

Cosmic Engineers – Gnome Press, 1950 (hc); Paperback Library 52-506, 1964 (pb)

Empire – Galaxy Novel #7, 1951 (digest-sized); something of an oddity in that Simak wrote the book based on an unpublished novel by a teen-aged John W. Campbell. In *Clifford D. Simak: A Primary and Secondary Bibliography* (G. K. Hall, 1980), compiler Muriel Becker quotes Simak: "*Empire* was essentially a rewrite of John's plot. I may have taken a few of the ideas and action, but I didn't use any of his words. And I certainly tried to humanize his characters." It was ultimately rejected by Campbell for *Astounding* for unknown reasons.

Time and Again – Simon & Schuster, 1951 (hc); Dell 680, 1953 as *First He Died* (pb, originally serialized as "Time Quarry" with a variant ending)

City – Gnome Press, 1952 (hc); Perma Book 264, 1953 (pb) "Epilog" added to the 1981 Ace reprint (**Winner**, 1953 International Fantasy Award for best fiction book)

Ring Around the Sun – Simon & Schuster, 1953 (hc); Ace Double D-61, 1954 (pb, bound with L. Sprague de Camp's *Cosmic Manhunt*)

Time is the Simplest Thing – Doubleday, 1961 (hc); Fawcett Crest D-547 (pb, originally serialized as "The Fisherman")

The Trouble With Tycho – Ace Double D-517, 1961 (pb, bound with A. Bertram Chandler's *Bring Back Yesterday*)

They Walked Like Men – Doubleday, 1962 (hc); MacFadden 50-184, 1963 (pb)

Way Station – Doubleday, 1963 (hc); MacFadden 50-198 (pb, Winner, 1964 Hugo award for best novel)

All Flesh Is Grass – Doubleday, 1965 (hc); Berkley Medallion X1312, 1966 (pb)

Why Call them Back From Heaven? – Doubleday, 1967 (hc); Ace H-42, 1968 (pb, Ace Science Fiction Special #1.)

The Werewolf Principle – Putnam, 1967 (hc); Berkley Medallion S1463, 1968 (pb)

The Goblin Reservation – Putnam, 1968 (hc); Berkley Medallion S1671, 1969 (pb, Winner, 1968 Galaxy Award, the first and only *Galaxy* readers' choice award)

Out of Their Minds – Putnam, 1970 (hc); Berkley Medallion 1970 (pb)
Destiny Doll – Putnam, 1971 (hc); Berkley Medallion, 1972 (pb)
A Choice of Gods – Putnam, 1972 (hc); Berkley Medallion 1973 (pb)
Cemetery World – Putnam, 1973 (hc); Berkley Medallion 1974 (pb, The 1983 DAW edition restores Simak's preferred text)
Our Children's Children – Putnam, 1974 (hc); Berkley Medallion 1975 (pb)
Enchanted Pilgrimage – Berkley/Putnam, 1975 (hc); Berkley Medallion, 1975 (pb)
Shakespeare's Planet – Berkley/Putnam, 1976 (hc); Berkley Medallion, 1977 (pb)
A Heritage of Stars – Berkley/Putnam, 1977 (hc); Berkley 1978 (pb, Winner, 1978 Jupiter Award for best novel)
The Fellowship of the Talisman – Ballantine/Del Rey, 1978 (hc); Del Rey 1979 (pb)
Mastodonia – Ballantine/Del Rey, 1978 (hc, also published as *Catface* by Sidgwick & Jackson in the UK the same year. Significantly expanded and re-written version of the short story, "Project Mastodon," originally in the March, 1955 *Galaxy*)
The Visitors – Ballantine/Del Rey, 1980 (hc)
Project Pope – Ballantine/Del Rey, 1981 (hc)
Special Deliverance – Ballantine/Del Rey, 1982 (hc)
Where the Evil Dwells – Ballantine/Del Rey, 1982 (hc)
Highway of Eternity – Ballantine/Del Rey, 1986 (hc)
Spacebred Generations – Wildside, 2009 (Book publication of the 1953 short-story)

Collections

Strangers in the Universe – Simon & Schuster, 1956 (hc); Berkley G-71, 1957 (pb, first edition collects eleven stories; paperback collects seven)
The Worlds of Clifford Simak – Simon & Schuster, 1960 (hc); Avon G-1096, 1961 (pb); also published in the UK by Faber and Faber as *Aliens for Neighbours* that same year. First edition collects twelve stories; US paperback collects six; Faber and Faber edition collects nine. In 1962, Avon published G-1124, *Other Worlds of Clifford Simak*, which collects the other six stories from the first edition.)
All the Traps of Earth and Other Stories – Doubleday, 1962 (hc); Macfadden, 1963 (pb).Bibliographically, this book is complicated. The first edition collects nine stories, the 1963 paperback col-

lects six; in the UK, the book was split into two separate books: the 1964 Four Square paperback with the same title as the US, which collected four of the original nine stories, and *The Night of the Puudly* from the same publisher the same year, which collects the remaining five. Geeks like me *live* for this kind of stuff.)

Worlds Without End – Belmont L92-584, 1964 (pb, collects three novelettes. First hardcover was the UK Herbert Jenkins edition of 1965)

Best Science Fiction Stories of Clifford D. Simak – UK, Faber and Faber, 1967 (hc); Doubleday, 1971 (hc); Paperback Library 1972 (pb, collects seven stories.)

So Bright the Vision – Ace Double H-95, 1968 (pb, collects four stories. Bound with Jeff Sutton's *The Man Who Saw Tomorrow*)

The Best of Clifford D. Simak – UK, Sidgwick & Jackson, 1975 (hc); Sphere, 1975 (pb, collects ten stories and a bibliography, with author's introduction.)

Skirmish: The Great Short Fiction of Clifford D. Simak – Berkley/ Putnam, 1977 (hc); Berkley, 1978 (pb, collects ten stories and author's introduction)

Des Souris et des Robots – French, J. C. Lattes, 1981 (collects nine stories. Title translates as *Of Mice and Robots.*)

La Croisade de L'Idiot – French, Denoel, 1983 (collects seven stories; can be considered as an abridgement of *The World of Clifford Simak*. Tile translates as *Idiot's Crusade.*)

The Marathon Photograph and Other Stories – Severn House, 1986 (hc); Methuen, 1987 (pb, UK, paperback as *The Marathon Photograph* only; contains four stories and compiler's introduction)

Brother And Other Stories – Severn House, 1987 (hc); Methuen, 1988 (pb, UK, collects four stories and compiler's introduction)

Off-Planet – Methuen, 1988 (hc); Mandarin, 1989 (pb, UK, collects seven stories and compiler's introduction)

The Autumn Land and Other Stories – Mandarin, 1990 (pb, UK, collects six stories and compiler's introduction)

Immigrant and Other Stories – Mandarin, 1991 (pb, UK, collects seven stories and compiler's introduction)

The Creator and Other Stories – Severn House, 1993 (hc) (UK, collects nine stories and compiler's introduction)

Over the River and Through the Woods: The Best Short Fiction of Clifford D. Simak – Tachyon Publications, 1996 (hc, collects eight stories and introduction by Poul Anderson)

The Civilisation Game and Other Stories – Severn House, 1997 (hc, UK, collects seven stories and compiler's introduction)
Eternity Lost: The Collected Stories of Clifford D. Simak Volume 1 – Darkside Press, 2005 (hc, dated internally as 2004; collects twelve stories and introduction by John Pelan)
Physician to the Universe: The Collected Stories of Clifford D. Simak Volume 2 – Darkside Press, 2006 (hc, collects twelve stories and introduction by Barry Malzberg)
Impossible Things – Wildside, 2010 (pb, collects four stories)
Hellhounds of the Cosmos – Wildside, 2011 (pb, collects four stories)

In addition to the two listings just above, there have been multiple publications of those few Simak stories which have fallen into the public domain, too numerous to mention here. Regardless of the quality of the various bindings and cover designs, the material remains well above average and the reader should not reject those publications out of hand. After all, one eats the sandwich, not the wrapper.

Non-Fiction Books

The Solar System: Our New Front Yard – St. Martin's Press, 1962
Trilobite, Dinosaur, and Man: The Earth's Story – St. Martin's Press, 1966
Wonder and Glory: The Story of the Universe – St. Martin's Press, 1969
Prehistoric Man: The Story of Man's Rise to Civilization – St. Martin's Press, 1971

Fiction and Non-Fiction Anthologies

From Atoms to Infinity: Readings in Modern Science – Harper & Row, 1965
The March of Science – Harper & Row, 1971
Nebula Award Stories #6 – Doubleday, 1971

Other Awards

Minnesota Academy of Science Award for distinguished service to science 1967
First Fandom Hall of Fame award 1973
Damon Knight Memorial Grand Master Award 1976
Bram Stoker Lifetime Achievement award 1988

Notes

1. William Crawford, the editor of *Marvel Tales*, would reprint the story as a 500-copy chapbook in 1946. It would see another chapbook publication 35 years later when Simak was the guest of honor at the 39th World Science Fiction Convention in Denver, with appreciations by Heinlein, Asimov, Williamson and Pohl added.
2. For years, del Rey claimed that his name was "Ramon Felipe San Juan Mario Silvio Enrico Smith Harcourt-Brace Sierra y Alvarez del Rey y de los Uerdes" or some combination of the foregoing. His real name was, in fact, Leonard Knapp. Why did he insist on that long string, or even the shortform? The quick answer is "Wouldn't you?", but the reality has more to do with a young man's desire to stand out from all the other faans, a desire I can fully understand and with which I can certainly sympathize.
3. Leaving aside sexuality, of course, and allow me to dispel a myth of very long standing. It turns out that no matter how much Campbell may have blamed his assistant, Kay Tarrant, for his refusal to allow hubba-hubba references in *Astounding*, it has become clear that it was Campbell himself who was the "prude" and not Ms Tarrant. That she was willing to accept the blame for his own puritanical predilections is an indication of how much respect and affection she had for the old (non)goat.
4. I've never cared much for Kipling, but to be honest I've never really Kippled that much. HAH! Oh, come on, you had to know I was gong there.
5. D-73, to be exact; the other side was *Adventures in the Far Future*. I've written about this little gem in detail in my "D-73—A (Sp)Ace Oddity" column, which is reprinted in the collection of those columns, *Anthopology 101: Reflections, Inspections and Dissections of SF Anthologies*, available from The Merry Blacksmith Press. Just so you'll know. Ahem.
6. Not all *Astounding* stories are upbeat adventures about human smart/tough-guys outsmarting hide-bound aliens, much as many people (including myself) tend to believe so. Campbell responded to darkness as well, as he proved only too well with Tom Godwin's "The Cold Equations" among others. A good story is a good story, regardless of tone.
7. They recorded "Yummy, Yummy, Yummy" back in 1968, the same year Frank Zappa released his Sgt. Pepper parody, *We're Only In It for the Money*. Rock 'n' roll is *funny*.

❑

Who?! San Diego Lightfoot Tom

In the field of science fiction/fantasy, there are the names that everyone knows, regardless of their age, and then there are the names that have been largely forgotten because of the graying of the readership and the indignities of publishing. Far too many Past Masters have been missed by entire generations of new readers simply because their books have gone out of print, and newer readers tend to shun the shelves of used book shops.

Then there are those authors who never got their shot at Masterhood. Some died too early and never built up a body of work that would take them beyond their life-span; this is unfortunate but in the actuarial scheme of things, inevitable. We can mourn them, and we can recommend their stories, but in the end, they become lost to the readers who follow.

Some live on, but give up writing for one reason or another: they become frustrated by the cold realities of publishing and quit, or find more lucrative means of earning a living (and believe me, your average vinyl siding salesman makes more money than the average writer), or, saddest of all, perhaps, they just flat run out of stories to tell.

This column, entitled "Who?!", will address these unjustly forgotten scriveners in a way (I hope) that will pique your interest and compel you to get up off the couch and track them down. When (and if) you do so, follow my lead and *talk* about them when appropriate. Tell your friends, your kids, and people at parties; point them to online sources for the books and stories, and if they make less money than your average vinyl siding salesman, buy copies for them on their birthday. I'd do it myself, but I'm your average writer and can't afford to. That's why I do *this*.

As some of you may already know, this is not the only venue I make use of in my endeavors to bring these unfairly ignored authors back to the attention of a reading public eager for "new" material to read. In fact, I already write one column on those once-mighty Past Masters I described in the first paragraph.

Here, though, I'll concentrate on those mentioned in the paragraphs following, the ones who never got their chance to shine as brightly as they deserved. My first subject is a writer whose work I enjoyed, and said "Wow!" about myself: Tom Reamy.

My very first exposure to Reamy wasn't a story, or a novel, but a copy of his brilliant fanzine *Trumpet*, specifically #5, dated June of 1967. Of course, in 1967 I was still in high school and blissfully unaware of fandom in any of its forms; I ran into this copy six or seven years later when I was given a box of old zines by a local fan who was moving and didn't want to pack them along.

I no longer have it, having lost it in one move or another myself, but I can recall at least some of the contents: andy offutt, John Boardman, George Barr's graphic adaptation of Poul Anderson's *The Broken Sword*, and Jerry Pournelle's political column, "The Bohemian Tory," all encompassed by Jim Cawthorne's fine covers.

Pournelle still has fond memories of both Reamy and *Trumpet*:

> Reamy was a pleasant chap and I don't recall him ever changing anything of mine although he did make a couple of suggestions. Trumpet was the elegant fanzine in a time when most were sloppy mimeograph. It was a professional looking publication.

Trumpet was certainly elegant. Although B&W throughout, it was slick offset instead of the usual run of Twill-Tone paper, hand-cut stenciled art, and/or purple spirit-dupe. Had its editors the budget it deserved, it would have rivaled the prozines at the time.

I bring all this up for a specific reason. Reamy the fan-ed was a significant influence on Reamy the author; his prose is as polished as the pages of his 'zine, and as meticulously crafted. His fan writing (and editing) influenced and informed his pro work, as was the case with many other fans. It didn't hurt that he'd been practicing his skill since his teens, refining his technique and finding better ways to tell his stories, and I don't doubt that his success with *Trumpet* attracted enough attention in prodom that it opened more than a few doors.

In a way, Reamy's stories resembled those by Terry Carr:[1] both were graceful and painstaking writers, presenting the reader with finely honed stories that nevertheless had an edge. This is not an easy thing to do, take it from me—I tend to craft my own stories by whanging them with various-sized hammers, a tool Tom Reamy neither wielded nor needed.

Thomas Earl Reamy was born in Woodson, Texas, on January 23, 1935. He stumbled over fandom in his teens, jumping into both conventions and fanzines, the latter as artist as well as writer. He began writing fiction, but struggled both with the process and his own lack of confidence and didn't submit.

In 1953, he formed the Panhandle State's first organized fan group, the Dallas Futurians, which attracted the attention of twins Jim and Gregory Benford. They put together very first SF convention in Texas, SouthwesternCon 6,[2] which featured Marion Zimmer Bradley as GoH, and Forry Ackerman as a surprise guest. Not bad for a two-day con in 1958.

(I feel it incumbent on me to mention that the Dallas Futurians, which Reamy co-founded, disbanded the day after the con for reasons having to do with fan politics that I won't bore you with. The story is out there to be found, but aside from the fact that it was actually done fairly cleverly, it's just fan politics as usual, and we all know how *that* stuff goes. And goes. And so it goes.)

In 1965, Reamy (then working as a technical illustrator for a Dallas aerospace contractor) began publishing his impressive fanzine, *Trumpet*. It ran for ten issues through 1969,[3] twice making the final Hugo ballot for Best Fanzine (it was judged ineligible in '66 because it didn't make the frequency requirement) in '67 and '69. He wouldn't win a Hugo for his fanac, but he did have an award or two in his future.

In 1974, after moving to Kansas City, he established a typesetting and graphic design business with Ken Keller called Nickelodeon Graphics.[4] In addition to a new fanzine, *Nickelodeon*, he also created the publications for the 1976 Kansas City World SF Convention, MidAmericon, featuring what is probably still the most elaborate program book created for any WorldCon. Full-size and hardcover, it featured a full-color jacket by George Barr. *Nickelodeon* was a worthy successor to *Trumpet*, with a twist: each issue contained a nude centerfold of a noted SF writer, the first being Steven Utley. *Nickelodeon* lasted only two published issues before Reamy's passing, with co-editor Ken Keller completing the unfinished third issue and publishing it as *Trumpet #12* in 1981.

Back up there a ways I compared Tom Reamy to Terry Carr, and the assessment is certainly valid, but a better side-by-side would be Ray Bradbury. Not that their stories are anything alike, because they aren't, but because both writers had a strong sense of the elegiac both in execution and in concept. Yeah, they both did circus novels (we'll get to them), but that's just the skin of it—two more different circus novels you'll never read.

Like Bradbury, Reamy settled on a melismatic style, one that flowed musically, with cadence and rhythm. Not all the music was tonal, but it didn't have to be in order to sing. They both wrote with a strong sense of the poetic, endeavoring to create from whole cloth imagery and chimeras that take the reader into places they might not otherwise go. This doesn't mean that they both sang in the same key, though. Reamy's stories are dark, dark in a way that Bradbury rarely approached. If Bradbury can be seen as a successor to Walt Whitman (consider Bradbury's "Where Robot Mice and Robot Men Run Round in Robot Towns" in terms of "I Sing the Body Electric"), then Reamy feels like Wallace Stevens—uncomfortable, vaguely disturbing, willing to probe the shadows in the corner where few of us are willing to look.

It doesn't make for easy reading, but then it isn't supposed to; not every fantasy story has to be birthday parties with wizardly fireworks. For every Shire, there has to be a Mount Doom; for every Gandalf, a Sauron. This is as it should be.

Reamy didn't slam you with it, however. His horrors (if that's the right word) were frequently intense, but never blundering shamblers. Writing of Reamy in *The Encyclopedia of Science Fiction*[5], co-editor John Clute said:

> The tales assembled in *San Diego Lightfoot Sue and Other Stories* (coll. 1979)… were notable for the threatening sweetness of their probing of unconscious material, often sexual, though they often ended at a point of healing uplift occasionally sentimentalized.

In his first story, "Twilla," for example, the monster isn't Dazreel, the sixteen-foot tall djinn with the enormous *schwanzstucker*, but the eternally thirteen year-old girl who uses him to… well, to relieve the boredom of immortality. Nasty little child, no matter how pure and innocuous she may seem:

> Miss Mahan had never in her life, even when it was fashionable for a child to look like that, seen anyone so perfectly… pink and… doll-like. She wasn't sure why she got such an impression of pinkness, because the child was dressed in yellow, and had golden hair (*that's* the color they mean when they say golden hair, she thought with wonder) done in, of all things, crop curls, with a big yellow bow in back. Twilla looked up at her with a sweet, radiant, sunny smile and clear periwinkle-blue eyes.
>
> Miss Mahan detested her on sight.

With good reason, too. This not-so-little girl proceeds to murder a fellow student horribly by means of Drazeel (who exists in an extreme and incessant state of horniness, and likes virgins) pretty much just because she felt like it. That's okay, though, Miss Mahan (her "teacher") takes care o' bidness in the end, turning just about every story Zenna Henderson ever wrote *straight* on its ear. And what a relief, too.

> This all began about ten years ago in a house at the top of a flight of rickety wooden stairs in Laurel Canyon. It might be said that there were two beginnings, though the casual sorcery in Laurel Canyon may have been the cause and the other merely the effect—if you believe in that sort of thing.

So begins his best-known story, "San Diego Lightfoot Sue." Published in *The Magazine of Fantasy and Science Fiction* (*F&SF*) just two years before his death in 1977, it was almost immediately celebrated by all who read it. It was the third of only nine stories published during his all-too-short life,[6] his second for editor Ed Ferman at *F&SF*.

This is not an easy story to describe, frankly. Fifteen year-old John Lee Peacock leaves Hawley (this is a connection between several of Reamy's stories and his novel, *Blind Voices*) after his mother's death for the wilds

of Hollywood in 1960. He falls in with typical Hollywood dregs: a prowling chicken-hawk, an engaging pair of trannies, and Sue. San Diego Lightfoot Sue, to be precise; an artist. John Lee poses for her, and that begins their (very real) emotional involvement.

It ends—badly—not much later. There is death, and destruction, and innocence is lost… no, destroyed. Utterly. There is no moral here, no wise adage to cushion or mitigate either John Lee's pain or the reader's. This is tragedy, fashioned by a writer who showed more than promise; "San Diego Lightfoot Sue" showed certainty.

> He was a writer getting better all the time, and there's no need to sloppify that, to moan and deify him, and to try to make his passing more "significant" and thus more deserving of our sorrow. He was as good as he was when he died, and that's enough to honor.

No less a luminary than Harlan Ellison wrote that about Tom Reamy in his introduction to Reamy's only collection, *San Diego Lightfoot Sue.* All but two of his published works are in this book, barring only an unproduced script, "Sting!", and "M Is for the Million Things", which appeared in an original anthology[7] four years after his passing.

Ellison, a close friend, goes on to describe Reamy as "… a teller of tales whose work had the heft and the graceful line and the vibration of creatures readying themselves to fly." Huh. All I could come up with was "elegant" and "meticulous." Which is why, of course, Ellison is what he is and why I'm still writing for six cents a word.

Ellison's description is colorful, but I can't—and won't—contest it.[8] The book was highly regarded by critics and readers alike, although its actual production and distribution was nightmarish. It was a small fan-press project done as a memorial, much as the Milwaukee Fictioneers had done for their late, lamented member, Stanley G. Weinbaum (*Dawn of Flame*, 1936).

While the stories included (see the bibliography at the end of this essay) are uniformly excellent, their individual elements vary widely. David Pringle, in his valuable readers' reference, *The Ultimate Guide to Science Fiction* (Pharos Books 1990), said:

> Angels, demons, gays, and country boys from Kansas walk the streets of Los Angeles, each as alien as the others. In the typical title story a naïve teenager… falls in love with a much older woman: it all ends in violence with a little black magic on the side.

There was a limited, edition of the book, slip-cased, and signed by Ellison, Howard Waldrop (who wrote the afterword) and artists Leo and Diane Dillon. As an artifact, it's handsome, well-bound, and the jacket illustration is (as one would expect from the Dillons) lovely and melancholy as befits the story, but the copy-editor's habit of using **bold** rather than *Italics* for emphasis is distracting and, after only a few pages, annoying as hell.

That's not the only annoying aspect of the book, though. There were a number of people—all Kansas fans - charged with selling it to both individuals and booksellers, and apparently they didn't consult each other. As a result, many who prepaid for the book never received it; a number of people who didn't prepay, did; and there are *still* individuals who never received their signed copies. Such are the perils of fan publishing.

Distribution (or lack of same) notwithstanding, the contents deserve careful perusal (or, if you weren't an English major, reading).

Reamy's only other book was a novel, *Blind Voices*, published not long after his death. Here is where the comparison to and contrast with Bradbury's *Something Wicked This Way Comes* (not to mention Charles G. Finney's *The Circus of Dr. Lao)* rears its not-so-ugly head.

Like his predecessors Reamy sends an odd-ball circus, Haverstock's Traveling Curiosus and Wondershow, into Hawley, Kansas during the Great Depression. As those earlier fantasists did, he uses the denizens of the Wondershow as a fun-house reflection of those who live there, three teenage girls in particular. Francine, Rose and Evelyn become involved with three of the circus folk: a centaur, a roustabout, and Angel, a melancholy albino who can fly. Haverstock has power over his employees, and he is definitely *not* a nice guy. There is a clear conflict between the innocence of the teen trio and the worldly tendencies of the show-folk, all centered on the withdrawn and frightened Angel.

Therein is the focus of *Blind Voices*: the triumph not only of good (no matter how seemingly powerless) over evil (no matter how puissant), but of Angel over his own inability to take charge of his own life. Pretty heady stuff for Kansas in 1920, *nicht wahr*?

Unlike the earlier stories, this is a tale of sexual awakening; an adultish theme infrequently encountered by most SF/fantasy readers in the mid-70s, but handled here by an author skilled far beyond most first novelists.

There is love (of a sort) here, danger, mystery and wonder, as they frenetically plot to free Angel and the others from Haverstock, the darkly inscrutable owner. The story culminates in... well, I'd as soon not reveal that. The book is currently available from Wildside Press, and I recommend it highly.

According to faanish legend, Tom Earl Reamy died the death of one intently concerned with his craft: he suffered a heart attack while bent over his typewriter (remember those?), finishing a story for Ed Ferman at *F&SF* on the fourth of November, 1977. As poetic as this may seem, and although the story has been repeated over and over in print and online references, there is *no* confirmation of it.

He left behind a small but intense body of work, readily available online from any number of booksellers. That I would urge you reading this to pony up the few bucks and add his two books to your library goes without saying, but I'll say it anyway. Go to AddAll.com, a website I use all the time, and (after clicking on "Used Books" at the top) plug Reamy's name into the "Author" field. You'll find multiple copies of both titles, at a price range that will suit your needs and resources.

(The following is as complete as I can make it with the resources I have at hand. Although a few of his semi-pro appearances are mentioned below, I haven't listed his faanish appearances for reasons of space. If you have corrections and/or additions, please feel free to contact me through Black Gate.*)*

Tom Reamy: A Bibliography

Short Stories

*"Twilla" – September 1974 *F&SF*

*"Beyond the Cleft" – in *Nova 4*, ed. Harry Harrison, Walker 1974

*"San Diego Lightfoot Sue" – August 1975 *F&SF*

*"Under the Hollywood Sign" – in *Orbit 17*, ed. Damon Knight, Harper & Row 1975

"Sting!" – in *Six Science Fiction* Plays, ed. Roger Elwood, Washington Square Press 1976

*"The Mistress of Windraven" – *Chacal* Winter 1976

*"Dinosaurs" – in *New Dimensions 5*, ed. Robert Silverberg, Harper & Row 1976

*"The Sweetwater Factor" – in *Lone Star Universe*, ed. George W. Proctor & Steven Utley, Heidelberg 1976

*"The Detweiler Boy" – April 1977 *F&SF*

*"Insects in Amber" – January 1978 *F&SF*

*"Waiting for Billy Star" – *Shayol #2* 1978

*"2076: Blue Eyes" – *Shayol #3* 1979

"M Is For the Million Things" – in *New Voices 4*, ed. George R. R. Martin, Berkley 1981

"Potiphee, Petey and Me" – unpublished

Books

San Diego Lightfoot Sue and Other Stories – collects eleven stories (marked "*" above), with an introduction by Harlan Ellison ("Embrace the Departing Shadow") and an afterword by Howard Waldrop ("Tom, Tom!"), Earthlight 1979

Blind Voices – novel, Berkley/Putnam 1978

Film Work

"The Goddaughter" (adult film, produced in 1972, only credited as Assistant Director)

"The Mislayed Genie" (adult film, produced in 1973)

"Sting!" (1975) (unproduced, subsequently published in *Six Science Fiction Plays* edited by Roger Elwood)

"The Screaming Night: A Screenplay" with Howard Waldrop (unproduced)

He also served as Property Master on the cult-movie "Flesh Gordon" (1974)

Awards: Nominations and Wins

Hugo: Best Fanzine nominee (1967) for *Trumpet*

Hugo: Best Fanzine nominee (1969) for *Trumpet*

Nebula: Best Novelette nominee (1974) for "Twilla"

Nebula: Best Novelette winner (1975) for "San Diego Lightfoot Sue"

Hugo: Best Novelette nominee (1976) for "San Diego Lightfoot Sue"

John W. Campbell Award for Best New Writer: winner (1976)
Nebula: Best Novel nominee (1978) for *Blind Voices*
Hugo: Best Novel nominee (1979) for *Blind Voices*

Notes

1. And Fred Pohl's, and Donald Wollheim's, and almost all of the other Futurians, not to mention the Hydras and the LASFS gang
2. That being the sixth incarnation of SouthwesternCon, a rotating con much like DSC (DeepSouthCon) is now.
3. There would be two more issues published after Reamy's death. #11 was finished prior to his death, and #12 was assembled from the final unfinished issue of *Nickelodeon* by Reamy's co-editor and business partner, Ken Keller.
4. They also employed Pat Cadigan, editor/publisher of the lovely semi-prozine, *Shayol*.
5. Compiled by John Clute and Peter Nicholls, St. Martin's Press 1993.
6. Four more stories would appear after his death, including two for Pat Cadigan's most excellent semi-prozine, *Shayol* (named after the Cordwainer Smith story "A Planet Named Shayol".
7. *New Voices 4*, edited by George R. R. Martin, an unfairly overlooked series by an important author.
8. I will, with your indulgence, admire it like a sumbitch.

❑

The Snouters

Originally published in the June 2003 F&SF

Professor Dr. Harald Stümpke had only 16 years to study the odd little creatures that inhabited the island of Heidadeifi in the Hi-yi-yi archipelago before he, they, and their island home were destroyed by A-bomb tests in 1957. Sic transit Stümpke, sic transit... the snouters. Or so says 1967's *The Snouters: Form and Life of the Rhinogrades*, in an epilogue penned by taxonomist Gerolf Steiner..

Well, truth be told, Steiner had a lot more to do with it. In fact, he made the whole thing up. With the goal of teaching his students something about how animals evolve in isolation, he decided that he'd give them something to really sink their teeth into: an order of mammals that walked and/or leapt on their noses. Some snouters fly, others hop, still others fish or lay in wait for their prey—but all use their nasal apparatus (or, in some cases, apparati) to survive.

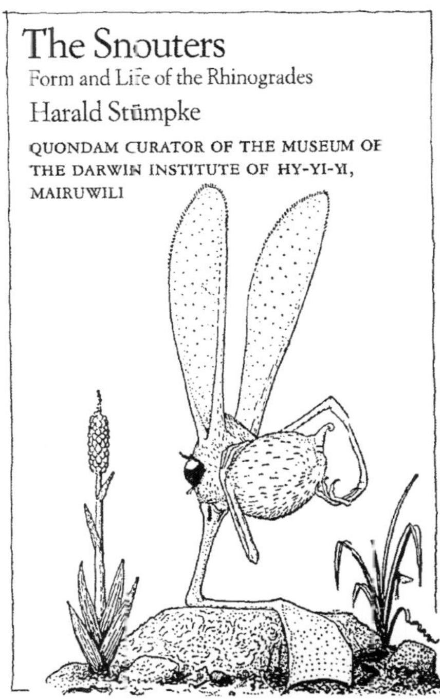

With the zeal typical of the Teutonic academic, he created a text that detailed the snouters and their physiognomy, habits, and reproductive cycles, all the necessary minutiae of Darwinian lore; then sprinkled it liberally with sketches and illustrations, not to mention an equally fictitious bibliography, all of it taken from his own fertile (some might say febrile) imagination. He did it so well that the book has been reprinted, is still being used in colleges, and has spawned a sequel of sorts by biologist Charles C. Davis.

It certainly would have kept *my* interest.

❑

Adventures to Come

Originally published in the January 2004 F&SF

J. Berg Esenwein. That's okay, he never heard of you either. He is credited, however, with editing the very first anthology of science-fiction; indeed, the very first *original* such anthology. Not that it mattered in the least; as an artifact, it's really cool, with a Buck Rogers-inspired jacket, but it had zero effect on science-fiction.

Adventures to Come (McLoughlin Bros. 1937) contained nine stories (none of which you've ever read) by eight authors (none of whom you've ever heard), one Berger Copeman being represented by two entries. Assuming, that is, that Berger Copeman, Norman Leslie, Burke Franthway or any of the other authors actually existed.

Between 1908 and 1928, Esenwein wrote six courses on writing for the Home Correspondance School, and that opens the possibility that a) he wrote the stories himself using pseudonyms; b) he culled the stories from students who never again published; or c) some combination of the above. My money is on "c."

The stories include "25 Miles Aloft," "Science Steals a March," and "It's Going to be True." Even for 1937, those titles were a bit ripe. Still, you'd think it would have had some influence, as hungry as fans were back then for *anything* stfnal, but you'd be wrong. The jacket blurb may give you an idea why: "This book contains a group of highly imaginative tales of the future... Space ships, adventure in the stratosphere, television figure in astounding events."

Thus, although it is undeniably the progenitor—indeed, the grandmother—of all SF anthologies, it sank into the genre morass with scarcely a ripple.

❑

Legal Daisy Spacing

Originally published in the June 2004 F&SF

SECTION 42B of the Floral Disobedience Act plainly states that daisies must be 25.5mm apart—no more, no less. Snowflakes must conform with Registered Snowflake Design # 65537f (mid-grey). You'd know that if you had a copy of Chris Winn's 1985 book, *Legal Daisy Spacing*.

Not that that's all it covers. Nothing less than a manual of world improvements issued by the Build-A-Planet program, it gives directions on how to disclipline barbaric deciduous trees, bottle tornadoes, bleach overly-colorful rainbows, and deal with those nasty Bipedal Growths.

Winn is primarily an advertising illustrator, but his imagination runs pretty wild throughout the book. Nearly every other page has a drawing showing volcanoes being freshened, or parish churches being compressed.

So, why a book about this subject? The easy answer is that it's a comment on environmental issues, what with instructions for oiling shorelines and such, but *Legal Daisy Spacing* goes so far over the edge that easy answers are suspect. Madness is what it is; the madness, perhaps, of an advertising illustrator who just has to let go from time to time and do something really bizarre.

That, at least, is the result, regardless of the intent. It's a delightfully twisted little book that begs to be read aloud, especially at parties, and that also teaches us the importance of Build-A-Planet's motto, "Order Through Vigilance, Decency Through Purification."

There's even a handy, bound-in ruler to help you comply with Section 42b.

❑

The Gods Hate Kansas

Originally published in the July 2004 F&SF

THERE ARE THOSE BOOKS whose titles are, in many ways, so spectacular that one fears they might overshadow the books themselves. There is Jack Butler's *Jujitsu for Christ*, for example, or *Dwarf Rapes Nun, Flees in UFO* by Arnold Sawislak.

And there's Joseph Millard's *The Gods Hate Kansas*. Right from the start you know you're in for something… different. First of all, the title begs the question: do the gods, in fact, hate Kansas, and if so, why? Well, don't hold your breath waiting for the answers. All we know is how the gods show their displeasure—by bombarding Kansas with more meteors per square mile than any other state.

Nine of them hit the Earth at the beginning of the story, the investigating scientists are zombiefied, and work begins on a spaceship. There's a beautiful (zombiefied) woman, loved by a (non-zombiefied) scientist, who, if not mad, is certainly awfully cranky by the end of the book, and there are aliens. What more could you want?

Well, how about a movie? It was filmed in 1967 as *They Came from Beyond Space*, but don't look for any better answers there. By comparison, the book is Great Literature.

Originally published in 1941 in *Startling Stories*, it did manage to predate other, better known aliens-take-over-our-minds yarns, but being first doesn't always mean being best. Millard himself went on to gain note as the writer of *The Cheyenne Wars* and other western non-fiction, none of which are as intriguingly betitled as this, his only SF novel.

❑

Codex Seraphinianus

Originally published in the April 2005 F&SF

Quick: What weighs a bit more than four pounds, measures 9" x 14" x 1 ¾", has about 190 pages, and contains only 111 words of any recognizable language—English, in the case of the example before me (well, a few words of French nonsense, but we'll let that pass)?

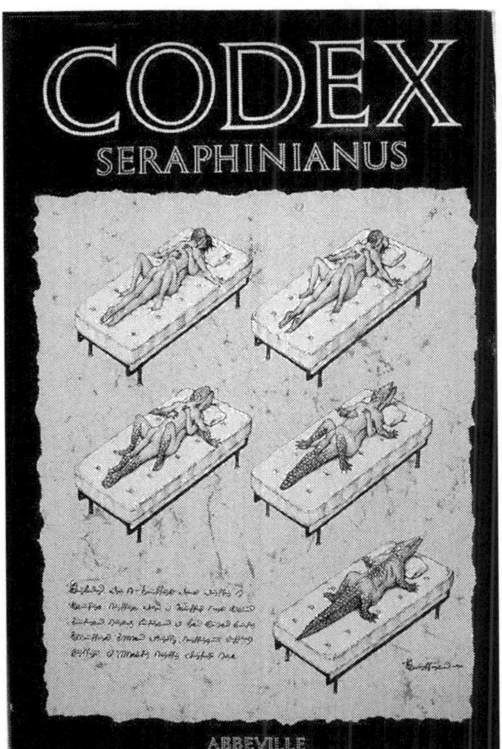

Give up? Don't blame you, I wouldn't have known either.

Back in 1981, Italian surrealist Luigi Serafini compiled a folio of flora, fauna, and persona that are... well, bizarre isn't too strong a word. Profusely illustrated in color pencil and with text written entirely in an alien script, the *Codex Seraphinianus* occupies a unique place in the art-book pantheon. I guarantee that you've never seen anything quite like it—unless, of course, you've seen the earlier Italian or French editions.

Few have. The book has never had anything like mass-market publication, only fairly limited editions. The US edition was heavily remaindered at the time, but finding copies now for under $300 is as difficult as finding your favorite *Codex* illustration, considering that the pages are numbered in the same alien script. It seems to be consistent, but who can tell?

As for the book-as-artifact, I think it's the bee's knees. The art is gorgeous (think Cirque du Soleil, but weird), there's wit on every page despite the fact that you can't read anything, and it's the sort of book that you can page through over and over and always find some new eccentricity.

It's well worth, er, reading.

❑

The Quest of the Gole

Originally published in the June 2006 F&SF

TALL, SLIM, ELEGANT, witty and eminently poetic—by no means, I admit sheepishly, a self-portrait, but rather a description of a wonderful little book by poet John Hollander. Illustrated by Reginald Pollack and published in 1966 by Atheneum, it's presented as an erudite literary study of an old myth as told by various cultures.

The story in and of itself is simple enough: a king is dying, his kingdom is under a curse, and his three sons must go in search of the Answer, which is made manifest in the Gole. The eldest son is brave and strong, the next is clever, and the youngest is dutiful, as is the custom in these tales.

What sets this apart from other, more traditional quest stories is the way in which it's told. We're given fragments of poetry, some long, some short. Each is presented as part of a longer saga of which the rest has been long lost. Connections are made between seemingly unrelated segments because of shared elements (a poet who reads bird-scratchings in rock, a book that writes the future as you watch), and the story is assembled from those disparate parts into a complete and delightful fairy tale.

The author's commentary is, for me, the most fascinating ting about this little book. Only a poet and teacher (Hollander is the emeritus Sterling Professor of English at Yale) could have done it this well, and I'm glad he did.

❑

Planet Big Zero

Originally published in the January 2006 F&SF

Russ Winterbotham, Jonathan Lethem. One wrote pot-boiler SF and comic books, the other is one of the most successful writers on the literary scene today. Is there a connection? I'll get to it, don't worry.

Planet Big Zero was a paperback original published by Monarch (the American International of paperback houses) in 1964, written by Winterbotham under the pseudonym Franklin Hadley. The delightfully-named hero, Ted Narly, lieutenant in the Terran Defense Corps, is captured by the Deotions and taken to their titular headquarters, a black nebula with but a single entrance: a funnel with a curtain of fire at the end.

Now, it would be easy to make fun of this one, but I won't. It's absolutely enjoyable, and if Winterbotham/Hadley isn't Cordwainer Smith, so what? As space opera goes, it's not quite Doc Smith, but it certainly comes close to Hamiltonian standards. I recall enjoying it when I was a kid, and re-reading it brought back warm memories of long bus rides home from school. It doesn't promise anything it doesn't deliver, unlike many of its contemporaries, and Winterbotham was nothing if not a professional writer. It pushes no envelopes and teeters not on the cutting edge, but any kid who won't put down his Game Boy to read this pulpy adventure of Lt. Narly in his fight against the Deotions is missing some good fun.

And that connection between an old newspaper guy and his literary opposite? Well, Lethem used Winterbotham's title for his own terrific story; it was just too good not to use again.

❑

The 27th Day,
by John Mantley (1956)

Originally published in the June 2007 F&SF

One of the most common—and hackneyed—stfnal concepts of the 1950s was our headlong descent into nuclear destruction, and the efforts of our Big Space Brothers to prevent it, either from altruistic motives or the purely selfish.

In John Mantley's only SF novel, five very different people are kidnapped by an alien race and each given capsules which they are told contain enough explosive power to destroy all life on Earth. There's a gimmick, though, one that actually places this book above most of the others, regardless of how many salt-grains it takes to swallow: in twenty-seven days, the capsules will be harmless—assuming that none of the five have used theirs before then. The capsules are keyed to the individuals so that if they die, the explosive is rendered inert.

Not a bad little conceit, all things considered, because it elevates what would otherwise be yet another dreary ideological cautionary tale to a character-driven story that actually has some power behind it. Each of the characters—American, British, German, Russian, and Chinese—cope with their responsibility as best they can; some tragically, some heroically.

One of the characters, a scientist, figures out something very important about the golden capsules and uses this knowledge to bring about exactly the outcome that the aliens wanted in the first place.

Perhaps that outcome is, in retrospect, a bit obvious, but Mantley does it as well as any and better than most. He wrote for film and TV, and *The 27th Day* is certainly cinematic enough. Filmed in 1957, the movie is even more blatantly anti-Communist than the book, which is saying something.

❑

Father of the Amazons, by Pete Lewis (?) (1961)

Originally published in the March 2008 F&SF

RIGHT OFF THE BAT you know you're not dealing with the majors when the spine and the title page don't agree on who wrote the book. "Pete Lewis" or "Peter J. Crown," whichever, is responsible for one of the more… interesting bits of space-age erotica to come from the early 1960s—if, in fact, you can call it erotic. Frankly, if the core of this one were any less soft, you could scratch it with Jell-O, but what can you expect from a publisher called Kozy Books?

The near-palindromic hero, Rev Oliver, is captain of Deep Space Probe A18-17 in the year 2607, with a crew of three (handsome) men and one (beautiful) woman. Of course, this being 1961 and Kozy being what it was, the woman seduces all the men (off-screen), then decides she can't take the pressure and runs off. Yeah.

As if that weren't enough to get your pulse pounding, their guidance system screws up, sending them hopelessly off-course to—wait for it—the planet of the Amazons, and he's the only survivor. No, really!

Of *course,* they treat him like a wimp. Of *course,* he resents being treated the way he treated "girls" back home. And of course, some of them fall in love with him. And I suppose they have some kind of sex, although the only way to tell is that Lewis/Crown's sentences get shorter.

As writing, well, one is tempted to wax critical, but one will restrain oneself. As an artifact, it certainly displays a reasonable level of Coolness, if you're into High Weirdness.

❑

Alvin Steadfast on Vernacular Island, by Frank Jacobs (1965)

Originally published in the May-June 2010 F&SF

THESE PAGES TEMPT THE WRITER to be cleverly snide, ironic, or cynical about the books we present, and it's quite nice to find one you can be enthusiastic about.

Written by *Mad Magazine*'s Frank Jacobs and published by Dial in 1965, this little book is a gentle spoof of the post-Victorian "boys' books" with resolute young heroes inventing or exploring (or both). Here, Our Hero travels the titular island with Dr. Thaddeus Cranshaw, searching for the Doubt.

Yes, it's a critter, and along with the Standing Ovation, the Running Commentary, and the Appropriate Gesture (this being Vernacular Island, remember) is part of the indigenous population, all wonderfully depicted by Edward Gorey, with nary a tennis shoe or fur coat to be seen.

Jacobs's delight in wordplay was one of the strongest characteristics of his work for *Mad* and is the best reason to spend a quiet hour with this little story. It's not the only one, though. *Alvin Steadfast* is filled with good-natured whimsy, gleefully conceived and described beasts (in addition to those listed above, we encounter the Glowing Report, the Small Wonder, and the Ill Omen), and a story elevated above the level of mere punning by Jacobs's obvious affection for the very material he lampoons here.

The story has all the necessary elements: a problem to be solved, difficulties met and conquered, characters driven by purpose and determination who win out against all odds, and even a Conditioned Reflex.

You'll have fun with this one, I promise you, and you'll have as much fun reading it to your kids.

❑

E-Books vs. Dead-Tree Books:
An Alternate Dialogue Between Bud Webster and Jerry Pournelle

Bud

There are those who eagerly promote the demise of paper books and the ascendancy of electronic text, and those who vehemently decry the idea and cling doggedly to their bound codices, no matter how cool electronic books might, in fact, turn out to be. Okay, that being said, where's the middle ground, and how does this debate illustrate the current state of flux in the publishing industry? For the past ten years and more the industry has shown few signs of stabilizing. Technology changes aren't likely to make it more stable.

Does the electronic format *have* to drive out paper, or is there room for both to co-exist peacefully? And what does it mean, not only to writers, but those of us for whom Real Books are a be-all and end-all?

I'll begin by coming to what is, for me, one of the most important advantages the printed book has over its electronic version: I find books beautiful. I find them sensually rewarding, corporeally gratifying, and visually satisfying. The feel of a fine binding against the palm, warming to the touch of the hand as you explore its texture, whether cloth or calf-skin; the impact of an intriguing jacket, protected (in my house, anyway) by Mylar, the light from an over-the-shoulder lamp reflecting off it against the wall and driving the cats mad; the aroma of old paper, sometimes comforting, sometimes alarming (depending on the degree of acidification); the rustle of the pages against your thumb as you riffle them to find the paragraph at which you left off last; the way they line up on the shelves alphabetically, chaos necessarily resulting from order as tall books and thick books alternate in wonderful randomness with short ones and fat ones.

The flashes of wild color, typography and images that whip across your senses as your eye skips from shelf to shelf, recalling the first time you read *that* one, the friend, now gone, who gave you *this* one, the roller coaster ride of nostalgia stopped dead in its tracks by the realization that the *other one* over there you haven't read yet—all these things are as important to me as the actual content of the book.

The foregoing is a little over the top, I'll admit, but I am first and foremost a recalcitrant bibliophile. Don't get me wrong, the content is *the* primary attraction of practically any book, physical or virtual, but I grew up loving the artifact as well as the information it contains. In Junior High School (what they call Middle School now, reluctant as they are to use potentially negative qualifiers), I remember trading a stack of comics for an old edition of Oscar Wilde's *The Picture of Dorian Gray*. Not the first, of course, but definitely 19th Century, with his signature stamped in gold on the cover. The binding was shot, the spine broken, and the front board dangling from the hinge by only a few threads, but it was *old*. I loved that book until it finally fell apart after a move.

(The comics I traded away were infinitely more valuable than the book was, even if it had been in fine condition, but I didn't care—I wanted the book.)

There are other, minor things as well, of course. You can't use an e-reader as a coaster, or to prop up the short leg of a wobbly table, and although I suspect that the injury done to your physical body were you to drop one in the bath would be minimal, I wonder how well the reader itself would hold up. If I drop a paperback, I'm out $7-8 max, assuming I didn't get it in trade or half-price at a used bookshop. How much do I stand to lose if I'm clumsy with an e-book? I'm told that the readers can hold hundreds of e-books. I can understand losing one's library in a flood or hurricane, but by dropping it in the tub?

For the moment, I'm going to pass over what is probably the most esoteric aspect of bibliophilia, the lore of the First Edition with its correlative arcana of edition points, variant issues and errata, since it's a position difficult to explain or justify to those for whom it has no attraction. But think about this: if your book is published electronically, what happens at a bookstore signing? Sure, they'll truck in your older novels and collections (assuming they're still in print), and the fans will bring in tattered paperbacks and the occasional well-preserved hardcover, but what about your newest one? Is there a way to personalize an electronic copy of a book that really only exists in phosphors? Will the electronic signature plate used by delivery services and cash registers become commonplace at in-store promotions? And if so, what kind of memento of the experience will that be for someone who may have driven from an hour or more away and stood in line patiently for longer than that? Or will they bring in CD-ROMs they've burned themselves to be signed?

That's enough in the way of questions for now, Jerry. None of them are rhetorical, by the way; I really am curious.

Jerry

We have no quarrel regarding the worth of hardbound books, but I don't know too many people who think hardbound books will or should be replaced by electronic books. Hardbound books still support a large economy. Publishers, distributors, and authors all make money. Oddly enough, enormous best sellers such as the Harry Potter books make a much smaller profit per unit than the majority of books, because of the huge discounts that best sellers get now; but even so, books are profitable, and book tours to promote books are still arranged.

There's also some profit in quality paperbacks. Less than with hardbound, but that is still a viable business.

It's different with paperback mass market books. Authors still do reasonably well from paperbacks, but neither publishers nor book sellers do. Moreover, there are few promotional tours arranged for paperbacks. When an author signs a paperback book, it is likely to be either at a convention, or as another book to be signed when promoting a new hardbound. Thus the intriguing question of what an author would sign when promoting an electronic book isn't likely to arise for a while.

The case for electronic books replacing paperbacks and other mass markets rests largely on two pillars: economics and convenience. On the convenience side: when going on vacation it's difficult to carry twenty books to read, whether hardbound or paperback. On the other hand, carrying twenty or even two hundred different ebooks is trivial. The economic case is similar: at the moment, publishers like to charge exorbitant prices for electronic books, but that practice is changing, due to competition from more savvy publishers, but also from pirate editions. Readers who would hesitate to steal a copy of a book and deprive the author of his due have fewer scruples about "ripping off a bloodsucking publisher" who wants twenty bucks for an ebook.

Electronic books now compete with paperbacks on price; and it's easy enough to make package deals. Buy one of the older Harry Potter books and get its predecessor as part of the package. Get three Kinsey Millhouse novels for the price of one. Buy this space opera, and receive a free copy of the first book in a new series. It costs nothing to add works to the package, and we can expect to see such deals pretty soon.

Of course, it all hinges on what you're reading it on. CDROM books didn't catch on even after CDROM drives fell in price from many hundreds of dollars to practically nothing because not many people want to read a book on a laptop or desktop screen. I have read perhaps a dozen books that way, all older works I didn't have—one was Samuel Butler's *Way of All Flesh*, and another was his disquisition on identifying Homer. This was before Amazon; if I'd had a simple way of quickly acquiring either or both of those, I'd probably have bought them as books—they couldn't cost much, being public domain. As it was they were free, but inconvenient to read.

But those days are gone. People do read books on laptops, and on Palm Pilots and iPAQ pocket computers, and some like to do that; but it's not very convenient. People read books on TabletPC systems, and that is convenient; I not only read works on my TabletPC, but often edit my own works on the Tablet. Reading on a TabletPC is comparable to reading a hardbound book; they weigh about the same, and it's about as easy to turn pages or browse with the one as the other.

But the TabletPC won't make major inroads into paperback book industry. It's too expensive, and there's no reason for everyone to carry one. It's also not the end of the technology trend. I have seen pocket computers: full Windows XP and XP and Vista computers, able to do everything a laptop or desktop can do, about the size of an open paperback book. They can be read in the dark, or in bright daylight; and it's easy to carry several hundred novels plus a bunch of reference works on the machine, and switch from one to the other as conveniently as you might fish into your brief case to change reading matter.

That still won't do it because not everyone wants to carry a pocket computer: but nearly everyone carries a pocket telephone. Present telephones aren't very good for reading books, but the next generation will be. The iPhone is getting lots of publicity. It's not very good as a telephone, but it has shown the way.

We will soon have telephones that are also pocket computers. I have seen the prototypes. It's a telephone (with Bluetooth or wired headset); Text message (Blackberry substitute); camera; GPS device; travel direction device; Yellow Pages; notebook; voice notebook; Personal Data Assistant; calendar; and probably some other functions I haven't thought of. Most people carry cell phones now; more and more carry several of these. I don't think it will be long before nearly everyone has the device I describe. I suspect that fashions will change, so that instead of hanging devices on your belt or stuffing them into pockets, both men and women will carry some kind of personal handbag to carry one's personal computer.

Your telephone will also hold 1,000 books you don't have to carry separately, and they will be as easily read on your telephone as they would be on paper.

When that happens, the paperback book will be as good as dead.

As to the other points: people don't usually carry their pocket telephones into the bathtub. Whether the convenience of reading in the bathtub will outweigh the inconvenience of carrying physical books that are already present in your telephone may be debated, but I suspect there is only one outcome to that. Electronic books have the possibility of backup copies; that's rather harder to do with paperbacks.

Bud

To hear a lot of people talk, the mass market paperback is already dead, what with distributor-dictated inventories and a returns policy that should have been abandoned decades ago, but let's let that lie for the moment. You can, of course, back up a copy of a paper book: buy another one. However, that's more glib than on-point, so let it pass.

Let me ask you this, though, since you bring up books-on-phones. How easy is it to read on a phone screen? How easy for someone who has to wear glasses? Who suffers from presbyopia? How visible is that screen in sunlight? How much text can a phone screen hold as opposed to the standard 4.5x7" mass-market paperback, or the increasingly common 5.25x8" trade paper? Does the convenience of having your library with you at all times outweigh the squints, and the inevitable headaches? I suspect that to many, at least those young or fortunate enough to not suffer from optical challenges, it will be, but I have to wear reading glasses as it is, and I'm fairly sure that reading on a small screen isn't going to make the experience enjoyable.

The tiffle-taffle about print books being replaced by electronic is primarily in the country of Blogistan. I see people posting gleefully that within five years (or two, or ten, depending on how their dice-throw came up, one supposes), books will have gone the way of the vinyl LP and everything will have magically become available only in easy-to-download MP3/PDF form. That there is an enormous industry devoted to printing and binding paper books with at least a century's momentum behind it seems to have slipped beneath their radar; these are the same sorts who, twenty years ago, were cheerfully predicting the advent of the "paperless office." Perhaps not the same people, but certainly the same Voice. I haven't noticed fewer paper shredders being marketed, or seen fewer copiers and laser printers in the offices I visit.

I have to bring something else up as well, and that's competing electronic formats. If I accumulate a library of 1,000 books to be read on the Mattel "My Li'l E-Reader" at a cost of a few dollars apiece, what happens when that breaks down and I have to switch to something else, like the Nerdstrom M-850, which has a proprietary software that won't run the Mattel books? I'm making those up because I don't follow the e-reader technology the way you do, but as the joke from *Men In Black* goes: "Looks like I'll have to buy the White Album all over again." How many times do I have to buy the same book just because the gizmos don't speak the same language?

I find it interesting that you cite piracy as a competitive factor in changing the price and availability of e-books, not to mention the perception of the publishers as "bloodsuckers," since essentially the same sort of thing happened in the post-war years with sound recordings. When that industry switched to the long-playing record, the Big Boys concentrated almost solely on contemporary material, ignoring the market for their earlier recordings. A number of pirate labels sprang up to reissue classic jazz on 10" LPs, one of them rather proudly dubbing itself "Jolly Roger." The majors did, eventually, bring their back catalogs into press, but not until after the pirates screwed themselves by bootlegging recordings that were then currently available.

Whether or not that will happen with books, I just don't know. Certainly the Internet is crammed with pirate sites, both domestic and foreign, offering scans (often imperfectly OCR'ed) of a writer's entire *oeuvre*, and eBay abounds with sellers flogging CD-ROMs filed with hundreds of stories and novels. Many of those are, in fact, in the public domain, but most of it is protected.

Which rather handily brings us back to our principal subject: the relative merits of print over phosphor. When one of these modern-day Bluebeards wants to upload last year's Hugo-winning novel, he has two options (well, three, but the third one—not to do it at all—isn't one he's likely to consider): he can either get a copy of the book and laboriously scan each page, perform the ritual OCR, and then convert it to his preferred format, or he can download a legitimate copy, hack the protection (if there is any), fiddle with the margins a bit and change the font, then offer *that* one to his eager customers/patrons. So, with a website waiting to be filled with literary "warez," which is he most likely to do? I know what I would do, but I'm lazy as hell.

Set piracy aside for now, though. You mention the possibility of bundling older titles on CD-ROM with current print books as come-ons. I have to ask, if only for the sake of form, if it doesn't make more sense for the publisher to not do this, but rather (as has been done in the past) simply to re-package the older titles, perhaps at a discount, and offer them? Series books were done like this for decades, with the newest Tom Swift or Nancy Drew being accompanied on the bookstore shelves by the previous volumes in new printings. Why would they offer them for free when they can still make money on them?

Well, for one thing, we have to decipher what the sales numbers tell us. We all know that there are more books being sold every year, but the question is how those sales are distributed: is it more copies of fewer titles, fewer copies of more titles, or (as is devoutly to be wish'd) more copies of even more titles? If the last, we're good to go and all this is moot; more people are buying more books, so all we have to do is keep writing them.

But the first two choices—either of which is far more likely than the last one—give your prediction a lot more weight. The publishers have to create a broader market somehow, and traditionally one of the most effective means of stimulating sales is to give stuff away. Loss-leaders, they used to be called, because although the producer might lose a little money on the freebie, he stands to make much more from the consumer because a) he's getting something for nothing, and is therefore more likely to spend the bucks he just "saved," and b) it promotes good will, which will keep the consumer returning to the producer, even when there's nothing free to be had.

Thus we come to a business model you certainly can discuss far more intelligently than I, so I'll toss the ball back to you by invoking the name of what is perhaps, for better or worse, a unique example in the publishing industry: Baen Books.

JERRY

You still do not understand. What people now carry as cell phones are not satisfactory for reading books; but the iPhone comes close, and what will come after the iPhone will be about the size of a paperback book. I have seen such devices, and they are as easy to read as any paperback. If you squint reading a paperback you probably will squint reading on the new screens—but maybe not, because the electronic medium will let you adjust the print size. Ginny Heinlein couldn't read books at all towards the end of her life, but she was able to read email letters on screen.

You do ask a number of unrelated questions, leaving me to organize the responses. I'll try.

I don't claim to be a marketing expert, and your guesses about marketing packages are likely to be as good as mine. I'm not a publisher. At the moment publishers are experimenting, and they make errors. There are multiple formats—just as there were multiple VCR formats. Note that the VCR itself has vanished, and there's competition between Blu-Ray and HD DVD; but the movie rental business hasn't vanished. There will be a single ebook format as soon as someone wins the competition for what device people will carry. It may be iPhone compatible, or something else. We'll just have to wait and see.

Baen makes small profits on paperback books, but fairly good profits on hardbound. I have a number of books with Baen, and I have been convinced that the existence of free electronic copies of books doesn't hurt the sales of paper copies—or hasn't so far. We can all hope that will continue, but it's not entirely clear. When Jim Baen was alive he built an on-line community of Baen Books readers, starting with the BYTE INFORMATION EXCHANGE (BIX) and continuing through Genie and then to the web. His successors have continued this practice. As a result, Baen buyers tend to scorn pirate editions.

Regarding piracy: this is a key question, but it affects the entire entertainment industry, not just book publishing. The mechanics of piracy get easier every month. There were pirated copies of the latest Harry Potter novel available before the official release date. Automatic scanning devices are quite accurate now and can only get better. They're relatively costly, but pirates seem to have access to them.

Pirates operate from various motives. Some use the lure of free books (or videos, or songs) to draw people to their web sites and collect money from advertisements; in other words, they use stolen material to draw a crowd, then sell their wares. Others have no profit motive at all. Some are genuine fans who want other people to read works they enjoyed. Some do it to impress their friends: I had Harry Potter on line before you could buy it in a book store! Another enthusiast has translated the last Harry Potter into French, and has it on line months before the official French translation will be published!

It hardly matters why they do it: we know there are people who will offer pirated works for free, and it's unlikely there will be fewer of them as it gets easier to scan in paperback works. Refusing to allow works to be offered in electronic form will not stop electronic piracy.

Baen books has shown that it's still possible to sell books in both electronic and printed form. I recently got significant advances for electronic rights to many of my older works. Clearly Baen thinks they can continue to make profits in this medium.

Other publishers haven't had such good experience, but many of them have not tried very hard. Some tried to sell eBooks for almost as much as they would charge for hard-bounds, then wondered why they had few sales. The result was predictable. That hardly means that publishers won't wise up, and many of them have already done so. Everyone is watching Baen.

The mass market book industry is in transition. One result of this is the author's death spiral. It works this way: a publisher ships 50,000 copies of a paperback book. It doesn't make any best seller list, and the sell through is 50% (which seems to be average). When the next book comes in, the publisher must decide whether this author is worth supporting at the previous level. All too often, the answer is no; so the press run for the next book is, say, 30,000 copies. That also gets a 50% sell through (again about average). The next press run is 20,000, and then it's decided that author isn't profitable. The author can decide to write under a pen name and try to start over, or get a day job.

Whether electronic book publishing will change this is an open question. It may help. It certainly offers authors an alternative way of publishing.

I don't think any of us has a working crystal ball. I do think there are vast changes coming. TV didn't entirely replace radio, but it did finish off the market for radio soap opera scripts. TV also ended the adventure magazine market. Stuart Cloete (*Rags of Glory*) told me he got $4,200 in 1948 for a short story in the Saturday Evening Post; he lived off that for the year it took to write his first novel. Breaking into the Post was the goal of most fiction writers, until the Post—founded by Benjamin Franklin!—essentially vanished. I have no doubt that we'll have equally significant changes in publishing as technology advances.

One thing I am sure of. Story tellers will always find a way to make a living. We always have.

Bud

From your mouth to the gods' ears, boychik. As a writer who practices only the short form, I've watched in dismay as market after market has fallen by the way, to be replaced—if that's the right word—by a plethora of on-line 'zines that seem to be run by fifteen year-olds in Mom and Dad's basement. Not all of them, certainly (I'm poetry editor and columnist for one of the better ones), but an infinite amount of web space, cheap bandwidth and easy software can make even the most amateur efforts look like the Big Boys—until you start checking the content. Haven't these people heard of spell-checkers?

Jim Baen managed to work his magic with the cooperation of most, if not all, of his authors, and by relying on his zealous and passionate online fan base, but mostly because he himself was convinced that it would succeed. Now that he's gone, it remains to be seen if the momentum he built will continue, or if literary entropy will take over. I respect his success, even if I don't care for some of what he published. I could, however, have said exactly the same thing about DAW books in the late 1970s, so *plus ça change*, if you will.

I agree about the silliness of charging high prices for e-books, and not just because people won't pay $29.95 for something they know damn well cost the publisher a penny apiece in bulk (for the physical disk, not the content). It has a bad tendency to cause resentment in your customer base, and when that happens, they're far more likely to buy used paperbacks or e-texts from some pirate site than from traditional retailers—and that goes for the publisher's entire catalog.

I wish I could deny the existence of the death-spiral, but I've seen it all too many times, even with people I know to be fine and reliable writers. And it does force a spiraling writer to consider alternate formats for his next book, assuming his "real" publisher won't take it. Case in point: Lawrence Watt-Evans and his Ethshar series. Tor, his current publisher, wasn't interested in the next book because sales figures for that series were lower than other titles he was doing for them. So, in the tradition of storytellers down through the ages, he took the then-new Ethshar novel to the web, posting each chapter only after he'd received a set amount of money in the form of donations. Those who had ponied up a certain amount were promised a paper copy of the book, I'll gleefully point out, and the only two readers who turned it down were one who preferred the e-version and another who didn't want to pay the postage to Australia.

Now, he didn't make nearly what he would have even from an advance from his publisher, but he proved that there were plenty of Ethshar/Watt-Evans fans out there who would, in fact, pay for the book in electronic form. The book is currently available as a trade paperback from

Wildside, as well as a limited edition hardcover, and will be issued by Cosmos in mass-market format soon as well.

The on-line magazine I'm involved with, HelixSF.com, does much the same, except that we don't cliff-hang the reader in order to get their pocket change. It's all there to be read and enjoyed, but we make it clear that unless donations come in, two things will happen: first, the writers won't get paid, and second, we won't be able to continue publishing. Thus far we've been at least as successful as any semi-prozine out there, and none of the story tellers have been paid less than three figures.

What I draw from all this is that books, both e- and tree, can co-exist, and that, whether or not I like it, e-books will become more and more common as the hardware/software evolves. I hope that publishers don't lose their enthusiasm for the physical book, because I cherish them beyond their content, but I'm only too well aware that I'm hardly their target demographic.

I'll pose one more question, then leave it to you to sum up. I know you see the e-reader, in whatever form it may take, becoming more and more available and usable in the next decade. What do you see for the bound codex in, say, 50 years? 100? Will they still grace the shelves of those of us dyed-in-the-wool bibliophiles, or will even that word change its definition?

Jerry

First, short fiction markets: I used to edit anthologies. John Carr and I turned out two or three a year, often buying first stories from new writers. There was enough money in the anthologies that John Carr could, and did, work with writers, doing the kind of editorial consultations that now come only with big novels and large advances.

That market is gone. There are anthologies, but they don't make enough to allow someone like Carr to make a living grooming writers. I can't afford to do anthologies for what they bring now. And yet: we are even now making deals for electronic rights to some of my older anthologies (*War World* almost certainly and possibly *There Will Be War*). They won't be reprinted on paper, but they'll still be available, and they'll still make money for the contributors.

It may be that ebooks will revitalize that market.

We can't predict the future, but we can invent it. Books are convenient and have been around a long time; there's no reason to suppose they will vanish in the next fifty years. However, there's good reason to believe the book business will change a lot.

There are many kinds of books. Some have only information and have to be revised often. That's an obvious candidate for an electronic book. Some are an aesthetic experience in themselves: Easton Press makes a lot of money with those, and so long as people will pay for leather and paper and color illustrations, they'll continue to do so.

The real question is mass market books. That especially includes magazines. Magazines have photographs and illustrations and color. They are expensive to print and are usually thrown away after being read. At one time *Byte* magazine was enormous, so thick that it could only be printed by the company that printed the Sears catalogue. It was tremendously profitable, and could afford to pay what in retrospect were wonderfully high editorial rates and generous expense accounts. Now it's gone. So are a lot of other magazines.

The instant that most people carry something like an improved iPhone, nearly all the rest of the magazines are doomed. A few specialty magazines may remain, but the notion of printing something both elaborate and ephemeral on dead trees is already bizarre.

But if printed magazines vanish, there will be competition among electronic magazines; that will almost certainly help the short story market. Of course the short story may have changed a lot. Writers may have to find ways to illustrate their stories, add maps, perhaps add photographs to set the scenes. There may be photos and even short action clips of actors portraying characters. We can look forward to a number of experiments as electronic magazines try to attract readers.

That's nearly inevitable once most people are carrying gadgets capable of displaying text, color pictures, action shots, video, and sound.

And that's our opportunity. Some of us will take advantage of it.

Mr. Heinlein told me two things about making a living as a writer. The first was, "It's a good racket. We work inside, sitting down, and there's no heavy lifting." The second was, "Never forget we're professional gamblers. Get your house and car paid for free and clear the first time you make a big sale."

I doubt that the new technology will change that much.

❑

Searching and Researching:
An Alternate Dialogue Between Bud Webster and Jerry Pournelle

Bud

Several years ago, I was on a panel at a convention in North Carolina that dealt with how writers research the subjects that they write about. There were four of us on the panel, all of whom fundamentally wrote the same things (SF, fantasy, some non-fiction) and all of whom wrote in widely divergent ways. A number of questions were posed by the moderator, and later on by the audience, and as someone who is keenly interested in process, I found the panel by far one of the most fascinating I've ever been on.

The basic thrust of the panel revolved around a dual axis—how do you do it, and what do you need to have in order to do it well. There are, of course, shades to both these, and we'll get to them, I promise.

Let me pose this question first and also its corollary, since to me it's one of the most important: how much research do you do? Is it possible to over-research a subject, and if so, what can go wrong?

My own feeling is that you do as much as it takes to ensure that what you're writing is accurate. This is especially vital when writing nutzen-bolts SF, where you not only have circumstances hinging on a specific point, but also a readership ready, willing and able to not only catch you out in a boner, but to write lengthy letters to your editor gleefully delineating which particular scientific pooch you screwed.

I'm convinced that it's vital for the writer to know at least as much, if not more, about a plot element than the reader does, all things being equal. Obviously this doesn't include the high end of the bell-curve—I'm never going to know as much about physics as Feynman did, or as much about conducting a symphony orchestra as George Solti—but it seems to me that you have to at least cover the lower 80% of that curve or you're not serving either the story or its readers at all well.

Too much research? Well, I assume that you could sink so deep into studying a subject that you never get around to writing the story/article you contracted to write in the first place, but other than that I'm not sure there's a down-side. If nothing else, over-researching a subject might just inspire you to write other stories, other articles, and spread the effort out over more than just one piece.

Before I turn this over to you, though, let me pose another question so you'll have more to talk about. When you're stuck on a point, and that point is necessary to the success of what you're writing, who you gonna call? Is it kosher to call the head of whatever department is appropriate at your local university, or the head honcho at the science museum downtown? How about the medical examiner for whichever county or municipality is your setting?

Let me give you a couple of examples from my own experience, then I'll hand the mike to you. When I was writing "Triumph in the Desert" for *Analog* a few years ago, there was a scene that took place at a Mojave airstrip in the late 1950s. I wanted to know what kind of small craft might be seen there and at that time, so I called the local air museum out by the airport here in Richmond. The guy I spoke to wasn't sure, but he knew *just* the fellow for me to talk to, and gave me his phone number. Sure enough, not only was he able to name a half-dozen or more small planes and give me details that would make the scene live and breathe, but when I asked (just for giggles) if there might be an auto-gyro there, he laughed and said, "Maybe, but only a madman would fly one of those in the desert!" Since this scene took place at a UFO convention, I figured it wasn't a stretch.

More recently, I had reason to contact the people who manufacture the Segway vehicles for information on turning one of them into a robot. I spent some time e-mailing one of their PR flacks and not getting much of anywhere with the questions I had, but then she put me in touch with one of the engineers and boy, did the info begin to flow then! Not only was he willing and able to think creatively and help me equip an alien artificial intelligence with arms and mobility, he was completely fascinated that a writer was actually consulting him before going off and writing something silly.

Same thing happened with NASA. The PR flack couldn't really be bothered with answering my questions, but he did give me the contact information for the Neutral Buoyancy Lab, and they almost fell over themselves to be helpful, even to passing me along yet again to an administrator who'd been up in the Comet and who was just as eager to make sure I got it right.

So, enough from me for now. What are your thoughts (and some examples if you will) on those two questions, Jerry?

Jerry

First let me state it simply: you can't do too much research. It's not possible to understand your subject too well. Having said that, there are limits. You owe your readers a good bit, but not the entire Earth. Obviously if you are doing a big book for a lot of money, you have a larger obligation than if you're doing a gimmick story for a magazine. We do have to make a living at this, and while giving the reader more than he has a right to expect is usually a good thing to do, we can't afford to do that every time.

Readers do count on you to be accurate. I got many of my notions about science—and scientific ethics—from science fiction stories I read in high school. Fortunately Hal Clement had a keen sense of scientific ethics, as did Mr. Heinlein, so I didn't learn the wrong lessons. If you assert something as fact in a story, it should be fact, unless it's part of the story. You don't throw in false facts just to be doing it.

Let me be clear on that: it's important not to make up details that have no relationship to reality. I know that's done often, particularly when the scene takes place in some obscure location, or in an organization that few know much about, such as a missile control center: but assuming that it's supposed to be a real location and a real organization, you have some obligation to get the facts straight.

An example of how not to do it: in the movie War Games, they have one missile launch officer threatening the other with a pistol. A very great number of people who ought to know better—big names in the national news media—act as if that scene describes a real missile control center. It doesn't. I happen to have been involved in the design of those control centers, and the first criterion was that it be physically impossible to launch the birds without the willing cooperation of both missile officers: they cannot threaten each other, because they cannot see each other when each is seated at his launch control panel. Moreover, the keys have to be turned simultaneously; you can't turn yours and rush over to threaten your partner. This was designed into the launch control system, as were some other failsafe precautions to prevent Armageddon on the whim of a mad major.

Of course this doesn't fall under the heading of bad research; I am sure the movie script people knew what the real situation is. This is more deliberate deception.

As to how much research is enough: You do have to balance the amount of effort you are putting in against what you'll get out of it. Even so, details can be important. *Lucifer's Hammer* had a number of themes, and required an enormous amount of research into astronomy, wilderness survival, synthesis of war gasses (and deciding which one to describe), nuclear power plant construction, the best theory of comet composition, as well as social structures of Los Angeles street gangs. In some cases a couple of scenes, a few dozen lines in the book, required hours of work so they'd be right. The result was worth it, and I doubt that *Hammer* would have sold millions of copies without all that work.

As to who you are going to call, once again, it depends on just how much you want. If you live near your sources, an afternoon or evening invested in buying some drinks at the local officer's club, or the faculty lounge, or the popular hot spot where the engineers gather will often get you far more information than you need, and usually will yield just the right nugget—an incident that illustrates the atmosphere and provides details. A bit more than artistic verisimilitude to an otherwise bald and unconvincing narrative, only this time drawn from real life. Of course that requires luck.

It also requires preparation. One of the major stocks in trade of the writer is a list of contacts in very imaginable field you might write about. Since science fiction writers can write about anything, there's hardly any limit. In my case, I used to go to conventions. In particular I managed a membership in the National Association of Science Writers, and went as press to the annual meetings of the American Association for the Advancement of Science. I even managed to wangle press credentials for Niven as a contributing editor, although he, and the AAAS press people, all knew that was sort of subterfuge: Niven wasn't going to write articles.

We worked those meetings. We bought drinks for speakers. We'd invite others to dinner. The result was a pretty good list of people we could call on for contacts when we needed to know how scientists and engineers might act in hypothetical circumstances—such as the discovery that the Earth was about to be smacked with something large, like a comet.

The Internet has changed a lot of this, of course. Now it's possible in two hours to use Google and the other search engines—do not neglect the other search engines!!—to find incidents, anecdotes, accounts, facts, and just plain daydreams about almost any subject whatever. Go backstage at the Met. Listen in on jury deliberations. Get some of the flavor of corporate decision meetings. It's all there if you search hard enough.

Once you have all that, you can go find an eager engineer who wants you to get it right; and Bob's your uncle.

Bud

And (as William Sanders is known to say) quite possibly your aunt as well, if you live in San Francisco.

I agree about the search engines. I use DogPile a lot, since it will return results from a number of others. I remember a time when WebCrawler was about the only one; I don't even know it it's still around now. Wait, I know! I'll log on and look. Yep, still there, and seems to do the same sort of thing that DogPile does. I miss that cute little spider they used as an icon, though.

Now, you and I differ quite a bit in our reference needs. Most of the time, I'm writing book-tweak stuff, not fiction (although I'm guilty of that as well, of course), and specifically I write with increasing frequency about the history of science fiction and fantasy literature. Much of what I need I can get on-line; for instance, Phil Stephenson-Payne's invaluable Index to Science Fiction Anthologies and Collections, Combined Edition located at http://www.philsp.com/homeville/ISFAC/0start.htm, or The Internet Speculative Fiction Database at http://www.isfdb.org/cgi-bin/index.cg. Both are well-organized and well-maintained, and if they ever charged me rent I'd go broke.

We are, of course, going to have to talk about Wikipedia and its Shadow, Conservapedia, but let it ride for a bit.

Since I write about the things I do, I've found it necessary over the years to accumulate a couple of shelves of on-point references: indices, bibliographies, encyclopediae, most of which are long out of print and have never been digitized. I've even written a couple, if only to keep my own collections straight.

Something I use very often—almost daily, and multiple times a day at that—is Donald Tuck's three-volume *Encyclopedia of Science Fiction and Fantasy* published by Advent and still available, I believe, from the NESFA website. It has information on authors, lists the books they've written and edited, and is as complete and definitive as a reference published in 1974 can be. There have been others, most notably *The Encyclopedia of Science Fiction* compiled by John Clute and Peter Nicholls, which update and expand that information. I find them to be at the top of a basic, required list of SF/fantasy references, admittedly a niche rather than general resource. The Clute & Nicholls, by the way, was still available on CD-ROM from St. Martin's a few years ago, if not now. It's a little clunky, but usable.

The New England SF Association—NESFA—produced a series of magazine and anthology indices covering 1966-1989, with a few years missing, cross-indexed by title, author and source, that is as useful in its own way as anything else I've got. Here again, these are intended to expand on the original magazine index, *Index to the Science Fiction Magazines 1926-1950,* compiled by Donald B. Day and published in 1952. Both Norm Metcalf and Irwin Strauss (aka Filthy Pierre) did independent updates to the Day to carry it through 1965, and if you want to be able to tell someone which issue of *Shouldn't Wonder Stories* that yarn by E. E. "Doc" Yogsothoth was in, or which volume of *New Orbiverse Visions* had the Hugo-winning story "I Have an Itch that I Can't Scratch" is in, those are the ones you pull down and look through.

Yeah, a lot of that is on-line now, but you have to go all over the place to find it; it's easier for me to just reach up and grab it off the shelf.

Okay, let's get into the various on-line 'pedias now, but I want to come back to paper later and mention one of my favorite ways to gather information on a subject—autobiographical memoirs.

Wikipedia strikes me as a wonderful idea. It strikes me further as a resource prone to error, one that should always be re-checked to make sure that somebody with a bug up their butt hasn't used the "edit" function to serve their own agenda. I've used it, and I've edited it as well, and I know it can be a valuable tool. But how do you know you can trust it?

Well, the answer is fairly simple—don't use it as your sole source of information. Confirm using other sources. This is a cornerstone mantra in journalism, or used to be, and we both produce what can be defined as journalism (you far more than I, I suspect). If there's something in Wiki that I haven't run across before, I make sure to find someone or some place that will verify that fact before I go blabbing it around William-Nilliam.

I know you've used it as well, but I don't know how you view it overall, so weigh in. I also know absolutely nothing about the technology involved, so feel free to elaborate on that, too. How did it get started in the first place? Yet another basement or garage?

You mentioned up there about the value of schmoozing to develop resources. I don't know about you, but I've found that many people are more impressed by our being writers than we are, and are only too happy to help out. That includes a local cop bar at a time when I thought I might be a mystery writer. I began hanging out there, a big, long-haired and bearded KID in T-shirt and jeans. I got a lot of funny looks, but finally one old hand came over and asked me if I was with one of the other precincts. When I told him I was a writer, and hoping to be able to pick up something about procedures and TOOs, he was more than a little suspicious but eventually became convinced that I wasn't trying to weasel out information on Baaad Cops for some tabloid exposé but legitimately looking to Get It Right.

That seemed to mean a lot to him, and he (and many of his fellow detectives) were a big help. The novel never got written, but I made contacts not only with the City of Richmond PD, but also some in the County and State departments as well. I even got an intro to the Chief Medical Examiner hereabouts, startling her with the question "If I hit somebody over the head multiple times with a tube-sock filled with wet sand, how much of the sand would lodge in the wound, and would the imprint of the weave-pattern of the sock be unique enough to be forensically valuable?" Her response: "Who did you say this was?"

Jerry

Like you, I tend to turn a critical eye on Wikipedia, and if there's any thing controversial at all I check with other sources, but I do find that it's the place I usually start. For those interested in the subject, probably the best introduction to Wikipedia is a long, and sometimes tedious, Wikipedia entry: http://en.wikipedia.org/wiki/Wikipedia. It gives history, intentions, and how the organization tries to control the reliability and accuracy of the entries. It also includes just about every criticism of Wikipedia ever made. It's worth the time to read.

Wikipedia tries to remain both accurate and relevant. In my experience, they succeed far more often than they fail. I often hear people denounce Wikipedia as useless, and I can only wonder why they do that. You'd think it would be due to personal experience, but generally it's not: it's generally someone who wants to be taken as an authority. Now I am sure there are some highly inaccurate entries on Wikipedia, but in fact I can't name most of them. One was easy enough: my own entry is often wildly incorrect. I used to correct that, but I no longer bother; in fact I don't even look at it.

Bottom line on Wikipedia: I generally start there when I begin a research project, or when I need some quick data, but unless the matter is either trivial or entirely lacking in controversy I go find another source just in case.

Regarding the cop bar, your experiences are not unusual. A great many people admire writers, and don't make a lot of distinction between successful writers and those just getting started. The very fact that you're taking such a gamble amazes people, including fairly tough guys like cops and firemen.

When I first started writing full time, I was fortunate in that Los Angeles had a very active chapter of Mystery Writers (MWA), and they had many speakers at their monthly meetings. Joseph Wambaugh, after New Centurions but while still a detective in LAPD, was one of them. They had arson detectives, and crime lab technicians, and a number of other experts. Needless to say, it's a good idea to take advantage of opportunities like that.

The bottom line is that writing is not a full time job, even if it is your only source of income. While you will not get paid until the words are on paper (or the electrons are on a hard drive), research is as much a part of the writer's job as writing. Ideally it never stops. Of course writers are curious people by nature, and we're always looking for new stuff to squirrel away for later use, so this isn't difficult.

On the other hand, many writers waste opportunities to make use of their curiosity: that is, they go looking for things, find them, but it's all for fun, and unless they have better memories than mine, they'll never be able to make use of the information. Now when I was younger and had lots of energy that didn't matter so much: I could always go do it again. At my present age that's not so attractive.

The secret here is to keep track of important sources in ways you can find them again. There are a number of tools for that purpose, and I've tried most of them: the best of the lot, for me, is a good TabletPC and a Microsoft program called OneNote. OneNote is a complicated program, and although it becomes quite intuitive after you've worked with it for a while, it does have a learning curve. There are several decent introductory books on OneNote, and it's worth while to go through one.

The advantage of OneNote is that it's easy to collect and organize research data, trivia, your own notes and thoughts, and location of source data, and label all this so that it's easily indexed.

Note that you don't need a TabletPC to use OneNote; I just find TabletPC's very easy to use, and once you get one trained to recognize your handwriting—it doesn't take all that long—then taking notes is very easy.

For those who don't want a Tablet or OneNote, it's possible to do the whole job with Word. After all, Microsoft Desktop Search is going to make an index of everything you have done, so it's mainly a matter of being intelligent about organization and labels. An example: Years ago I found some articles on the Venice Arsenal in 1500, when Venice could assemble and launch a war galley in a single day. I made notes on this, in Word, because OneNote didn't exist then. My notes included the sources of the information, many of which were not on line at the time. A year or so ago I discovered that for Janissaries I need a scene set in a place that looks a lot like 16th Century Venice. Since I have the habit of transferring all of my research data files from whatever machine I have been using to any new machine I adopt, it was easy enough to find my old notes. Microsoft Desktop Search had indexed them. The notes were buried among hundreds of other entries Search turned up—finding clever and unique headers is one skill worth developing—but it was still a lot faster to find the old notes than to start from scratch.

Once I found my notes I was able to chase down the original stories. Some of my sources were now on line, so I didn't have to go down to the library or make do with the notes I had taken. The result was that I had my scene written by evening, without a lot of work; all that at the cost of making proper notes a decade ago.

Another important tool for writers is a pocket camera. The one in your cell phone will do, but I carry a Sony DSC T-100. Woot—www.woot.com—had reconditioned Kodak Easy Share cameras as one of their daily specials recently. I like those, too. The point is that you get pictures with the camera you have with you, and there are now so many small and inexpensive shirt pocket cameras that there's really no excuse to not have one. The camera alone isn't quite enough: you also need a good voice recorder. I carry the Olympus WS-100 because it's easy to use, runs forever on a single battery, and makes files that can be sent to Dragon Naturally Speaking where they get transcribed with better than 90% accuracy. The result is that it's easy to do annotated photo journalism, as for instance the night that Niven and I were taken for a tour of Mount Wilson Observatory by the late Robert Jastrow. Once we got down to flatland it took less than an hour to move everything—pictures, sound files and all—over to OneNote. I could then allow Dragon to transcribe the recorded notes at my leisure.

There are other combinations of equipment that will do the job; the point is to be aware that there such things exist, so that most of the fun things you do in life are also "doing research."

Bud

Get a machine to recognize my handwriting, Jerry? Hell, it's all *I* can do to recognize it. I'd never put a machine through that kind of torture.

Now, OneNote intrigues me, but it's going to have to wait until I've done some other hi-tek things, like upgrading my primary computer from Windows 98. God, I miss DOS. Still, I like the idea of being that organized, even if I have to use Word to do it. As it is, my notes start out at the bottom of whichever document I'm working on, then, after the page count gets to be high enough, I cut-and-paste them into a new doc so that all I have to do is Alt-Tab back and forth.

See, you're far more conversant with the new technologies than I am. I used to think I was hep to the jive back when everything ran from batch-files and you could hit a key and little ANSI bugs would start clearing the text off your amber monitor (boy, was I ecstatic when I got my first RGB! Now those bugs would be in *color!*), but things got past me while I was napping one afternoon, and I've never been able to catch up. I'm only just now getting to where I can use this InterWeb thingie right.

I used to carry a micro-recorder, too, back in the day. It worked quite well, too, recording story ideas and snippets of imagery and even dialogue, but somebody who broke into my car one night decided they needed it more than I did, and I just never had the free cash to replace it.

Now, a camera...! I've still got an old Canon SLR with a good selection of glass, but I never really used it for research. I have a camera-phone now, like everybody else, but I use it to take cute pictures of my cats and outlandish Christmas decorations around town more than anything else.

But they are tools, aren't they? If I were a full-time writer, instead of doing it as an avocation (not, I will point out, a "hobby"), I would clearly be at an advantage if I learned to use them effectively. Any cost could be written off, and more permanent records kept of whatever subject I was researching just then.

Getting back to Wikipedia, I, too, have an entry, albeit a tiny one. I haven't added to it (there's not enough of it right now for there to be any errors to correct) because...well, I feel a little funny about it. Like I should make stuff up, really outrageous stuff, just to see if any of it disseminates across the web. But then they'd just put it back the way it was, and I'd get in trouble, and have to go to the principal's office or something. No way, José.

However, I have added to and corrected other entries such as Groff Conklin's and Nelson Bond's, and I've added some of my on-line articles on classic writers who have slipped from print and therefore from memory to the External Links sections of the appropriate entries, because I want *other* researchers to be able to Get It Right. I've also been cited several times in entries I had nothing to do with, and believe me, that's a hoot.

I want to move on now to an area I have a definite affection for, and that's autobiographical memoires by writers and editors in the field. In particular, I would like to mention Fred Pohl's invaluable autobio, *The Way the Future Was*, published by Del Rey in 1978. Anyone who has even a passing interest in the science fiction world of the pre-and post-WWII period can benefit from this one, and if you are, like me, struggling to become the new Sam Moskowitz, it's absolutely necessary to own it. Same goes for the late Sir Arthur Clarke's *Astounding Days*, which covers much more than just what he did for Campbell. This is living history, told by those who were there and did just about everything there was to do. Damon Knight, Jack Williamson, and Lester del Rey also did books devoted to their careers, and the insights you can get into the way things worked back when the American News Company still controlled magazine distribution and there were dozens of fiction magazines on the stands is truly astounding.

And then there's one I turn to over and over again, *Grumbles from the Grave*. I read it mostly for fun, and a look into Heinlein's process (so different from mine), but also to get a sense of what even a writer of his stature had to go through in order to make a living at this jazz. Not to mention the light it casts on the work itself, which alone is worth the price of admission.

Books, people, cameras and software: it takes all this now to research well, but more than that, I think, it takes an inquisitiveness not always found even in writers. Some best-selling authors pay other people to do their research, working from their notes instead of actually seeking out the information and, you know, learning something. It's still necessary, though. Even if you're writing magic realism, you have to research the stuff you're planning to make up.

And you have to like it, really *like* it. I do, and that's one reason why I'm willing to work cheap (well, cheapish); for me, the research is part of the fun, part of the joy of writing. I mean, how else could I get paid for sitting at a desk with books piled all around me (as I now am), or in front of a computer screen, on-line and with dozens of research sites listed in my Favorites (as I now am)? Am I lucky, or what?

So sum this one up for us, Jerry. Do you enjoy research, even when it doesn't mean schmoozing rocket scientists and military honchos (honchi?) or using the technology at hand to use decade-old notes? Is research a means to an end for you, or can it be an end in itself?

Jerry

First, I am in complete agreement about Fred Pohl's wonderful *The Way the Future Was.* It's a wonderful book and every SF writer ought to read it. Fred is one of our national treasures. And congratulations and thanks for your bibliographic efforts.

Second, I only have one viewpoint for a summary. I have had several reasonably successful careers: in aerospace, then in academia, and even as a political manager; but I have been a full time writer with no day job since 1972, and that's really all I know how to do now.

When I went to work at Boeing in Human Factors and Reliability, and thence to Systems and Operations Research, one of the job requirements was that you have the right tools for the job. Boeing insisted on that: if you were a flight line mechanic, for example, you were expected to have a complete tool set. Boeing would issue specialized tools, but the basic tool sets, some worth thousands of dollars, were up you. Boeing made it easy to acquire those tools. They\d loan you the money, and take the payments out of your pay; but they insisted that you have them.

In my case, one requirement was the best slide rule available in 1957, a log-log Decitrig. I still have it hanging on the wall, although I haven't looked at it in years. I also had a large circular slide rule that would find answers to four or five figures. When I left Boeing for Aerospace Corporation it was pretty clear that I would be expected to write large and complicated reports, and I made it a condition of taking the position that not only would I have the perquisite office furniture for my rank in the company, but also an IBM Selectric Typewriter and typing table, and the best Olivetti desk calculator available. In other words, that Aerospace would provide me with the best tools of the trade. Aerospace not being in aircraft construction wasn't accustomed to requiring their technical staff and managers to provide their own tools, so they were willing to get them for me.

The point was that I got in the habit of acquiring and using the best tools available for the job I was doing; and the habit stuck when I became a full time writer. I always had the best stuff available: an IBM Selectric with correction tape built in; the best Texas Instruments logs and trig calculators, upgraded annually as better ones came out; and so forth.

I first met Robert Heinlein in 1960, when I was still in the aerospace business. When I decided to write full time, he was very helpful with advice. He used to say that as writers we got to work inside, and sitting down, with no heavy lifting. He also invested in the best tools of the trade he could find, and advised me to do the same. Productivity is key to making a living in this racket.

When small computers and word processors came out, I was among the first to use them: indeed, old Ezekial, my first computer, is on display at the Smithsonian Museum of American History (Hall of Communications and Computers) as the first machine anyone used to write a novel on. Old Zeke cost me $12,000 dollars in 1978. (Half of that went for the Diablo daisy-wheel printer). I had to borrow the money, and my wife wasn't pleased; but Zeke increased my productivity enough that I earned it all back within a year, and doubled my income while cutting back on the expense of sending my work out for a final clean draft.

Now this stuff is cheap. That Olympus WS-100 is available from Amazon for under $60 bucks, and I'd be willing to bet I could find one for half that by looking harder. The Woot blowout of the Kodak Easy Share was under a hundred dollars. The combination of a pocket camera—as I said the one in your phone will do—and a decent voice recorder makes a potent research tool. I use both on my daily walks: the other day I got a good set of pictures and notes on a movie shoot going on down on Cantura Street.

A good sub-laptop that you'll always have with you can be got for about what we'll be paid for this article. The best tools of the trade can cost more, but a basic productivity tool set is well under a grand for everything you need. Moreover, every bit of it is deductible, and the IRS will never even give it a thought (provided that you report some writing income).

So sure: I enjoy hell out of having the latest and greatest equipment, and I enjoy leaning the best use of the tools of my trade. I probably over invest: I don't really need a MacBook Air and iPhone, but they're gloriously cool, thoroughly deductible, and easily carried: and the tools you have with you are the ones you will use. I use both a lot. Sometimes I haul out the MacBook Air and just sit on a wall during my morning walk and jot down notes on things I thought of while walking. Other times I tap in notes to myself on the iPhone while I continue to walk. The point is to preserve those ideas, preferably in a form that lets me find them again whenever I want them. The other day I had reason to find the notes I took about workmen repairing a pot hole on the Kalinengrad in Moscow in 1989. I found them easily.

Writing is like any other profession: you can study and learn a lot about how it's done, and the more you learn, the easier it becomes. Research isn't an end in itself, but it sure helps if you like doing it. As you note, most writers do love it; and it's sure a lot more fun if you have the proper tools and know how to use them!

❑

In the Good Old Days:
Another Alternate Dialogue Between Bud Webster and Jerry Pournelle

Bud

It is a truth universally acknowledged that two SF writers in possession of a good number of years, must eventually speak about the Good Old Days. At any convention you go to, from the smallest relaxacon to World Fantasy and/or the Nebulas, you will find a couple of pros of a certain age at the bar or more likely in the SFWA Suite saying that Things Were Different When We Were Coming Up.

It's true enough. Things change, technology not the least of them, and even someone as forward-thinking as a SF writer will eventually find them changing faster than s/he can keep up. Most of the time, I think, it's for the better—if we're honest about it. I don't have to tell you, Jerry, how much easier the Internet has made research (assuming you can separate the wheat from the chaff); you've watched the whole thing from close up. Word processing has it all over typewriters for producing readable manuscripts, and even if they didn't, most markets are perfectly happy with electronic transfers. You can even get paid that way, no fuss, no bother, and within minutes.

There are still changes that have happened in our insular microcosm, though, that are both perturbing and perplexing. What I'd like to talk about now is the apparent Balkanization of the field of fantastic literature.

There was a time not so long ago when an author could turn out a couple of hardcore, nutzenbolts SF novels, then sell a high fantasy to the same publisher, and nobody blinked. It's just the way it was done. The same readership would read them, talk about them, review and/or revile them, but always within the context of the World of Science-Fiction and

Fantasy. Poul Anderson did it all the time. So did Clifford Simak. Even so recent (as we reckon it) writers as Lawrence Watt-Evans and C. J. Cherryh did it, early on in their careers.

I grew up thinking that this was the way it was, and I was perfectly happy with it. I looked forward to the variety, wondering if *Glory Road* would be as good as *Double Star*, or if *Tau Zero* could possibly be as much fun as *Three Hearts and Three Lions.*

Then, it changed. I'm not naïve enough to think it happened suddenly, these things never do, but I honestly don't know what happened to split the genre into two ever-polarizing sub-genres. These days writers are strongly urged by their agents and editors to write one or the other, but not both. Bookstores even have separate shelves for SF and fantasy, and newer readers cling stubbornly to whichever side they've chosen, rarely venturing to try the opposition.

You were there during the process as a professional writer, Jerry; I was just a faan, and not plugged into the system deeply enough to be able to make a reasonable assessment. What's the view from Chaos Manor?

Jerry

Partly I think it was *Lord of the Rings* and Harry Potter. For a very long time fantasy was the younger brother of science-fiction. *Astounding* always had a larger circulation than *Weird Tales* and *Fantasy and Science-fiction*, and while fantasy stories were acknowledged at SF conventions, they were not the real stuff. Fantasy didn't win Hugos and Nebulas.

In those times, though, science-fiction wasn't a very good option for a professional writer looking to make a living at his craft. Robert Silverberg got rich from writing, but not from his SF: he got his venture stakes from non-fiction about archaeology and lost cities, and made some excellent investments. When I was President of SFWA back in the 70's there were no more than twenty writers making a living at science-fiction. I know, because Spinrad and I tried to make a list of them, and to get even that number we had to include Larry Niven, who didn't need the income from SF due to a fortunate choice of grandparents, and Isaac Asimov, who hadn't written any fiction in about ten years despite an almost incredible output of words.

Then SF got popular. Niven and I will take some of the credit: *Lucifer's Hammer* got what was then an enormous advance and was for 14 weeks the #2 fiction best-seller (just below *The Thorn Birds*). Star Trek novels began to take up a lot of rack space in drug stores and supermarkets. The truck drivers who actually filled the racks began to notice science-fiction, and the genre took off. We had a major boom in SF.

But Star Trek and Battlestar Galactica changed the rules of the game. They weren't fantasy, but they certainly weren't the older kind of science-fiction. Even Doc Smith and L. Ron Hubbard had rules to their stories; the media tie-in novels didn't. I was paid decent money to make a novel out of "Escape From the Planet of the Apes" (done as a work for hire, of course) and I tried to make it at least self-consistent and to reduce the number of direct conflicts with known science, but I wasn't really able to do that. The entire concept was fantasy.

Of course this was during the era of the "New Wave" stories, which were "speculative fiction" and flouted the absence of rules and made no attempt to conform to hard science or anything like it. The notion of science-fiction that tried to conform to scientific reality and employ "what if" concepts that might actually come about vanished under the flood of "New Wave" concepts. New Wave took over much of academia, and many critics were New Wave. This didn't help the Pure Old Stuff much. There were some hard science best sellers—*Footfall* by Niven and Pournelle managed to hit the number one slot on the best seller list, and our *Oath of Fealty* made it to number five - but for the most part hard SF languished while the field went through some rapid expansion.

And somewhere in there, straight fantasy caught on. SF and the media tieins had opened the way to more rack space, but for reasons not entirely clear to me, fantasy began to fill much of it. Pretty soon there were fantasy best sellers. Robert Jordan began shipping an unprecedented number of hard bounds, and continued to sell in mass market. Jordan was an interesting case: his background was nearly perfect for a hard science-fiction author (he was a Navy nuclear engineer), but he preferred fantasy. He wrote good stories, and they caught on. Of course it didn't hurt his distribution to be married to Harriett McDougal, one of the best known and most powerful editors of the time. Some editors might not have realized that the wheel had turned and it was fantasy's time for a place in the sun; she did, and her husband's books made a lot of money for her publishers.

Fantasy has always done well. For example, although *Inferno* by Niven and Pournelle never hit a best-seller list, it went into 20 printings, and in actual sales topped Sagan's *Contact* as well as our own *Oath of Fealty*. I had the opportunity to look at Simon and Schuster/Pocket Books sales figures for SF and fantasy a few years ago, and the results were instructive. Their top seller in SF was *Mote in God's Eye*. Number two was *Inferno*. *Contact* was third.

And then came Harry Potter, and all bets were off. Fantasy, the younger brother of science-fiction, became the 800 pound gorilla; and of course the Potter sales not only took up rack space but brought in more fantasy to fill more space, just as the distribution system began to collapse, and there was less rack space to fill.

That, at least, is my recollection of what happened. As to why there are few writers who do both SF and fantasy, it takes less training and education to write fantasy. I don't mean that as insult, it's just true. And there are a few writers who carry on the old tradition of going back and forth between SF and Fantasy. Larry Niven always did that. Our *The Burning City* and *Burning Tower* novels are set 14,000 years in the past, just after Atlantis sank, and they've done well. Alas, not Robert Jordan well, but then few works do.

And, as always, the story tellers prevail. The character studies of the New Wave have pretty well vanished. Good stories, SF or fantasy, continue to sell.

Bud

I'd add another name to your Tolkien/Rowling duology: Terry Brooks. I was working in a major chain bookstore when Del Rey brought out the first Shannara book, and it was heavily promoted both inside and outside the genre. Having devoured the Tolkien books as a kid, I read it, and found it okay, but derivative. I wasn't the only fan who found it so, but watching the sales of the book (and the sequels) told me something that both pleased me and dismayed me. Twenty people making an actual living from writing about spaceships and robots is a pretty dismal figure, although I don't doubt its veracity. I wonder what percentage of the still fairly new SFWA that might have been, and what percentage of our current SFWAns are free and clear of day jobs or generous (and patient) spouses? If the ratio is about the same, then has anything changed, except the gross numbers?

Here's what I saw from the vantage of one employee in one store in one city during the mid-'70s blitz: long-time SF/fantasy readers weren't the only ones buying Terry's books, they were being bought in very large numbers by people who had never read much in the genre, and who were certainly not aware of what had gone before. They saw it as new, groundbreaking, exciting, and because they didn't read the reviews in the genre pro- and fanzines, raved about it to their friends and families as the Latest Thing.

I was pleased that the numbers on the book were high - in those days, I was happy for anybody writing the stuff who made it big - but I began to notice something that worried me; when these readers came back, a lot of them didn't want Tolkien, or MacDonald, or even *Glory Road*, they wanted the next Shannara book. They wanted *only* the next Shannara book.

It was the same with the tie-ins. They came in droves to buy the movie and TV books, but try and steer them to *Childhood's End* or *Mission of Gravity* and their eyes glazed over. A few did, in fact, move on to more mainstream science-fiction and/or fantasy, but not enough of them to do more than encourage a few of the braver publishers to reissue a handful of then-OP titles from the Classics.

You mention the Apes books. You're right, of course, that they were bad SF if they were SF at all (yours excluded), but then the Pierre Boulle original wasn't so much science-fiction as it was allegory, and allegory is, perforce, fantasy. Which brings us to the question, what happened back in the beginning (I'm talking about the 1930's-40s now) that made SF subsume fantasy? *Astounding*, first under Bates, then Tremaine and finally John Campbell ruled the pulpish roost from 1930 to 1950, when *F&SF* and *Galaxy* introduced a more literary feel into the mix, and in those two decades the fantasy magazines just didn't keep up. Leaving aside *Weird Tales* and *Argosy*, most of the best-selling pulp magazines were SF (or at least super-science). What happened that allowed them to shove fantasy aside like a red-haired stepchild?

Coming back to the mid-70s, I remember the wave of attention that greeted *The Mote in God's Eye*, from the (now forgotten) fanzine reviewer who called it "the best novel Heinlein never wrote" to the flared-nostril disapprobation of those who still thought that the New Wave was what science-fiction wanted to be when it grew up. It may have been both hailed and reviled, but it was as solid a nutzenboltzer as anything Hamilton or Clement ever did, but in view of our topic, I have to ask what may very well be the key-question here: was it, in fact, the beginning of sciencefiction's last gasp? Again, what changed?

I seem to recall—and I welcome correction if my hindsight is blinkered—that much of the change(s) came from Ballantine/Del Rey. It was, I believe, Judy-Lynn del Rey who fostered Terry Brooks, even though she was in charge of the imprint's SF, while Lester edited their fantasy titles. It was very much like the later hype about Bruce Springsteen being the "New Dylan," a promotional tack that Columbia Records (which was also

Dylan's label) took with a vengeance. There was some rather heated backlash on the part of some critics, and anecdotally I knew a lot of people who were cold towards Springsteen because of it, but in the long run, it didn't matter: the Boss transcended the marketing department's rather clumsy attempt to cast him as usurper prince and he found his own place.

In much the same way, Del Rey was pushing Brooks as the "New Tolkien," to much the same response from those who saw nothing wrong with the old one; again, though, Brooks carved his own niche.

You say the numbers went up, and so have others, so I accept that as the truth. Perhaps it was my own consternation at the way those Star Trek/Wars books flew out the door that caused me to imagine dust on the classics.

But it did change, and it seems to me that it changed from the top down. Writers didn't stop writing SF, or at least wanting to, and readers didn't stop reading it (and wanting more of it). When did the in-house editors and the publishers send down the word that one could do this or that, but not both?

Jerry

In the following I hope readers will forgive me: I'm going to talk a lot about myself and my books. This isn't egotism: it's what I know and can be authoritative about. I really don't know a lot about other writers' sales and income. I would say we are a long way from science-fiction's last gasp. Niven and I both make enough money to live on from writing what looks to nearly everyone I know as hard science-fiction. In 1985 *Footfall* was the Number One NYT best seller. There were those who said that *Lucifer's Hammer* - Number Two on the NYT list—was not really science-fiction, but only a big disaster novel. *Footfall* had two-trunked elephants from Alpha Centauri invading Earth in a universe without faster than light travel; it would be pretty hard to say that wasn't science-fiction!

My Falkenberg stories are science-fiction. They still sell. *Starswarm* is a science-fiction juvenile. *Oath of Fealty*, Number Five NYT best seller, is science-fiction. I did almost a score of anthologies on *War World* and *There Will Be War*, all science-fiction. Now true, Niven and I wrote *Fallen Angels*, which is science-fiction satire, and took some time to do the *Burning City* novels - admittedly in the hopes of cashing in on fantasy's popularity - but most of what we do is SF of the old school. Both of us have other incomes - journalism in my case - but we could make a living on SF if we had to.

I don't know enough about other writers' incomes, but I would guess from what I hear of their sales figures that there are at least twenty full time science-fiction writers in addition to about a score of full time fantasy writers. Some do very well. I know that Greg Bear supports a house on a lake and two children in college. Fred Pohl continues. Baen has brought up a dozen new full time writers, and some do very well indeed.

Some "full time" SF writers have "day jobs" but that's always been true: Cliff Simak was a newspaper editor to the day he died, and even Jack Williamson had an academic stipend. Surely they were science-fiction writers?

The problem, I think, is that the New Wave encouraged SF writers to learn neither science nor story telling, and a number of people came into the genre with literary credentials and didn't do well; so they went off in a huff to become critics.

It all happened before. When I was just getting into the SF business, we were coming out of a bust. The bust followed a boom. What had happened was that SF boomed; critics and editors wanted to buy SF; but unlike Bob Gleason who bought *Mote in God's Eye* at S&S/Pocket and *Lucifer's Hammer* at Playboy, they wanted "literature", stories that would get good academic reviews and high praise from critics. They bought many of those (one editor paid six figures for a book about a chicken). They didn't sell.

Meanwhile, the old hard stuff continued to sell. Heinlein became self- indulgent and stopped editing his work, but his story-telling ability never changed. If the frontier planet sequence with the intelligent dogs had been teased out of *Time Enough for Love* and published as a stand-alone novel, it would have not only been a best seller but have won all the SF awards there are.

Niven and I not only sold but got record breaking advances for stories that were considered schlock by the critics and academics. I recall the de Lap and Lupoff reviews of *Mote*. Thomas M. Disch wrote a scathing review of *Janissaries* for New Republic (on the internal evidence of the review, he hadn't bothered to read past page 40 of the book since he thought that Cuban communists were part of the main story).

The conclusion among some editors was that good science-fiction didn't sell, but schlock did; and since there were plenty of writers who would deliver schlock on demand, it wasn't necessary to pay decent advances. The result was a period in which lots and lots of true schlock was published, and there was another bust because the public wasn't buying science-fiction schlock.

What I am trying to say here is that good story telling with good science continues to sell. Many of the writers who can deliver the old goods have other careers - Greg Benford comes to mind—so they're not very productive. That's been true for me: I made six figures a year from doing 10,000 words of computer journalism a month, and that does cut down on the number of novels I could write. I made more per word from fiction, but the BYTE checks were regular and steady, and I had four boys to put through college.

Fiction writers are, as Mr. Heinlein repeatedly told us, professional gamblers. He believed that until the day he died: I recall that about a year before his death he visited Chaos Manor and remarked on my 18 inch Lavalamp: "We have one of those, but we could only afford the 12 inch." Now of course Robert hadn't been hurting financially for many years, but he still ran scared all his life.

I am not sure I've answered your question, but I think the real answer is that authors and editors don't have any more idea of what sells than anyone else. I mean, can you imagine an author coming in to Del Rey and saying "Hey Lester, let me pitch you a fantasy series about an anti-hero who has leprosy!"?

Writers work for different reasons. Some are content just to be published writers: they are authors, not shop clerks or financial analysts or housewives. They are concerned about sales only to the extent that they sell enough to keep getting published. When the Author's Guild did a survey of members' annual incomes from writing, the average was about $2,000 a year. If that's the average, and Niven and I make what we make, there must be a lot who make even less than $2,000 a year.

Sales aren't everything. Nathaniel West's *Day of the Locust* sold 450 copies in hardbound. But if you're trying to make a living at this racket, you do have to worry about sales, and you write what you think will sell. Sure, you do the best you can with the story you're writing; but you choose what story to write by sales potential if you're a full time writer.

No one ever said that SF writers would get rich at it. A few of us have, but we still have to run scared.

As to SF vs. Fantasy, it has become pretty clear that I know more about making a living from the old hard stuff. Niven and I did well from the *Burning City* novels, but not as well as we had hoped. In our next book we'll go back to the most lucrative thing we ever did: we'll hit the Earth with something big...

Bud

Give me a minute to catch my breath, Jerry, I'm a little croggled by the idea that Robert Heinlein owned a Lavalamp—and wanted a bigger one. It would seem that he and I had more in common than I thought.

If you didn't specifically answer the question I asked back up there a ways, you've certainly given me the data I need to answer it myself: for all the hoopla about fantasy, and its success in the marketplace, there's still a largish hard-core readership for the nutzenbolts, and that's not only gratifying, but reassuring.

I'm never going to be able to write science-fiction without going to experts to check my math and physics, but I knew that from the beginning. In fact, even if I were a working scientist of some sort, I'd still get somebody to go over my notes, because it has to be right in order to serve the story well.

Much of what I write isn't science-fiction as much as science-fantasy, in the way that Nelson Bond and others like him wrote. It doesn't pay very well—little of this does, unless, as in your case, there's outside work, too—but it's become clear to me recently that regardless of the fact that I help balance out you and Niven way down at the low end, I could no more give up writing something than I could give up breathing or sleeping. Or root beer, but that's my baggage, not yours.

I was told at the start, lo, these many years ago (by you, amongst others) that instead of trying to anticipate the next Big Thing, I should simply write what I like to read. That's been pretty good advice for me. When I read over a story I've just finished and feel like it's the sort of thing that Groff Conklin would have reprinted, I'm satisfied.

I don't write novels, at least I haven't yet, so sales on that level are not even on my radar screen, but it nevertheless concerns me. Clearly, the more hard SF that is written and published, the more space there is for more of it, some with my byline, hopefully.

In this Alternate Dialogue, I suppose I'm self-cast in the role of B. Malzberg, what with my Eeyorish fear of the gradual disappearance of that which I grew up reading and loving. These days I look on the bookshelves, even at the local specialty shop, and wonder where Pangborn went, and Clement, and Tenn. I go to conventions to sell used books, and I'm gratified that people buy Poul Anderson and Heinlein (even Niven & Pournelle), but I'm still saddened by the occasional youngster (well, relatively young, anyway) who stops by my table and asks, "So, who's this Simak dude?" Of course, that's my opportunity to sell him a copy of *Way*

Station or *City*, depending on what I have in stock, but I'm only one person. I can't change it all.

To wrap this segment up—and before I yield to the almost irresistible temptation to beg you for the title of that chicken book—let me lay aside my Malzbergian *penchant* for the nonce and say that I hope you're right about things stfnal. No matter how much I may love visiting my hobbit friends and hanging out with teen-age wizards, my life continues to be bounded not by magic and Faerie, but by crashing suns and generational starships.

And that's just fine with me.

Jerry

A couple of points for clarity. First, science-fiction in the Old Days really was pretty sharply divided between the fans and the pros. While some pros like Simak had day jobs, most didn't. Anderson, Cogswell, and Dickson starved in garrets together. Poul and Gordy went on to become full time SF writers with no other source of income. Cogswell, in my judgment as good a writer as Dickson and nearly as good as Anderson, couldn't keep up, and went to teaching. In those days SFWA had requalification requirements: to be an active member you had to publish one short story a year, or one novel every three years. Ted couldn't meet that requirement and became an associate member. Of course that wasn't exile and death: the Associates voted for the Nebulas and pretty well dominated that, and Ted was the editor of the SFWA Forum.

Of course for some not being a full time writer really was exile and death. Beam Piper, one of the best old line story tellers we ever had, thought he was finished when his agent delayed in telling him that Beam's last Fuzzy book had sold. Beam couldn't pay the rent, and rather than get a day job on the local newspaper - stop being an author and become just one more guy who used to write—he shot himself. The tragedy was that the book had sold and the check was in the agent's desk, never delivered to Beam Piper.

In 1974, of perhaps 150 Active Members, about 20 were more or less full time writers. There were about 200 Associate Members, some like Cogswell and Rotsler quite "active" in that they did much of the work that kept SFWA going, and others who no longer wrote but still paid dues and showed up at conventions to be on panels and hang out in the SFWA suite.

In those days the status gap between fans and pros was pretty clear. That difference has largely vanished now, along with the SFWA requalification requirement. It's just as well. The fan who had a couple of good stories and sold them is likely to be more interesting than the old pro who exists largely by never paying his bar bill and often ducking his share of the dinner tab. But since anyone regardless of output can be a "pro" now, I do wonder if that hasn't been partly responsible for the fantasy boom. The old Hard Stuff required a lot of work to make the stories hold together. The laws of physics don't change, and while your story may be about a new physical law, or about bending an old one, the others are still there, and can't be ignored; which means the writer has to be aware of them and know something of their implications and how they influence the rest of the universe.

The best fantasy requires considerable research into myth and legend and the "laws" of magic and wizardry. Tolkien was of course very much the scholar, and worked as hard at understanding myth and legend and how they influenced beliefs as any physicist; but many fantasy writers make it up as they go along, which is why many of the big multi-volume fantasy novels begin to bog down: it's just too hard to cover up the internal contradictions. If Lord Foozle is so powerful and smart, why hasn't he squashed the protagonist like a bug before the quest ever begins? But if you make the story interesting enough, you can get away with a couple of volumes before losing control.

You will note that Pratchett and Rowling were able to hold it all together and make their worlds internally consistent. That's hard to do, harder in many ways than the Old Hard SF ever was because the universe keeps track of the SF writer's internal consistency; the fantasist has to do it for herself. On the other hand, it's a lot easier to turn out a couple of fantasy stories without ever building in the nuts and bolts, which is why, I think, we have so many new fantasy writers appear every couple of years.

Having tried both, I find I agree with you: I like writing the old Hard SF with big things crashing into the Earth, or computers implanted in the hero's head, better than magic, wizards, and elves; or at least I'm better at the Hard Stuff than fantasy. On the other hand, I can regard people like Pratchett, an old friend, and Rowling, whom I never met, with complete awe. And I love reading their books.

Bud

You had to mention Pratchett, didn't you? We could go on for another 2000 words about the remarkable artifact of the Discworld, and just how science-fictional it really is. Fantasy, my not inconsiderable butt. Pratchett is, as you say, every bit as meticulous in his backgrounds as Clarke was in his, and for exactly the same reason: it serves the story well. Just about anything that serves the story well is acceptable, and just about everything that doesn't, isn't.

But I see out editor tapping his foot and glancing pointedly at his watch (not to mention his checkbook), so let me make one more comment and then come to an end.

A good story is a good story, regardless of whether its trappings are wands and pointy hats or nano-bots and Bussard ram-jets. And does a good story really give a tinker's dam whether it's told fantastically or science-fictionally? I think not.

When there's a Big Thing getting ready to hit the Earth, it doesn't matter if it's thrown by an angry Thunder-God, or just passing through on its way from the Oort Cloud. I can't wait for that new book, Jerry. Thanks for writing it, and all the others.

❑

In the Beginning
(or, The Communiqué of the Communité)

(Please note: in writing this history of the SFWA Bulletin *my intent is not to examine the early days of the magazine in a strictly chronological format, but rather to open the pages here and there to show you how it looked, how it read, and what it contained. Sure, I'll cast my eyes in a roughly sequential manner, but I hope you'll forgive me if I skip around a little from time to time in an attempt to share my excitement at being able to examine them at all. Please bear in mind that any history of the* Bulletin *must necessarily include a partial history of the organization itself to be even minimally comprehensive, so if I move off the primary subject to discuss* SFWA *itself, there's a good reason.)*

> Send us any news items you may have, about yourselves or other s.f. writers—honors, promotions, marriages, job changes, unusual accomplishments outside the field....If you have special knowledge of any area of our field and are willing to write an article about it for the Bulletin, let us know.

That's "D.K.", or Damon Knight, writing in the very first issue of the *SFWA Bulletin* as part of the only real editorial content in those eight 8.5x11" pages[1], aptly titled "From the Editor." He goes on to add this:

> At the recent Milford S.F. Writers' Conference, those present were asked, "What's bugging you as a writer?" The answers were illuminating: Ignorance of the market. Poor relations with agents; inability to get an agent. Unauthorized editorial changes. Delays in reporting on manuscripts.

> Low rates and advances. Lack of respect from editors, publishers and agents: the feeling of being low man on the totem pole. SFWA is moving toward solutions of all these problems. What's bugging you? Tell the Bulletin.

That may have been simply stated, but it's eloquent and comprehensive. Leaving aside piracy, which was not quite as common then as now, D.K. didn't leave much out. This was what the founding members of SFWA wanted it to be: a force that would advocate for authors against any others who would try and act against them. Not a union, as such, but a professional organization devoted to protecting (hell, *establishing*) auctorial rights and to giving its members both a heads-up about events and problems and a centralized medium for sharing information.

That medium was the *SFWA Bulletin*, and it's been going strong in one form or another for nearly half a century now.

Why was this important, you ask? Simple: until 1965, the field had no real gathering place for its creators. There were conventions, yeah, but worldcons come only once a year and even the big regionals had only a relative few pros in attendance. Fanzines? Those were the last outlets that Knight and his fellow pioneers wanted to use as a means of input; in many case, the negotiations between writers and publishers were loaded with details that, well, they wanted to keep between themselves.

It's true, of course, that plenty of SFWA business leaked into the faanish environs, but this was to be expected. Many pros came up through the faanish ranks and kept

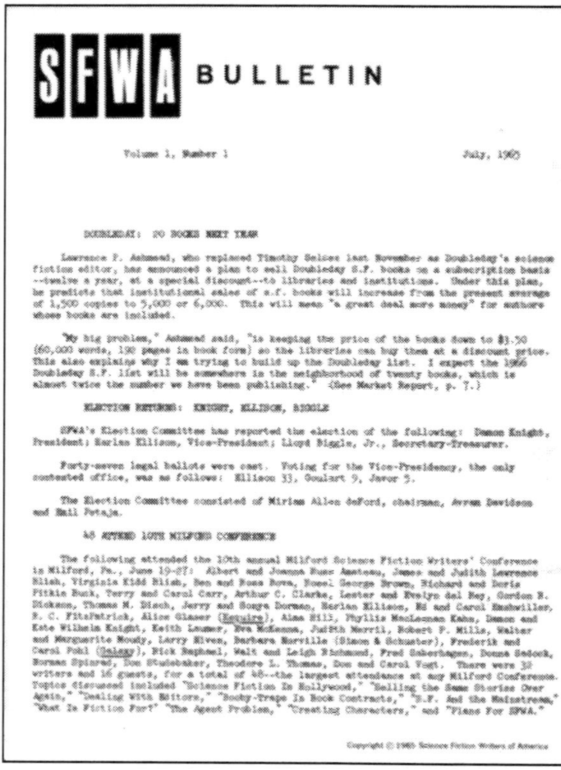
SFWA BULLETIN

Volume 1, Number 1 July, 1965

DOUBLEDAY: 20 BOOKS NEXT YEAR

Lawrence P. Ashmead, who replaced Timothy Seldes last November as Doubleday's science fiction editor, has announced a plan to sell Doubleday S.F. books on a subscription basis --twelve a year, at a special discount--to libraries and institutions. Under this plan, he predicts that institutional sales of s.f. books will increase from the present average of 1,500 copies to 5,000 or 6,000. This will mean "a great deal more money" for authors whose books are included.

"My big problem," Ashmead said, "is keeping the price of the books down to $3.50 (60,000 words, 190 pages in book form) so the libraries can buy them at a discount price. This also explains why I am trying to build up the Doubleday list. I expect the 1966 Doubleday S.F. list will be somewhere in the neighborhood of twenty books, which is almost twice the number we have been publishing." (See Market Report, p. 7.)

ELECTION RETURNS: KNIGHT, ELLISON, BIGGLE

SFWA's Election Committee has reported the election of the following: Damon Knight, President; Harlan Ellison, Vice-President; Lloyd Biggle, Jr., Secretary-Treasurer.

Forty-seven legal ballots were cast. Voting for the Vice-Presidency, the only contested office, was as follows: Ellison 33, Goulart 9, Javor 5.

The Election Committee consisted of Miriam Allen deFord, chairman, Avram Davidson and Emil Petaja.

48 ATTEND 10TH MILFORD CONFERENCE

The following attended the 10th annual Milford Science Fiction Writers' Conference in Milford, Pa., June 19-27: Albert and Joanna Russ Amateau, James and Judith Lawrence Blish, Virginia Kidd Blish, Ben and Rosa Bova, Rosel George Brown, Richard and Doris Pitkin Buck, Terry and Carol Carr, Arthur C. Clarke, Lester and Evelyn del Rey, Gordon R. Dickson, Thomas M. Disch, Jerry and Sonya Dorman, Harlan Ellison, Ed and Carol Emshwiller, P. C. FitzPatrick, Alice Glaser (Esquire), Alma Hill, Phyllis MacLennan Kahn, Damon and Kate Wilhelm Knight, Keith Laumer, Eva McKenna, Judith Merril, Robert P. Mills, Walter and Marguerite Moudy, Larry Niven, Barbara Norville (Simon & Schuster), Frederik and Carol Pohl (Galaxy), Rick Raphael, Walt and Leigh Richmond, Fred Saberhagen, Donna Sadock, Norman Spinrad, Don Studebaker, Theodore L. Thomas, Don and Carol Vogt. There were 32 writers and 16 guests, for a total of 48--the largest attendance at any Milford Conference. Topics discussed included "Science Fiction In Hollywood," "Selling the Same Stories Over Again," "Dealing With Editors," "Booby-Traps In Book Contracts," "S.F. And the Mainstream," "What Is Fiction For?" "The Agent Problem," "Creating Characters," and "Plans For SFWA."

Copyright © 1965 Science Fiction Writers of America

their contacts for one reason or another, and face it: writers love to get together and gossip about themselves and each other, and there are always fans around the hotel bar and at room parties. A little more than two years later SFWA would deal with that by creating the *Forum*, but I'll get to that anon.

Or I could do it now, I suppose. The first *Forum* was dated October 1967, and was edited by Terry Carr, whose duties at the time also included heading up the *Bulletin*. It was mimeographed by SFWAn Richard Lupoff, and was available only to members. There was a *lot* of heat and light in the *Forum* over the years. Silverberg recalls:

> Damon intended the *Bulletin* as the public face of SFWA, available to outside subscribers, libraries, etc., as well as to members, and so care was taken by all the various editors to keep the dirty laundry out of it. The *Forum* was founded specifically for in-group discussion, as a successor to Cogswell's privately published *PITFCS*, and many of the funny *PITFCS* feuds were carried right over into the *Forum*. Attempts were made to keep the *Forum* from falling into non-member hands.

Until it went public, the *Bulletin* was pretty unprepossessing. The first nine issues (dated July 1965 through November 1966) were large format (like the first), but with the January 1967 issue (#10), production and mailing costs convinced them to halve that; saddle-bound, it measured 8.5x5.5" and with the typefaces suitably reduced, they could pack twice the content into the same basic space.

There was little in the way of graphics in the early large-format issues aside from the SFWA logo and a bare few photos. The reason was simple: reproducing photos cost money, money SFWA didn't have and wouldn't have until Doubleday began publishing the *Science Fiction Hall of Fame* books in 1967. Remember, there were fewer than 150 members in the early days, and dues were $3 or so. The solution, as Kate Wilhelm recalls, was literally to produce it in-house:

> I know he had a mimeograph setup, no printing press. Later he used a local printing company, but not in the beginning.

(I relish the image of Damon Knight typing directly onto stencil, it's so deliciously faanish. Don't forget, though, that Knight was instrumental in creating the National Fantasy Fan Federation or N3F back in 1941 when he was first starting out, produced his own fanzine titled *Snide*, and had been both a Futurian and a member of the Boston-based fanorg, the Stranger Club, so cranking out an ish or two by hand was most likely not outside his wheelhouse.)

To give you an idea of what the members of this new writers' society were to find in their mailboxes, here's a quick look through volume one, number one:

> DOUBLEDAY: 20 BOOKS NEXT YEAR (Larry Ashmead, D'day's SF editor, reports that the number of books they will publish will double in '66, and will offer them at a subscribers' discount to libraries and institutions.)
>
> ELECTION RETURNS: KNIGHT, ELLISON, BIGGLE (President, VP, and Secretary-Treasurer respectively. 47 ballots were cast.)
>
> 48 ATTEND 10TH MILFORD CONFERENCE (The list includes the Usual Gang of Non-idiots, as well as Doris Pitkin Buck, *Esquire*'s Assistant Editor Alice Glaser, and Barbara Norville of Simon & Schuster.)
>
> A MODEL AGENT-AUTHOR AGREEMENT (Knight's creation, a boiler-plate contract that offered more clarity and advantages to the writer.)
>
> SCIENCE FICTION CLIENTS OF U. S. AND BRITISH AGENTS
>
> FROM THE EDITOR (Knight outlines what the SFWA member can expect to see – and not see – in the ***Bulletin***.)
>
> PEOPLE AND PLACES (Announcements, including the death of T. S. Stribling.)
>
> MARKET REPORT (Very much the same as Cynthia Ward's, this one announces the first volume of a new original anthology series, *Orbit*.)
>
> NEW MEMBERS (Including Judith Merril and J. Francis McComas.)

Subsequent issues didn't vary too much. There were reviews of nonfiction titles related to the field, articles on applying science to fiction (one in particular, "How to Build a Planet" by Poul Anderson, takes up fully half of the 12-page #9, dated November 1966), more market reports and letters from members. There was, beginning in the first few issues,[2] an irregular feature titled "Meet the Editor(s)." The earliest example I have on hand is in the June '66 issue (#6), an autobiographical sketch by Ian and Betty Ballantine, who ran one of the most important paperback[3] publishing houses, Ballantine Books. Later installments would include Fred Pohl, Donald A. Wollheim and Terry Carr (this was during their tenure at Ace, remember), and Harry Harrison.

These pieces are of particular interest because they were written by the editors themselves. This gives them added value as self-portraits intended as much as advertisements as bios, but more than that they offer the current reader an inside look at some of the people who played equally vital roles in creating modern science fiction.

When the *Bulletin* went to the smaller size, more photos began to appear. The cover of #11, dated April 1967 (the Nebula issue), is emblazoned with the images of Daniel Keyes, Samuel R. Delaney, Mrs. Eva McKenna[4] all holding their Nebulae, and Damon Knight handing Gordon Dickson the Lucite block of shiny for his novelette "Call Him Lord." The center spread of that issue has nine more photos of that year's Nebs, credited to "Ross Photos; H. V. Schoepflin." Harold Vincent Schoepflin wrote under the penname Harl Vincent, and died a year after the date of this issue.

I've been unable to confirm any involvement by Schoepflin as a photographer, or the identity/identities of "Ross Photos." I know that the majority of photos in those early issues were taken by, and credited to, the late Jay Kay Klein. As always, I invite correction on this point.

In preparing for this article, I contacted several of the original members. One, Robert Silverberg (a past president as well), told me of a document he had saved that predated not only the first issue of the *Bulletin* but the actual formation of SFWA itself. It consists of the proposed bylaws, and was sent to those SF/fantasy writers who had expressed a willingness to join the new writers' organization. Silverberg was kind enough to scan a page, as it included two important things: first, and foremost, a list of the 72 writers that Knight declares is "the charter members of SFWA." Of those 72, I count at least a dozen who are still with us; another dozen of them, interestingly enough, are names that are almost completely forgotten now, and to be honest, never terribly well-known to begin with. SFWA was never limited to famous names, after all.

The second important thing the page offers is dates. The document itself is dated February 28, 1965. According to Knight's comments, the initial letter to potential members was sent on January 15 of the same year. He solicits the recipients' comments and suggestions, asking that they return said by March 26. He further says:

> During the first week of April, the by-laws will be mimeographed again together with any amendments received, and you will be asked to vote.

Considering that the first *Bulletin* was dated July 1965, things moved quickly, if not precipitously, towards the inauguration of something special. Six months between proposal and launch is an indication of several things, all of them very much facets of the single-mindedness of the group's organizer, coordinator and self-described "benign dictator," Damon Knight.

He wanted this latest attempt to start a genre writers' association to be the one that finally worked. He wanted every aspect of it to work, to be the best it could be within the constraints of time and budget.

With the house organ of this association, the *SFWA Bulletin*, he wanted more than just a market report and a place for members to carp/crow about their careers. He wanted a clearing house of information about how

those markets treated their writers, how agents treated their clients, how the members themselves could become better at what they did – not just the nutzenbolts of writing, but how to get the best out of their contracts; how to spot a bad publisher and avoid dealing with them; when to draw the line against unfair demands from editors and when to give in graciously; even how and where to live where the rents and food are cheaper. In other words, how they could be more professional.

Looking back through these early issues, I'm struck by the realization that they represent an accurate assessment of what it was like to be a science fiction writer in the mid-sixties, from almost every perspective. However much help they were to the membership Back in the Day, from my viewpoint they're an illuminative and irreplaceable insight, snapshots of the small things that would add up to what is perhaps the greatest professional genre writers' organization. It's like holding history in my hands, exciting and humbling at the same time.

There are, of course, individual issues which stand out, and we'll take a look at some of them now. Please note that I do *not* have the space to scrutinize more than a very few of them, as there are a few other articles of importance that my editor wants to include in this very important *Bulletin*, but I'll see if I can keep your interest.

Pull up a chair and make sure your root-beer is sufficiently chilled, and we'll begin.

January 1967 – Volume 3, Number 1: Whole Number 10

This was the first directory issue, done back before that was a separate publication. There are 268 names listed, along with agents where applicable. No full addresses, though Knight promises to forward any mail to members. From the brief header:

> This list is intended to be of use to editors and anthologists, who frequently need to know who an author's agent is, as well as to SFWA members who would like to make contact with other members. (Two s.f. writers lived in Okemos, Mich. until recently; neither knew of the other until both had moved away.)

I, for one, am dying to know who they were. No way of knowing at this point, I guess. Also present are an article by Robert Silverberg titled "Tax Breaks for Self-Employed Writers: The Keogh Plan Pension" (a piece which could be updated to very good effect now) and an informative piece by Asimov titled "There's Nothing Like a Good Foundation" in which he talks (in part) about his frequent meetings in the 1940s with John W. Campbell at the *Astounding* offices at which he would pitch a story idea and then rush home and write it if Campbell green-lighted it:

> On this subway ride, I had no story idea to present him with so I tried a trick I still sometimes recommend. I opened a book at random, read a sentence, and concentrated on it until I had an idea... By the time I reached Campbell I told him I was planning to write a story about the breakup of the Galactic Empire.

Thus, o my droogs and only friends, was the Foundation Trilogy born, from a chance opening of a collection of Gilbert & Sullivan plays to *Iolanthe* and an illustration of the fairy queen bowing before Pvt. Willis of the Grenadier Guards.

There is a letter column, too, something I dearly wish the current *Bulletin* incarnation had, with letters from Milton A. Rothman (concerning Campbell's Dean Drive and psionics obsessions); and Fred Pohl, Jerry Sohl, Harlan Ellison, and Gene Roddenberry (then listed as a SFWA member) who all jump into a big pile over—what else?—*Star Trek*. And, let me add, whatever their relationship might have become after the date of this issue, Ellison defends Roddenberry quite strongly.

Rounding out the number is a short piece from Knight about donating manuscripts, a descriptive listing of science periodicals by Tom Purdom, and "Forthcoming SF Books," which in this instance includes Clement's *Needle* from Avon, Hubbard's *Slaves of Sleep* from Lancer, and Conklin's anthology *Seven Come Infinity* from Gold Medal.

April 1967 – Volume 3, Number 2: Whole Number 11

This was the first Nebula issue, and the biggest one to date, fully 32 pages. Inside we learn that there were *two* Nebula Banquets, one in LA at McHenry's Tale O' the Cock and the other in NYC at Le Champs. Speakers included Ian and Betty Ballantine as well as Ed Ferman of *F&SF* in New York; Alan Armer, producer of *The Invaders*, held the podium in the City of the Angels.

In a piece titled "UKONOMICS: Being a rough guide to the cost of living in London in 1967 67" [sic—I haven't the foggiest where Knight's proofreading skills were that day], John Brunner spends more than five pages explaining how one can live relatively cheaply in London, complete with figures: rents, autos (a Jaguar E-Type Zephyr could be had for $5200 tax-free), food, pub beer, haircuts, clothing, canned beer, paper, typewriter ribbons, bottled beer, soap, even (*blush*) brassieres. Did I mention the beer?

President Knight's major contributions to this issue are an eight-page examination of the Ballantine contract and the reprint of the speech he gave at the fourth Boskone (then a semi-annual event), suggesting ways that fans could use to convince retailers and wholesalers to carry more SF.

The rest of #11 is taken up by James Blish's testimony before the Senate Subcommittee on Patents, Trademarks and Copyrights; letters from Avram Davidson, Poul Anderson and others; and more Presidential musings on simultaneous submissions and foreign rights.

July-August 1971 – Volume 7, Number 2: Whole Number 35

Half the size of the last number we looked at, this one is notable for the obituaries of John W. Campbell (1910-1971, written by Gordon R. Dickson) and August Derleth (1909-1971, written by E. Hoffmann Price). Knight, no longer president, writes about warranty clauses and going out of print without really trying.

At some point in late 1972 or early '73 (here's yet another gap in my personal holdings), the *Bulletin* went from the small size back to 8.5x11", although it was still B&W inside and out. I'll give you a brief look at a couple of these, just to emphasize the changes.

Summer 1973 – Volume 9, Numbers 2-3: Whole Numbers 47/48
Fall 1973 – Volume 9, Number 4: Whole Number 49

The first of these two issues is, as you may have guessed, a double issue devoted to the '72 Nebulas; the second covers the Hugos. These are slick issues with heavy cover stock, rife with photos and artwork inside and out.

The cover of the double issue features photos of Asimov, Clarke, Anderson and Russ, all proudly holding their Nebulas. Inside, there are reports on all three—count 'em, *three*—Nebula banquets. The first, by photographer Jay Kay Klein, might ramble a bit but at seven pages is more than informative, not to mention his invaluable photos of the attendees at the New York banquet, fronted by Harlan Ellison as toastmaster and Poul Anderson as keynote speaker.

The second report, by Chelsea Quinn Yarbro, is very short, consisting mostly of photos by Paul Turner, taken at the Berkley do with Richard Lupoff and Peter Beagle at the helm.

The third of this Nebular triumvirate took place in the Big Easy[5] and featured founder Damon Knight and Lloyd Biggle, and the brief report was written by Texas SF author Joseph F. Pumilla, who mentions that the attending SFWAns included R. A. Lafferty, Daniel Galouye, and Richard C. Meredith, writer of the brilliant novel *We All Died at Breakaway Station.*

Think about that for a minute. The reports don't mention dates, but one assumes that the banquets were held simultaneously, as the report on the Southern gathering mentions the presence on Sunday of "Piglet", aka George Alec Effinger, "after helping produce the N.Y. banquet..." That's one, two, three banquets held in widely spaced cities on the same weekend. Consider the amount of planning and coordinating that had to take place, and then bear in mind that all that was done by volunteer members who were also writing for a living. Whoosh. Silverberg, as ever a veritable font of valuable information, told me:

> In the days of multiple Nebula ceremonies, they were held simultaneously, with allowance for time-zone differences, and sometimes we tried to set up phone hookups between the East Coast and West Coast events, not such an easy thing to do then. Southern banquets were rare, but we did try to have one on each coast.

The photos in these two issues are remarkable; not necessarily in composition or layout, but for the people they depict and the stfnal history they represent: Asimov, Clarke, Pohl, LeGuin are well-known faces made even more so by the ubiquity of the Internet, but figures like R. A. Lafferty, Joanna Russ, Raymond Z. Gallun, Frank Belknap Long, and A. E. van Vogt are not so well-represented online. Here, these giants still stand tall, engaged in conversation or at the various podia accepting their rockets or shiny blocks as if they walked among us still. History, in my hands.

In each year for which I have copies, those numbers that cover the Nebula and Hugo awards are not only bigger and more photo-filled, but also contain material above and beyond the regular *Bulletin* fare. The July 1972 Nebula issue, for example, presents the reader with "The New Readers of Science Fiction" by James Gunn, who was then President of the organization. It's his keynote speech for the 7th Annual Nebulas, and as befit his gig as English prof at the U. of Kansas it concerns the benefits (and disadvantages) of college SF courses, and their potential effects on the field as a whole.

The same issue gives us tributes to two major figures upon their demise. First, Brian Aldiss writes about his friend and colleague John Carnell, who not only was a powerful literary agent in the UK, but an important editor and anthologist. Aldiss is journalistically proper through most of the piece; names, dates, achievements all the order and just as one would expect from the *Times*, but the last few paragraphs are heart-felt, a man saying goodbye to a long-time friend. Lovely, as one would expect from Aldiss.

This is followed by comments by Michael Moorcock, whose early work was published by Carnell and who took Carnell's place as editor of *New Worlds* in 1964. His own feelings about his friend and mentor are exemplified by his final words: "For most of the present generation of writers Ted had always been there. We took him for granted. I wish he was still alive."

Fredric Brown, master of the very short story, was the subject of his friend Mack Reynolds' memorial accolade. It's filled with anecdotes of their times together, including his discovery that Brown had, as a young man, been employed by the Pinkerton Detective agency to infiltrate the Young Communist League on the behalf of

> ...[S]ome right-wing organization or other, so he could attend their meetings, get the names of their members and report on their plans... Fred wasn't quite believable as a private eye.

Lest you think that Reynolds, a self-described "life-long radical" was offended by Brown's finkery-for-pay, let his last lines reassure you that he wasn't:

> So long, Fred. See you in Xanadu, where all good SF writers go. At least, I hope I make it. You'll be there. You were one of the best.

Over those first few years, there were more than a few recurring articles which still hold an intense grip on the reader. I mentioned above the "Meet the Editor" pieces, and I'd like to look at a couple of these before we're done, but there were other articles just as useful to the professional SF/fantasy writer.

Some of these directly addressed the very things that Knight had in mind when he founded the organization, of course. There are detailed examinations of contract language, more discussions like the Anderson I mention above of the (then) current state of the sciences and how a writer might apply that information to fiction, various bits and pieces about dealing with the IRS and other financial matters, and so on.

One of my personal favorites was an irregular column by divers hands called "What Works for Me." In these wonderful little articles a SFWA member (always a different one) would set forth his method(s) of turning out salable prose. As you can imagine, this is revelatory for a combined stfnal historian and process geek like Your Humble Narrator.

In the first installment (the August 1967 issue, #13), Founding Father Knight says in part "If I know anything for sure about writing, it is that I don't know anything for sure about writing." He goes on to list and discuss these rules/suggestions/incantations, with my brief explanations in brackets where necessary:

1. Write what you like.
2. Counterpunch. [Write what others aren't writing.]
3. Take Chances.
4. Look for challenges.
5. Pyramid. [Build on things that work.]

6. For Christ's sake be honest.
7. Listen to your subconscious.

For a guy who didn't "know anything for sure about writing," true *dat*. James Blish follows up in the same issue with his own list:

1. Learn the mechanics.
2. Write spare. [Don't get cute.]
3. Sit down. [I.e., just do it.]
4. Cue your unconscious. ["…solutions from the unconscious often don't just 'float up,' but have to be cued."]
5. Make somebody feel it.
6. Don't talk it out.
7. Don't over-produce.

Interesting to note the differences there as well as the similarities. Two widely disparate writers, and two widely dissimilar critics, to be sure; however, there's enough agreement there, at least in spirit, to highlight one of the things that helped make SFWA work from the beginning: strength from contrast.

By 1974, it had evolved into "How To," at least in #51-52 and 53b in which no lesser giants than Poul Anderson, Clifford Simak, R. A. Lafferty and Katherine Kurtz wrote not so much for beginning writers (who most likely wouldn't have seen these articles anyway), but more just to share their perspectives with their colleagues.

In Lafferty's "It's Down the Slippery Cellar Stairs"[6] he says in his typically Laffertinian voice:

> And whence come the ideas? Where do you find them? You just go down the slippery cellar stairs, and there will always be several good ideas lying around down there. These are the slippery stairs down to the cellar of your own mind.

Me, I don't go down into the cellar of my own mind. Too many cobwebs and spiders, and there's a leak in the corner over there. By comparison, Anderson's "How To" starts out with a direct and honest declaration of intent:

> This article is not for the seasoned professional writer. He already has his own ways to go about his business... Nor is it necessarily a guide for the beginning writers who comprise the majority of SFWA's membership. They will develop their personal ways too, and the odds are much against all of these resembling mine. However, somebody may find useful one or two of the practical procedures I've come upon in the course of years. If so, this piece has served its purpose.

Indulge me for a moment, if you will. Why am I so all-fired fascinated by Process? I've asked myself this same question more than once. I can pinpoint the origins of my interest easily enough, and did so in the Robert P. Mills installment of 'Anthopology 101' last issue, but that's only where it started, not *why* I fixate on it.

That quote up there by Poul Anderson is a big reason, I think. I'm always looking for new ways to improve what I do, new perspectives and insights on how others—especially my heroes—get 'er done. Some of them have worked, most haven't, but as long as there's a chance that one of those insights can make it easier for me to produce pay copy[7], I'm willing to give it a try.

That's not the only reason, of course. There's a part of me that loves to know how other creative types operate, and when I can compare their work to one of these "How To" pieces and find correlations and connections between them, it engages me on a very basic level. That's true for me, at least; I realize I'm not typical.

I wish there had been more of these informative articles, but there were others just as enlightening to come. In the August '69 issue, for example, the late Harry Harrison (tongue firmly grounded in cheek) tells us "How to Sell to John W. Campbell, or Psionics in One Easy Lesson." Witty though it may be, let me assure you that Harry knew whereof he spoke. In the words of the then-editor of the *Bulletin* (our very own Barry Malzberg, by the way) "I think that this is one of the most useful pieces to ever be published in the *Bulletin* and I invite reader response to it." Yea, verily.

Harry also delivered a brief report on the Second International Film Festival in Brazil in the June '69 issue, titled "Flying Down to Rio."[8] It's chatty, unpretentious, and—dare I say it?—almost faanish.

I mention that for a reason. Although the whole point of the Science Fiction Writers of America (as it was originally called) was to bring

together the needs and experience of professional SF/fantasy writers, this was at a time when a majority of those writers came not from outside the field but up through fandom. Many of the charter members had pubbed their own ishes, or written LoCs to someone else's 'zine, sent multi-page letters to the pro-zines' lettercols, and/or spent hours in con-suites arguing about ScientiFiction or whether or not Yngvie really was a louse. This leaves aside all that brouhaha about Courtney's boat.

Quite a few of those whose articles and letters graced these early *Bulletins* also put in their time in the amateur press. Many of them became pro writers *because* they were first of all fans. Whether they saw what was being published and said "Oh, hell, I can do better than *that*," or just got excited by the idea of writing for Real publication, they made their first bones (however small they may have been) in small-run mimeoed or spirit-duped cranked out by fan-eds and sent through the mail to 2-300 people at best.

Many of them, in fact, would continue to write for the better-known fanzines, including Damon Knight and James Blish, both of whom wrote criticism for the amateur press, Blish under the pen-name of William Atheling Jr. Why? Well, why not? For one thing, it was easier on those far-off days for a writer to make a reasonable living[9], and it's not outside the realm of possibility that at least a few of them felt they owed the odd article to the even odder fan-ed. After all, if they weren't SF fans they'd be writing about bacon or real estate.

"People and Places" (sometimes "Notes and News") was another feature in the early *Bulletins* that I find fascinating. F'rinstance, in the April '69 number, we read that:

> Ray Bradbury will be appearing in a Chung-King Chow Mein commercial with Stan Freberg.

Well, not really, it was a Sunsweet Prune ad which you can easily find at YouTube. Still pretty funny. The same issue tells us:

> Folk-rock performer Richie Havens has bought screen rights to Arthur C. Clarke's *Childhood's End* and plans to begin production in June. Havens will write the music and play the role of the last man on Earth.

According to Wikipedia, Havens announced his involvement with the project in the magazine *Ebony* "Months before his performance at Woodstock in 1969..." There were screenplays created, but it never came to fruition. No surprise there; the only other classic SF title to be optioned and never produced more often than the Clarke is *Stranger in a Strange Land.* I forget who wrote it.

Other announcements in "People and Places" included changes of address, changes of representation, editors' changing jobs, and (inevitably) the deaths not only of members but of any figures involved in the field, including fans.

Looking wildly about through my collection, I find the following one-offs which caught first my eye and then my attention: "The Idea Factory" by Ben Bova (Summer 1974 again), his "Meet the Editor" installment detailing his first two years of helming *Analog* after Campbell's death, and the changes in the magazine not only during that brief period but throughout its existence.

A lengthy (10pps, almost half the total page count of the double issue #38/39) essay by Joanna Russ titled "The Wearing Out of Genre Materials," reprinted from the October 1971 issue of the academic journal *College English* centers on her contention that:

> ...[F]iction is *a wish made plausible* [Italics Russ's]. (I have developed this formula out of my own experience in writing and personal acquaintance with some two dozen living writers.) The written story is a compromise between the germinal wished-for situation...and the surrounding fictional circumstances which make the original *X* possible...

It goes on in a very scholarly fashion which might deter some casual readers, but only to their disadvantage. Collegiate as it is, this is an important hypothesis by an important writer.

Speaking of academia, I would be remiss if I didn't mention an important (if short-lived) *Bulletin* department: Dictics, now more commonly spelled "Deitics," meaning "proving directly by means of logic."[10] This department was handled by Bruce McAllister (author of the acclaimed novel *Dream Baby*), who described it thusly:

> ...[T]he 70's were the era during which SF got "academized" (partly but not exclusively because of the New Wave's "literary qualities"), i.e., suddenly there were 1,500 SF courses at colleges around the nation; and the SFWA BULLETIN wanted to recognize that arrival of SF in academe and academe in SF. Fred Pohl asked me to be the DICTICS editor....I'd been writing and publishing SF since 1963, but now had a graduate degree, had used my first SF novel as my MFA thesis (making history in the process), was teaching SF; and I seemed a likely candidate for the DICTICS editorship.

I can dig it, myself. However, it would be remiss of me to point out that academic writing can be...well, academic and not necessarily the most exciting stuff to read if you're not an academic yourself. McAllister was only too aware of this:

> I was, however, too young to know what I was doing (I'd do it differently now, but that's hindsight with 25 years of university teaching between it and me now); not knowing I should probably do something else, I ran long academic articles that put us all to sleep, and Fred finally dropped the section and with no argument from me.

As someone who has advised a couple of university professors about how to set up a SF study program, I can sympathize. Nevertheless, no matter how stodgy the Dictics articles might seem to the casual reader, they contain a wealth of good, solid information. And frankly, no member of SFWA should ever be a "casual reader."

The October 1967 number features a short piece (apparently by then-editor Terry Carr), "The SF Writer's Basic Library," a compendium of fifteen stfnal references suggested by James Blish, Damon Knight and Richard Lupoff. Divided into "Critical" and "Historical" volumes, I won't name them here[11], but I find it quite satisfying to note that I own all but four of them.

I'm getting perilously close to my editor's word-count limit, and there's still so much to bring to your attention.

Here's a fascinating article by A. E. van Vogt in the otherwise slim Fall 1973 issue (#49), titled "The Joys of Science Fiction." He talks not only about his working life as a SF writer but the peripheral things which influenced that work. MENSA, hypnotism, General Semantics, Campbell's psionics; all these cast their shadow on his books and stories. What I find most interesting, though, is that his single reference to his early connection with Hubbard and Dianetics consists of the sentence "During my 15 years involvement with a study of human behavior, I did only fix-up novels and one original, *The Mind Cage*." One wonders why he couched his terminology.

I'll end with this brief mention of the transitional issue of *The SFWA Bulletin*, even though it falls well outside the scope of this retrospective. In going through my (incomplete) set, I note that the first issue which bears a cover price ($3) is Fall 1979, #71. This was the first issue to be available to non-members and non-subscribers, with a price of $3 proudly emblazoned on the cover and perfect-bound.

Editor John F. Carr really beefed this one up, featuring the theme of "Science-Fiction Future Histories" and including articles by Heinlein, Anderson, Niven, Bradley, Asimov, Pournelle, Varley, and

Dickson, as well as a very thorough piece on H. Beam Piper by Carr.

Think about how that must have looked to an unsuspecting fan, browsing the magazine rack at his or her local SF bookshop or at a convention. Small, unassuming, B&W throughout it might be, but oh, those *names*!

There are features in these old issues that I would dearly love to see returned, if only on an occasional basis: How I Do It, Meet the Editor, the letter column, and especially how to live on the cheap. We could all benefit from that last one.

History. In my hands. There are few things more exciting, more immediate, than periodicals that were written back then for what was at the time, NOW. Most of the writing in these was never intended to be read 45+ years later, it is very much the Present Tense. *The SFWA Bulletin* (or *The Bulletin of the Science Fiction Writers of America* as it became in 1971) is an anchor to our origins, a time machine whereby the Founders of this organization can visit us with their wisdom, their experience, and their dialogues. Through them, those Past Masters speak to us, and speak volumes.

There is room in the world for a book, print or electronic, which collects the very best of the *Bulletin*. If you'd like to see such a thing, let the SFWA Officers know.

Notes

1. Well, 11x17" folded to 8.5 and unbound. No corner staples here, by Ghu!
2. Sorry, but my own collection of *Bulletins* is incomplete.
3. They did bind some of their titles in hardcovers in the early years, small handsome books printed from the same plates as their mass-market avatars with the cover art reproduced as wrap-around dust jackets in very small print runs, primarily for sale to libraries. These days, copies of even marginal titles in decent shape with no library markings can bring prices in the mid-three figures.
4. Widow of Richard McKenna, author of the Nebula winning story that year, "The Secret Place." McKenna was a brilliant writer who gained more fame outside the field by writing the historical novel *The Sand Pebbles*, serialized in the *Saturday Evening Post* in the winter of 1962. It won the Harper Prize Novel contest for 1963, and was later made into a very successful film. McKenna died of a heart attack in '64, and one can't help but wonder what else he would have done had he survived.
5. New Orleans, or N'Awlins, in case you don't watch TV.
6. Later collected in the chapbook of the same title by Chris Drumm in 1984 (Drumm Booklet #14) and two reissued two years later by Borgo Press, and highly recommended in whichever edition you turn up.
7. "Pay copy" doesn't indicate hackwork, I hasten to add. It's not enough for me to get a check in the mail, the story has to please Mary and the three

damn cats as well.

8. You can read another report on this important festival, this one written by J. G. Ballard, at http://www.jgballard.ca/deep_ends/jgb_rio_convention.html.
9. There were a number of articles in various issues which gave solid advice to others about how to make their writing dollars stretch, always a good thing for a scrivener.
10. Or, as is more often spelled these days, "deictics."
11. If you really want to know what they are, contact me and I'll reveal all.

❑

Index

In this index, magazine and book titles and publishers are listed only where they appear in the body of the text. For other appearances, please refer to the various bibliographies as listed by authors' names.

8054709R00222

Printed in Great Britain
by Amazon.co.uk, Ltd.,
Marston Gate.